# 1636
## FLIGHT OF THE NIGHTINGALE

## DAVID CARRICO

T0026058

## 1636: Flight of the Nightingale

This is a work of fiction. All the characters and events portrayed in this book are fictional, and any resemblance to real people or incidents is purely coincidental.

Copyright © 2019 by David Carrico

An earlier version of "Prelude" appeared in *Grantville Gazette* Volume 26 (copyright © 2009). An earlier version of "Adagio" appeared in *Grantville Gazette* Volume 27 (copyright © 2010). An earlier version of "Interlude" appeared in *Grantville Gazette* Volume 28 (copyright © 2010). An earlier version of "Etude" was serialized in *Grantville Gazette* Volumes 67, 68 (both copyright © 2016), and 69 (copyright © 2017). This is the first publication of "Toccata" (copyright © 2019). This is the first publication of *Flight of the Nightingale* (copyright © 2019).

A Baen Books Original

Baen Publishing Enterprises
P.O. Box 1403
Riverdale, NY 10471
www.baen.com

ISBN: 978-1-9821-2506-6

Cover art by Tom Kidd
Map of Northern Italy & Switzerland by Michael Knopp
Maps of Magdeburg by Gorg Huff

First printing, November 2019
First mass market printing, December 2020

Distributed by Simon & Schuster
1230 Avenue of the Americas
New York, NY 10020

Library of Congress Control Number: 2019029060

Pages by Joy Freeman (www.pagesbyjoy.com)
Printed in the United States of America
10  9  8  7  6  5  4  3  2  1

# FOR WANT OF A WHEEL...

There was a bone-rattling *crunch!* followed by the carriage abruptly slowing as the left rear corner sagged, accompanied by the sound of something large being hideously scraped along the road. Francesca's heart sank.

The carriage scraped to a stop in a cloud of dust.

*"Merda,"* Davit muttered. He opened the door on the side away from the sag, and climbed out. A few moments later, he stuck his head back in the door. "The wheel is broken. You'll need to dismount."

Marco was out the door in but a moment. Francesca took her time, and descended with some care. She saw that Antonio and Benvenuto were crouched, examining the damage.

Davit had the look of a man who had bitten into an apple and found half a worm. "We have a spare wheel, don't we?"

"Yes."

"Get it on, then."

As they got to work, Francesca stepped over beside Davit. "We're not going to make Cremona tonight, are we?"

"No." Francesca followed Davit's gaze to the afternoon sun. "This," he gestured toward the work with a thumb, "will take a few hours at best."

"Or longer," Francesca muttered, wondering how close behind were her pursuers...

# ERIC FLINT'S RING OF FIRE SERIES

*1632* by Eric Flint • *1633* with David Weber • *1634: The Baltic War* with David Weber • *1634: The Galileo Affair* with Andrew Dennis • *1634: The Bavarian Crisis* with Virginia DeMarce • *1634: The Ram Rebellion* with Virginia DeMarce et al. • *1635: The Cannon Law* with Andrew Dennis • *1635: The Dreeson Incident* with Virginia DeMarce • *1635: The Eastern Front* • *1635: The Papal Stakes* with Charles E. Gannon • *1636: The Saxon Uprising* • *1636: The Kremlin Games* with Gorg Huff & Paula Goodlett • *1636: The Devil's Opera* with David Carrico • *1636: Commander Cantrell in the West Indies* with Charles E. Gannon • *1636: The Viennese Waltz* with Gorg Huff & Paula Goodlett • *1636: The Cardinal Virtues* with Walter H. Hunt • *1635: A Parcel of Rogues* with Andrew Dennis • *1636: The Ottoman Onslaught* • *1636: Mission to the Mughals* with Griffin Barber • *1636: The Vatican Sanction* with Charles E. Gannon • *1637: The Volga Rules* with Gorg Huff & Paula Goodlett • *1637: The Polish Maelstrom* • *1636: The China Venture* with Iver P. Cooper • *1636: The Atlantic Encounter* with Walter H. Hunt • *1637: No Peace Beyond the Line* with Charles E. Gannon (forthcoming)

*1635: The Tangled Web* by Virginia DeMarce • *1635: The Wars for the Rhine* by Anette Pedersen • *1636: Seas of Fortune* by Iver P. Cooper • *1636: The Chronicles of Doctor Gribbleflotz* by Kerryn Offord & Rick Boatright • *1636: Flight of the Nightingale* by David Carrico

*Time Spike* with Marilyn Kosmatka • *The Alexander Inheritance* with Gorg Huff & Paula Goodlett

*Grantville Gazette I–VIII*, ed. by Eric Flint • *Ring of Fire I–IV*, ed. Eric Flint

**To purchase any of these titles in e-book form, please go to www.baen.com.**

To all those teachers in
schools and churches and private studios
who strive to awaken in children the love of music.

May your tribe increase.

# Contents

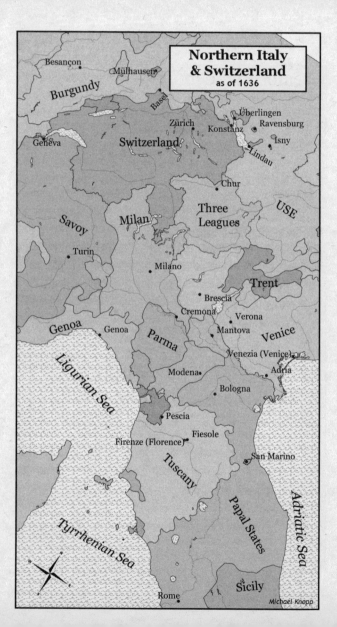

**Northern Italy & Switzerland**
**as of 1636**

Besançon

Mülhausen

Burgundy

Basel

Zürich

Überlingen

Konstanz

Ravensburg

Geneva

Switzerland

Isny

Lindau

Chur

Three Leagues

USE

Savoy

Milan

Trent

Turin

Milano

Brescia

Verona

Cremona

Mantova

Venice

Genoa

Genoa

Parma

Venezia (Venice)

Adria

Modena

Ligurian Sea

Bologna

Pescia

Fiesole

Firenze (Florence)

San Marino

Tuscany

Tyrrhenian Sea

Papal States

Adriatic Sea

Sicily

Rome

Michael Knopp

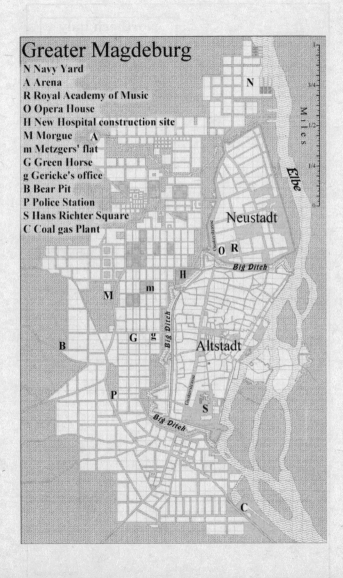

# Greater Magdeburg

N Navy Yard
A Arena
R Royal Academy of Music
O Opera House
H New Hospital construction site
M Morgue
m Metzgers' flat
G Green Horse
g Gericke's office
B Bear Pit
P Police Station
S Hans Richter Square
C Coal gas Plant

Neustadt

Altstadt

Elbe

Big Ditch

Big Ditch

Big Ditch

Miles

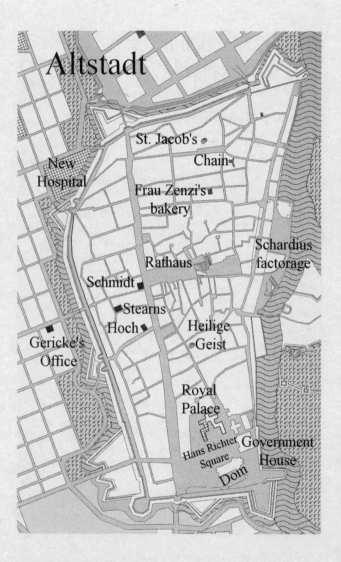

Altstadt

St. Jacob's

Chain

New
Hospital

Frau Zenzi's
bakery

Schardius
factorage

Rathaus

Schmidt

Stearns

Hoch

Heilige
Geist

Gericke's
Office

Royal
Palace

Hans Richter
Square

Government
House

Dom

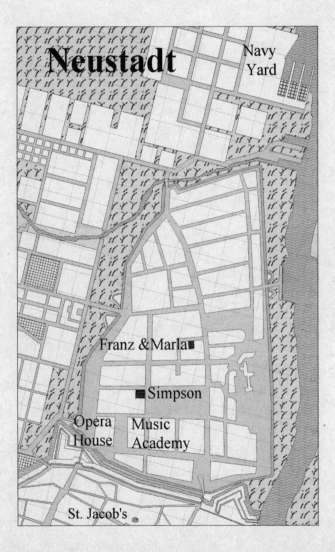

# Flight of the Nightingale

# Chapter 1

*Firenze*
*September 1636*

Francesca stuffed the last folder of paper into her bag and forced it closed, fastening the closure and making sure the hasp stayed put. The last thing she wanted or needed right now was that bag flopping open and all the pages inside spilling out. She looped the strap over her left shoulder and tucked the bag under her left armpit.

She looked around the room. So many memories here, good and bad. So many things that were being left behind. Pinching the bridge of her nose to forestall welling tears, Francesca took a deep breath, then dropped her hand to smooth the front of her skirt. It was very common, much less ornate than her usual wear, made of rougher linen and dyed with cheaper dyes. Picking up the dark cloak that was much richer than her dress, she swirled it over her shoulders. She looked to the slight figure that stood by the door.

"Who are you again?" Her voice was curt.

"Marco Sabatini."

Her new attendant's voice was smooth, sexless, and of a moderately low pitch. It sang well to her ear, but more importantly, it wasn't a voice that was very familiar to anyone in the palace tonight. That was important—critical, even—to their success.

"Yes, you are. Remember that. And what is the plan?"

"You go out the door. I set the bar in its brackets, then go out the window and close the shutters behind me, making sure the latch falls into place."

"And where do we meet?"

"At the north end of the garden loggia just before the small gate."

Francesca gave a nod. "Good. And you have the wine?"

Sabatini nodded at a small wineskin leaning against the back wall of the room by the open window.

"Good," Francesca repeated. She took a deep breath, then said, "Let's do it."

Sabatini turned and pulled the door open enough to stick his head out into the corridor and look both ways. Then he straightened and gave an urgent wave of his hand. Francesca pulled the hood of the cloak up over her head and stepped past Sabatini into the hallway, which was empty for the moment.

Of course, it was supposed to be empty. They had planned on it being empty, because at that hour of the night it usually was. But there was always a possibility that some drunken member of the court, slacker of a servant, or lost visitor could wander into sight around one of the corners. Francesca hurried down to the next cross corridor. Behind her the light dimmed as the door closed, leaving her just the faint illumination from the lantern hanging at the far end of the corridor. A moment later she heard the bar drop into place on the door. So, that part of the plan was working.

Francesca turned into the cross corridor and released the breath she hadn't realized she was holding. Now she was in the back halls of the palace, the ways usually only traveled by servants, and at this hour of the night this stretch was usually empty. In a few more hours it would be bustling, but for now it was as quiet as the catacombs in Roma... and almost as dark.

She walked as quietly as she could, but she was wearing sensible solid shoes tonight, not her usual palace slippers, and they made enough noise that Francesca was constantly looking around to see if anyone had heard her go by. But it didn't take long before she reached the outside door where servants could exit to pass into the gardens or take a more direct route to another part of the palace than through the various hallways.

Here Francesca had no choice. She had to unbar the door to get out, and once she was out she would have no way to put the bar back up. She would just have to hope that no one would come by and discover the situation until she was well on her way away from the palace.

She gently slid the bar out of its brackets, and equally gently set one end on the floor and leaned the other into the nearby corner, out of the way, where it wouldn't go sliding down the wall or fall over.

The click as Francesca tripped the latch seemed to resound in the empty hall, and she froze for a moment, shoulders hunched. But there was no sound, no query, no outcry behind her triggered by the noise, so she opened the heavy door with care. She had surreptitiously spread a little olive oil on the hinges a few days before, and it seemed to have paid off, as the door opened with little noise. She slipped through the doorway as soon as the opening was large enough, then pulled the door closed behind her, striving to minimize the noise. The noise as the latch engaged was less noticeable out here in the open air, and she hoped that no one had come by to hear it inside.

She gathered the cloak around her. It looked like she had beat Sabatini here, so she stepped into the shadow of the loggia to wait for him.

Sabatini closed the door and slipped the bar back into place. He stepped to the doorway of the bed-chamber to make sure the bundle under the blankets still was in place. He knew it wouldn't fool anyone who closed on the bed, but it might distract anyone who just gave a quick glance into the room.

He crossed to the table where the small candle stand was placed. Before he blew the candle out, he looked around the room one more time. Francesca Caccini—La Cecchina—The Nightingale, as she was known in the Medici court in Firenze—had lived and worked in these rooms off and on for a long time, except for the years of her second marriage to Tommaso Raffaelli, a very minor nobleman, where she had mostly resided in his homes in Lucca. But even then, she had returned for visits to the court from time to time, at which times she would reoccupy the rooms for as long as she needed them. It was one of the advantages of being a favorite of Grand Duchess Christina. So in this Year of Our Lord 1636 few in the court could remember a time when she hadn't been in those rooms there, especially after she had returned to the court full time in 1633 after Tommaso's death and the ravages of plague in the country. It was hard for her to leave, but it was her decision to go. After the death of her son, there was nothing left to hold her here, and Sabatini couldn't blame her.

Everything that was left behind was in its place: pens, rules, parchment, cheap paper for drafting; all lay in boxes on the table. Fancy court clothes were in the chests in the bedchamber. Her lute hung from a peg on the wall. That had almost broken Francesca's heart to leave behind, Sabatini knew, but it would have hampered her flight, and made it much easier for someone—or someones, he thought—to track her. In the end, he had been able to convince her to leave it. He crossed to it and ran his finger across the top of it. For luck, he told himself.

Sabatini turned back to the table and blew out the candle, then moved to the window. He pushed open the shutters, thankful that they had thought to apply some olive oil to the shutter hinges the same day they had oiled the kitchen door. They opened silently because of that. He reached down and picked up the wineskin and hefted it through the window, setting it on top of the rosebush that sat just to the left of the window opening. Then he sat down on the window ledge, swung his legs up and through the opening, and dropped off it to the ground, ducking his head as he did so to clear the top of the window frame. It was a superior apartment—ground floor, at that—in the Palazzo Pitti, one of the major residences of the Medici family in Firenze, but still was for one who was considered—mostly, even after her marriage to Raffaelli—a servant, after all, he thought. The window accordingly wasn't very large. Francesca had been promised a glass casement in the window for the last several years, but somehow the palace major never seemed to find the monies in his budget to make it happen.

He brought the two shutter leaves close together, ready to shut them, but before he did he checked to make sure the thread he had run in the late afternoon around the latch arm on the left shutter was still in place running up and over the top of the shutter. It was there, so he closed the shutters, pulling slightly on the thread ends to lift the latch arm. It took a couple of tries before he heard the click as the latch arm settled in place.

A quick pull on the shutters confirmed that they were properly latched. Sabatini pulled one end of the thread until it was all free of the shutter, winding it into a small ball which he tucked into a pocket. One never knew when a nice long piece of thread might be handy, after all.

Picking up the wineskin, Sabatini headed around the perimeter of the courtyard toward the loggia. He didn't want to keep Francesca waiting. Their plan was pretty tightly scheduled.

Francesca stepped out as a shadow moved by the loggia pillars. She was tense, but relaxed when the light from a nearby torch flickered over Sabatini's face.

"Any problems?" she whispered.

"After all the practices? No." Sabatini's voice was just as hushed. "You?"

"Didn't see or hear anyone," she replied.

"But did anyone see or hear you?"

"No."

They looked back down the loggia, then toward the gate that was their goal.

Francesca took a big sigh. She reached up and folded her hood back, revealing her face, her put-up hair, and the dangling earrings that swayed as she moved her head. Sabatini held up the wineskin, and Francesca took it. "Time for the next step, I suppose."

Sabatini said nothing, simply faded back into the shadows. Francesca took another deep breath, then headed for the gate.

The guards tonight were Giuseppe and Ercole, two of the regulars who usually had the night shift on *Martedì*. They were rascals, at best, whose accents and remarks indicated they were not from Firenze originally. Francesca thought they were from one of the northern regions.

They also just happened to be the two guards who had the most regular arrangements with those who supplied certain comforts to members of the court without necessarily going through the proper channels for import duties due the city and state of Firenze in the person of Grand Duke Ferdinando.

Francesca was an occasional client of one of their suppliers, so she knew the two guards, and they knew her. More importantly, they knew her as a customer, not an interloper. That was important.

"Maestra Caccini," Giuseppe called out when she stepped into the pools of light cast by their lanterns. "Are you expecting someone? We hadn't heard."

"No, no," Francesca replied. Her short laugh sounded

a bit forced to her, but neither of the guards seemed to notice anything. "Or, not exactly. Benito sent me word that he might have something small for me tonight or tomorrow, so I thought I'd stop and see."

"No, Maestra," Ercole said. As usual, Francesca had to bite her lip to keep from laughing at the thin reedy tones his voice produced. If ever a man could say that he was cursed by his name, it was Ercole. Francesca had never met anyone who looked less like a Hercules than Ercole: thin, bony, round-shouldered, long-necked, jug-eared, and above all, short. It made him the inevitable butt of rough jokes from his fellow guards, but from what Francesca had seen, he kept a good humor about it, and gave as good as he got.

"No, we have not seen Benito tonight," Ercole continued without realizing her thoughts. He looked at his partner. "And we hadn't heard that he planned on coming by any time this week." Giuseppe nodded in agreement.

"Ah, well, I must have misunderstood, then. Do let me know if you hear from him."

"Certainly, Maestra," Giuseppe said. "We certainly will."

The guards were on their best behavior. Francesca was well aware of the fact that if she had been a simple serving woman or kitchen worker, their attitudes would have been considerably more casual and would have involved physical contact. Even though the Grand Duchess was now dowager and no longer the regent over the duchy, she still had a great deal of power and authority behind the scenes, and a certain amount of protection flowed from her to cover Francesca. It would take rank and standing much higher than these men would ever possess to counteract that. Which didn't mean that there weren't those in the court who might try. A knot in her stomach reminded her of that fact.

Francesca looked down almost as if surprised, and lifted the wineskin that she was holding. "I believe I promised you good men some wine a couple of weeks ago. Sorry it took me so long, but I do keep my promises. This is yours."

"Madonna bless you, Maestra!" Ercole exclaimed as Giuseppe reached out greedy hands for the wine. "We were late to supper, and all they had left to drink was some really sour beer. We are dry as a desert, standing here."

Francesca laughed and handed the wineskin to Giuseppe, who popped the stopper out of the neck of the skin and lifted it up to pour wine into his open mouth with a very practiced motion. After a moment, Ercole reached up and pulled his arm down. "Pig! Swine! Glutton! You will not swill it down before I get my share."

Giuseppe coughed, wiped his mouth on his sleeve, and surrendered the skin to his partner. "*Delizioso*, Maestra! Very fine, very sweet, the blessings of all the saints upon you for remembering poor Giuseppe and poor Ercole standing lonely watch in the middle of the night."

There followed bows, first by one of them, then by the other, then by both together, until Francesca held up her hands laughing, saying, "Enough, enough. You like it, that's good. Just keep an eye out for Benito, all right?"

"*Si*, Maestra," Ercole said as Giuseppe snagged the wineskin again. "We will certainly do that. Give me that," he snarled at his partner the next moment, grabbing for the skin.

Francesca turned and retreated into the shadows again, moving back to where she had left Sabatini. When she heard his "Psst," she stepped sideways into the darker pool of shadows around one of the loggia columns, pulling her hood back up over her head to help shade the lighter skin of her face.

# Chapter 2

They watched the two men pass the wineskin back and forth, until it was empty enough that Ercole held it above his face and let the last few drops drip onto his tongue before he threw it to one side and began to curse Giuseppe for drinking the lion's share of the wine.

"How long will it take?" Sabatini murmured.

"Not long," Francesca whispered back. "The opium is strong."

"And will they stay asleep?"

Francesca smiled. "There was enough in the wine that they could sleep for two days."

"Is that why you mixed so much honey in it?"

"Partly, and partly because it helped hide the fact that it was good wine, not the cheaper stuff they usually get. Lots of wine sellers mix honey with cheap wine to make it sweeter and mask the taste, and guys like this who only get the cheap stuff get used to it."

"There they go," Sabatini said as Giuseppe dropped onto a stool and leaned back against the wall by the gate.

"Wait," Francesca said, placing a hand on Sabatini's shoulder as he started to move forward. "Ercole's not down yet." And indeed, the scrawny guardsman was staggering around in a drunken circle, lurching first to one side then the other, before he finally made contact with a wall and slid down it to end with his feet splayed before him and his head lolling to one side. "Wait," Francesca said again. She counted over sixty heartbeats before she lifted her hand. "Now, quietly."

The two of them slipped back into the lamplight before the gate. Francesca stepped carefully through the tangle of feet and leaned over to relieve Giuseppe of the large key that hung from his belt. Her heart stopped when he snorted as she pulled the key free, but he just turned his head to the other side and began snoring.

Picking her way back out again, she stepped over to the gate where Sabatini was already lifting the bar out of its brackets. She opened the large clumsy lock with the key, and pushed the gate open. They walked through it, then closed it again. She examined the gate in the moonlight. There was no sign of a lock on the outside, so she pulled the gate open again, enough that she tossed the key to land in Ercole's lap, then closed it again.

"Come." Francesca turned and hurried down the path that led from the gate toward the city. They passed through the gardens until they arrived at a portal through the garden wall. That one she had a key to. An unofficial key, needless to say, but probably all of the senior servants of the palace had one. Everyone needed a private way to leave and return from time to time, after all.

Once they were outside the wall, she looked to her right. The Forte di Belvedere loomed from that direction. It was still referred to as "the new fort" by all residents of Firenze, even though it was nearly as old as she was. Tonight, it was a landmark, large and mostly dark and silent.

"You know this would have been a lot easier if we could have taken the corridor," Sabatini whispered.

The *Corridoio Vasariano*—the Vasari Corridor— was an enclosed corridor that ran from the Palazzo Pitti to the Palazzo Vecchio, the main governmental palace, crossing the Arno River atop the Ponte Vec- chio bridge. And yes, it would have been very much easier to make their way out of the palace and cross the river using it.

"Easier to cross, but impossible to escape," she hissed back. "And you know it. So stop talking stupid."

There was no more talk. Francesca led the way down Via de Bardi and its successor roads until they reached the Ponte di Rubaconte. It was a moonless night, and they were able to slip across the bridge without attracting attention.

Once on the northern bank, they headed back to the west. Francesca didn't slow down until nearly to the Ponte de Vecchio. Once she could clearly see the Torre dei Mannelli, she felt some of her tension drain away, and she stopped.

"Come on," Sabatini muttered, taking her arm. "We need to keep moving. The night watch might come by."

"All right," Francesca said, gathering herself up and getting her feet moving again. "This way." She led them down to a cross street and around another corner.

"Where are we going?" Sabatini asked.

"To the Teatro Mediceo," Francesca replied.

"The theatre?" Sabatini's voice raised in astonishment, the first time Francesca had heard an emotion from him. "Why?"

"Because that's where we're going to meet Barbara and get our packs."

"Ah." Sabatini was silent for the rest of that part of the journey.

Francesca knew this part of town well, as she had more than once been involved in a production by providing either newly written music or arrangements of existing songs to be performed in conjunction with plays. The Medici family had given her a certain amount of latitude as she grew older, and was no longer the almost-notorious older girl/young woman musician that her father had trotted out before the wealthy of Firenze, Tuscany, and France. And she had saved much of the money she had earned, which was one of the reasons she was able to do what she was doing now.

"Hsst," Francesca said as Sabatini started past the mouth of an alley. "In here." She turned up the alley, and heard him coming in behind her.

Francesca had to slow down. The alley was so narrow that the moonlight wasn't penetrating its darkness well. She stayed to one side of the alley, avoiding the muck and noisome debris that she knew was in the middle, even if she couldn't see it. "One..." she counted a door as she went by, "two...three..." At "four..." she stopped and knocked gently on a door, in a staggered rhythm.

After a moment, the door opened a handsbreadth with a scraping sound from its bottom edge. "In whose name?" a voice whispered roughly through the gap.

"San Giovanni Battista," Francesca whispered back. The door opened wider. "In," the voice urged.

Sabatini snorted at the password—using the name of the patron saint of the city of Firenze didn't seem to him to be very secret or secretive. Then he shrugged— on the other hand, it would be easy to remember, and who expected secret signs on an event like this, anyway?

Once they were in, the door closed softly behind them, and someone opened a gate in a lantern to release a flood of golden light. He blinked, and discovered that they stood in the backstage of the theatre, in a corner filled with tied-off ropes that ran into the darkness above them.

Holding the lantern was a large woman with plump flushed cheeks and obviously hennaed hair. From behind Sabatini slipped a stick of a woman not much taller than himself, whose hair shone a brassy gold in the lantern light. That also seemed to be an improbable color to occur naturally.

"Barbara," Francesca said.

It took a moment for Sabatini to recognize the other woman as a popular actress in the Mediceo Theatre Company who was usually proclaimed as "Isabella." Of course, probably every fourth actress in northern Italy used the stage name "Isabella," as a link to the famous actress of the previous generation, Isabella Andreini, who had trod the boards before every noble family of Italy and France in her time. Her name still carried a certain weight in theatre circles.

The large woman reached out a hand to her. "This way, Maestra..."

"No names," Francesca interjected hurriedly.

"As you wish," Barbara said as she drew Francesca to a nearby stool beside a rickety table. "Here, sit, let us transform you. Renata, take the cloak."

Francesca threw back the hood and undid the throat fastening so that the smaller woman could whisk the cloak away before Francesca sat on the stool. Renata returned in a moment, and unbound Francesca's hair so that it hung loose, then took a comb and began to attend to the hair to smooth it out.

Meanwhile, Barbara looked at Francesca, then took her hand and grasped Francesca's chin to move her head slightly into different angles in the light. "Hmm," she muttered. She turned away and picked up a few things from the table. Turning back, she said, "Open your mouth." When Francesca did so, she inserted something on each side, then stepped back. "Close your mouth."

Sabatini moved far enough back that he could see all of Francesca's face. It looked different, somehow. Barbara looked at Francesca, then gave a definite nod.

"Here's the deal, dear. You've seen us do stage makeup, and we could teach you to do that, but it wouldn't serve your purpose. Stage makeup is designed to make an impression from twenty, thirty, fifty feet away, with bold colors and lines. Up close, in a room or on the street, it would look horrible and would attract attention, which is the last thing you want. So what we're going to do is just change you a little bit, so that you look normal, but don't look like you did. To begin with, those pads I put in your mouth change your cheek lines. Someone might look at your eyes and forehead and think it's you, but when they get to the cheeks they'd decide it can't be you. That's one change."

Barbara picked up a small round jar. "This is a bit of goose grease mixed with a bit of gray ash. A smidge of that rubbed in just below the eyes will create a shadow that makes them look older and very tired." She proceeded to apply it lightly. When she stepped back, Sabatini could see the shadows that had been created under Francesca's eyes, which did indeed create an effect of weariness. He nodded. That, combined with the cheek pads, really made her look different.

Meanwhile, Renata has finished combing out Francesca's hair and had plaited it into a single braid which she coiled around the back of her head and thrust a long hairpin through it to hold the mass in place. Barbara looked at that, and quirked her mouth.

"If you were going to stay in Firenze, or in any of the nearby large towns where you could find supplies, you could always put henna on your hair, or one of those herbal rinses that change the color a bit. But if you're going to be on the move, you can't count on finding the supplies quickly to make that change. So I suggest that you leave your hair its normal color, and just wear it in the simplest styles, like any woman of the country would do. Don't present it in a courtly style, in other words, and it shouldn't call anyone's attention to it. But if for some reason you desperately need to change the color a bit, then rub some of this..." she held up the ash and goose grease jar "...into your hair. The grease will darken the color, and the ash will dull it a bit. Just don't get your hair near a torch or candle until after you get it washed out, or you will become a living candle."

Sabatini shivered at that thought...goose grease–laden hair would indeed light up like a torch if even lightly touched with a flame for a moment. He swallowed.

"Stand up," Barbara said. Francesca did so. Sabatini noted that she hadn't said anything since right after they'd entered the theatre. That wasn't like her. Francesca normally had plenty to say, and was well known for wanting to have the final word in any conversation. He kept an eye on her, just to make sure she wasn't getting sick or something.

Barbara walked around Francesca, slowly, looking her up and down from every angle as she did so. "The blouse, the vest, the skirt...they are right for what you are trying to do. And the other clothes in the bag we packed will work with them...you can swap pieces in and out to change appearance easily. But you need something else...Renata, bring me the miller's wife's apron."

The other woman spun on her toes and scurried off into the gloom. Barbara turned back to Francesca and waved at the stool. "Sit, sit. And take off your shoes."

Francesca did so, handing them off to Sabatini, then received another pair of shoes from the actress. "Try those to see if they fit."

Francesca slipped them on, and nodded. "Well enough. A bit loose, maybe, but if I'm on my feet all day, it won't take long for my feet to swell up and they'll be snug enough then."

"Right," Barbara said with a chuckle. "Tell me about swollen feet. A three-act show that has a double performance on *Sabato* or *Domenica*, and they almost have to cut my shoes off my feet by the end of the day." She held out her hands. "Take my hands and stand up. Take my hands," she said sharply as Francesca started to move without doing so.

Francesca frowned, but did so and rose, only to lean and almost fall to one side. Sabatini moved to take that elbow to support her. "What..."

Barbara held her hands strongly, and said, "That's why I wanted you to take my hands. The shoes are not the same height, and the first time people wear something like that they get off-balance very easily. Steady now?"

Francesca nodded, still frowning. "I think so, but why am I wearing mismatched shoes?"

Barbara dropped her hold and backed away a few steps. "Walk toward me. Carefully!" That last was uttered in a snap as Francesca lurched and tilted again as she tried to move. Sabatini stayed at her side. They made their way with care across the space, until Francesca was again standing right before the actress.

"You, Sabatini," Barbara said, "bring the stool over here."

Sabatini did so once he was certain that Francesca wasn't going to fall over when he let go of her elbow. She sank onto the stool with obvious relief.

# Chapter 3

Francesca looked up at Barbara. "And what was that in aid of?"

"One of the best ways to appear to be someone different is to change the way you walk. Take the shoes off, please." After Francesca kicked them off, Barbara picked them up and held them out before her. "But even trained actors have trouble remembering which leg to limp with over a long performance, so the best way to do it and make sure you don't draw unwanted attention is to do something to the shoes. Some actors put a small pebble or stone chip or a small stick in their shoes. That works, but you can't do it for long without rubbing sores on your feet. So the smart ones do this."

The actress flipped the shoes over so they were bottoms up, and Sabatini could see that the heel of one of the shoes was built up a little more than the other. "See, the difference in heel height doesn't have to be very much at all to make the illusion of a very convincing limp. The bigger the difference, the more you'll limp. A finger's breadth will make you lurch like a cripple."

"How do you know all this?" Sabatini asked. He was absorbing all that was being said, but his head was beginning to spin.

"Part of it is stagecraft," Barbara said with a chuckle, "and part of it is experience. Actors are probably second only to gypsies for needing to know how to get out of town without attracting attention, official or otherwise." That got a cackle from Renata from where she stood behind them.

"Put your shoes back on and stand up, dear," Barbara said as she turned and placed the limping shoes in a worn bag that was sitting on the floor by the table. Francesca looked around for her shoes, and Sabatini picked them up and handed them to her. While she was fitting them to her feet, Barbara said, "Those are good common sensible shoes. They won't give anything away, and no one looks at a poor woman's shoes, anyway, so you shouldn't have to worry about that. Clothes, we've got covered. Renata." She looked at the other actress, who handed her a length of cloth. Barbara took it, shook it out, and it was revealed to be an apron. To be specific, a very dirty apron, with a very unfortunate stain right in the middle of it.

"And for a quick change if you ever need it," Barbara said as she wrapped the apron around the now standing Francesca, "you take off your coat and throw it to the boy, take the scarf off your head, pull a bit of your hair out of the bun or braid to fly around your face, take both cheek pads and put them in one cheek, and put this on. A little creative swearing as you march down the alley or street, and no one would believe it was you."

Sabatini goggled a bit at the thought of Francesca creatively swearing, but there was no doubt that the apron really changed her appearance.

Francesca looked at Sabatini. "Really?"

He nodded with a grin. "Everything she says changes the way you look and the way you move. I think she's right."

Francesca quirked her mouth. "All right." She smoothed her hands down the apron, and paused halfway through the motion to peer at the fabric. "Paint?" She looked up with a quizzical expression on her face.

Barbara nodded with a smile. "Only the best artistic work in our costumes," she said. "Heavens, if we'd used real meat juices and kitchen dirt, the mice would have consumed that years ago."

"Are you going to get in trouble for giving me these things?" Francesca asked about a half a beat before Sabatini started to ask the same question.

"No," Barbara said over another cackle from Renata. "The shoes are mine, so no problem there. As for the apron, Renata is our costumer. She'll just conveniently 'lose' it." She shrugged. "*Merda* happens, and it wouldn't be the first time. By the time we might need it again, we can replace it."

"And besides," Renata contributed in a reedy voice, "that cloak you're leaving behind is worth more than everything you're taking. The velvet, the color of it . . ." She kissed her fingertips.

"Truth," Barbara confirmed with a nod.

Francesca got a worried look. "That might be recognized . . ."

"Pfaugh," Barbara said with a wave of her hand.

"Go teach your grandmother to suck eggs. Renata will have that reworked into a costume or a gown in a couple of days. Nobody will ever see the cloak in it."

Sabatini watched as Francesca relaxed and removed the apron. Barbara took it and rolled it up with a practiced motion, then stuffed it in the bag on the floor.

"Now," the actress said, "coat or cloak?"

Sabatini saw Francesca hesitate. "Coat," he interjected. After a moment, Francesca nodded in agreement.

"Going north, eh?" Barbara remarked. Sabatini saw Francesca start, and Barbara laughed. "Dear, if you're going to run, it's either go south or go north, and if you want a coat, you're probably going north. And for what it's worth, I agree. If you need to get out of the reach of the court, go north."

Renata offered a coat to Francesca. She stood and pulled it on. Barbara reached out to tweak the collar and opening, buttoning the top button, then stepped back to examine the effect. "A bit old-fashioned, a bit frumpy, definitely out of style . . . perfect. Nobody will look at you twice in that."

Renata came forward and folded one of the front panels of the coat back. "This is fully lined with a different material, so it can be turned inside out and worn that way to change your look as well."

While Francesca was examining her coat, Renata handed one to Sabatini. "Here, try this on."

Sabatini slipped it on. It was a bit large on him . . . he could feel the extra room in the shoulders, and the sleeves hung almost down to his knuckles. He held his hands out before him with a grin.

"Perfect!" Renata exclaimed. "You look like you're

wearing your older brother's hand-me-down. And no one will take you seriously when you look like that."

Even Francesca had a smile on her face at that. Sabatini pushed the sleeves up his arm, and put his hands on his hips.

Barbara hoisted the worn bag off the floor and set it on the table. "There are two more blouses, a reversible vest, and another skirt in here, plus the limping shoes and three or four scarves. You need to look at those, so you'll know what you have. And when you arrive at a new town, look at the poor women in the streets to see what kind of scarves they're wearing on their heads and how they're wearing them and with what kind of knots they're tying the ends down, and switch yours to as close a match as you can make. It's a little thing that will help you blend in and not be as obviously an outsider." She went to close the bag, and stopped to pick a small clay pot off the table and add it to the bag. "And your goose grease with ash mixed in is in here as well."

Renata brought a smaller bag over and set it on the table. She looked at Sabatini. "A change of clothing for you, plus a scarf and some gloves. You go far enough north, it will start getting cold."

It alarmed Sabatini that the women knew that much of their plans. He looked at Francesca, and he knew his eyes were wide, but he couldn't help himself. She held a hand out and patted the air.

"They know nothing, Sabatini, and what they might guess they will never tell."

Barbara nodded firmly, and Renata pulled a shiny cross on a thin necklace out from under her blouse and kissed it. Sabatini still wasn't comfortable with it, but he nodded anyway. He stripped off the coat and rolled it up. It just barely fit in his bag on top of the clothes already there, but that was good. It was too warm to be wearing it now, and he wanted the freedom of movement as long as possible. He touched the hilt of his belt knife just for a moment.

Francesca went to pick up her bag, and Barbara held up her hand. "Your earrings, dear."

Francesca's hands went to her ears, and Sabatini saw the disgusted expression she got. "Stupid me, I forgot about them." She very carefully took them out of the holes in her ears and laid them on the table. Then she pulled a thin wooden case out of her pocket. After she worked it with her fingers for a moment, a piece of it slid up, exposing a small flat compartment. The earrings were carefully picked up and laid in the compartment, which was then closed up. "My daughter will want these."

She turned it over and slid a piece on the other side up. That exposed two sewing needles stuck through a wisp of cloth. "My mother's etui," Francesca said with a sad smile. "I'm not sure where she got it, but she used to hide little things in it from time to time." She closed the case again and handed it to Sabatini. "Here, you hide this."

Sabatini took it and tucked it in an inner pocket of his jerkin.

"Now," Barbara said, drawing their eyes back to herself. "At dawn, you need to be in the Piazza di San Sabatini, where you will meet with Giulio and his cart. He will take you, dear, out of the city and to the nearest village. You, lad," she looked at Sabatini, "will have to walk by yourself until she gets out of the cart. But there's usually enough traffic that you can keep close to the cart without seeming odd."

"Dawn. Piazza di San Sabatini. Giulio," Francesca repeated.

"Sounds like you have it," Barbara said. She looked around. "You're probably safe enough here. No one is supposed to be here until almost noon today."

"You can rest here," Renata said. "I'll make sure you awaken in time. I'm always up with the roosters."

"She is that," Barbara said. "Disgusting."

She turned and picked up a cloak from a chair that stood behind her, to swirl it around and settle it on her shoulders. "I'm off, dear. Be very careful, and when you get where you're going, please send us word."

Francesca reached under her vest, and fumbled with something for a moment, then pulled out a gold florin and held it out. "Here. You deserve this."

"I can't take that, dear," Barbara said, aghast. "How in the world would I be able to explain having one of those? And besides, we didn't do that much."

Francesca laid it on the table. "Take it for the help you've provided, and to provide help to the next person who comes to you."

Barbara looked at her solemnly. After a moment, she picked up the coin and made it disappear into her own layers. "All right, dear. On those terms, I'll take it."

"Go to old Mosè the moneychanger," Francesca said. "He'll change it for you and keep it quiet."

"Aye, he would," Barbara said. She reached out and laid a hand on Francesca's shoulder. "Go with God, and be careful."

"We will."

A moment later, Barbara had slipped out the door they had entered by. Sabatini looked around.

"Sorry, no beds here," Renata said. "But you can stretch out on the floor. We swept it earlier, so it's pretty clean."

Sabatini looked at the floor with a frown, but a yawn suddenly split his face. He was tired . . . more tired that he'd realized. He looked at Francesca, who had sat back down on her stool. She waved a hand. "Sleep if you can. The morning will bring another long day."

Sabatini hefted his pack, then dropped it on the floor and stretched out himself, rolling onto his left side and propping his head on the pack. Another yawn cracked his jaw. He closed his eyes, and the last thing he recalled was the thought that Francesca looked worried.

# Chapter 4

Sabatini awoke at a nudge.

"Marco," he heard Francesca say as he was opening his eyes. "Time to go."

He shook his head to clear the cobwebs from his thinking, and rolled to his feet in a limber motion.

"Oh, to be young again," Renata murmured. She pointed toward a door. "Chamber pot's in there."

Sabatini took advantage of it, making sure the door closed firmly and that he threw the latch. He was glad to see the latch, actually, but he figured that actors being both lively and often bawdy, everyone would insist on the latch for self-preservation. There was no candle or lamp in the cubby, but enough light leaked in under the door and from a gap in the outer wall just above the ceiling to let him see what was what. It didn't take long before his business was done and he was back in the backstage area, checking his clothes to make sure that they were straight.

Francesca was waiting, toe tapping. She had her new coat on and was holding the bag with clothes. The other bag, the one with the papers, must be under the coat, much as she had carried it under the cloak. Sabatini understood that. Those papers were more important to her than almost anything.

"Ready?" she said. Sabatini nodded as he scooped up his own bag. "Let's go." She looked at Renata, and gave a nod that was almost a bow. "Thank you for your help, and thank Barbara again for me when you see her next."

"It was our pleasure, dear," Renata said in what Sabatini thought of still as a reedy voice. "Santa Cecilia bless you, and go with God."

A moment later, they were outside the theatre in the predawn light.

"Which way?" Sabatini asked. He knew about where the Piazza di San Sabatini was, but he wasn't sure what the best way was to get there from the spot where they were standing.

"This way," Francesca said, turning and leading the way farther down the alley in the faint light. It ended abruptly in a cul-de-sac, which took Sabatini aback, but Francesca walked over to a door set in the left-hand wall. It opened at her touch, and Sabatini followed her into a rather dark hallway. He kept his hand on the wall as he followed almost blindly.

Sabatini stumbled as they crossed a threshold into what seemed to be another building based on the brickwork. There were a couple of candles in the room, which seemed to be a small taverna. An older woman who was wiping down tables looked up and nodded as they walked by. Francesca nodded back, but said nothing as she walked to another door. That door also opened at her touch, and let them out onto a street.

Three corners and several short blocks and they

turned onto the large piazza before the Cathedral of Santa Maria del Flore. They crossed the piazza and entered Via de Martelli, which immediately fed into the Larga.

Francesca was walking briskly in the slowly growing light. She said nothing, and gazed straight ahead, but Sabatini was certain she knew what was going on around her. There were servants and tradesmen on the streets, either hurrying to work or carrying loads for deliveries. In their common clothing, carrying their bundles, the two of them just seemed to blend into the crowds.

Two long blocks and they entered Piazza di San Sabatini. Now at last Francesca stopped for a moment— or rather, hesitated to look around. Just as her eyes seemed to locate what she was looking for, a loud voice called out, "Aunt Maria!"

A large and burly individual hopped down off of a cart and bounded toward them, arms spread wide. "Aunt Maria! Here you are! It is so good to see you." He wrapped his arms around her, even though she stiffened for a moment in surprise. Sabatini stepped back a couple of paces, to create a little distance. Based on what they were supposed to be doing, he needed to not be a part of this scene. He turned to his left a bit, and walked over to gaze at the basilica, but keeping Francesca in the periphery of his vision.

Giulio—that must surely be him—gave Francesca a resounding kiss on the cheek and released his embrace. "Oh, Aunt Maria, I am so glad Cousin Giovanni was able to convince you to come. Uncle Umberto needs tending badly, and he won't accept anyone but you." He took Francesca by the arm, and gently urged her toward the cart. "But please, he is hurting so badly, we must be on the way. The sooner you get there, the sooner he will listen to sense."

Francesca climbed up into the cart, boosted by Giulio, looking over her shoulder at Sabatini as she did so and giving a bare hint of a nod and smile. Sabatini relaxed a little. If this was indeed Giulio, then things were going according to what he knew of the plan, anyway.

There was a sleepy little donkey standing before the cart, who looked around reproachfully when Giulio climbed up into the cart as well, took the reins in hand, and shook them.

"Get along, Rosario, you lazy thing," Giulio called out, shaking the reins again. The donkey faced forward, seemed to sigh, and leaned into his collar. The cart started moving with a hint of a squeak from the wheels. Sabatini's mouth quirked at that—that kind of noise would drive Francesca mad.

Giulio kept up a running thread of conversation, mostly on his own. Sabatini could see Francesca nodding as the cart pulled away. He waited for it to travel a distance, before following in its track.

Giulio took Via degli Arazzieri out of the piazza, the Street of the Tapestry Makers, but the street was only a block long and its T was crossed by the larger Via San Gallo, where Giulio turned the cart to the right, to the north, and headed for the city gate. Sabatini followed, and he caught a glimpse of Francesca looking over her shoulder for a moment to make sure he was still in sight.

It was a fair distance to the gate, and a grumble from his stomach reminded him that he hadn't eaten anything yet today. He kept an eye out, and sure enough, before long he saw a baker's boy carrying a towel-covered tray the same direction he was going.

"Got bread under that?" Sabatini asked.

"No, I'm carrying rocks," the other boy retorted. "Of course I have bread."

"Marco," introducing himself.

"Guido."

"Sell me one?"

Guido looked around. "I don't know . . . these are supposed to be going to . . ."

"Tell them a dog jostled you and a loaf dropped off. I'm starving, and I've got a long way to go today."

Guido looked around again, and shrugged. "Show me the coin." Sabatini reached into an inner pocket of his jerkin and pulled out a soldo. Guido looked horrified. "I can't change that. I don't have anything on me."

"Fine," Sabatini said. "Give me two loaves, then. I'll want something to eat this evening, too." He was overpaying, but he didn't care. He was hungry.

Guido stepped close beside Sabatini as they walked. "Fine. Pick up the towel, put the coin on the tray, and take the two loaves on the edge."

Sabatini did exactly that, tucking one of the loaves inside his jerkin, and tearing a bite out of the other with sharp teeth.

"Mmm," he mumbled past the wad of dough he was chewing. "Good."

"Should be," Guido said. "My master is one of the best in Firenze. Good travels to you."

"Thank you," Sabatini replied after he cleared his throat. "San Giovanni watch over you."

With that, Guido split away from Sabatini and

headed toward an upcoming cross street. Sabatini continued on. He was lagging farther behind Giulio's cart than he wanted to be because he and Guido had slowed down a bit while they exchanged words, coin, and bread, so he stepped up his pace.

The bread was fresh, and even still had a trace of warmth inside it from the baking. The crust was dense, but the inside was light and a bit moist, which was good, as Sabatini didn't have a water bottle. But he strode along with a will, enjoying the fresh bread, and watching as they drew closer to the Porta de San Gallo, the northernmost gate out of the city.

Sabatini was close enough to the cart now to hear that Giulio was still talking. He must have been doing it on purpose. Sabatini had to admit it attracted attention to him, and as long as Francesca limited her responses to nods and the occasional quiet word, she was just background to Giulio's performance. And performance it was.

The gate was open today, and those guards in view stood to one side or the other, simply watching as people entered and left, but focusing mostly on the former. Sabatini saw that he had caught the eye of one of the guards, so he flashed him a big grin after he popped the last of his bread in his mouth. The guard returned the grin with a thumbs-up sign.

Sabatini took a careful sigh after he moved out from the shadow of the gate to stand on the road outside the city walls. First milestone of their very long journey reached—they were out of Firenze. A lot of miles to go, but that was a matter of putting one foot in front of another for a lot of days. Or at least, he hoped it was.

✧ ✧ ✧

The cart crested a low hill. They were in the foothills of the Apennine Mountains, and Francesca was now glad of the cart. The thought of her legs having to go up and down hills wasn't comforting. She kept checking on Sabatini, but he was still keeping pace with them.

"And there is Fiesole," Giulio remarked. Even his volubility had run down after the first couple of miles on the road, and after the traffic had thinned out some. These were the first words he had said in some time.

"Finally," Francesca said with some relief.

Giulio looked at her and chuckled. "Surely my repartee was not that bad."

"My feelings have nothing to do with you and everything to do with the hardness of the seat in this lurching excuse for a conveyance." She put her hand out to the side as one of the unsprung cart's wheels rolled over a small rock in the roadway. The track to Fiesole, although not bad as most roads went, was certainly not as good as one of the old Roman Empire via roads. Francesca was ready to get off and walk on her own feet.

"Well, I suppose we could have borrowed—"

"Stolen," Francesca interjected.

Giulio waved a hand. "What's in a word? As I was saying, we could have borrowed the dowager duchess's carriage, but I'm afraid that would have defeated your purpose."

"Indeed." Francesca's tone was dry enough to serve as a desiccant. Giulio chuckled again.

Francesca turned to look at her companion. The angle was far enough around that she could get a glimpse of Sabatini still trudging along some distance behind them. She faced back to front, content to know that he was still with them.

After another furlong, Giulio said quietly, "You will be missed, you know."

Francesca looked at him out of the corner of her eye. "Right," she said. "A fifty-year-old woman singer who has lived in the shadow of the court all her life will undoubtedly be missed."

"Maestra," the actor responded, "you are valued by many in Firenze—perhaps more than you know—and you will be missed. Even Salvator Rosa has said he will miss you, because no one can talk him into a corner like you can." That drew a snort from Francesca, which engendered a grin on Giulio's face. Rosa, an artist and writer, was a recent transplant from Roma, but was originally from Napoli. Like most artists Francesca had met, he was a walking stick of ego and arrogance. However, she had to admit in his defense that he was almost as good as he thought he was. And he had upon occasion made her laugh.

"I'm sure he said that," she said in her dry tone again.

"He did," Giulio protested. "I heard him say it with my own two ears." Francesca shook her head. "It's true!" he asserted.

"Fine," Francesca said. "He said it. Whether he meant it or not..."

"He is an artist and a writer," Giulio said with a grin. "Of course he meant it...for the moment."

That evoked a laugh from Francesca.

# Chapter 5

The rest of the ride occurred in silence, but it wasn't long before the wheels of the cart rumbled onto the streets of Fiesole.

"Take it slowly," Francesca murmured. "He must be able to keep us in sight."

"No fear of that," Giulio said in return, his voice equally quiet. "I forgot today was a market day. We'll be lucky to get to the taverna in an hour."

And there was indeed a throng of folk on the streets, mostly carrying packages or net bags filled with produce, none of them moving very fast. Conversations were being shouted down the lengths of streets and across piazzas; so many that it wasn't really necessary for the two of them to lower their voices. It was all they could do to hear each other in their normal tones, and they were sitting next to each other on the cart's seat.

Francesca turned to look behind, but couldn't see Sabatini in the crowd. She turned back, now worried, but there was nothing she could do. He knew the plan; she had to trust that he would be able to find her after she stopped.

"There's the taverna," Giulio said, nodding his head toward a sign painted in a blob of faded purple that Francesca guessed was supposed to be a bunch of grapes.

"So what do you do now?" she asked.

"After you drop off, I leave the cart with Alessandro the carter for him to return to Luigi the carter in Firenze in the next few days, and then hustle back down the road to try and make it back to the city in time for the evening's performance."

"Ouch," Francesca said. "I don't envy you."

"Ah, not so bad," Giulio grinned. "I have long legs, and it's basically all downhill from here. I should make it in plenty of time."

Francesca slipped a hand inside her coat and felt in the inner pocket of her dress. She pulled out several soldi and slipped them into his jacket pocket. Giulio felt the movement, and looked at her out of the corner of his eye. "For you and Alessandro and Luigi," she said. "It's not much, but I want you to have it."

"Not necessary, Maestra," he protested. "We agreed on this already."

"You will take this as a courtesy to me," she insisted. "Unless you want me to frown at you."

"Oh, San Giovanni," Giulio said after a snort of laughter, "*Dio* forfend that you should frown at us. Very well, Maestra, it will be as you have said. And here we are."

They had finally arrived at the taverna, and Giulio brought the cart to a halt. He slipped off the seat and hurried around to help Francesca alight. Once her feet were on the ground, he enfolded her in an embrace, then released her, saying "Go with God, Maestra."

The actor bounded back up onto the cart, shook
the reins at the donkey, and in a bare moment was
moving down the street.

Francesca started when Sabatini appeared at her
elbow. "Don't do that!" she snapped. The young man
just returned a cheeky grin to her. She took a deep
breath, then nodded at the door to the tavern. "In."

Once through the door, Francesca realized that
the outer part of the taverna was more piazza than
building. Tables were scattered in the sunlight within
the small paved area, and a few more were nestled
under a broad loggia that crossed the front of the
building. In the center of the loggia were doors to
the interior of the building itself.

Francesca led the way to a table in the sun set
near one of the side walls. She settled into a woven
wicker chair, which settled and creaked a bit under
her weight. Sabatini took the chair most between her
and the piazza, and tilted his head at her.

Recognizing a query, wordless though it was, she
responded, "I am tired of dim and dark rooms. I want
to sit in the light as much as possible."

"You will need a heavier coat when we get farther
north, then," Sabatini said with another of his irre-
pressible grins.

"May be," Francesca said with a not-so-feigned
shiver. She really didn't like being cold. "So I will sit
by the fire and dream, then."

Sabatini nodded to acknowledge the point. "Where
from here?" he continued in a low tone.

"We wait for a friend of Mosè's to show up."

At that moment a server appeared, a woman with

a lined face, which made her look older than her probable years. "What'll you have?"

"I was told you have a good red wine and a decent soup," Francesca said, emphasizing the last two words slightly. "We'll have two of each."

"Half a soldo then," the woman said.

Francesca showed her the coin she had palmed out from under her coat, and the server turned away. She stopped a younger serving girl who was about to enter the door to the taverna with empty mugs, took them from her, and apparently gave her some directions, because the girl turned and went down the loggia and around the corner of the building. The older woman took the empty mugs into the taverna proper.

"Some kind of message?" Sabatini guessed, barely moving his lips.

"What I was told to order," Francesca murmured. "And don't ask by whom."

The boy sat back, mouth twisted a bit in dissatisfaction, but he didn't pursue it. They sat in silence, Francesca enjoying the morning sun, until the serving woman reappeared with a tray carrying two small bowls, two small rolls of bread, and two small cups. Francesca smiled at the presumed pretensions of the taverna, serving the soup in actual pottery rather than a bread bowl.

In a moment, the contents of the tray were set before them, and Francesca and the woman exchanged a whole soldo for a half. Francesca tucked the coin bit away and pulled her pewter spoon out of her inner pocket, wiping it with her thumb to make sure that there was no lint in the bowl of it. She dipped it into the soup, and conveyed a bit of it to her mouth.

Lukewarm, which was to be expected. A bit thin—also to be expected. But it had bits of vegetables in it, and had from the taste of it had been exposed to at least the sight of a chicken in the recent past. She'd had worse, even in the Medici palaces.

Across from her Sabatini had a wooden spoon out and was slurping the soup up as quickly as he could. She smiled slightly, and ate her soup almost as quickly, if a bit more sedately, tearing pieces of bread off the fist-sized roll to dip into the soup. The bread turned out to be barley, which was fine with Francesca. She actually preferred barley bread to wheat, probably because she had eaten so much of it as a child in those times when her family hadn't had the money to buy the more expensive wheat bread.

When Francesca finished, she wiped the spoon off on the sleeve of her coat and tucked it back into her inner pocket, then picked up her cup. The first sip almost took her breath away. She expected ordinary table wine, or even something a little less in quality. But what hit her tongue was better than that—better than anything she'd had in the palace at Firenze, if not as good as what she had had with her late husband Tommaso in his residences in Lucca. She held it in her mouth and let it trickle down her throat, with a small sigh of satisfaction at the end.

"Gently," she murmured to Sabatini as he reached for his cup. "This is the good stuff." She watched as he took a cautious sip, and saw his eyes widen as the taste registered. "Not too much," she cautioned. And after a second sip, Sabatini set the cup back on the table.

They sat together in the sun, Francesca taking slow sips of the wine, separated by spaces of sunshine and silence. Francesca enjoyed it while she could, suspecting that before long she would be longing for times like this again.

"What are we waiting for?" Sabatini finally said.

Just at that moment, a third person sat down at their table, jarring it as he did so. Francesca looked over to see an older man, small in frame, gray-shot hair sticking out from under his hat and tinting his beard, dressed in clothing that at first seemed nondescript, but under a second glance was revealed to be good quality.

"Good day to you, Maestra," he said with a nod. "And to you as well, young man."

"Good day," Francesca replied.

The stranger dropped his voice to not much more than a murmur. "I have an associate in Firenze who tells me that you are interested in a passage to Venezia."

Sabatini opened his mouth, but Francesca lifted a forefinger, so he closed it and settled back in his seat.

"It is under consideration, if it is the right time of the month," she said in the same manner, responding to the signal given in the older man's statement.

The man shrugged. "For those with enough ducats, it's always the right time of the month," he said. Then he smiled. "So, you are the Firenze maestra who needs to go someplace else."

Francesca simply nodded.

After a moment, his smile widened. "A woman of wisdom and restraint, I see. I believe you can be seen in the last chapter of Proverbs."

"And you are?"

"Let us say, an associate of Mosè of Firenze. You may call me Bigliamino."

"Maestro Bigliamino, then," Francesca responded with a small smile. The mention of the moneylender in Firenze caused her to relax a bit more. He was well-known to her, and was the man she had approached when she first began laying her plans to transfer herself to the northern climes.

"And since you are here in Fiesole," Bigliamino said, moving his head a small increment to scan the area around them with his eyes, "the logical assumption is that you want to go to Bologna."

"Farther than that," she continued in the quiet tone, "but Bologna first, yes."

"Keep your goals immediate," Bigliamino said. "A woman of wisdom, indeed. So, I have arranged a conveyance for you." She raised an eyebrow at him, but said nothing. "There is an ox wagon leaving very soon for the cardinal's palace in Bologna with a cargo of spices and sundries. It will have a couple of guards riding with it, and you can ride inside the wagon box among the cargo and attract little attention. And since the cargo is for the cardinal legatus, it will not be seriously inspected by anyone. Very private. You will see."

The cardinal legatus in Bologna, the papal nuncio who was the Pope's governor over the city-state, was nobody Francesca wanted to see. Regardless of who it was today—and that had changed a couple of times recently, due to the upheaval within the church and Urban VIII's leaving Rome—whoever it was would be known to the dowager duchess, so avoiding his attention would be key.

"I'm not going to the cardinal's palace." Francesca leaned forward, and for all that her tone was quiet, her expression apparently spoke volumes, because Bigliamino held up both hands.

"Oh, no, Maestra, you misunderstand. The wagon goes to the palace, but you will part company with the wagon before it reaches the city gates."

Francesca relaxed and sat back. "Good. So when does this wonderful conveyance of yours leave? When should I be there?"

Bigliamino grinned. "Now would be good. The drover is waiting impatiently."

"Then let us not keep him waiting longer." Francesca finished her cup of wine.

# Chapter 6

Ferdinando, grand duke of Tuscany, second of that name, looked up as his grandmother Christine, dowager duchess of Tuscany, swept into the room through the arched doorway.

"Ferdinando, have you seen La Cecchina today?" The duchess's voice was shaky. Today was obviously not one of her better days, the duke thought. Her addressing him informally in public was another indication. His grandmother was normally the height of formality. He knew that the musician was one of the duchess's favorites in the court, and one of the few people who could help calm or soothe her when she got upset about anything.

"No, Grandmama," he responded in matching informality. "In fact, I don't think I've seen her in at least a couple of days. Why do you ask?"

"She was supposed to come to me an hour ago and sing her new song for me," the duchess said with a frown. She looked back at her attendant lady. "Isn't that right, Maria?"

The middle-aged lady who acted as the duchess's seneschal nodded. "She said three days ago that she would come today an hour before noon and play the new song."

"Maybe she forgot, or was interrupted," the duke suggested, looking back at the new lenses on his desk that had been ground for a new telescope. He took one carefully between the fingertips of his left hand and picked up a magnifying glass with his right to make a careful examination of it.

"No, no," his grandmother said in a querulous manner. "She always comes when she says she will, or she sends word if something prevents her. Something is wrong."

Ferdinando suppressed a sigh. He was fond of his grandmother. She had been one of his regents after his father died in 1620, and had been effective at it. And when Ferdinando achieved his majority in 1628, she had relinquished the role with some grace. But there was no denying that her last year or so had not been good to her. She had reached the age of seventy-one within the last few months, and unfortunately her wits were beginning to wander. Poor Maria was becoming as much a keeper as an attendant or steward.

"Have you sent to her rooms to see if she is ill?" he asked.

"No, Your Grace," Maria murmured.

Ferdinando sighed, set his magnifying glass down, and raised his hand to beckon with a finger. A quiet unassuming figure stepped forward from where he had stood against a wall. "Piero, go check on Maestra Caccini in her rooms."

The page hurried out of the room. Ferdinando looked toward his grandmother. "I suspect that she has been ill, and simply not left her room."

"Even so, she should have sent word," Christine said petulantly.

Ferdinando narrowed his eyes, and gave a direct glance at Maria. She sighed, and said, "Come, Duchess, it is time for your posset."

The dowager duchess smiled. She did that a lot these days whenever someone flattered her, Ferdinando recalled. And a smiling dowager duchess was usually a pleasant dowager duchess, which helped keep the peace in the palazzo. Ferdinando wasn't going to object. And since he was the grand duke and it was his palazzo, that meant no one else was likely to object, either. Even the occasional figures of the church who passed through Firenze, cardinals and nuncios and the like, did the same. Of course, for them, it was for political reasons, dating back to when the dowager duchess had been one of Ferdinando's regents after his father's death. Flattering the dowager duchess had been the rule, then.

Of course, back then, when her mind was still sharp and focused, his grandmother had understood exactly what they were doing, and why. And she had taken some pains to teach Ferdinando some of the truths of being a ruler, including the proper use of flattery.

"All right, Maria." The duchess looked to her grandson. "I do want to see La Cecchina, Ferdinando."

"Yes, Grandmama. As soon as we can find her."

The duchess turned toward the door, and Ferdinando rolled his eyes. His grandmother's retreat into senility seemed to be a little worse every day. He shook his head after she left the room, trailed by Maria, and picked up the magnifying glass again.

Sometime later, a small noise penetrated Ferdinando's

concentration, and he looked up to see Piero standing in front of his desk. He raised an eyebrow.

"I went to Maestra Caccini's rooms, Your Grace. Her door is barred, and no one answered my knock, even when I pounded very hard."

Ferdinando frowned, and after a moment set the magnifying glass down. "Go find Palace-Major Roberto and tell him I want to see him."

Piero bowed, and again hurried from the room. Ferdinando carefully slid the lens he had been examining back into its pocket in the velvet cloth spread on his desktop. He sighed. Always other things required his attention whenever he tried to focus on his love of science and optics. His old tutor Galileo Galilei had warned him there would be days like today.

Piero ducked back into the room and flattened himself against the wall beside the door. Roberto Del Migliore, the palace-major, appeared in the doorway. Ferdinando was, as always, struck by just how sinister the palace manager could appear. He was dressed, as usual, in a very dark color—a very dark forest green today—with a small collar and very little ornamentation or jewelry but for his badge of office hanging from a heavy gold chain and a very functional looking dagger hanging from his belt. The dagger was in a very nicely tooled sheath which was adorned by a gemstone or two. But the plainness of the serviceable hilt made it very clear that this was a serious weapon, and not some nobleman's equipage that was more flash than utile.

With his iron-gray hair and the patch that covered his left eye socket, Del Migliore gave much the same impression to Ferdinando as that dagger did. The palace-major had spent much of what Ferdinando had once heard an English cleric call his "salad days" as a mercenary soldier. And he had apparently been a good one, having ended his career following close behind Ottavio Piccolomini, the well-known Firenzan condottiere who had been heavily involved in the warfare north of the Alps.

Having lost his eye in some skirmish in 1630, Del Migliore had returned home to Firenze, where a tidy sum had been saved from the spoils of his wars, and where Ferdinando had presented him with the prestigious (and lucrative) palace-major position when its previous occupant of the position had been caught with his hand too deep into the duchy's coffers. That appointment had come about to a great degree because Roberto was a cousin of some sort to Ferdinando Leopoldo Del Migliore, a noted historian and scholar in Firenze that the grand duke had taken a liking to due to the coincidence of their names.

Del Migliore served well in his position, having noted on occasion that running the palace was no more difficult than running a mercenary company that was short of wine and hadn't been paid in three months. And the grand duke was certainly both aware and appreciative of the competence of his new palace-major. Nonetheless, the presence of the occasionally grim and frequently dour palace-major sometimes made the duke uneasy.

"You summoned, Your Grace?" Del Migliore said with the slight bow that Ferdinando allowed all the senior palace servitors in private.

"Yes. This is a matter for which I might ordinarily utilize the talents of Lieutenant Bartolli, the grand duchy's consulting detective, but he is traveling back to Grantville and Magdeburg to report to the owners of the borax operation and will be gone for some time. This cannot wait until he returns."

Ferdinando stopped to make sure that Del Migliore appreciated the seriousness of the situation. When the palace-major nodded and murmured, "As you wish, Your Grace," he was assured that the proper understanding had been reached.

"The dowager duchess has noted that Maestra Francesca Caccini has not made a promised appearance. Piero tells me that the door to the maestra's chambers is barred shut, and no one answered his attempts to rouse a response."

"Indeed," the palace-major said. "I've not seen her myself in some days. I shall see to the resolution of this matter, Your Grace."

"Your attention will be appreciated, Messer Del Migliore. The dowager duchess will be most appreciative. La Cecchina is one of the few bright spots in her life as it draws to its close." After a moment, Ferdinando added, "You needn't repeat that last to her, of course."

"As you direct, Your Grace," Roberto murmured. "With your permission, I shall see to this small matter."

"I leave it in your capable hands, Messere," Fernando said.

The palace-major gave another of the slight bows, and left to see to "the matter."

Ferdinando relaxed. He did so appreciate competent service.

The grand duke reached for the nearby wine cup. Empty. When did that happen?

"Piero, my wine cup is empty. A dolorous condition, that is. Please alleviate it."

"Immediately, Your Grace," the page said as he stepped away from his station by the door. "Would you prefer the red or the white?"

"I believe the red."

And as Piero busied himself with filling the empty wine cup, Ferdinando removed a new lens from its velvet pocket and held it up between his eyes and the light. *Beautiful*, he thought. *Flawless work... as good a lens as I've seen anywhere from anyone.* He picked up his magnifying glass and lost himself in the detailed examination of the lens. He wanted his new telescope to be perfect.

# Chapter 7

Roberto Del Migliore strode toward the back of the palace. "You," he called out to a servant crossing the hallway before him, "Ernani. Come here."

"Yes, sir," the servant said, pivoting in the intersection of the corridors and approaching the palace-major, obviously wondering what he might have done.

"I need Alessandro Nerinni and Cesare Falconieri to meet me at the quarters of Maestra Caccini immediately. And that means now, not a quarter-hour later." The palace major twisted a simple ring off a finger and handed it to the servant. "Take this. They'll recognize it and won't argue with you. Alessandro should be in our offices, and Cesare will either be in the armory or the stables. Find them, and then meet me at the maestra's quarters. If you see Paolo Gagliardi, tell him as well. And don't be the last one to arrive."

The servant swallowed, and took off at a near run. Roberto quirked one corner of his mouth up in amusement, then continued on his way.

No surprise, Roberto was first to arrive at the maestra's rooms. He tried the door's latch. It moved easily, and he could feel it disengaging, but when he pushed on the door, it moved very little. He tripped the latch again, placing one hand on the door about shoulder level and leaning into it. The door seemed to move more above his hand than below it. So Piero's observation about a bar on the door was probably correct.

"Consulting detective, indeed," Roberto muttered. "I believe we can do this without the aid of the up-timers."

Roberto stood back and crossed his arms. He took a deep sniff of the air. Nothing out of the ordinary, other than a hint of someone's chamber pot being in need of a cleaning. Of course, that didn't signify anything. The servants' quarters on some of the back hallways didn't get as much cleaning sometimes as they needed.

It did concern Roberto, though, that the maestra had been out of sight for perhaps two or three days, and the door was barred. It wouldn't be the first time someone died in their sleep and wasn't found for a few days. He made a wry grin to himself. He could face the prospect of battle with its attendant bloody casualties with a very calm spirit ... almost placid, even. But let him be faced with perhaps finding the two- or three-day-old corpse of a woman who died quietly in bed, and his stomach tied itself in knots. God had a sense of humor, there was no doubt.

The sound of approaching footsteps registered. More than one set of feet, it sounded like ... two pairs, at least, maybe more. Roberto looked around as two men rounded the corner of the corridor and headed toward him. Alessandro and Paolo—good—his assistant as palace-major and his longtime attendant both on the battlefields and off.

"What happens, Roberto?" Alessandro said. "Ernani didn't say." As an ex-condottiere, Roberto allowed a certain amount of informality from his staff.

"That's because he didn't know to say," Roberto said. "At the moment, all I know is Maestra Francesca Caccini has missed an appointment with the dowager duchess, which has Her Grace unhappy. It appears that she may not have been seen for some time, and the door to her room is barred."

"Barred?" Paolo asked in his gravelly tones. "Not locked?"

"See for yourself," Roberto said. "No lock on the door."

Paolo's mouth twisted as he examined the door. "Right. No lock. Solid frame. Solid door. Not so good, then. She might be dead in there and we wouldn't know it."

"*Dio* forfend," Alessandro said, crossing himself. "She's not that old, I don't think."

"A bit over fifty," Roberto said after a moment's thought. "I remember asking when she came back to the palace and resumed her place at court after her husband's death and the passing of the plague years."

"She doesn't look it," Paolo said. "I would have called her no more than late thirties, myself."

"She has children," Alessandro said. "A daughter by her first marriage, and a son by her second."

"Twice-married?" Roberto asked. That bit of information surprised him. "I didn't know that."

"First to another musician in the court; second to a Luccan nobleman," Alessandro said. "Twice a bride, twice a mother, twice a widow. After her second husband died in the recent round of the plague, she eventually came back to the court here. His family was not very accepting, apparently."

"Ah," Roberto said with a nod. "He married outside the normal ranks, and some of them resented it?"

Alessandro shrugged. "That's probably the root of it. But a lot of people don't need much excuse to be nasty, especially to anyone not of their social rank."

Paolo snorted. "Right. Me and the capitano," he nodded at Roberto, "seen more than our fair share of that over the years."

Roberto grimaced slightly at the reference to their mercenary days, but Paolo had been his sergeant, attendant, and companion for most of those years, and the notion of Roberto being his captain was so ingrained in him that it couldn't be removed. Paolo knew his place in the order of things.

More steps were sounding, and the three of them looked to the corner in time to see the servant Ernani scurry around it, followed by Cesare Falconieri a moment later. Roberto gave a small smile as he saw Ernani holding out the ring and hurrying it to place it in his hand. And he had made an obvious effort to not be the last one to arrive, in accordance with the palace-major's instruction. Whether he did so out of fear of the consequences if he did not—or more likely, out of certain knowledge of the consequences—made no difference to Roberto. Obedience was the desired result; obedience was what he received. That was as it should be, he thought.

Falconieri, the head of the palace guards, joined them as Roberto accepted the ring from Ernani. The servant started to turn away, only to freeze at a gesture from the palace-major. "Sorry," Falconieri said. "I was in the stables checking the new horses. They'll do for now, but we need to find some better ones."

Roberto grimaced, and Paolo chuckled. "Every horse that isn't locked up is being sent north," the attendant said. "Between rebuilding regiments that have been hammered to dust in the Swede's campaigns, the fighting that happened in Poland and Bavaria, and now the Turkish onslaught, all of them—the Swede, the Austrians, and the Americans—are paying top prices in florins, ducats, guilders, or dollars for horseflesh right now. You'd best post extra guards over the stables to make sure ours don't wander off."

"Go teach your grandmama to spin, Gagliardi," the guard leader said with a rude gesture. That brought a round of chuckles from all the men.

"So why are we here, Roberto?" Falconieri asked.

"Maestra Francesca Caccini's quarters," the palace-major said, nodding at the door. "She hasn't been seen in a few days. The door is barred. And no one responded when His Excellency's page Piero came banging on the door a little while ago."

Awareness dawned on all the men's faces at the same time. "You think she may . . ." Alessandro began.

"It is a possibility. Regardless of what we find when we enter, since we will likely be reporting to the dowager duchess, I want unimpeachable witnesses." Roberto turned to Paolo. "Can you open the door?"

Paolo walked over and leaned one hand against the door, feeling its weight against the bar. He bent down and examined the door and doorframe in the area where the bar crossed behind them.

"Probably," the attendant said, straightening again, "but it might mess up the door." He looked up and down the hallway. "Let's try something else, first. There's a window in this room, right?" Alessandro nodded. Paolo grabbed Ernani by the arm. "You, come with me."

They went down the hallway in the other direction and turned into a different cross corridor. Roberto looked to Alessandro. "So how long has the maestra been a part of the palace musicians?"

"Oh, for years," his assistant replied. "Way before my time here. She started as a child, if I remember what someone told me correctly. The dowager duchess liked her so much that she even refused to let the king of France hire her when her family was touring there a long time ago." He shrugged. "Or at least, that's what the duchess's ladies say. I wouldn't know. Way before my time."

"In you go." They all heard Paolo's voice sounding through the door. "Get the bar off the door, and don't touch nothing else, *chiaro*?" A few moments later, they heard the grating sound of the bar being slid out of its brackets, and a moment after that the door swung open.

Roberto was the first through the door, followed closely by the others. Paolo stared at them for a moment from where he stood outside the window, flashed a grin, and disappeared, obviously on his way back. Roberto looked to where Ernani stood, still holding the bar. "Put the bar there," he told the servant, pointing to the nearest corner, "then go stand in the hallway. I may need to send you someplace else in a moment."

Ernani almost dropped the bar, he moved so fast

to get rid of it and get out of the room. He nearly ran into Paolo as the attendant entered the room, but managed a fast side-step and disappeared into the hallway.

"Look around," Roberto ordered, "all of you. What do you see?"

"Neat," Falconieri said after a long moment of surveying the outer room. "Clean."

"Too neat," Alessandro added. "Looks like a presentation, not a room that is lived in." He waved his hand at the table. "Everything organized and in its place. Like an accountant lives here, not an artist."

"Capitano," Paolo called from the bedroom. "Come see."

Roberto led the way through the narrow arched doorway. He found Paolo standing at the head of a bed where a figure lay covered by a blanket. For a moment, he thought his fears were realized, but then Paolo flipped the corner of the blanket back to reveal that the figure was nothing more than a couple of sacks of . . . he stepped closer . . . straw.

"So, no maestra here, even though the door was barred and the shutters were latched," Roberto said in a musing tone.

"Her court shoes and dresses appear to be here," Alessandro said, his voice muffled from inside a wardrobe.

"Any plain clothes?" Roberto asked. "Any practical shoes?"

Alessandro rummaged around some. "No."

"This looks like a jewelry box." Falconieri held up a box he'd picked up from a table.

"Anything in it?"

Falconieri had it open and stirred the contents with a finger. "Some lead pilgrim medals, some brass chains. A couple of broken silver coins, and a small tarnished crucifix with one arm broken off. Trash."

Paolo spoke up. "The candlesticks are wooden, painted with silver paint." He set them back on their table.

"Hmm."

Roberto walked back into the front room. He scanned the room again. "What's missing?"

The others looked around with furrowed brows. Alessandro finally held his hands up in a "who knows" gesture.

"Maestra Francesca Caccini, La Cecchina, is a musician. So where is her music?"

"*Merda*," Paolo muttered. "There's none here."

"Exactly," Roberto replied. "And whoever saw a musician's room without scraps of paper or parchment with scribbles on them?"

"You're right," Alessandro said disgustedly. "It's like no one lives here."

"Exactly. She's left." The others looked surprised, and Roberto shook his head. "Look at it: no sensible or practical clothes in the room, no jewelry worth anything—and don't tell me a wife of even one of the minor nobility wouldn't have some jewels—and most importantly, not a scrap of music. She's left. She's run, without telling us, the grand duke, or the dowager duchess."

"But this is still here," Alessandro said, walking over and placing a hand on the lute that hung on the wall. "This was her favorite. I heard her call it her bambino. She wouldn't leave this behind."

Roberto considered that, and after a moment began to nod. "Yes, she would if she was truly planning to break all ties and move fast and far. A woman traveling with a master-class lute such as that would attract attention on the road, wouldn't she?"

"Undoubtedly," Alessandro said, nodding himself.

"The maestra sacrificed it to gain speed and invisibility," Roberto said.

"She's serious about this, then," Paolo said. "That's a lot of gold hanging there on that peg."

"Indeed."

Falconieri snapped his fingers. "Her children. She wouldn't have run without them."

Roberto looked to Alessandro. "He's right."

Alessandro shook his head. "Her son died a year or so ago."

"Plague?"

"No. At least, I don't think so. It was before she came back from Lucca." Alessandro's eyebrows raised. "Come to think of it, it was right before she came back from Lucca. That may be what caused the break with her dead husband's family."

"And that may have been what started her thinking about leaving altogether." Roberto crossed his arms on his chest, then took his chin between his right thumb and forefinger, stroking the dagger-pointed beard that was there. "But didn't you say she had a daughter? What of her?"

Alessandro shrugged. "I think I heard that she had been placed with a convent. In any event, I haven't seen her around here for months, and I haven't heard mention of her."

Roberto pointed a finger at Alessandro. "Find out

what convent, and send to see if the girl is still there. What's her name?"

"Marcella, Marietta, Madalena ... something like that."

"Find that out as well. Now. If the girl is still in the convent, she's probably somewhere not too far away. If the girl is gone, she's almost certainly with Maestra Caccini, and *Dio* only knows where they're on the way to. Gagliardi," the palace-major turned to his henchman, "you go with him, and as soon as you have the name and the convent, you go find out if the girl is there. Bring word back as soon as possible.

"Falconieri," he looked to the guard leader, "put the guards on alert. If they see anything, if they know anything, if they hear anything, no matter how silly or stupid it might seem, I want to know it."

"Right."

Roberto looked to the hall. "Ernani!" The servant popped into the room instantly. "You can go. But you keep your mouth shut about all of this. Not a word to anyone, anywhere, anytime. Got it?"

Ernani said nothing, but his head pumped up and down several times.

"Go." Ernani vanished.

"He won't keep his mouth shut longer than two weeks," Paolo said in a calculating tone, brow creased.

"Do you think so?" Alessandro asked. "Myself, I think it will be three weeks at least."

Paolo looked at him from the corner of his eye. "Five soldi?"

"Ten."

"Done." Paolo looked at Falconieri. "You want in on this?" The guard chief shook his head. "Your loss."

"That's what I'm afraid of," Falconieri said with a laugh.

Roberto sighed. "If you gentlemen are through placing your wagers, you have tasks to pursue. And I," he stressed that last syllable, "must go inform the grand duke that his songbird has taken flight. I expect he will not be thrilled."

# Chapter 8

"Watch your step, Maestra," the drover said as Francesca edged down the steps. If the wagon was stable, it would have been no problem to descend the steps, but the wagon was not stable. It was moving, and that made Francesca very nervous. The fact that Marco had skipped down the steps and alit on his feet with no problems was no comfort.

He was walking beside the bottom step now, holding his hand out to her. "Come on," he called. "You can do it. You walk faster than these oxen every day."

Francesca kept a tight grip on the rope that served as a handhold as she stepped down to the bottom step. The distance from there to the ground really wasn't very far . . . not much more than a span, less than a half cubit. She took a deep breath and held out her hand. Marco gripped it tightly, which gave her some assurance. Francesca bit her bottom lip for a moment, then hopped from the bottom step to the ground, landing on one foot and advancing the other enough to start the stepping movement. She almost stumbled, but between her grip on the rope and Marco's grip on her other hand, she remained steady and fell into the rhythm.

"See?" Marco said. "I told you you could do it." He dropped her hand and moved ahead.

Francesca continued to hold onto the rope as she took a few more steps.

"Are you all right, Maestra?" the drover said, leaning out of the opening slightly.

Francesca looked up at him and smiled. "Yes, I believe I am. Thank you."

"I need to close this up again, then," the drover said, laying a hand on the rope.

"Oh," Francesca said. She dropped her hand and moved away from the steps. As the drover pulled on the rope to pull the steps back up into the side of the wagon and latch them into place so that they disappeared from view and the wagon just looked like a wagon again, she moved ahead to catch up to where Marco had turned around and was walking backwards in the road ahead of the slow-moving oxen, waiting for her.

Francesca moved past the oxen. Marco turned and fell in beside her as she stepped past him. "They must move more than just goods," he muttered.

"Does this surprise you?" Francesca replied with a small smile. Marco just shook his head.

The road from Fiesole to Bologna moved through the foothills of the Apennine Mountains, going up and over some of them and around others. It was one of the reasons Francesca had been so glad to hear about the ox wagon.

"We should see Bologna from the crest of this hill," Marco said, gesturing at the one they were advancing on. "At least, that's what Ricardo the driver said."

"Good," Francesca said.

"We made good time," Marco offered after a few steps.

"Better than I had hoped," Francesca admitted quietly. "But the oxen were strong, the load was light, and the weather's been good. That shaved at least a full day off the trip. We're getting to Bologna in three days, when I expected it would take at least four, maybe five. That's good, because I expect the palace has figured out I'm gone by now, and it won't be long before they start looking."

"Are you sure about that? The looking part, I mean." Marco's voice was quiet, but his face was troubled.

"It's an almost absolute certainty," Francesca replied, looking back at the ox-drawn wagon which was flying the papal nuncio's banner and was trailed by two guards in Bolognese colors on horses. She and Marco were slowly drawing away from it. Healthy adults could outwalk an ox any day if the terrain was reasonably flat or not too hilly. But over the long haul, oxen would usually outwalk humans if not overloaded.

"Why?"

"I told you before," Francesca said.

"So tell me again. No one's close enough to hear."

"I've been performing since I was a child," Francesca began. "My father took our family around from noble house to noble house to palace to perform. By the time I was fourteen I was essentially committed to perform on demand for the Medici family. And that controlled my life, even after I was married, for my first husband, Giovanni, was also a musician in the court."

"Did you love him?"

"I was twenty when I married him. I'd known him around the court for a few years. Was I madly, passionately infatuated with him? No. And he was no paragon of a husband, either. He spent too much of our money on new clothes and on wine. But he wasn't mean or cruel, and he could be gentle. And he was the father of our daughter, our only surviving child, whom he loved dearly. So, yes, I came to love him, even though he originally married me mostly to try and use me as a ladder to acclaim."

She shook her head. "So many years of singing, of playing, of writing music on demand, and never being more than a servant in the eyes of the court, never being more than an ornament at best and a possible whore who wouldn't even have to be paid at worst. Giovanni was a large man, and our marriage was protection enough for most situations. But I was so tired of all that by the time that Giovanni died, that I quickly acceded to the desire of Tommaso Raffaelli to marry him. And he was noble enough, and well-off enough, that I could leave the court and retire to his Lucca townhouse. Unfortunately, that ended with his death a few years later, not long after the birth of our son, also Tommaso. His family rejected all of us, including little Tommaso. And they could hire more lawyers, and better ones, so I was forced to return to Firenze and to the Medicis, to resume my place as their musical ornament."

They marked off more steps before Francesca spoke again. "The dowager duchess, she was oh-so-glad to see me return. I could tell that to her it was like the return of a valued bauble that she had loaned out. I teach the Medici children; I come at the duchess's call and perform for whichever little group of friends and associates has come in on any particular day. And, oh, I cherish the few nights when I am able to retire to my chambers alone, and read, and play the music I want to hear, or write the music that yet rings through my mind."

More steps.

"The circles of my life are almost a canon. At fifty, at least I am old enough now that men no longer want to paw at my body. I could have stayed there, and just slowly drifted into the background and faded away, especially after the dowager duchess dies."

"Is she on the verge, then?" Marco sounded surprised.

"Yes...no...I don't know. She's much older than I am...over seventy, by God's grace. But she is drifting more and more into senility, and even if her body continues to breathe and house her spirit, her mind, all that made her the redoubtable woman she was, will soon be gone, and she will be relegated to the keeping of a nanny. And people would have forgotten me."

"So if that was your desire, why..."

"Why leave? Why now? Why this way?"

"Yes."

Still more steps before Francesca replied.

"Because little Tommaso died a year ago, of a winter's cough, so I need no longer care for him. The blessed Madonna has received him. But my daughter, my sweet Margherita, she is now fourteen. She is the same age as I when I came to the Medici court; her voice is every bit as good as mine was then; and she is as comely."

Marco shook his head. "She thinks she is not as pretty as you."

Francesca laughed. "Girls always think that. She is my very image. If I were her age again, we would pass as twins. She will grow into beauty, and she will be a songbird of note. But if I do not make another road for her, she will do so in the Medici court, where she will live the life I lived. Her life would be filled with the motifs and themes I have experienced, and I will not have that."

Francesca's voice had darkened and hardened, and her last few words rang like a hammer on an anvil.

"I did not know this," Marco said after a moment.

"It was not necessary for you to know."

"But if that is your desire, why is your daughter not with you?" Marco's voice held a tone of uncertainty.

"Because she is safer where she is. And when I have achieved my journey, when I know I have found safety and refuge, then I will bring her forth for the world to see. But not until then."

In silence they finished cresting the hill, and saw the gate of Bologna before them.

"And now, we take the next step," Francesca said, looking at a scrap of paper Bigliamino had given her as she had climbed into the wagon back in Fiesole. "We need to find Jachobe the moneylender."

# Chapter 9

"Your Grace," was said in a quiet voice. Ferdinando looked up from where he was comparing two of the lenses to each other, to find Roberto Del Migliore standing two paces away from his desk. As soon as the other man saw that he had the duke's attention, he gave a bow, somewhat deeper than the bow he had given earlier in the day.

Ferdinando sighed. It was going to be bad news—he could already tell that. He set the lenses down on the velvet with care, then folded his hands together and looked at the palace-major. "Yes?"

"At your direction, Your Grace, I went to the chambers of Maestra Francesca Caccini, taking with me Alessandro Nerinni, Cesare Falconieri, and my attendant, Paolo Gagliardi."

"Such a redoubtable group of men," Ferdinando murmured.

Del Migliore responded with a nod, and continued. "Her door was indeed barred, but Gagliardi was able to open the shutters and boost a servant into the room to withdraw the bar."

There was a moment of silence, before the duke observed, "And was the maestra in her chambers?"

"No, Your Grace. From all the signs, she had not been there in some time—certainly at least a day, probably two, possibly three."

Ferdinando sat up straight. "You are telling me that she may have left the palace two or three days ago?"

"Very possibly, Your Grace. Captain Falconieri is checking with the guards now to see if any of them recall seeing her leave the palace, and Alessandro is checking with the servants, but based on what was reported and based on what we have seen, then yes, it appears she left the palace as much as three days ago."

"*Madonna mia,*" Ferdinando muttered as he sat back in his chair. "Grandmama will have a fit."

The palace-major wisely did not respond to that.

Straightening, Ferdinando said, "Find her. If she is in Firenze or the surroundings, find her and bring her here to me. If she is not to be found, report that as soon as you have made that determination."

"Yes, Your Grace." Del Migliore gave an even deeper bow in acknowledgment of the commands.

Ferdinando waved his hand. "Go. Go."

Roberto headed for his office. He found both Alessandro and Paolo waiting on him when he arrived.

"The daughter's name is Margherita," Alessandro said. "Her father was the maestra's first husband, one Giovanni Battista Signorini, another musician in the court. And the last anyone knew she was residing in Convento della Crocetta, as were some of the other daughters of members of the court. Her son was named Tommaso, after his father, Tommaso Raffaelli, the maestra's second husband. The boy died a year or so ago. A winter flux, one of the women said."

"And the convent is located..." Roberto said.

"On the Via Laura," Paolo replied.

"Then what are you still doing here?" Roberto demanded. "I believe I gave you an order." The smile on his face belied the sternness in his voice.

Paolo straightened from where he leaned against a wall. "On my way." A moment later, his footsteps were receding down the hallway. Roberto looked to his assistant.

"I suppose it is possible that we will find the maestra somewhere in Firenze, but I have a feeling in my gut she's run farther than that. Accordingly, I think we need an inventory of what is left in her room. Take one of the clerks and see to it. And do a deeper search than we did. There's always the possibility that something was left behind that we will find useful."

"Right." Alessandro rose from his seat. "That shouldn't take long. And you're going to be busy for the next little while, anyway."

Roberto raised his eyebrows.

"The dowager duchess wants to talk to you as soon as I find you," Alessandro said with a smirk.

"Joy."

"So I'll just go see about that inventory you wanted," Alessandro said as he went out the door.

Roberto stood alone in the room for a moment, after which he took a deep breath and betook himself to the quarters of the dowager duchess. He was met at the door by none other than the duchess's trusted companion Maria, and was ushered to a room where the duchess obviously held court at times. There was a throne-like chair at one end of the room, he noted, albeit one somewhat less ornate and regal than that possessed by the grand duke. But all those present in the room were clustered around a lounge set to one side of the room, on which the dowager was reclining.

Maria escorted Roberto through the numbers of women standing around, taking him through to the dowager herself.

"Duchess," Maria said, "here is Palace-Major Del Migliore, come in answer to your summons."

"Messer Del Migliore," the dowager said, opening her eyes and holding out her hand.

Roberto took her hand and dropped to one knee beside the lounge. "Duchess," he said as he bowed his head.

"Have you found La Cecchina for me?"

"No, Duchess, we have not. She was not in her quarters. We are looking through the rest of the palace now, but I suspect that she is not within its walls."

The dowager's eyes opened wide, and she struggled to raise up, aided by a young woman in servant's clothing who stood at the head of the lounge.

"You mean she has gone to the city and not returned? How long has she been gone?"

"It's not certain she has left the palace," Roberto replied. "Until we have verified that, I would rather not speculate about anything else."

The dowager's hand tightened its grasp on Roberto's hand with surprising strength. "You find her, and bring her back to me. She is like a daughter to me, and I want to see her safe."

Releasing his hand, the dowager settled back on the lounge. "You may leave, Messere. I am weary."

Roberto rose to his feet and gave a courteous bow, aware of all the eyes upon him. He locked eyes with Maria for a moment, and quirked the corner of his mouth. Her own lips tightened in response. Message now sent and received, the palace-major retired from the chamber. Once in the corridor outside the chamber, Roberto stood, shook his head once, and returned to his office.

Roberto sat behind his desk and reviewed the current ledger of palace expenses. It looked like he was finally going to have to speak to Grand Duke Ferdinando about the expenses being incurred by his grandmother. The dowager duchess was outspending the budget for her maintenance by a noticeable amount. Until recently he had been able to smooth it out by transferring some underspent discretional funds from other accounts, but those were gone. The duke was going to have to either authorize some significant changes to the budget and accounts, or he was going to have to rein in his grandmother. Either way, Roberto wasn't looking forward to the conversation.

Footsteps sounded in the outer room. "The capitano in?" Roberto heard addressed to the clerk outside his office. Paolo was obviously back from his errand.

"In here," he called out. He looked up from the ledger as his attendant entered the room. "Well? Tell me you have good news."

"I could tell you that," Paolo said, taking his plumed hat off and lodging it on a peg in the wall near the door, "but I'd be lying."

"*Merda*," Roberto muttered.

"That and more," Paolo agreed.

"So what is the news?"

"Margherita Signorini was indeed lodged with the sisters of the convent for a period of time. She was receiving tutoring in several subjects, as well as singing as one of their choir and occasional soloists."

Roberto held up a hand. "I know the sisters and their reputation for music. She was that good?"

"From what I could gather," Paolo replied, "she was. Not surprising, perhaps, when you consider whose child she is." Roberto waved his hand to continue. "Maestra Caccini would visit the convent often to provide lessons to the lay students and the younger sisters, and she would always spend time with her daughter when she did. But about six weeks ago, she withdrew her daughter from the convent and took her away. No one there knew why it was done or where she was taken. The abbess was actually somewhat unhappy that that had been done, I think because she had hoped to convince the girl she had a vocation."

"Six weeks ago," Roberto mused. "One wonders what might have occurred about then or right before the time that would have brought the maestra to the point of leaving Firenze."

"You are sure she has left the city?"

"Oh, yes," Roberto said. "If this had only been about leaving the court, there were other ways to go about it. Not least of which would have been joining the convent herself. No, something occurred that pushed La Cecchina to abandon everything she knew. I wish we knew where her daughter went. That would help us track them down."

More footsteps sounded, and Alessandro and Cesare appeared in the doorway together. Cesare's face was grim, but Alessandro had a small smile on his face. Roberto pointed at that smile, and said, "Tell me what you've found."

"Well, I found the maid servant who usually cleans and straightens Maestra Caccini's chamber," Alessandro began. "She looked over the contents of the wardrobe, and stated that it looks to her like all of the maestra's court dresses and shoes were there. She didn't know about any plain clothing, but she did say that there were two pair of outdoor shoes that had been there before that aren't there now."

"Confirmation of that much, at least," Paolo muttered. Roberto waved him silent and pointed at Alessandro again.

"She also was shocked at the state of the outer room. She said that every time she had been there before there were pages and pages of music scattered around, and that the maestra had cautioned her to leave the music wherever it was, even if it was on the floor, if she valued her life. The sight of the straightness of the chamber almost caused her to faint. She definitely paled, and I had to assure her that she had nothing to do with it, and if the maestra were to lodge a complaint against her, I would defend her. She was almost pitiably thankful after that."

"Anything else?"

Alessandro's smile widened a bit. "I took young Antonio with me, and he made a discovery. He examined all the paper and parchment in the boxes, and as you might expect, none of them had any writing on them. He did, however, discover a piece that had been below another piece of paper that had been written on, and he was able to find this."

He withdrew a folded piece of paper from inside his jerkin and handed it across the desk to Roberto. The palace-major unfolded it and laid it out on the desk-top. At first glance, it looked like nothing but a smear of charcoal on the paper, but as Roberto studied it he began to perceive the faint traces of symbols. He looked up at Alessandro.

"Antonio apparently had a sideline in learning how to send invisible messages while he was in school," Alessandro said. "And one of the simplest ways is to simply stack two pieces of paper, then write on the top one with a pen or pencil or stylus, pressing hard enough to leave faint indentations on the second sheet. Once received, you rub the sheet with charcoal, and behold!" He waved at the page.

Roberto looked at the page again, and this time could follow the chain of symbols well enough to determine:

$$F \rightarrow F \rightarrow B \rightarrow M \rightarrow M \rightarrow C \rightarrow B$$

"But what is it?" he muttered.

The smile slipped from Alessandro's face. "I don't have the faintest idea. Do you?" He looked at the other two men in the room.

Roberto spun the page and pushed it toward the edge of the desk for them to view it. Cesare shook his head after a few moments. Paolo, however, stood with creased brow for a moment, then turned without a word and walked over to a large cabinet against the side wall, rummaged around inside of it, and pulled out a roll of parchment, which he brought over to the desk. Roberto rescued the piece of paper just before Paolo plopped the parchment down on the desk and untied its ribbon to unroll it.

The parchment turned out to be a map, one of Italy north of Roma. Paolo spun the map to make it orient to Roberto's eyes, then plucked the paper out of his hand and laid it on top of the map. His blunt square-tipped forefinger stabbed the map.

"Firenze," he said, "being F. To Fiesole, another F." His finger traced that line. "To Bologna." His finger traced farther. "To Modena..."

"To Mantova," Roberto interjected as Paolo's finger moved again.

"To Cremona," Alessandro added, making the next jump as the finger continued to move. "But where's the B?"

They all looked at the map, until Paolo's finger stopped moving. "Here."

"Where's here?" Cesare demanded. "I can't read that scrawl."

Alessandro leaned over to peer at the map closely. "Brescia? That's the B?"

"Has to be," Paolo said. "There's not another town with a B name anywhere close to that line."

Roberto picked up the paper and angled it around in the light. "There are no other letters. Why would she go to Brescia? I could understand Milano. I could understand Venezia, definitely, although I would have gone via the Ferraro road for that. I could even understand Genoa, although I think that's too close for her purposes. But Brescia? Why Brescia? That's almost in the mountains, for the Heavens' sake."

There was a long moment of silence, then Paolo said, "Look beyond Brescia, Capitano. It is but the gateway, I would wager."

"The Swiss? The Austrians? Why would the maestra go to them?"

"No, Capitano. The Germanies."

"She is a good Catholic," Alessandro remonstrated. "She would not go to the Swede. She would not join with the Protestants."

"Gustavus Adolphus is not the only power in the north these days," Paolo said.

Roberto looked at the map, and imagined what lay north of the Alps and the Swiss cantons. "Grantville," he said slowly. "You think she means to go there."

"The only reason for one like her to go that direction," Paolo said. "To the northeast or northwest there are other large cities to provide refuge, but to go to Brescia... there is nothing north of there in Italy for her. So..."

Roberto considered his attendant's words. He and Paolo had worked together for years, and he trusted the other man's knowledge of both strategy and tactics and how people worked. It certainly made sense. They still didn't know the why, mind you, but the what and the where seemed to be pulling together.

"Grantville."

# Chapter 10

"Keep hold of that thought," Roberto said. He looked to Cesare. "You look like you have unhappy news."

"With what you now consider, perhaps less unhappy and more confirming." And the guard commander's expression had indeed eased a bit. "The short tale is that most of the guards have no recollection of seeing Maestra Caccini in the last several days. Given what you now suspect she has done, that comes as no surprise. But..."

"But?" Roberto arched his eyebrows.

"Two of the guards claim to have seen her a few nights ago. But I don't know that I believe them."

"Which guards?"

"Giuseppe and Ercole."

"Of course," Roberto said, sitting back in his chair. Alessandro rolled his eyes, and Paolo gave a snort but said nothing else. "It wanted only those two to be involved to make this a matter of earthshaking importance."

"Now, Roberto," Alessandro said, "you know that Vesuvius has been quiet for several years, but there is no need to tempt fortune."

Paolo made the sign of the horns with his off hand to avert the ill luck. The palace-major pointed at him. "Paolo, bring those two here."

"With pleasure," the attendant said with a grim smile. He looked at Cesare.

"They were caught asleep on night duty a few nights ago, and are in the holding room at the back of the stables," the guard commander said. He pulled a key from his belt and tossed it to Paolo, who nabbed it one-handed in midair and stalked out the door.

"I can almost feel sorry for them," Cesare said.

"Almost," Roberto replied.

Alessandro said nothing, but gave an evil-sounding chuckle.

The guards of the palace were all somewhat leery of Paolo Gagliardi. He was by far the hardest, toughest soldier any of them had ever met, and he wasn't shy about demonstrating that on some hapless guard who happened to rouse his ire. Consequently, when the door to their holding cell swung open in a few minutes to reveal Paolo standing there, it was certain that the two miscreants would suddenly realize that their lives had just gotten more complicated.

The three of them observed the map and discussed the virtues and shortcomings of the path that La Cecchina had apparently mapped out. They had pretty well decided that for two people on foot, it was perhaps the easiest way to take once they got over the Apennine Mountains to Bologna. That stretch would be a hard hike, once they got past Fiesole. But after that, relatively easy walking, perhaps two days between each of the major stops noted in the path.

"Of course, if she has the money to buy horses, it could be done faster than that," Cesare said.

"Don't remind me," Roberto replied. "But if she had that kind of money, would she have taken off on the sly like that?"

"Since we still don't know why she ran, maybe." The guard commander's voice was matter-of-fact.

"And she may have more money that anyone knows," Alessandro said. "Remember, Tommaso Raffaelli was a nobleman with property in Lucca. His family may have forced her out, but who knows what she came away with?"

"Thank you for making the picture even darker than before," Roberto said dryly.

"My pleasure," Alessandro said with a smile.

Paolo appeared in the doorway, turned sideways, and waved a hand toward the inner office. "In," he said brusquely.

Giuseppe and Ercole slunk into the office, and bunched together to one side of Roberto's desk, opposite where their commander and the assistant palace-major stood, both with their arms folded and matching glowers on their faces. Ercole tried to edge behind Giuseppe, but Paolo cleared his throat, and both of them jumped forward and stiffened.

"Commander Falconieri, tell me what is pertinent in this matter, please." Roberto leaned back in his chair and folded his hands together, resting the steepled index fingers on his chin.

Cesare cleared his throat, causing the two guards to flinch. "These two had the night duty on the garden gate three nights ago. They were found sound asleep in the middle of the night with an empty wineskin between them. I've had them stored away, waiting for some little task to come up that they can undertake, some little punishment detail that can put them in the proper frame of mind for the next time I put them on duty somewhere." The guard commander's voice was calm, but there was an edge beneath it that caused both Giuseppe and Ercole to flinch when he said "punishment detail." "Oh," he said almost as an afterthought, "the gate was also unlocked. We found the key on the piazza beside Ercole's slumbering body."

Roberto raised his eyebrows in surprise. He hadn't heard about this . . . not that he necessarily would. It was up to the commander to control his guards and handle the day-to-day operations and infractions. Yet Cesare usually told him of anything serious. He tilted his head a bit toward the commander, and Cesare did quirk the corner of his mouth up in a rueful acknowledgment.

The palace-major stood and walked around his desk, then leaned back against it and crossed his arms, keeping the two miscreant guards in his gaze all that time. He let the silence build. Giuseppe and Ercole both wilted under the gaze, and began to fidget.

"Messere," Giuseppe began, only to stop when Paolo slapped him on the back of the head with one of his very calloused palms.

"You were not told to speak," the attendant snarled. Giuseppe ducked his head, and stared at the floor. Ercole kept his mouth shut, and tried to edge away from his companion in whatever mishaps they were guilty of. Roberto knew they were guilty of something. It was just a question of what.

"Asleep on guard duty," Roberto finally said in a musing tone. "Tsk, tsk. A signal failure of responsibility.

Ah, in the old days, that would have been grounds for some serious punishment. What did we do to the last detail that slept while on guard, Paolo? Did we flog them?"

"No, that was the detail before last, the ones who fell asleep on the night before the battle and were supposed to be guarding the camp." Both the miscreants gulped at that pronouncement. "No, the last detail were the ones in that garrison we posted in that little village in Bavaria. Them we just slapped around a little bit and put to permanent stable duty for the duration of the time the garrison was there." He gave a remarkably evil grin. "And I made sure they took care of their work. Nothing like swinging a hay fork and a manure shovel for over a hundred horses to keep them too busy to fall asleep."

"Hmm," Roberto said, his hand on his chin. "Do we have a hundred horses, Falconieri?"

"Sadly, we do not," Cesare replied. "And even if we did, I'm reasonably certain I would not want these two caring for them. I'm sure I can find a couple of village idiots who would do the work just as well, and cause less trouble while they were about it."

Ercole nodded strongly at that, causing Roberto to smile just a bit. Giuseppe's eyebrows started to draw down in an incipient frown...until Paolo spoke up.

"You can leave that to me, Capitano."

Both Giuseppe and Ercole were now looking a little sick. Ercole looked up and said, diffidently, "Please, Messere..."

Roberto raised a hand in time enough to prevent Paolo from administering a correction to the second of the two miscreants. "Yes, Ercole?"

"We didn't mean to fall asleep. And we can't figure out why we did. I mean, we've had night duty lots of times, and never fell asleep before, even when we'd had lots of wine before going to the gate."

Roberto looked to Cesare, who nodded in confirmation of Ercole's assertions. He picked up on something Ercole said. "So were you drunk? Is that what you're saying?"

"No, Messere," Ercole raised his hands in protest. "That was the night there was no wine with supper, only bad beer. We were ready to drink water, we were, when Maestra Caccini brought us a sack of wine."

"Oh?" Roberto's ears perked up at that, but he kept his tone level. "And just why would she do that? What would the court's leading musician have to do with the like of you?" He let a bit of scorn edge his voice.

"But she did," Giuseppe interjected. "She said she owed it to us, and she brought us a skin."

"But it was a small skin," Ercole continued. "It might have gotten one of us drunk if he drank all of it. But not enough to pass out. And split between the two of us, no. That could not have happened."

"This wineskin," Cesare said. "Where is it? I don't remember seeing it, and it wasn't with you in the holding room."

Roberto tensed a bit as Giuseppe stuck his hand inside his jerkin, then relaxed as he pulled out a flattened wineskin. Paolo pulled it out of his hand and stalked over to stand beside the palace-major. He held the wineskin up, commenting, "It's not very large, at that. Nice piece of work, though."

"'S why I kept it," Giuseppe muttered.

Paolo pulled the stopper out of the mouth of the

skin and took a sniff. "Wine. Probably cheap wine, because it's been mixed with honey." He stuck a finger in the opening, then pulled it out again and licked it. His eyebrows drew down, he frowned at the wineskin, and stuck his finger back in. He tasted the result again, and smacked his lips a couple of times. Still frowning, he looked up to Roberto. "They may be right, Capitano."

Roberto was surprised at that. "How so?"

"There's a taste there, one that's not wine or honey." Paolo repeated the finger taste a third time, and this time he nodded afterward. "Poppy."

"Opium?" Roberto asked sharply. "You're sure?"

"Sure there's something there not wine, and pretty sure it's poppy. That one field surgeon that was with General Piccolomini a few years ago liked to use that with the badly wounded, and he would mix it with cheap wine."

"I remember," Roberto said. He also recalled that Paolo had taken a saber cut in a skirmish that had been intended for him, so had reason to remember that surgeon. He looked back at the two miscreants, eyes narrowed. They stiffened at that. "What hour of the night did this happen?"

"Does this mean you believe us?" Giuseppe asked, only to receive another slap on the back of his head.

"Idiot!" Paolo snarled. "Don't blather. Answer the question, and otherwise keep your mouth shut."

"It was about second hour of the night watch," Ercole offered. Giuseppe nodded sullenly, hand on the back of his head.

Roberto leaned back again. After a moment, he said, "Return them to their holding space."

"Right." Paolo bent a glower at the two hapless guards. "You know the way. Move." Moments later, they were gone, and their footsteps were receding.

"*Per Dio*," Cesare shook his head. "The maestra, she plans like a general. She must have read Machiavelli."

"No need," Alessandro said. "She grew up in the grand duke's court, and was watching Duchess Christine for years. She needed no other lessons."

"Indeed," Roberto agreed. "As you said. Sly, subtle, sneaky, yet restrained. She did nothing more than she had to do."

There was a long moment of silence, eventually broken by Alessandro. "This was planned, of course." His voice was dry.

"Of course it was," Roberto said. "And for quite some time, from appearances. Although I would like to know why she picked those two for her escape route."

"Because they are the ones that everyone goes to to bring little things into the palace that may not have tariffs properly paid or may not have their provenance documented fully." Paolo's voice was dry as he walked back in the door. "The maestra was undoubtedly a past customer; she would know them, they would know her, she could approach them, they would take a wineskin from her. And she undoubtedly knew them for the kind of men they are. She knew they would drink the wine immediately, and with the poppy in it, they would go to sleep very quickly. She undoubtedly stood and watched it, and left at her leisure afterward." The attendant shook his head. "Cold and hard. Don't make wagers with this woman."

Roberto began to laugh. "See, see? Maximum confusion, maximum obfuscation, with minimum effort.

What a condottiere that woman would have made." He shook his head in admiration, still smiling.

The smile trailed off a moment later. "So, the maestra has apparently been gone from the palace for over three days now, and her daughter has been missing longer than that. Her room has been cleared of everything of value to her except her lute. She's not at Convento della Crocetta, or Paolo would have discovered her when he went to look for her daughter. And this," he waved the paper, "makes it look like she planned to leave Firenze and head north." He straightened, feeling his mouth set in a grim line. "The grand duke and the dowager duchess must hear what we have discovered, and I suspect they will *not* be happy."

There were no smiles from the other men.

"I need to report this to the duke," Roberto said. "And you," he said, forestalling whatever Alessandro had opened his mouth to say, "will all be coming with me. Now." And with that, he led the way out of the office, hearing them all fall in behind him.

It took them a while to locate the grand duke, but they finally located him out on the back terrace of the palace, testing one of his new telescopes.

"Your Grace," Roberto said as he drew near. The others stopped a few steps behind him.

"Excellent," Grand Duke Ferdinando exclaimed. For a moment the palace-major was startled, but then he realized the duke was referring to the new telescope. "I can see the Forte di Belvedere quite clearly. Make a note, if you would, to send word to the fort commander that the roof of the central keep has several broken tiles on it."

"As you direct, Your Grace," Roberto said. He pointed at Alessandro, who nodded. "In the matter of Maestra Francesca Caccini, Your Grace..."

The grand duke lowered the telescope and looked back at the palace-major, then around the terrace. "Is she ill? Is she...dead?"

"Neither, Your Grace." Roberto saw the duke relax a bit.

"Is she with Duchess Christine, then?"

"No, Your Grace."

The grand duke looked around and frowned. "She is not here, either. Where is the maestra, then?"

Roberto took a deep breath. "She appears to have left the palace, and probably Firenze, altogether, Your Grace."

The grand duke turned and faced Roberto and his associates. "She what?"

"She appears..."

Ferdinando waved his hand. "I heard what you said, Piero," he snapped. The page sprang up from a nearby bench. "Go to the dowager duchess, tell her we have word of La Cecchina, and I request her presence in the small reception room as soon as she can make her way there. Once you see that she is on her way, return to me there at once."

Piero bobbed his head and took off at a run.

"You," the duke said, almost snapping at them as well, "with me."

# Chapter 11

The walk to the reception room was made in silence. The grand duke led the way with very firm steps, almost stalking. Behind him came a couple of his guards, followed by Del Migliore, who was in turn followed by his companions. A couple more guards brought up the rear of the little procession. They trooped across the piazza and back into the palace, then down hallways and around corners until they arrived at the small reception room.

The palace-major followed Ferdinando into the room. The guards spread out and took their positions against various walls. The grand duke stalked over to a very ornate chair standing in the center of one of the side walls and seated himself. Roberto started to say something, but Ferdinando held up a hand, so the palace-major closed his mouth and settled himself to wait.

It wasn't long before Piero hurried into the room. He paused before the grand duke long enough to bow, then moved to his own place against the back wall behind the chair. That meant that the dowager duchess shouldn't be long in coming. Roberto hoped it did, anyway.

And it was only a short time before the duchess swept into the room through the doorway the rest of them had used. To Roberto's eye, she looked ill: skin pale even below whatever she had applied to her face, and leaning on her companion's arm. Nonetheless, she was walking with some energy, and strode to another chair set beside Ferdinando's that was only slightly less ornate than the one that the grand duke was occupying. She turned and settled in the chair, then looked over at the grand duke.

"You requested my presence, Your Grace."

Her voice was a bit cold. Roberto decided to be circumspect during the next discussion. He had no desire to get caught up in the middle of a ducal-level family tiff.

"Yes, Duchess," Ferdinando replied, looking at his grandmother. His voice was level and controlled, if not quite as cold as his grandmother's. "Messer Del Migliore has things to tell us that he has discovered about La Cecchina. I thought it best that we both hear them at the same time." He faced forward again and gestured toward Roberto. "Proceed."

"As you direct, Your Grace," Roberto said with a slightly deeper bow than what he had been using during their earlier conversations. Their current setting seemed to warrant a little greater formality. "After hearing of Maestra Caccini's possible . . . indisposition from your lips earlier today, Your Grace, I undertook to determine what her condition was. We found the door to the maestra's quarter barred and the shutters locked. No one responded to our serious knocking on the door, so my attendant," Roberto gave a graceful gesture to indicate Paolo, "was able to open the latched shutters and sent a servant in to unbar the door. I had summoned my assistant Alessandro Nerinni and guard captain Cesare Falconieri to assist in the process and if necessary serve as witnesses as to what we discovered."

Roberto paused there to give his hearers a moment to absorb what had been said and ask questions. Ferdinando made a short sharp gesture that the palace-major took to mean "get on with it."

"The maestra was not in her quarters."

"Then where is she?" the dowager duchess demanded. "She was supposed to come to me this morning, but she didn't, and no one has seen her, and now you are saying she is not in her rooms. Where is she?"

The duchess's voice was shaking, which alarmed Roberto more than a bit. He waited a moment, then responded in a quiet tone, looking only at the grand duke.

"When we examined the maestra's quarters, Your Grace, we found that although all her court clothing and shoes were there, other plainer clothing and shoes were not there. Nor could we find any money or jewelry. In fact, everything of value was gone, except for her lute. And perhaps most telling, all of her music is gone."

Ferdinando stiffened. "Her music? All of it?"

"Gone, Your Grace."

"I begin to understand. Continue, Messere."

"Based on everything else we have found, Your Grace, it appears that Maestra Caccini has left the city."

"She's left Firenze?"

"That's what we believe, Your Grace. As I said, she appears to have taken everything she values, plus we discovered that she has removed her daughter from the care of the sisters at La Crocetta, and no one knows where the child is now located. We think they are together, and are headed for another city."

"Where?" Ferdinando demanded.

Roberto held his hand out, and Paolo placed the carbon-rubbed piece of paper in it. Roberto stepped forward and handed it to the grand duke, then spent the next several minutes explaining the significance they had assigned to the letters.

"Brescia?" Ferdinando said after the account was finished. "Venezia I could understand. Milano I could understand. Roma I could understand. But Brescia? That makes no sense."

"Unless she is planning on going beyond the frontiers, Your Grace." Ferdinando raised an eyebrow.

"That *puttana*!" Duchess Christine suddenly erupted. "That little whore! After all these years of promoting her, of preferring her, of giving her support and freedom and protection to do her music, and she throws it all over to run north of the mountains. She's going to France, I'm sure of it! They tried to hire her away from us before, and we rejected it. Now they're trying again!"

Roberto felt his eyebrows rising pretty much of their own accord. That was certainly a possibility he hadn't considered. But it wasn't one he wanted to take seriously. It just didn't feel right. Grantville still seemed like the only thing north of the Alps that would have much attraction for the maestra.

The duchess stood up and turned on her grandson. "You send after her, Your Grace! You send someone to find her, and drag her back by her hair, if necessary. I want her back here, before us, so I can explain to her what an ungrateful sow she is! I'll have her well-striped, I will. The impudence. Whore." Her voice dwindled away to inaudible mutterings.

Roberto noted that the dowager duchess was literally panting, almost hyperventilating, and her eyes were wild. The grand duke stood as well. He took his grandmother by the arm. "As you say, Duchess." He looked to her attendant. "Lady Maria, the duchess is weary. Please escort her to her rooms, and see to it that she gets some rest."

Maria dipped her head, took the duchess's other arm, and began guiding her toward the doorway, murmuring softly to her with every step. After resisting the first step or two, the duchess seemed to change her mind and went along willingly. The others watched until she left their field of view through the doorway, then looked to each other.

It seemed to Roberto that the dowager duchess Christine was beginning to fail. Certainly, that outburst would never have occurred even six months ago. She was ordinarily much more controlled than that. Or she had been.

Ferdinando ran his hand down his face slowly, then resumed his place on his seat.

"I ask that you wipe the last few moments from your minds, Messrs.," the grand duke said. His tone and posture indicated that he was speaking as grand duke and that, though phrased as a request, this was an order.

There was a responsive collective, "Yes, Your Grace," from those in the room.

"Nonetheless, Duchess Christine, speaking as a member of the Medici family and as the dowager grand duchess of Tuscany, is correct that if the actions of Maestra Caccini are as you say, she has certainly cast a great insult on our family. That being the case, the most correct course of action would be to bring her back to stand before us and present her defense before she is, as the duchess indicated, thrown out onto the street."

The grand duke was silent for a moment. "It is unfortunate, perhaps," he finally resumed, "that our consulting detective is not available to us for this work."

Roberto felt a flash of irritation at the reference to the up-timer. "Your Grace," he said, "what we have now is not a matter of chemistry or deduction. There are no tests to be performed. What is before you is a hunt, not a puzzle, and you have some very fine hunters in your train that you can release to run the quarry to ground. Not all problems can be solved with a hammer."

Ferdinando sat back in his chair. After a moment, he gave a slow nod. "You are correct, Messere. Very correct. Although your final statement should perhaps be more wittily phrased as, 'Not all problems can be solved with a microscope.' But your point is well taken. So if I am to send out the huntsmen, how would you recommend organizing the hunt?"

Roberto had already done that consideration in his mind, and now he set it forward for the grand duke's consideration. "Let Messer Nerinni and Captain Falconieri remain here in Firenze to search the city and the immediate surroundings, to ensure that she has not remained here, and to look for anything that might confirm our thoughts or substantially alter them. Meanwhile, I will take your warrant in hand and take a small group of guards and companions and will pursue this trail," he lifted the paper, "trusting that a mounted group of experienced soldiers and riders can outdistance a woman traveling with a girl. I believe that we will catch her up before Brescia."

Ferdinando sat again for a long moment, obviously mulling over Roberto's recommendations. "Let it be as you have stated," he said at length. "And you will have your warrant. But all of you," he looked around the room, "I want her returned alive and well and with no damage. She is a talent given by God, one who graced our court for decades, and despite her recent actions, she is worthy of respect. See to it that she is so treated. Is that understood?"

Another rumbled collective, "Yes, Your Grace," was heard.

"Good." The grand duke stood. "Be about it, then."

# Chapter 12

Francesca led the way down the Bolognese street. It had taken a bit of time to get directions to the street of goldsmiths. Then it had taken a bit more time to find someone who could direct her to the place of business of Jachobe the moneylender. But they were finally on the right street, and she was counting doors under her breath as they moved down it.

"...Four...five...six..." Francesca stopped in front of a door. "...Seven..." She looked up and down the street, and at the painted signboard swinging from an iron rod overhead. "This is it."

Marco pushed the door open and led the way in. The interior of the shop was lit by a number of large candles—beeswax, from the faint scents on the air. An older man, perhaps close to Francesca's age from the looks of the gray in his hair, was seated at a table writing. He looked up as they entered.

"Yes? Do you have an appointment?"

"I was told to seek Jachobe the moneylender," Francesca said quietly. She reached inside her vest and brought out a folded paper which she handed to him. He unfolded it, and read the contents once, then laid it flat on the table and brought out a magnifying lens to read it again.

Putting the lens away, the man folded the paper back up. "Both Maestro Mosè and Maestro Bigliamino speak well of you. Wait here, please." With that, he stood and left the room through a door behind the table.

It wasn't long before he returned, this time ushering an older man with very white hair and a thick white beard that flowed down his chest. The younger man walked him to the chair behind the table and helped him settle, then stood to one side.

A couple of large men dressed in sober clothing also entered the room from the rear door and flanked the door on either side, standing against the wall. Francesca wasn't intimidated by them, exactly, but they looked as if they would be very capable at dealing with any kind of physical threat that might arise. Oddly enough, that gave her a certain sense of comfort.

"Good afternoon," the old man said in a breathy tone. The Jewish mark was prominently displayed on his clothing, and he wore a skullcap over his thinning hair. That was not unexpected. Francesca looked at the other men, and noted that they also wore the Jewish mark.

"Good afternoon," Francesca responded.

The older man held out his hand, and the younger man put the paper into it. The older man opened the paper and held it before his face for a long moment, then lowered it to the table and folded his hands atop it. "Maestro Mosè was careful to not name the bearer of this note," he observed. "I assume, Donna Incognita, that you are the person he wishes aid and assistance granted to."

Francesca nodded, but said nothing.

The older man smiled after a moment. "A woman of wisdom, I see. The less you say, the less can be used to trace you or against you."

"A hard-bought wisdom, I'm afraid," Francesca said with a slight nod.

"Most wisdom is acquired at high prices, I find," the older man said. "The wisest know that, and pay the prices willingly, for wisdom is invaluable; rarer than finest pearls and richer than much fine gold."

Francesca nodded, again in silence.

"I am Jachobe, Donna Incognita. This is my son, Davit." He gestured to the man who had greeted Francesca when they had entered the shop. "And this," he said, tapping a fingernail on the paper, "is an unusual document. It is not often that one of our people will request unconditional assistance for a stranger."

"For one of the goyim, you mean," Francesca said in a dry tone.

"Not to be too sharp about it, yes." Jachobe folded his hands and rested them on the paper. "Do you speak Hebrew, then, Donna?"

"Read it to some extent," Francesca said, "but speak only a few words with any facility."

Jachobe smiled. "Nonetheless, I will warn all to be wary of how they speak around you. I suspect your facility is better than you will admit."

Francesca shrugged.

"Maestro Mosè only says that you travel, and wish to travel swiftly, but even more travel unnoted. Why?" Jachobe was not smiling now. He tapped the Jewish mark on his breast. "What risks would I or anyone within my sphere of influence be running to aid you? You know who we are, you know how we live now only on the sufferance of the princes of the land and the princes of the church. Why should we risk anything for you?"

"I gave Maestro Mosè ten florins to get me to Bologna as quickly and quietly as possible," Francesca said. "I will give you twenty florins to get me to Brescia ahead of pursuit."

"Pursuit?" Jachobe's voice grew a little colder as Davit's eyes narrowed. "And who would be pursuing?"

"Agents of the grand duke of Tuscany, I fear. And no, I have stolen nothing from them, and harmed no one in their family or in their employ. I simply wish to . . . be free."

"And they will have reason to object?"

"They may view it that they have a claim on me."

"And do they?"

"No legal claim," Francesca said, her voice shading toward iron. "No moral claim. They have had nearly forty years of my life. It is enough. I would spend my remaining years my own woman, and bring my daughter out of bondage as well."

"Ah." Jachobe brought his hands up, placed his elbows on the table, and rested his chin on his thumbs. "To be free of an unlawful bondage . . . that, I—we—can relate to." He looked to Davit, and received a nod in reply. "Very well, Donna Incognita. We will take your commission, and see you to your destination. But why Brescia? Why not Venezia? Or Marseilles?"

"I have my reasons," Francesca replied.

Jachobe tilted his head at a slight angle as he considered her. Then his eyes widened, and a smile appeared on his wrinkled face. "I . . . believe I see. Well played, Donna Incognita; well played, indeed."

He looked to his son. "Davit, they are your charge. See to their commission." With that, he levered himself back up to his feet. "I will not see you again, undoubtedly, Donna Incognita, but I look forward to hearing of your reaching your goal. Go with God." The last was in Hebrew. He turned, and made his way through the rear door.

"Do you ride, Donna?" Davit inquired.

"Not really," Francesca confessed. "I have ridden a donkey and a saddle mule before, but it has been a very long time since I have done so. And Marco Sabatini, my attendant," she gestured toward Marco, "is no better a rider than I am."

"That is unfortunate," Davit murmured. He eyed Sabatini. The name identified one of bastard birth, and he was obviously trying to decide if the name fit or if it was a nom de guerre. After a moment, he gave a minute shrug, and continued with, "I suspect any pursuit will be coming on horseback."

"I think we have two days on them, maybe as much as three," Francesca said. "I laid a false trail that will take them a bit of time to uncover."

"But you cannot count upon that," Davit said. "We need you on the road as soon as possible, because men on horseback can travel much faster than even a light carriage, especially if they are willing to buy or rent fresh horses every few hours."

Francesca felt a ball of ice form in her gut. "I know."

Davit turned to the other two men. "Sansone, go tell the stable master to harness the two best horses to Jachobe's light carriage, and stock it for a week's journey. Tell him to have it ready in an hour." One of the men nodded, and left out the front door. "Bartolomeo, have a message sent up the road immediately. Use the path to Modena, Mantova, and Cremona. We will want fresh horses, good horses, waiting for us at each location. We have no time to spare. But it is to be done as quietly as possible, not be obvious." The other man left by the rear door.

"Donna," Davit said as he turned back to Francesca and Marco, "please, come with me. It will take a little while to have all ready, and you should rest and have some food before we start."

He beckoned them around the table, and they followed him through the rear door. Another younger man slipped through the door in the other direction, and Francesca caught a glimpse of him settling into the chair at the table as the door closed behind them.

Davit led them down a hall, turning two corners as he did so, until they arrived in what was undoubtedly a kitchen. "Clara," he called out.

A stoutish woman, with her hair pulled back under a scarf, turned away from a table where she was sorting carrots and put her hands on her hips. She, too, wore the Jewish mark on her vest. "And what is it now, Maestro Davit?"

"These are a couple of guests of Father," he said with a gesture to Francesca and Marco. "They will be leaving shortly, but Father wishes them to be fed and given a chance to rest while preparations are being made."

"Preparations, is it?" Clara gave a ladylike snort. "I remember some of those preparations. You, go." She waved a hand. "I'll see to them."

Davit grinned at her, and said to Francesca, "Clara is very good, and she will see to you. It will probably be about an hour before we come for you, but it might be a bit longer."

"Go," Clara ordered.

Davit went, still grinning.

"Sit," Clara pointed to a couple of stools pulled up to a counter. Francesca sank onto one of them, sighing to get the load off her feet. Marco took the other, and even he made a sound of relief.

Clara bustled about, loading a couple of pewter plates with a couple of apples, a couple of bunches of raisins still on the stem, some slices of a creamy cheese, and two sections of a golden bread cut off of a large loaf. These she placed before them with instructions to "Eat! Eat! You look to be ready to fall down from hunger. Eat!"

The two of them tucked into the food, while Clara filled a couple of wooden cups from a bottle of wine standing on a back counter. "Here. This will give you strength."

Before Francesca was done with the first apple, Clara was placing bowls of soup before them. The liquid was thick and filled with vegetables, while the aroma rising from them testified to the presence and influence of chicken in the recipe. The bowls were porcelain, among the finest that Francesca had ever seen, and the spoons that Clara presented to them were works of silver artisanry to match the bowls.

Francesca took the first spoon of soup into her mouth, and closed her eyes in sheer pleasure. Based upon the soup alone, Clara was the finest cook she had ever experienced, even considering the Pitti Palazzo in Firenze, the house of her deceased husband Tommaso in Lucca, and the houses and palaces she had encountered in France as a young woman. She ate slowly, savoring every morsel and drop of the food.

The wine was the equal of the food—dark, rich, sweet, yet with a fine flavor. That, too, she savored, looking around the kitchen and almost marveling at the contrast between the humble setting of the rough furniture and the kitchen and the simple food that was fine enough to grace the highest tables in Europe.

Francesca was cradling the wine cup when Davit reentered the room. "We are ready to leave, Donna," he announced. She sipped the last bit of wine from the cup and set it down, then slid down from the stool, hissing as her tired feet made contact with the floor.

Turning to Clara, Francesca smiled. "Maestra Clara, the food was most excellent, and the fact that it was served from such a gracious heart made it even better. Thank you."

"'Twas nothing," Clara muttered, her hands wrapped in her apron.

"A cup of water from your hand would be a blessing," Francesca said. "But food such as that . . . a miracle, an act of grace, a blessing upon a blessing. Thank you."

Clara nodded once, apparently unable or unwilling to speak. Francesca smiled again, and turned back to Davit. "Lead on, Maestro Davit."

# Chapter 13

Once they had withdrawn from the reception chamber and returned to the palace-major's office, Paolo looked to Roberto. "I'll just see to packing our things and getting the horses ready, shall I?"

"Not quite yet." Roberto looked to the two other men. "Business as usual while I'm gone. Alessandro, you have authority to do whatever I would do for any situation that comes up. And do have our eyes and ears look for both the maestra and her daughter."

"But you don't expect us to find them," Alessandro said.

"No, I don't. But look anyway. Keep yourself before the grand duke at least every couple of days, and reassure him that you are looking everywhere diligently. Cesare," Roberto turned to the captain, "I need at least four of your men, maybe six. All men who can ride well."

Cesare nodded. "I expected that. I can let you have four. Any more than that will leave me shorthanded for the gate shifts."

"Can your two miscreants ride?" Paolo asked.

"Giuseppe and Ercole?" Cesare replied. In response to Paolo's nod, he said, "Giuseppe is about average for the guards. He can stay on at a gallop, and he can draw his sword while the horse is moving without cutting either the horse or himself. But he's not a lancer, nor would he make a formation rider. Ercole, on the other hand," the captain spread his hands, "turns into a centaur in the saddle. He's the best rider in the guards. If he was only better at being a guard, I'd probably have made him at least a sergeant by now, if not an ensign or cornet."

Paolo gave an evil grin. "Give us four good guards and those two. I'll deal with them for you while we're gone. A couple of weeks' hard riding should serve to shape them up."

Alessandro and Cesare grinned to match Paolo. "They are yours, with my blessing," Cesare proclaimed.

"Well, I'll just go get them out of their confinement, then, and share the good news," Paolo said. He looked at Roberto. "Anything else you need me for right now, Capitano?"

"No." Roberto waved his hand. "Go get us ready." Cesare followed the attendant out the door, leaving Roberto and his assistant.

"Do you think you'll catch her?" Alessandro asked.

Roberto shrugged and juggled his hands. "It's possible, but I'm not going to place any wagers on it. I am planning on driving hard to Brescia, without spending a lot of time in checking the cities and towns as we go through them. She has too large a lead to lose that much time. If we spot something along the way, or if she has some kind of mishap, well and good. But my plan at the moment is to trust the paper and ride for

Brescia. I don't intend to kill horses doing it, mind you. The duke would not appreciate that, either. But eight trained men on good horses should be able to run down a woman over a week and a half, even if she has a three-day start and has a horse of her own and is a good rider. She won't be conditioned for that kind of ride. And if she's walking, it will be that much faster."

"Makes sense," Alessandro said with a nod.

Roberto headed for the doorway. "I've got to get out of these velvets and silks and into some canvas and leather. And hope that my best boots are still in the back of the wardrobe and haven't been stolen or thrown out by one of the servants. Draw me a hundred florins from the ready cash for expenses and bring it to my rooms. Also, for emergencies write up a letter of credit that I can take to a moneylender, and have that ready for me as well. I've seen too much *merda* happen to even the best plans to not have some backup plans available."

Three hours later, Roberto led his little company through the Porta di San Gallo. It was late in the afternoon, but there was enough time to get down the road. They should be able to make it to Fiesole before it was full dark, and Roberto and Paolo between them knew that city well enough to know where they could find an inn with rooms.

Once they were well clear of the gate, Roberto sighed. He leaned forward and gave his mount a couple of light slaps on the shoulder, then sat back in the saddle and felt tension drain away. This wasn't his old campaigning horse. That had been a bay that he had named Fulmine, or Lightning. That poor old horse had been aging when Roberto was in the skirmish which had cost him his eye. It had also cost him Fulmine. And with his decision to leave the wars after that, he hadn't bothered to find another war mount. This was one of the mounts that Falconieri had acquired for the guards, and while he was a solid animal, willing but not overly temperamental, he wasn't the mount that Fulmine had been. But even so, it felt good to be back in the saddle, despite the twinges that told him that he was going to regret not having ridden more.

Being in campaign clothes felt good, too. Heavy breeches, high-top boots, buff coat, wide-brimmed hat with a plume, sword at his side and pistols in the saddle holsters . . . it all felt so right. Roberto started wondering if he had made a mistake leaving Piccolomini's staff.

This wasn't the first time in the last few years that he had wondered that, of course. But it was the first time he had felt seriously tempted to go back to the mercenary life.

"Feels right, don't it, Capitano?"

Paolo's voice came from Roberto's left, where the former sergeant customarily rode. Roberto's mouth quirked a bit, then he said, "Old times, Paolo. Old times."

"Good times, too."

"That they were," Roberto said. "That they were. But they're behind us now. As much as I'm tempted, I'm not going back to them."

Paolo shrugged. "I'll ride with you wherever you say, Capitano."

They rode a ways farther down the road. After they crested a slight rise, Paolo rose up in his stirrups and looked back over the riders following them two by two. He settled back into the saddle with a grim chuckle.

"They all still in place?" Roberto asked, keeping his eyes on the road ahead.

"They are," his companion said. "Even Giuseppe and Ercole."

"Good." After riding a little farther down the road, Roberto asked, "You going to make them ride the tail the whole distance?"

"For a few days," Paolo chuckled. "They can stand to eat a little dust. But I'll start switching them around some before long, just to keep everyone alert."

They rode another mile or so before Paolo said, "So, Fiesole tonight, then what—two days to Bologna? Three?"

"Three," Roberto replied. "These horses are strong enough to do it in two, but they'd need a rest after that. I'd rather make the steady progress than rush, then rest, then rush, then rest, and run the risk of injuring any of the mounts."

"Right," Paolo said. "No guarantee of what kind of horses we could find to replace any of ours."

"You were the one who told Captain Falconieri about the demand for horses."

"Yes. Still, these are good strong horses. We might make it past Bologna in three days. Some village or small town on the road to Modena."

Roberto nodded. He looked ahead. "Road's level, traffic's light. Let's trot." He nudged his mount with his heels, and the horse responded by moving into the easy motion of a trot. Paolo caught up with him after a moment, and behind him Roberto could hear the increased drumming of horse hooves hitting the road.

# Chapter 14

Francesca looked at the carriage with distaste. After three days of riding in it nonstop, her body was beginning to rebel at the thought of mounting into it again. She shuddered to think of what her bottom and back would be saying to her if there were not some rather thick cushions in the carriage.

"Come, Donna Negri," Davit said as he came alongside her. For a moment, she forgot that she was Donna Negri—that they had agreed on that alias when they began the journey. "Antonio says all is ready."

"Not all is ready, I fear." Francesca placed a hand in the small of her back, and gave a slight moan.

Davit smiled for a moment. "I fear that we are not made for sitting in one place for extended hours."

"Especially on a conveyance going over roads at speeds. Most especially when we are past the first bloom of youth." Francesca's tone was very dry, and she felt her face moving to a wry grin.

Davit outright laughed at that. "My bones are old enough and I have enough silver threads in my hair and beard that I completely understand and fully agree with you, Donna. Yet," he gestured toward the carriage, "it is your necessity we serve, and we should be on our way. We should not waste daylight."

"True, Maestro Davit," Francesca said. "Very true. So, on we go." She handed her clothing bag to Marco and made her way to the side of the carriage, where she stepped stiffly up into the carriage and settled herself in the corner of the rear seat, carefully arranging the cushions before she settled down with a sigh. Moments later she was joined by Marco, who had seen to stowing their bags, and Davit.

Davit waved a hand to the driver before he closed the door to the compartment, and just as he settled on the forward bench, the carriage lurched forward as the horses began moving and took up the slack in their harnesses. Davit handled the motion with a practiced manner, but uttered a sigh. "Antonio still has somewhat to learn about being a carriage driver, I fear."

"New to the work, then?" Francesca asked.

"Oh, he is an experienced driver," Davit explained. "But he has heretofore brought only barrels and boxes and bales in his wake. But our usual driver broke his leg and is unable to serve, so Antonio was brought in to travel this route, with little chance to learn that a cargo of people should receive some gentler consideration than his usual hardware."

"He seems skilled to me."

"He is, or we would not have considered him. But he and Benvenuto both are new to Father's direct service, so we are giving them some new experiences with this trip."

"Benvenuto? The one who rides with Antonio?"

Davit nodded. "Our guard."

"I wondered at that," Francesca admitted. "I hadn't seen any weapons."

Davit's face took on a slight smile. "You wouldn't. For those of our folk," he obviously meant Jews, "to be seen with obvious weapons could lead to...problems... in some locations. But with the right connections, and a certain amount of gold, one can obtain new weapons, in the up-time designs, from points north. Weapons that are smaller and easier to conceal than what has been available until recently, yet at the same time are more reliable and more effective."

"The influence of Grantville, I assume," Francesca said. "Reliable, effective, and undoubtedly more deadly."

"Indeed," Davit replied, "as with so many other ideas from that place...or so I have heard."

"It is good to know we are so well protected." There was a moment of silence, then Francesca continued with, "You do not wear the yellow signs."

"There is some confusion in the decrees as to whether they are required when one is traveling." Davit shrugged. "And even if there weren't, it is still often worth the risk to be able to move without notice or remark. I am not ashamed of being a Jew, but..."

"I am sorry to have drawn you out." And she was. It was beginning to dawn on her just how much oppression was visited on the Jews of Italy, in the heartland of the Church.

"It is of no moment," Davit said with a smile. "I have some business in the north, anyway."

"You travel often, then?"

Davit shrugged again. "I am a merchant and a banker's son." His tone was matter-of-fact, as if it should be self-evident. Which, Francesca realized, it should be.

She changed the subject. "We are well along?"

Davit nodded. "We will reach Mantova tonight. Four days from there to Brescia, if the weather holds and we have no mishaps with the carriage or the horses."

"*Dio* forfend," Francesca said.

"From your mouth to His ear," Davit said.

"Bologna," Paolo said as they crested a small hill and saw the city in the distance. "Three days' hard ride it's been. My arse is tired."

"You say that?" Roberto said. "You? The iron sergeant?"

"That's what I get for lolling around behind you in a fancy palazzo every day." Paolo spit to one side. "We got soft, is what we did. And don't tell me you're handling this any better than I am, Capitano. I saw you moving this morning."

"Not moving, would be more like it," Roberto muttered. He peered at where the sun was riding in the later afternoon sky. "Should we press on, try to gain distance?"

"I would say no," Paolo said matter-of-factly. "By the time we get through the city, it will be dusk, and we won't make much time after that. Better to stop a bit early and give the horses a bit of extra rest and some grain. That will pay off more in the long run."

"Wish I knew where La Cecchina is," Roberto muttered.

"At worst she's three days ahead of us," Paolo said. "But now that we're out of the mountains, we'll be able to gain on her. Especially now that we're getting toughened up again." He shifted in the saddle. "I think," was his final statement, muttered.

Roberto chuckled. He looked at the angle of the sun again, and decided that Paolo was right. "Send one of the men ahead to the Golden Cockerel to bespeak rooms and stable space for us."

"Right." Paolo turned in the saddle, stuck his index and little fingers in his mouth, and whistled shrilly. "Ercole!" he bellowed then. "Here! Now!"

Within a moment, Ercole was pulling in alongside the attendant's horse. "You called, Sergeant?"

"I am not a sergeant, you horrible little man," Paolo said.

"Once a sergeant, always a sergeant," Ercole said with a toothy grin from where he rode easily beside Paolo.

Roberto could see that Falconieri's judgment of Ercole's riding skills wasn't far short of the mark. The man rode like he was a part of the horse.

"He has you there," Roberto remarked with a chuckle.

"Fine," Paolo growled. He repeated Roberto's instructions, ending with, "And you make sure they know it's Capitano Roberto Del Migliore that's coming. They should still remember us...him. Now, repeat that back."

Ercole rattled the instructions back almost verbatim, ending with, "...Capitano Roberto Del Migliore."

"Good enough," Paolo growled again. "Off with you."

In an instant Ercole's horse was flying down the road ahead of them. "The man can ride," Paolo muttered.

"You won't be telling him that, of course."

Paolo turned a glower on Roberto. "Do I look like a fool or idiot, Capitano? Of course not."

Roberto chuckled again, and they continued to watch the city gates grow larger as they approached.

# Chapter 15

There was a bone-rattling *crunch!* sound, followed by an immediate slowing of the carriage as the left rear corner sagged somewhat, accompanied by the sound of something large being hideously scraped along the road. Francesca's heart sank.

The carriage scraped to a stop in a cloud of dust.

"*Merda*," Davit muttered. He opened the door on the side away from the sag, and climbed out. A few moments later, he stuck his head back in the door. "The wheel is broken. You'll need to dismount."

Marco was out the door in but a moment. Francesca took her time, and descended with some care. Once out, she walked around to the rear of the carriage, where she could see that the left rear wheel had indeed broken. Antonio and Benvenuto were crouched before the wheel, examining the broken section. They finally stood, dusting their hands off.

"One of the felloe sections was not good wood, Maestro," Antonio said. "It looks good from the out-side, but on the inside it's like it was worm-eaten or something. Anyway, it held up for a while, but finally gave way here. And once it broke, that caused the strakes to bend, and here we are."

"Did the wheelwright know of this?"

Antonio shrugged. "Maybe."

"Probably," Benvenuto said at the same time.

Davit had the look of a man who had bitten into an apple and found half a worm. "We'll discuss it with him later. We have a spare wheel, don't we?"

"Yes."

"Does it match this wheel?"

Antonio shrugged. "It looks close. Close enough to get us to the next town or inn, anyway."

"Get it on, then."

Davit's tone was resigned. Antonio nodded, and he and Benvenuto took the bags out of the luggage carrier and pulled up the flooring under that to show an assortment of tools. Shortly a couple of pry bars were on the ground alongside a large mallet, followed by a short-handled shovel and several pieces of wood of various shapes.

As they got to work, Francesca stepped over beside Davit. "We're not going to make Cremona tonight, are we?"

"No." Francesca followed Davit's gaze to the afternoon sun. "We wouldn't have made Cremona today anyway. Now we probably won't even make the halfway point tonight. This," he gestured toward the work with a thumb, "will take a few hours at best."

"Or longer," Francesca muttered.

"Or longer," Davit conceded, "if things don't go well."

Francesca turned away, her stomach knotted, only to see the expression of worry on Marco's face. She felt her own lips tighten. They were in the middle of the countryside...hours north of Mantova...not in a town or city. There was nothing she could do about this, not even hire another conveyance.

"Do we start walking?" Marco asked.

"We may have to," Francesca said. "We can't sit out here for a long time." She thought for a moment. "I think we could make Brescia in three days, maybe a bit more."

"Three long hard days, right?"

"Three long days with very tired feet at the end," Francesca said. "Or at least a day, maybe plus a bit, to get to Cremona. Once there, maybe I can find another conveyance to rent. But I don't have connections to anyone in Cremona, so it would be hard to do."

They turned to watch as Antonio and Benvenuto had assembled some of the wooden pieces into Francesca couldn't tell what and started to put it under the back of the carriage. Benvenuto, being the burlier of the two, crawled out from under the carriage and, stepping around to the broken wheel, grabbed two spokes, one on either side of the wheel hub, set his feet, and lifted. From underneath, they could hear the sound of the mallet beating on something, and with each blow the carriage would jerk a little bit and raise a bit more. They were obviously putting some kind of lift under the carriage.

Two or three more hits, and Antonio called out, "That's got it." He rolled out from under the carriage himself, and clambered to his feet, mallet still in his hand. Taking the wheel in his other hand, he gave it a spin and watched it turn in its unbalanced, limping, lopsided manner clear of the ground for a couple of revolutions before it settled to rocking back and forth. "Right. Let's get on with it."

Benvenuto picked up a pry bar and approached the broken wheel.

Francesca watched, the knot in her stomach turning to ice at the thought of pursuers riding while she was stalled here.

Roberto took a deep breath as they exited the Modena city gate. "We're gaining on her," he said. "I can feel it." His focus and anticipation went up another notch.

Paolo nodded. "I can, too." His mouth quirked. "Feels like old times, Capitano. Been a long time since we were on the trail of someone."

"Still no sign of a woman and a girl, though, or even a woman by herself."

Someone moved up on the other side of Roberto. He looked over at Ercole and raised his eyebrows.

"Messere," the guard began, "one of the gate guards we just went by thinks he saw Maestra Caccini a couple of days ago...he thinks."

"And how did you get that piece of information?" Roberto asked, astonishment mixed with disbelief.

"How would he know it was her?" Paolo added.

"I showed them this," Ercole said, pulling a piece of folded parchment out of his jerkin and handing it over.

Roberto unfolded it to see a remarkably good likeness of the maestra sketched in charcoal, even though it was somewhat smudged. "Where did you get this?" he demanded.

"Giuseppe did it."

"He has undiscovered talents, then." Roberto passed it over to Paolo, who grunted and passed it back. "If

I had known you had that, I would have had you showing it to all the guards at all the gates."

Ercole smiled. "I've been checking, Messere. This is the first time someone had even a bit of a memory."

"So what did the guard say?"

"He thinks it was two days ago, and it was a carriage that went through. He said it was kind of like one of the new-fangled Hungarian coaches. Painted brown, with undyed linen curtains, but they had been pulled back, and he saw her through the window as it rolled through the gate. He remembered her because she looked a bit like one of his aunts."

Roberto felt his eyebrows go up again. "A carriage? How many horses?"

"Two horses."

"*Merda*. Was he sure about that?"

Ercole nodded.

"*Merda*," Roberto repeated. "They'll be making good time, then."

"As long as the roads are good," Paolo said. "Once they're north of Mantova, though, that may not be the case."

Roberto shook his head, then looked back at Ercole.

"Did you think to ask if anyone else was in the carriage with her?"

"A dark-haired man and a youth."

Roberto's curses this time were longer and harsher. "That's why no one has noticed her. She's not traveling with her daughter. She's traveling with a different group." He slapped his thigh in frustration. "I should have thought of that."

"Where's the girl, then?" Paolo asked.

"*Dio* alone knows," Roberto snarled. "In hiding, in a

different convent, on a ship to America. Who knows? I tell you, Paolo, this woman is a better strategist than half the condottieri of Europa—no, more than half. We're busy chasing her phantom while what should have been our best hope of finding her, her daughter, has disappeared off the board altogether. I am a fool! *Idiota! Grullo! Citrullo!*"

Roberto handed the parchment back to Ercole, and gestured him back into his position. He could tell his face was set in a frown, because even Paolo was looking at him sidelong and not saying anything.

Roberto considered distances, times, horses, carriages. "We will press harder," he said, nudging his horse into a trot.

Paolo caught up with him in a few moments. "You will wear the horses out faster, Capitano," he said.

"A chance we'll have to take," Roberto said. "We need to make up more time now."

His face still grim, Roberto faced ahead and thought, trying to anticipate what other stratagems Maestra Caccini could have devised.

Ferdinando heard steps behind him. He was out on the rear piazza of the palazzo again, trying another combination of lenses for his telescope.

"Who is it, Piero?"

"The Lady Maria, Your Grace."

Ferdinando sighed, and lowered the telescope as the steps came to an end behind him.

"What is it, Lady Maria?"

"Your Grace . . . the dowager duchess . . ."

The grand duke heard a tone in the lady's voice that he'd not heard before. He wasn't sure what it signified, but he knew it was a marker for something different.

Ferdinando turned, only to find the lady sunk in a deep curtsey. Before he could speak, she said a single phrase.

"*Se n'e' andatai.*"

He froze. "Gone? Are you telling me that my grandmother is . . . dead?"

Lady Maria raised her face, and he could see the tears on it. That got through the shock. "Yes, Your Grace."

"How? Why?" Ferdinando pushed the telescope into the arms of Piero and stepped toward the lady. "Are you certain? Call the doctor!"

"Doctor Rinaldo is there now. The duchess had complained earlier that she didn't feel well, so I got her to lie down and rest while I sent for the doctor. She seemed to go to sleep, but when the doctor arrived, we were unable to awaken her, and he said she was . . . dead."

The next hours were dark to Ferdinando, chaotic, blurry in later memory. He had rushed to his grandmother's chambers, to fall to his knees beside her bed amidst the weeping and wailing women of her suite and take her cold hand in his. It did not warm in his grasp. And the slackness of her chin and throat was proof enough that she was gone.

He had stood and backed away. "Tend to her," he had said, then left the room to wander through the palace. He had eventually ended up back on the piazza. He didn't know how long he had been there, when his focus returned, and he felt himself again. It was growing dark.

Ferdinando sighed, then turned around. Faithful Piero was there. That did not surprise him. But also there was Alessandro Nerinni, the palace-major while Del Migliore was gone. He had a goblet and a bottle of wine in his hands. A moment later, he had poured some of the wine into the goblet and handed it to the grand duke without a word. Ferdinando took the goblet, also without comment, and drained most of it in a single gulp. He held it out, and Alessandro refilled it.

Taking a more moderate draft of the wine, Ferdinando lowered the goblet after a moment and said, "I need you to send a message, Maestro Alessandro."

"Immediately, Your Grace. To whom?"

"Send it to Del Migliore."

Ferdinando spent a long moment dictating the message. When he was done, he waved a hand and said, "By fastest messenger."

"As you will, Your Grace."

Alessandro bowed, then left to carry out that order.

Ferdinando turned and looked out over the Boboli Gardens as dusk turned to night, holding his goblet out from time to time for Piero to refill from the bottle that Alessandro had left with the page.

"The end of an era," he murmured with the last cup. Even more so than the death of his mother five years earlier was the death of his grandmother.

The carriage rolled to a stop in front of the village taverna. This wasn't even the halfway point on the road to Cremona. It was simply the first village they had come to after getting the wheel replaced on the carriage.

Francesca sighed. It was very close to dark. They could not drive farther, not with the light gone. But they were behind their schedule now—hours behind. She was tense with fear at the thought of looking over her shoulder and seeing men in the colors of Firenze riding up behind them.

Davit dismounted from the carriage, then held out his hand. "Come, Donna Negri," he said. "This is as far as we can safely go tonight. We will arise early tomorrow and begin our travels with the earliest rays of dawn."

"We should have walked," Francesca muttered as she stepped down.

Davit shrugged. "It would have occupied some time for you, but it would not have saved any. It would have taken you just as long to get here."

And that, Francesca realized, was the truth.

"Well, roust out the village wheelwright or blacksmith and make sure the new wheel is on solid." Francesca knew she sounded angry. She was so tired, and so worried, that she didn't care. "We can't afford to have this happen again."

Davit nodded in dour agreement.

# Chapter 16

"Cremona at last," Francesca murmured as they rolled through the city gates. It was nigh on to full dark, and they had barely made it to the city before the gates closed. It had been a long day. They had all been up with the first glimmer of predawn light, and they were on the road as soon as Antonio could see his horses clearly.

Antonio had pushed the horses all day, knowing that they had to make up for lost time. They had made up the time, at the cost of exhausting the horses. Even Francesca could tell that they were weary, heads drooping.

"Good horses," Davit said, as if he was reading her mind. "We will exchange them for fresh horses here, and leave them to be rested and fed well. They should be good to go when we come back through a few days from now."

"Good," Francesca replied. "I'm glad we've reached Cremona, but I'm also glad we didn't kill the horses to do it. So, two days to Brescia from here?"

"Yes, Donna," Davit replied. "Again, barring bad weather or more problems with the carriage or new horses. And I will have everything checked over again tonight while we rest."

"Good," Francesca said as she shifted position on her cushions, trying to find a position that eased the ache in her back and hips.

"Nearly there," Davit said, obviously trying to reassure her.

"Good." Francesca pulled a rosary out of her pocket, and went through a decade, murmuring the prayers. As she completed it, she looked up to see Davit staring at her, face expressionless. "Sorry," she said as she slipped the rosary back into its place, "I needed some comfort."

Davit nodded, but said nothing more. She realized she had offended him, but she was so weary that she had no strength left to discuss it with him.

The carriage rolled down the cobbled street. The rumble of the wheels on the stones seemed to resonate in Francesca's bones.

Giuseppe and Ercole brought their mugs and came to stand in front of the table where Roberto and Paolo were sitting back in the corner, away from the other people in the common room of the Mantovan taverna where they were stopped for the night.

"What do you two want?" Paolo growled.

"Capitano," Ercole said to Roberto, giving a bob of his head as he said it. He and Giuseppe had picked up that address from Gagliardi. "You told Bastiano and Donato today that we were headed next to Cremona. Where are we headed after that?"

"Why do you want to know?" Roberto said after taking a sip of his wine.

The two guards looked at each other, then back at the leaders.

"My name is Giuseppe Landa," Giuseppe began, then jerked a thumb at his partner, "and his is Ercole Brenzona. We're from Mantova, Messere..." which explained their accents, "...or actually, a couple of little villages north of here. We know the land around here well. If you'll tell us where we're going, we may be able to get you there faster."

Roberto heard Paolo expel a breath with some force, and he felt like doing the same. He restrained the urge to curse, and focused on the two guards standing before them.

"Sit." He pointed at the chairs on the other side of the table. The guards sat with some alacrity. They had the good sense to keep their mouths shut as he thought through everything, all the while staring at them with a stony gaze.

"It's no great secret," Roberto finally said. "Our goal is Brescia. That is where we think Maestra Caccini is going."

"Brescia? Why Brescia?" Giuseppe looked and sounded confused.

"It doesn't matter. We have information that indicates that's where she is headed, and she started out about three days ahead of us. We're following the path she laid out."

"Brescia?" Ercole said. "Capitano, if your goal is Brescia, you have no need to go to Cremona. We can get you there from here much quicker."

"How much quicker?" Paolo interjected, placing his elbows on the table and leaning forward.

The two guards looked at each other, and Giuseppe shrugged. Ercole looked back at the leaders.

"From here, on horseback, if it doesn't rain, maybe

two, two and a half days. It will take four if you go through Cremona."

"Then why is she going through Cremona?" Paolo demanded.

"Don't know," Giuseppe said. "It is a wider road, better, more well-known. It would take a carriage or wagon better than some of the backwoods trails we would use, too. But it is definitely longer."

Roberto turned his mug in his hands while he thought. When it stopped turning, he frowned at them. "Are you certain of this?"

"Yes, Capitano," Ercole said. Giuseppe gave a firm nod.

"How certain?"

"Very certain," Ercole said. "We know the lands around here." Roberto stared at them. The two guards looked back at him steadily. If they were shading the truth, they were doing a very good job of it, he decided, and he wasn't at all certain they were capable of that. "Gagliardi?" he asked.

"Your decision to make, Capitano," Paolo growled. "But if they're not lying, it could really save us some time. Not to mention wear on the horses."

Roberto tapped one fingertip on the table, thinking. The finger stilled as he made a decision. "If you two can deliver me to the gates of Brescia in two and a half days from tomorrow morning, I'll give you each a florin, above what your pay usually is. But if I'm not under the gates of Brescia at noon on that day, you won't get a florin, you'll lose all your pay since Capitano Falconieri took you off duty. And," he lifted a finger, "I'll have you beaten with rods."

A moment of silence was allowed to extend. Ercole

finally spoke. "Is it true that we're chasing Maestra Caccini?"

Roberto nodded.

Ercole snorted. "Good. I'd like to get a bit of my own back after what she did to us." Giuseppe nodded strenuously in agreement.

"You'll have to settle for capturing her," Roberto said severely. "The grand duke specifically ordered that she be treated with care and consideration and not harmed."

The two guards definitely appeared disgruntled, but they nodded in recognition of the orders.

Roberto finally spoke again. "Do you understand what I want? Get me to Brescia in that time, and you'll be rewarded. Fail me, and you will be punished, harshly."

They didn't flinch. Roberto was somewhat pleased by that.

"We can do that," Ercole said in a firm tone. Giuseppe nodded.

"See that you do."

# Chapter 17

"What is that?" Davit said as they crested a rise near to Brescia.

Francesca stuck her head out the other window of the carriage, blinking to settle her eyes in the wind of their passage. She immediately saw what her companion was remarking on, and her heart gave a jump. "That is—must be—the airship." The great lumpy thing in the sky was slowly sinking toward a location outside but near the city walls.

"The...airship..." Davit said in tones of wonder. He gave a sharp shake to his head, then turned narrowed eyes upon Francesca. "This...*this* is why you come to Brescia, not other places."

"Yes," Francesca admitted with a smile. "If I can buy us passage, in four days we will be on the other side of the Alps, and two days later either in Magdeburg or Grantville."

"Four days." Davit turned his gaze on the airship. "That would put you so far ahead of the pursuit that you could disappear before they would catch you up."

"Exactly."

Marco scrambled to stick his head out the other window so he could see the airship. After a few moments, he pulled his head back inside, and turned widened eyes on Francesca. She nodded at him, still smiling. He swallowed, then returned a shaky smile of his own.

"The airship," Davit muttered, eyebrows lowered as he stared at the floor, thinking. "This will change many things. Papa must hear of this."

"Oh, I suspect Maestro Jachobe already knows of the airship," Francesca said, remembering the conclusion of the conversation she'd had with the old money changer.

"Ah," Davit said. "I see. That must be something he learned from the Cavrianis."

"The who?" Francesca was confused.

"The Cavrianis. A goy merchant family that has become very intertwined with some of the affairs of or surrounding the Grantvillers. Papa has had dealings with them before, and speaks well of them. I know that one of them had approached Papa recently."

"I thought the papal rulings..."

"Very quiet dealings," Davit said dryly. "There are only so many ducats and florins available, so sometimes even Jewish money is useful. That is why even though most of the Jews of Bologna have been expelled, our family and a few others remain. The ghetto is almost empty, but we remain, we few, because without us the business life of Bologna would collapse."

"I didn't see that in Firenze," Francesca observed.

"Because the grand dukes of Tuscany, despite their attachment to the popes, have also done a better job of protecting the interests of their Jewish residents than most of the rulers in Italy. Maestro Mosè operates more freely than any of the rest of us."

"I am sorry." Francesca's tone was quiet and sad.

"It is the way of the world," Davit said in a resigned tone.

"Not all the world," Francesca said. "Not in Grantville. Not in the USE. Or at least, so it is said."

Davit shrugged. "Perhaps. But there have been times—even generations—of tolerance and encouragement here, and in Spain, and in other lands, but always it changes. Always the face of the leaders turns against us. Always the persecutions begin."

"So move to Grantville and support the change. Lead the change. Make yourselves so useful that they cannot turn against you."

Davit looked at her with hooded eyes. After a long moment, he said, "Would that it were that simple."

There was a long moment of silence, then Davit clapped his hands together and changed the subject. "Well, what would you do now? We near Brescia."

"First, take us to where the airship is coming down," Francesca said. "I would talk to the people who make that happen."

Davit nodded. "Strike while the iron is hot, yes. By all means." He leaned out of his window and shouted at the driver, and got a shout back. Pulling back inside the window, he said, "Antonio will try to find a way there without going through the city. If there is a road or a path, it would be more direct."

"Good."

Francesca settled back against her cushions, but still kept her eyes directed out the window toward the airship, which had now settled to the ground. She attempted to suppress her excitement. Her deliverance was visible. She was almost free, and she trembled at the thought.

Marco looked at Davit, tilted his head a bit, and made a motion with his left hand down beside his left thigh, so that it was hidden from Francesca. When Davit saw it, he thought for a moment, then showed his right hand beside his right thigh and rubbed his thumb along his fingertips. Marco slipped his hand inside a jacket pocket and pulled something out of his pocket which he displayed to Davit for just a moment, then slipped it back inside his pocket.

Davit looked at the youth for a long moment. Marco stared back at him, stony-faced. After a moment, Davit nodded. Marco returned the nod, then crossed his arms across his chest and looked out the window.

"We won't make Brescia today, Messere," Ercole said. "We are two, maybe as much as three hours from the city, no more, but we cannot get there before they close the gates. It would be better that we stop in one of the village inns that we will see soon and give the horses some rest tonight, then push on at first light. We will be there early in the morning."

"Two hours, you say?" Roberto queried.

"No more than three hours, Messere," Ercole replied. "On my mother's grave and the Madonna's throne, I swear it."

Roberto looked to Paolo and raised his eyebrows. "Let us ride until we run out of daylight," came the growled response. "Every foot we travel now is a foot we don't have to travel tomorrow."

"Agreed," Roberto said. "But tomorrow...be ready."

The carriage came to a stop. Davit dismounted immediately, even before Antonio or Benvenuto could come back and open the doors. He turned and helped Francesca descend, her feet carefully fitting into the steps that hung down from the opening.

"Are you sure about this, Donna?" he murmured as they walked toward several men who were clustered at what appeared to be the nose of the airship, Marco following behind them.

"Never more so," Francesca replied just as quietly. "Besides, what choice do I have?"

The men they were approaching looked their direction as they neared. "Yes?" said the one who was holding one of the new up-time inspired clipboards. "Do you need something?"

"I need to speak to whoever is in charge of your operation," Francesca said boldly.

"You're talking to him," the same man responded with a pronounced Venetian accent. "Marcello Bonaro, from Venezia originally, now from Grantville and Magdeburg. Do you have business with us?"

"I would like to have business with you," Francesca said with a wide smile.

Bonaro's eyebrows rose, and he handed off the clipboard to one of his companions with an aside of "Finish the checklist." He faced Francesca directly, and nodded to her. "What are you seeking, Donna..." he tilted his head in inquiry.

"Call me Donna Negri," she responded. "I have a

pressing need to be in Magdeburg as soon as possible. I am willing to pay quite well for the carriage of myself and my attendant Marco," she gestured toward the youth, "over the Alps."

Bonaro eyed the two of them, and pursed his lips. After a long moment, he said, "We don't ordinarily accept passengers who are not from the USE..." Francesca pulled a florin out of her pocket, and let the golden edge of it show. Bonaro's lips curled up just a bit as he caught sight of that, and he continued with, "...But there were a couple of men that were supposed to go back with us that we've been informed won't be making this trip. And since you and your... attendant...are not large people, we can accommodate you. The trip will not be luxurious, mind you."

Francesca chuckled. "After eleven days in ox carts and carriages, I doubt that your airship will be any worse."

Bonaro smiled at that. "I will concede that. Six florins. Each. One way."

"One way?" Francesca was confused by that.

"Six florins buys you carriage from here to Nürnberg only. No ticket or provision for a return trip."

"Ah. That will not be an issue. I will not be returning soon. But too much. Four florins each."

The resulting round of bargaining was almost desultory, as if they were going through the motions because they were expected to. There were no other airship services yet to offer competing prices, and Francesca had already admitted she had a serious need to get across the Alps fast, so she really had little leverage to affect the prices. Bonaro was actually being generous when he settled for five florins apiece.

"And here is one to bind the agreement," Francesca said as she handed Bonaro the florin in her hand.

"Witnessed," Davit said.

"And you are?" Bonaro said as he took the coin.

"Davit ben Jachobe from Bologna."

"Are you now?" Bonaro said. "I've heard of you... or at least your family." He stuck the florin in his pocket, and held out his hand.

Davit looked a bit surprised, but took the offered clasp and shook hands firmly. "I would have been a bit surprised if you hadn't," he said.

"When do you leave?" Francesca asked.

"Tomorrow early," Bonaro said. "As close to dawn as possible. We're waiting on one shipment, and we'll leave as soon as both it and you are on board."

"Good. We will be here." She turned to leave, only to turn back when Bonaro spoke.

"You can't bring anything large with you, Donna. No large cases or lockers, nothing heavy. And you'll need to bring your own food and wine."

"A couple of small bags of clothes and one of papers," Francesca said. "We have been traveling light. And we'll take care of provisions."

"Then be here at first light tomorrow with your nine florins," Bonaro said with a grin.

"We will be."

# Chapter 18

It was cool for a late September morning. It was barely light out, and there was a brisk wind blowing down out of the mountain. Roberto was glad for his buff coat. It cut the chill—for where it covered, anyway. His fingers and ears were cold, but he was able to ignore that.

His little company had gotten an early start that morning. Paolo had pointed out to Roberto the previous evening that the moon was going to be up and visible late in the night into the dawn light, and with the cloudless days they had been having, they could probably make their way along the roads pretty well.

And so it had proved. The moonlight was good enough to light the way along any established road, as long as they moved at a walk so that the riders could see ahead and guide the horses around obstacles or holes.

No one spoke. Roberto suspected that most of the guards, all of whom had some experience in the wars, were asleep in their saddles, trusting their horses to follow the lead of the horses before them. An occasional raspy sound from beside him indicated that Paolo, that most experienced of troopers, certainly was.

Giuseppe and Ercole led the way. Roberto could make out their outlines in the dim light ahead of him. He watched as the light grew from the east and the way ahead became clearer and clearer. All thoughts of drowsiness fled his mind the moment that both the advance riders stiffened and shaded their eyes. He felt Paolo snap to full awareness at that same moment.

"Messere," Ercole turned and called out, pointing ahead, "what is that?"

Amid the jingles and clanks of all the riders rousing and focusing on what lay ahead, Roberto peered in the direction Ercole was pointing. At first all he saw was the bulk of the city, but then off to the side a bit... what was that lump, swelling up into the sky...

Roberto realized that he had pulled to a halt, and everyone else was gathering around him while he considered what he was seeing. "What is it, Capitano?" Paolo breathed from where he had drawn up beside Roberto. "Some kind of fortalice? Some kind of device or engine?"

Device... engine... those words resonated through Roberto's mind and pulled a thought from his memory. He swore, bitterly and viciously, then said, "The airship! That is the airship everyone has been passing rumors and stories about. She has planned this." More swearing. "La Cecchina is the equal of every general of the age! Ercole! Giuseppe! Get me there now! Now, do you hear me!"

Ercole said nothing, simply spurred his horse into movement. Everyone else did likewise and bent forward in the gallop, following the tail of Ercole's mount.

Roberto's mind was reeling through every curse and blasphemy he knew, and a few that he invented. He saw it now. Her plan was utter simplicity...simply stay ahead of the pursuit until she got to Brescia, then board the airship. Once the airship took flight, the trail would be broken. It was reportedly four days to Nürnberg on the airship, a trip that would take more than a week on horseback through the Alpine valleys and passes. Once the airship left, they would never find her, never catch her.

But the airship hadn't lifted yet, and they weren't that far from it. If they could get there quickly enough...

He bent forward, and urged his horse to greater efforts, while still swearing at and admiring his quarry's stratagem.

"Where were you for so long last night?" Francesca murmured as she opened the jar of ash-tinged grease and used a finger to dab it around her eyes, especially under them.

"Talking with Maestro Davit," Marco said in just as low a tone.

"What about?"

"His business," came the reply. "He makes it sound exciting."

Francesca's mouth quirked a bit. "Given who he is, and even more who his father is, I imagine he's had plenty of exciting times. Just remember that times that are exciting to read about or hear about are usually very unpleasant to live through."

"He kind of hinted at that a couple of times," Marco said. "Why are you bothering with that? We're almost done. None of that stuff about hiding or disguising has been needed. Why start now?"

"Because we're not out yet," Francesca said. "And now is when the fortune could turn against us. So better to be somewhat prepared. Hold still."

She took his chin in her hand and used a finger to dab a bit of the grease under his eyes, and to draw faint lines from the corners of his nostrils around the corners of his mouth to right above the jaw line.

"What did you do that for?"

Francesca cocked her head to one side and looked at Marco. "It makes you look older and a bit harder. Almost makes you look like you have jowls."

"Enough."

Francesca chuckled at that reaction. She had already changed to one of the older outfits and turned her coat inside out to present a different color and fabric to the world, and she had tied one of the very different scarves that Barbara had given her around her head in a style very like that of Brescia and very different from that of Firenze. Pulling out her inner purse, she transferred nine florins to an inner pocket of the coat, then laid five more on the tabletop before she restored the inner purse to its place under her bodice. The bag of her music hung inside the coat, as it had done for the entire trip.

"Tuck those inside your shirt somewhere," she said. Marco didn't argue, but did as he was told, pulling out a little purse of his own and loading the golden coins into it before he tucked it away beneath the layers of his own clothing.

Once that was done, Francesca looked at Marco with a very somber expression. "I know things have gone very well for this whole escapade," she said. "But I can't help feeling that they will somehow catch up with us and cause trouble. I pray to *Dio* and to Santa Cecilia that they do not, but I have this ache in my gut that it will happen. So, if something does happen, whatever happens, you get on that airship. You understand?"

Marco had a very stubborn look on his face. He didn't say anything; but then, he didn't need to. Francesca pointed a finger at him.

"You do as I say, understand? If something happens to me, you get on that airship and get out of here."

She held that pose until Marco gave a very reluctant nod.

The last thing Francesca did was pull out the staggering shoes, as Marco called them. The jar and her other shoes went into her clothing bag.

"You really think you need to use those?" Marco asked with a rather pained look on his face as she slipped them on. "You know how much that's going to slow us up?"

"Not all that much," Francesca said. "I practiced walking around in them last night while you were talking with Maestro Davit." She stood and essayed a few steps to the end of the room and back again. Her gait was definitely irregular, but she was able to keep on her feet and move with some regularity. Marco shrugged.

There was a tap on the chamber door. "Donna Negri," Davit's voice sounded. "It is growing light outside. We must be on our way if you wish to keep your appointment with the airship."

Davit's eyes widened as the door opened to reveal Francesca's changed appearance. He said nothing as they left the house and made their way through the streets to the gates closest to the airfield.

They didn't use the carriage, as it would have attracted more attention than Davit thought they should deal with at that point in the journey. It had been stored in a stable in the Jewish ghetto. But Davit, Antonio, Benvenuto, and a local acquaintance of Davit's that hadn't been introduced to Francesca were all nearby. The driver and the guard were walking together some distance ahead of them, wearing long coats in the style of the *lefferti*. Davit, in his usual attire, flanked Francesca with Marco on the other side carrying the clothing bags. The anonymous acquaintance, dressed in somewhat scruffy clothing, loitered some distance behind them. He carried the bag with bread and a couple of bottles of wine.

It wasn't long before they walked out through the gates to the city. Once they were clear of the gatehouse, Davit glanced over to where Francesca was limping along. "Are you injured?" His voice was very low pitched—so much so that it barely carried to her ears.

"No. Special shoes." Her voice was no louder than his.

"Ah. They don't look very comfortable."

"They're not, and I will lose them at the first opportunity."

Davit chuckled, then said, "Interesting transfiguration you made."

"Hoping for no last-moment problems, but attempting to prepare for them anyway."

"Prudent."

The remainder of the walk was made in silence, with only the sound of her staggering steps to accompany them.

# Chapter 19

"Good morning to you, Donna Negri." Bonaro was standing beside the loading door, seemingly ubiquitous clipboard in hand, checking things off as boxes were carried aboard.

"And a good morning to you, Maestro Bonaro," Francesca said as she came to a stop beside him. "Are you ready to leave?"

"Now that you are here, all that wants is to finish loading this shipment," Bonaro said, checking items off on his clipboard. "And the little matter of nine florins." He flashed a smile at her.

Francesca reached into her inner coat pocket and withdrew the coins she had put there for this purpose. She waited as the last of the boxes and packages were carried aboard, then handed them to Bonaro.

The airship officer counted the coins under his breath, ". . . Six, seven, eight, nine." He looked up. "As agreed. Give them just a moment to finish tying the cargo down, and we'll be ready to leave."

At just that moment, the sound of drumming hooves filled the air.

✧    ✧    ✧

The horses were tiring, Roberto could tell. Even Ercole's mount had slowed enough that it had dropped back to be barely a head's length ahead of the rest. But they had held up long enough. The staging area for the airship was before them. They would be on it in moments. There were only a few people in the area. The novelty of the airship had apparently worn thin for the citizens of Brescia. But one of those people was a woman. He couldn't yet tell if it was Maestra Caccini, but he couldn't assume it wasn't.

"Ercole! Giuseppe! Take her, now!"

Suddenly there was a group of horses plunging toward them. Davit wasn't certain how many, but most of them pulled up short of the airship loading area. Two of them, though, rode straight up to the airship and their riders threw themselves off their mounts' backs to reach out and try to grab Donna Negri. She began to hit at them and shrieked curses. They were slightly restrained in their actions until her clawed fingers left furrows in the face of the skinny one right below his eyes.

"Whore! Sow!" he swore as he swung an open-handed slap at her. She stumbled at just that moment, though, and the slap, instead of smashing into her cheek, landed on her throat instead.

Donna Negri dropped to the ground, hands grasping her throat, and her young attendant went mad. He pulled his dagger and stabbed the skinny rider twice, once in the leg and once in the lower back. Leaving his dagger there, he reached into a coat pocket and pulled out a pistol, with which he immediately shot the other rider in the leg.

At the sound of the shot, everyone else in the area either froze or dropped. Davit and his companions were exceptions, as they pulled weapons out from under their coats.

"Still!" Davit bellowed. "Hold!"

There was the sound of metallic ratcheting all around them, and Roberto looked around to see four men with long guns standing around them.

"Still! Hold!" one of them yelled.

Roberto decided that was a good idea, and reinforced that with an order of his own.

"Stand!"

Everyone took that to heart, except for one person. The scrawny youth that had stabbed Ercole and shot Giuseppe took two steps forward, and raised his pistol to point it at Roberto. He could see it well enough to see that it was nothing like any of the pistols he had ever used as a condottiere. It had a very unusual appearance with a skinny barrel, which meant it almost had to be an up-timer-patterned weapon, which meant that he was staring at the barrel of death, for it would hold several loads, not just one.

Roberto had enough time to see that the face of the youth was very hard. He marveled at the hate on that face, for one so young should not have enough experience to hold that much.

His eyes widened as he saw the woman that he assumed had to be Maestra Caccini somehow stagger back to her feet and lurch forward to place one shaking hand on the youth's shoulder while the other still clutched at her throat. She shook that shoulder. The youth looked back at her for a moment, and she shook her head, even though it was obvious that it caused her great pain to do so and fresh waves of tears washed down her face.

A man with a clipboard in one hand stepped up beside the youth. "Don't waste your ammunition," he said. "Get her aboard."

The youth snarled, but put his pistol back in his pocket and turned to help Maestra Caccini to lurch to the entryway into the airship and help her climb aboard. The man turned to face Roberto over the moaning Ercole and Giuseppe.

"You want to tell me what this is about?" he said in a pronounced Venetian accent.

Roberto looked around. The four long arms pointed at the six of his pack that were still on their horses were being held rock steady, and the faces looking at him were not very forgiving. From the look of them, they were also up-time designs, which meant they probably had capability for multiple loads as well. He hadn't survived as a condottiere without learning to assess threats, and right now his senses were held taut at their highest level. It was a throw of the dice as to whether or not they were going to survive. He saw out of the corner of his eye that Paolo was sitting very still on his mount, hands in plain view. Obviously his read of the situation matched Roberto's.

"I am Capitano Roberto Del Migliore, officer of the court of the grand duke of Tuscany. I have a warrant for the detainment of Maestra Francesca Caccini and the returning of her to Firenze. I believe that is the woman who just entered your airship. The grand duke greatly desires to see her and have certain conversations with her about her behavior."

"Has she been convicted of a crime?" the clipboard holder said.

"Noooo," Roberto drawled the syllable out, "but the grand duke greatly desires—"

"To see her and talk to her," the clipboard holder interrupted. "I understand that." Another man descended from the airship, claimed the clipboard, and reboarded the craft. The speaker stuck his hands in his pockets. From the bulge that was made there, Roberto suspected there might be more in his pockets than fingers. The airship man continued, "But you see, Messere Capitano, was it?" Roberto suppressed his irritation and simply nodded to the other man. "You see, you are not in the grand duchy of Tuscany. You are in the province of Brescia, which looks to Venezia for its leadership. Without the signature of a Venetian official or magistrate, your warrant is not worth the parchment upon which it is written. And so, in assaulting this area and one of my contracted passengers, who has paid for her passage and is now my responsibility, you are acting as no better than a common brigand."

Paolo stirred at that, but Roberto held up a hand and he settled back in his saddle.

"Surely not a common brigand," Roberto said.

That brought a brief smile to the other man's face. "Perhaps not so common as all that." The smile disappeared. "But this territory, this piece of ground where we are standing at the moment, is leased to Upward, LLC, incorporated in Magdeburg, United States of Europe. This is like a piece of the USE, and your warrant is really worthless here without having been validated by a USE judge's signature. You have no standing here. I suggest you pick up your men and leave." Left unsaid was the terminal phrase, "...while you still can." Roberto heard it nonetheless.

Roberto looked over at Paolo and jerked his head toward the moaning Ercole and the cursing Giuseppe. Paolo motioned to a couple of the other guards, and the three of them swung down out of their saddles and converged on their two prostrate fellows. It only took a few minutes to roughly bandage the two of them, although Ercole was roused to vituperative cursing when the dagger was pulled from his back. Fortunately it was not a critical wound, and he and Giuseppe were both bound up and boosted back in their saddles.

While that was going on, another of the airship men exited the craft long enough to pick up the bundles that the woman and the youth had dropped. One of the men with the long guns nudged another bundle toward him, so he detoured to pick it up as well, then hurried back aboard the airship.

Once Paolo and his assistants were back in their saddles, Roberto faced toward the airship man. "This isn't over," he said. "I'll be back, with a countersigned warrant, and you'll cooperate with us then, or you won't do business here. Firenze is not without influence, even in lands ruled by Venezia."

"As the up-timers say, whatever," the airship man said. He walked over and picked up the scrawny youth's dagger where it had been tossed aside after it had been pulled out of Ercole's back. He straightened, and said, "We'll be back in eight days or so. If you want a ride then, come see me. But it will only be one of you, and it will be ten florins to carry you over the Alps one-way. You'll have to cover all your other expenses yourself. Now clear off, because we're leaving. Now."

With that, he turned and walked over and entered the airship gondola himself. The door was firmly closed behind him. Moments later, at a signal that Roberto hadn't seen, several men standing by the stakes the airship was tied to released the mooring cables, and the airship began to rise. When it was thirty feet above them all, the engines were started, and the ship began to move, turning in the air until it pointed to the north.

Roberto sat his horse and watched as the airship dwindled away in the distance until it was just a very small blob barely visible against the distant Alps. He took a deep breath and looked around. It didn't surprise him to see that the men with the long guns had disappeared while they were focused on the departing airship.

"Something to tell Duke Ferdinando about, anyway. Know a good inn here, Paolo?" Roberto asked. Receiving a nod in reply, he said, "Lead the way."

Paolo turned his horse toward the city gates and let the weary animal find its own pace.

Davit looked at the other men walking with him. "Split up. Antonio, you get to the stable, get the carriage, and drive to the first curve of the road outside the eastern gate. Take Benvenuto's gun with you and put them back in their places in the carriage.

"Benvenuto, you trot back to the inn, gather our things, and make your way on foot out the eastern gate and meet up with Antonio there. And both of you stash those long coats as soon as you can.

"Carlo," Davit turned to the fourth man who had been loaned to them the previous night when they arrived, "give your master my thanks for your standing with us. Get back to him now, and forget that you saw or did anything this morning."

That worthy gave a gap-toothed grin, stealthily passed his own gun to Davit, and took off in a different direction at a trot.

Davit looked at the other two. "Go. I'll meet you at the curve."

"What will we do after that, Maestro Davit?" Antonio asked.

"Do you know, I suddenly have a great desire to visit some cousins in Venezia," Davit said with a broad grin. "So get going. We need to be on the road before the Firenzans get settled."

# Chapter 20

Francesca had stumbled to the rear of the compartment, backed up against the wall or partition, then slowly slid down it to the deck. Her hands were loosely wrapped around her neck. The pain was severe. She could feel the tears continuing to course down her cheeks. She wanted to cry out, to moan, to make even little squeaks of pain, but the slightest attempt to speak or utter sound sent fresh spikes of agony through her damaged throat. She could breathe, but it hurt to breathe hard or gasp. And swallowing was almost out of the question. The movement of the pharynx that caused the larynx to close off was the source of an even greater spike of pain.

"Do you have someone who knows anything about physicking or injuries?" she heard Marco asking, urgency in his voice. "Please! Anyone? Maestra Caccini is hurt badly!"

"She's not dying, boy," Bonaro said from the other end of the compartment. "She'll have to wait until we're safely aloft and moving. Then we'll see what we can do."

Francesca opened her eyes a bit long enough to see Marco crouch by her and hold his hand out to touch her, only to stop as he realized he didn't know what to do and anything he did might make things worse. She closed her eyes and focused on holding her neck and throat still, although a moan spasmed through her throat when the engines started up and added vibration conducted through the hull to jar her. She opened her eyes and held one hand out to Marco, who took it. She grasped it tightly and used the leverage to pull her back away from the rear wall, reducing the feel of the vibration, but not eliminating it by any means.

It seemed like an eternity, but was probably less than half an hour before Bonaro and a crewman turned up and crouched down beside Francesca on the opposite side from Marco. She opened her eyes, which were still oozing tears.

"So what happened, boy?" That was Bonaro.

"I think she got hit or slapped in the throat when she was struggling with that one guard," Marco said. She could hear the almost panic in his voice and see the strain on his face even through her tears.

The other man whistled. "That is not good," he said in gravelly tones. "Maestra, I need to see your throat. Can you move your hands, please?"

Francesca held herself very still, and slowly lowered her hands, trying very hard not to tense up and cause the pain to flare up again. It had settled to a dull hurt as long as she didn't move.

"This is Guillermo," Bonaro said. "The insurance company insisted that every airship crew has to have at least one crewman who has had advanced medical training for wound treatments and other medical conditions. Guillermo is it for this crew."

"Can you lift your head any at all?" Guillermo said

as he moved about, trying to view her neck from every angle. "Your chin is shadowing your throat." Francesca breathed slowly and steadily as she tried to raise her chin a bit more.

"Relax," Guillermo said as he sat back. "There is some swelling on the throat, and some bruising. I can't tell for sure, but it looks like her larynx—her voice box," he said in response to the quizzical expressions he got from both Bonaro and Marco, "—is pushed over to the side a bit, which would indicate some pretty serious damage under the skin. But I don't know anything about that. About all they taught us about the neck and throat in the medic training is how to clear out an obstruction from the trachea, how to start an IV in the neck if absolutely necessary, and how to do a tracheotomy to restore breathing and bypass damage or an obstruction. But none of that applies here, because she is breathing on her own."

"So what can we do?" Bonaro said.

"Just trying to apply some common sense," Guillermo said, "she probably should be lying down to rest. No talking, no eating for the next several days. No more drinking than she has to do. If I had some opium, I would give her some of that to alleviate the pain. Best we've got is some cheap brandy. She can take a little of that at a time. I'd guess it's going to hurt like the fires of hell for her to swallow."

Francesca raised one hand back to her throat, and pointed emphatically at Guillermo a couple of times with the other before it joined the first.

"So there's nothing more we can do?" Bonaro asked.

Guillermo shook his head. "Nothing I can splint or wrap or suture. We don't have any ice to use for cold compresses. No opium. All we can do is make her as comfortable as we can. When we get to Chur, she needs to see a doctor and spend a couple of weeks resting."

Francesca took her right hand off her throat and made a short sharp horizontal gesture.

"I'd guess that means 'No,'" Bonaro said with a twisted grin. "Why don't you go see if you can find that cheap brandy, Guillermo, while I try to find out what's going on here?"

Guillermo rose and moved toward a door in the rear compartment wall. Bonaro looked at the two of them. "You named yourself as Donna Negri when we bargained, but that Firenzan officer said you were Maestra Francesca Caccini and this young man called you Maestra Caccini. After having to face down that Firenzan and his lackeys, I think I deserve to know who you are and what I may have gotten my company in the middle of." He shifted his gaze back and forth between them expectantly.

Francesca pointed to herself, then pointed to Marco and waved her hand at Bonaro.

"You want me to tell him?" Marco asked.

Francesca pointed at him twice, with emphasis. Marco sighed. "All right."

He turned to look at Bonaro. "Her name really is Francesca Caccini. She has been Maestra Caccini, one of the greatest musicians of northern Italy, for longer than I've been alive."

"I know that name," Bonaro muttered. "Caccini, Caccini..." he snapped his fingers. "La Cecchina. Right?"

"Yes," Marco admitted. "She has been called that."

"But that would make her part of the court musicians of the grand duke's court in Firenze, wouldn't it?"

"One of its leading musicians for years," Marco said.

"Then why..." Bonaro spread his hands.

"The maestra is very tired of being an ornament and being treated worse than many of the servants," Marco said. "She has broken no rules, injured no one, stolen nothing. She brought nothing with her but the music she has written, a few items of clothing, and the money she has saved over the years and from her marriages. She left quietly, hoping to relocate to Magdeburg to join the musicians' colony forming there without trouble. Yet the court has sent this Del Migliore after her."

"Ah," Bonaro said. "I begin to understand. A case of wounded pride, most likely."

Marco nodded.

"Well," Bonaro continued, "I stand by what I told the officer. I—we—owe him nothing, certainly not in a case of harassment of a private individual."

He looked at Francesca with some concern from under lowered brows. "You need to see a doctor, maestra. You really need to offload in Chur and stay there." Francesca repeated her right-hand horizontal gesture. "That means 'No,' I take it." She pointed at him emphatically.

"Your passage is paid through to Nürnberg," Bonaro said. "But he," pointing at Marco, "says you need to get to Magdeburg. Yes?"

Francesca pointed at Bonaro twice.

"Ah. Well, we may be able to help with that, as well. Let us wait and see what develops. Meanwhile, here is Guillermo with his brandy. I will leave you in his hands."

❖     ❖     ❖

Marco rose and moved aside at Bonaro's beckon. He watched as Guillermo held a small flask to Francesca's lips and tipped small amounts of brandy into her mouth, followed by flashes of agony crossing her face as she swallowed.

Finally, she pushed the flask away, and Guillermo put a stopper in it. He rose and crossed over to Marco and handed it to him.

"Try to get some more down her later. She needs whatever little relief from pain she can get."

Marco took the flask. "I'll try."

"I'll come back later and check on her."

With that, Guillermo turned away and began to talk to one of the other crew members.

Bonaro looked at Marco. "Ask you a question?" At Marco's nod, he said, "If you're from Firenze, how did you lay your hands on an up-time-style pistol? Those aren't easy to acquire south of the Alps yet."

Marco's mouth quirked. "Maestro Davit sold it to me. Five florins of gold it cost me, but it was worth it. I just wish I'd gotten it out even a half a minute earlier."

"Hmm. I may need to maintain connections with Maestro Davit," Bonaro mused. "A man of some means and resolution, it would seem, for all that he is a Jew. And one who made you a sweet deal. An up-time-style revolver would ordinarily run ten florins. Eight, at least."

"Five was all I had," Marco replied, eyebrows drawn down for a moment. "But Maestro Davit is a good man," Marco observed, "a very good man. He helped us more than we deserved."

"I'll remember that," Bonaro said. "You should, too. Meanwhile, it looks like the brandy is working. Let's help your maestra lie down."

# Chapter 21

Roberto Del Migliore stood on the edge of the airship field, Paolo at his side and two of the guards at his back. He was ready to confront the airship crew and force his passage back up the route in pursuit of Maestra Caccini. His warrant had been countersigned by the local Venetian governor, in exchange for a surprisingly small number of golden florins. He had the legal authority now; he simply needed to catch up with the woman, and he had no doubt he could do that, even with the delay of the airship returning.

He was unhappy at one thing. The airship crewman had said it would be eight days before they returned. It turned out to be ten, and Roberto was well aware of just how much that added to Maestra Caccini's time to run.

On the other hand, it had allowed extra time for both Ercole and Giuseppe to begin healing from the wounds they had taken at the hands of the scrawny youth who had been at Maestra Caccini's side. He still wondered who that was, but whoever he was, he had watched over the Maestra with some passion.

He watched, hands behind his back to keep his fingers from drumming on his belt or from seeking his sword hilt, as the airship came to a halt and drifted lower, dropping mooring ropes as it neared the ground. Within a few minutes, the airship had lowered to the ground and had been snugged down.

The first man out of the airship was the airship crewman who had confronted Roberto ten days ago.

"I thought you said you would be back in eight days," Roberto said in an accusing tone of voice.

"We strive for the schedule," the man said, "but between weather and other issues, sometimes we slip a bit. Messer Del Migliore, isn't it?"

"Yes," Roberto bit the response off. "And who are you?"

"Plain old Marcello Bonaro," the man replied with a slight bow, "originally from Venezia, now from points north."

"Well, plain old Bonaro," Roberto said in a voice of iron, "I have my countersigned warrant, so you will take me and at least one of my men back along your route and set us down wherever you released Maestra Francesca Caccini."

Bonaro shrugged. "I think I can take one," Bonaro said. "I'm not sure I can take two. That will depend on what else has been contracted for to go north. That will be ten florins a head, however many go, payable in advance in valid coin."

"Fine." Roberto wasn't especially angry at the man. His irritation level, however, was beginning to rise.

He turned to Paolo, vaguely aware of a disturbance that had happened behind him. "Pay the man."

"You may want to read this first, Capitano," Paolo said, handing him a sealed dispatch. Roberto frowned at him. Paolo shrugged. "I don't know about it, Capitano, but the only people who would be sending that are the grand duke or Alessandro." He jerked a thumb at the dust-covered and obviously exhausted courier who was standing behind him with one of the other guards they'd left at the inn. "Either way, for them to have sent it fast enough to catch up with us this quickly, it must be important."

Roberto's mouth twisted. "I wish I could say you were wrong, but we both know you aren't. Open it, please."

Paolo pulled a thin-bladed knife from his sleeve and broke the seal on the folded page, then handed it to Roberto. Flipping it open, Roberto read through it once, stiffened, then read through it again slowly. When he was done, he folded it up and tucked it inside his tunic.

"*Merda*." Roberto's voice was quiet, but still had the hard sound of his days as a condottiere.

"What is it, Capitano?" Paolo frowned at the sound of his leader's voice.

"Dowager Duchess Christine is dead. The grand duke has ordered us to stop our pursuit of Maestra Caccini and to return home 'to resume our duties.'"

"And?" Paolo asked. "Do we finish our task first?"

"No," Roberto said with a hard exhale of breath. "Alessandro wrote the communication, the grand duke signed it, but Alessandro added a bit of a postscript to the bottom of the note: 'He means it.' That means

I'll be risking almost royal displeasure if I continue the hunt. If I could bring it to an end in a couple of days, I'd do it. But with this thing in play," he jerked a thumb at the airship, "I'd be lucky to get back to Firenze in a couple of months, and that the grand duke would not appreciate."

Roberto gave another hard exhale. "So..." He turned to Bonaro. "I will not be needing those passages after all. And you can tell Maestra Caccini that the grand duke of Tuscany has decided she is not worth bothering with and no one will be looking for her."

With that, he pivoted on his heel, not exchanging farewells with the airship commander, and strode toward the gates into Brescia.

# Chapter 22

Marco looked at Francesca. "Are you sure about this?"

Francesca was nervous for the first time in she didn't know how long, but she hadn't come this far to falter now. "Yes," she husked.

"All right."

Marco pushed open the door and gestured Francesca into Walcha's Coffee House. He followed her through, and closed the door behind them.

Francesca looked around the room. Every table was occupied. Every table was fully occupied. A couple had people sitting in concentric rings around them. But she didn't see who she was looking for—not at that table, or that one, or that one, or... She saw a face in profile that she thought was the man she was looking for. She tapped Marco on the shoulder and pointed toward the table.

Marco led the way, threading between the backs of people in the many chairs, even having to turn sideways in some places to make his way through.

160

Francesca followed him. No one paid any attention to them. Apparently tight quarters was nothing unusual here, she mused.

They arrived at the table in question. In addition to the man she sought, there were two couples at the table: two men that she could tell were down-timers even though they were wearing some up-timer-styled clothing, and two women who were, without a doubt, up-timers. Francesca had spent enough time in Grantville on her way north to be able to recognize them. There was just something about the way the up-timers carried themselves, especially the women.

Her quarry looked around at them. "Yes?" he said in a very cool soprano voice, which confirmed Francesca's identification of him and sent a wave of relief through her.

"Are you Maestro Andrea Abati?" Marco asked.

Abati blinked his eyes. "Yes, I am. Why do you ask? Do I know you?"

"No, you don't know me," Marco said, "but may I make you known to Maestra Francesca Caccini?" He bowed and gestured to Francesca.

Abati shot to his feet, knocking his chair over onto the floor behind him. "La Cecchina! Here?"

Francesca felt a broad smile growing on her face, and she nodded, holding out her hands to him.

Abati took her hands and raised them both to his lips, giving them both kisses. "Dear Francesca, how wonderful it is to see you again after all these years. But what are you doing here, and why didn't you let me—us—know you were coming?" He waved at the table. "Let me introduce you to my friends. Here you see Marla Linder, the prima soprano of Magdeburg, and her husband Franz Sylwester, *dirigent* of the Magdeburg Symphony Orchestra, and Maestro Giacomo Carissimi, whose name I'm sure you recognize, and his wife Elizabeth Jordan."

They all smiled and nodded, and Francesca felt some warmth flowing into her. This was what she was looking for.

"My friends," Abati continued, "you see before you Maestra Francesca Caccini, La Cecchina, the Nightingale of Firenze, the crown jewel of the musical crown of the court of the grand duke of Tuscany, the finest singer of northern Italy and one of the three best musicians of all of Italy." He turned back to Francesca, and said again, "But what are you doing here?"

"I have come to make my future," Francesca finally spoke, husking the words out.

She saw the surprise appear on Abati's face: the shock, followed by the horror at the sound of her ruined voice.

"What . . . what has happened . . ."

"An injury suffered in escaping the attentions of the court," Francesca said, the tones of her mutilated voice grating on the ears of them all, she could tell.

"Oh, my God," Marla Linder breathed. "How horrible."

"Not so much, Maestra Linder," Francesca said. "My sun is setting. My years of singing were about to pass anyway. I will not miss the singing . . . much." She swallowed at that moment of honesty, and felt the phantom of pain of days past. "The doctors in Grantville said that if I had been able to be seen by them, especially Dr. Nichols, right after the injury, they might have been able to repair the damage. But by the time I—we—managed to make our way to

Grantville, the healing had already progressed to the point where they could not promise any improvements with their surgeries. So, it is what it is. But I can still play, and still compose, and still hear, so there is much I can do yet in the autumn of my years. But my future, now, that is still bright."

Francesca reached out a hand to draw Marco to stand in front of her. She took Marco's cap off of his head, and tossed it on the table before the others. "This is my future. Behold my daughter Margherita, whom I have brought out of Firenze and Italy to this land, to place in your hands, to grow and bloom and blossom into the musician she should be without paying the prices I have paid. Cherish her."

Marla Linder was on her feet and circling the table to come stand before them. She stared first into Francesca's eyes. "Absolutely. She will be cherished. Count on it. The more so, because of the price you have paid to get her here." Francesca could read the iron determination in the other woman's eyes, and she smiled in acceptance.

"And you, young woman," Marla said, looking to Margherita, who had almost slumped to the floor now that her role was ended, "you are a very special gift, and you are very welcome. Call me Marla, and call on me whenever you need anything. Got it?"

It took a moment to puzzle out what the up-timer meant, then Margherita nodded tentatively.

Elizabeth stood and followed Marla around the table. She came to Francesca, and without saying a word, simply enfolded her in a strong embrace. Francesca felt tears starting in her eyes as she returned the embrace as best she could.

After a long moment, Elizabeth released Francesca, only to place her hands on her shoulders and say warmly, "Welcome home."

And at that the tears began flowing freely.

Home. She was home. Finally, after all these years, Francesca had found home.

# Bach to the Future

# Prelude

*Magdeburg*
*July 1634*

### Magdeburg Times-Journal
### July 18, 1634

*The Royal Arts Council announced today that the contract for designing and constructing an organ for the new Royal Opera Hall and Fine Arts Complex has been awarded to Johann Bach of Wechmar. Herr Bach is a musician and organist of note who has studied under Herr Johann Christoph Hoffmann, Stadtpfeifer in Suhl. He has served as organist at Suhl, Arnstadt and Schweinfurt, where his responsibilities included maintenance of the organs. This is his first commission to construct an organ.*

"Impossible."

The word seemed to echo in the room for a moment. Johann Bach heard it, and folded his hands together before responding. "It had better not be impossible, or there will not be an organ in the opera hall."

"But the plans are finished, the detailed drawings are almost complete, they've begun digging the trenches for the foundations." Josef Furttenbach the architect, senior partner of Furttenbach and Parigi, clamped his jaw after making that statement. He and Carl Schockley, the general contractor's project manager for the building project, glowered at Johann in concert. Alfonso Parigi, the other architect in the partnership, had a trace of a smile on his face.

Johann smiled back at them all. "I am sorry that you seemed to have received bad advice before now. The space you have allotted for the organ is adequate as far as the organ cabinet and pipe space and the wind-chest, but you have left little room for the bellows. Without the bellows, there is no wind for the wind-chest. That would be like God making Adam without lungs."

Furttenbach and Schockley continued to glare across the table at him. Lady Beth Haygood cleared her throat. "You're serious." There was a hint of question in her tone.

Johann suppressed a sigh. "Very serious. An organ without bellows is like a flute that has been hung upon the wall: it may be made of the finest materials and the greatest of the craftsman's art, but without moving wind it makes no music."

"Can't you..." Lady Beth moved both hands in the air as if trying to shape something, "...reduce the size somehow? Can we use electric fans or something?"

Johann did sigh now. "Perhaps. I will study it. But it would be best if we plan now for what I know will work. If another approach can be adopted later that will save space..." He shrugged.

"So what would we do with the wasted space then?" challenged Furttenbach.

"Make storage closets," Johann smiled. "If musicians and artists are going to be using the building, there will always be a need for more storage."

No one else smiled, but Lady Beth did jot a note on the pad in front of her. She looked up at the architects and contractor. "Fix it."

"But Lady Beth . . ." Schockley began.

"Fix it, Carl. I'm not going to explain to Mary Simpson when she gets back from her trip that her opera hall doesn't have an organ in it."

"All right, but you know that changing plans after they've been finalized and the work's begun is the first step to cost overruns. This one's not our fault, and I don't want to hear about it later." Now he bent his glower on Lady Beth, who was singularly unaffected by it as far as Johann could tell.

"Then I suggest you get word to your excavator operator and stop digging until you know what the changes are going to be. I don't want to hear about you pouring foundations in the wrong place, either." She closed her pad and gathered her jacket and purse. "Send me word when the revised plans are ready and I'll come and go over them with you." She left the room.

Schockley ran his hand through his hair and looked to Furttenbach. "Fix it, she says." He shook his head. "Well, like she says, I'd better go get the digging stopped." His glance now included Johann. "Work it out as soon as you can. I really don't want to lose any time if we can help it." He followed Lady Beth out the door.

Furttenbach looked at his partner, jerked his head at Johann and left. Parigi looked at Johann, sighed, and flipped through the drawing packet until he found the sheet he wanted. "Okay, show me what you need."

The two men bent their heads together over the page. "See, this wall is too close." Johann traced a line with his finger.

"How much room do you really need?"

"Well, I was planning on twelve bellows, each about eight feet by four feet. And we'll need at least two feet between each to get between them."

Parigi looked horrified. "*Mio Dio*, Signor Bach. Excuse me, please, but that's over one hundred and twenty feet!"

"No, no," Johann laughed. "I was not clear, my friend. The narrow end of the bellows connects to the wind-chest. The length of them will go this way," and his finger traced on the plan again.

"So, it is a mere seventy-two feet that we must allow for." The Italian smiled and snapped his fingers. "That is nothing. A piece of cake, as Carl would say."

"Perhaps a bit more difficult than that," Johann said. "To get the most even wind pressure, it would be best if they were lined up on each side of the wind box."

Parigi's brow furrowed. The two of them bent over the plans again. Fingers pointed and drew lines and thumped emphatically several times before they reached agreement. The architect laid a very thin piece of paper over the plan and traced out the new dimensions that would be needed. "It is fortunate," he said, "that this is actually outside the main support wall of the auditorium. If it had been necessary to move that, *ai*, old Josef would throw a fury such as would make my old papa proud."

"Is Master Furttenbach difficult to work with, then?"

Johann was not looking forward to working with the man if the answer was yes.

"No, not so much. He dislikes changes after things are supposed to be final. He's German." Parigi gave a fluid shrug. "He is a good architect, though, very good. He studied with my father in Italy years ago when he was young. When I told Papa I was going to come north to work with him, he harrumphed and said that I could do worse."

"You will get the changes made, then?"

"Two days for the foundations and walls. We will not need to settle things like doors and crawlspaces just yet."

"Good, because I have not yet done the details for the wind chambers and wind trunks yet."

"Well, come by my office and maybe I can help with that. I would really like to understand this organ stuff in case I have to deal with one in another design."

"Good. Meanwhile, go tell Herr Schockley where he can dig and then let's go find an ale."

*"Un' idea eccellente!"*

The Green Horse Tavern was busy, as it was every evening when Marla Linder and her husband Franz Sylwester and their friends came to play and sing. Johann Bach sat at a table near the front of the room. His command of up-time English was improving, so he understood most of the words, and where he didn't he just enjoyed the music. He especially enjoyed what they called the Irish songs. There was a lilt and a bounce to them that was unique in his experience.

Marla was singing one of the best of them now. It was a song that could easily have been dreary, but somehow in her hands, with her voice, it was fun.

The song was drawing to its close. Marla, eyes sparkling, was grinning at Franz as he played his violin like a dervish.

> *When the Captain came downstairs,*
>     *though he saw me situation*
> *In despite of all me prayers I was*
>     *marched off to the station*
> *For me they'd take no bail, but to get*
>     *home I was itchin'*
> *And I had to tell the tale, how I*
>     *came into the kitchen*
> *With me toora loora la and me toora*
>     *loora laddie*
> *And me toora loora la and me toora*
>     *loora laddie*

Franz grinned back at his wife. Marla turned back to the audience and sang the last verse.

> *Now, I said she did invite me, but*
>     *she gave a flat denial*
> *For assault she did indict me, and I*
>     *was sent for trial*
> *She swore I robbed the house and in*
>     *spite of all her schreechin'*
> *And I got six months hard for me*
>     *courtin' in the kitchen*
> *With me toora loora la and me toora*
>     *loora laddie*
> *And me toora loora la and me toora*
>     *loora laddie*

*With me toora loora la and me toora*
   *loora laddie*
*And me toora loora la and me toora*
   *loora laddie*

They finished the song with a flourish. Marla joined
hands with Franz to take a bow to loud applause.
She waved as the applause crested and died. "We'll
be back in a while to sing some more."

Violins were put in cases, pipes were wiped and
a harp was hung from a peg in the wall. Marla and
company crowded onto the benches around a table
at the front.

"Johann!"

He looked up to see Franz beckoning to him.

"Is there room?"

Franz looked around, then nodded. "We will make
room. Come." Johann picked up his mug and squeezed
onto the end of the bench next to Rudolf Tuchman,
exchanging a nod with the young Hanoveran.

Marla and Franz were across the table from him.
He bowed to them with a grin. "Well sung, Frau
Marla. Very sprightly. But was that not a man's song?"

She laughed, then said, "You got me there. But it's
so fun to sing I just had to do it."

"Fun it is," Johann's smile widened. "One could
dance to it easily."

Marla started laughing again. Johann looked to
Franz with raised eyebrows. That worthy sighed.
"For all that she likes to sing sacred songs, she has
a devilish sense of humor, and we never know what
will set it off." Franz leaned over and poked his wife

in the ribs. "Enough, woman. Either tell us the joke or leave off your laughing."

Marla managed to stifle her laughter, wiping her eyes as she did so. "Oh...oh, my. That just caught me off guard."

"So, tell." Franz growled with a fierce expression. Marla poked him back in his own ribs.

"Okay, it goes like this: When my parents were kids, there was a television show for teenagers on Saturdays. They'd play rock and roll music for the kids to dance to, and every week they'd play at least one new song. Then they'd get a couple of the kids in the studio to come up and rate the song. And the comment they heard most of the time was..." She paused for effect, causing Franz to raise a finger and aim it at her. "...'It's got a good beat and it's easy to dance to.' Then he hears a song I know darn well he's never heard before," she pointed at Johann, voice unsteady as her laughter threatened to break out again, "and what does he say?"

Everyone around the table, including Johann, chorused, "One could dance to it easily." And laughter reigned supreme for a time.

Once they settled down to mere chuckles, Franz looked back over to Johann. "So, Johann, how goes the organ building?"

"Well enough, for a start." He looked across at Marla. "I reviewed the plans for the organ spaces with the architects, and it is a good thing I did." He shook his head. "They had not allowed enough room for the wind-chest and bellows, and it took a bit of talking to get them to see the need for the change. In truth, if not for Frau Haygood, we'd probably still be arguing."

"Ah, Lady Beth to the rescue," Franz drawled.

Johann considered that statement. "Indeed." He shrugged. "Anyway, once that got settled, I started looking for craftsmen. As it happens, the main builder, the 'contractor' I think they called the company, has already found most of the people I will need to build the organ. They have a good cabinetmaker, and of course regular carpenters abound. So I am down to two craftsmen that I need: a bellows maker, and a whitesmith."

"Bellows?" Marla asked.

"For the wind-chest," Franz leaned over.

"Ah. I never thought of that. The only pipe organ I've ever been close to is the one in the Methodist church in Grantville, and it uses electric motors and fans to force the air. I've never seen an old-style organ."

Johann was taken aback for a moment. He was planning on using the best and latest approaches to organ building, and to hear them called "old style" caused him a moment of disorientation. But he made note of the electric motors. This was the second time that had been mentioned. He would need to look into that.

"I know what a blacksmith is," Marla continued. "What's a whitesmith?"

"A metal worker who works with metals like tin." Johann regained his aplomb.

"And you need him why?"

Johann struggled to keep incredulity from his face. "To make the pipes for the organ, of course."

Marla giggled. "Sorry. I never thought of tin being used for that. I think of tin, I think of cans with food in them." She giggled again.

"When do you think you will be able to begin building the organ?" Franz asked.

"We will start making the pipes and other pieces as soon as we can. Putting it together will have to wait for the building shell and roof to be complete enough to keep the weather off. That will be a while yet; several months."

"They keep saying it will be ready in a year." Marla made a rude noise. "Ha! I bet it takes longer."

Johann shrugged. "It will take as long as it takes."

A thought crossed Johann's mind. "Frau Linder, can I ask you something?"

"Call me Marla, and sure."

"Why do all the up-timers, when they first hear my name, get such strange expressions on their faces?"

The whole table broke into laughter again, with Marla's voice skirling over the top of them all. Johann sat back and crossed his arms, offended.

"We're sorry," Marla said as the laughter dwindled into chuckles. "It's just that your name... Have you had a chance to study any of the music history from the up-time yet?"

"Not really, no." Johann knew he sounded surly. He uncrossed his arms and continued. "Mostly I just know what I have seen in the concert programs and heard from those of you who have been to Grantville."

"Umm, well, you see, Bach is a pretty familiar name to us."

Johann sat back again, this time in astonishment. He knew the Bach family was well-known in Thuringia, but how would the up-timers know of them?

"We consider Johann Sebastian Bach to be one of the greatest musicians who ever lived."

Johann... *Sebastian* ... Bach... Johann shook his head. "I do not know that name," he murmured.

"That's because he hasn't been born yet."

Now Johann was truly confused. *Has not been born yet? How...?*

Marla and Franz both looked at him with sympathy. "Yeah, now you're starting to understand just how weird this whole Ring of Fire thing can be," Marla said. "You think this is weird, go talk to *Kapellmeister* Schütz about how he felt when he read a biography of his whole life."

That thought had never crossed Johann's mind—he might be able to read about his future. "Do you think I..."

"I don't know," Marla shook her head. "There might be a little information about you in the library, but probably not a lot. No offense, but I'd never heard of you before you showed up at the concert a few weeks ago."

"But this Johann Sebastian..."

"Lots of information about him, sure."

"And he was famous?"

"Yep. Wrote tons of stuff." She frowned. "I don't know how much of it came back through the Ring of Fire. Grantville wasn't exactly a hotbed of musical culture, but I know some of it did. If nothing else, there are a lot of recordings, especially of the organ music."

"Organ music?" Johann sat up straight.

"Oh, yes," Marla grinned. "The greatest organ music ever written. I envy you," she sighed, "getting to hear the Toccata and Fugue in D Minor for the first time."

Johann sat silent for a moment. "How do I find this organ music?"

"Go to Grantville," everyone at the table chorused.

*Grantville*
*Early August 1634*

Johann looked at the book in front of him. "Johann Sebastian Bach. German Musician. 1685–1750." Somehow seeing it in print in a book from the future seemed to have more weight than just hearing Marla and the others talk about it. He looked up at the young monk who was assisting him in the library. "This is the man?"

"You asked for Johann Sebastian Bach. This is the only article about him in this encyclopedia." The monk looked apologetic.

Johann began reading the article, but after a paragraph or two realized he was struggling. The typeface, the spellings, the English of it, made for hard going for him. "Please, Brother..." he realized he didn't even know the monk's name.

"I am Brother Johann." A smile crossed both their faces at the realization that not only did they have the same name, but so did the subject of their hunt.

"Please, can you help me read this?"

Brother Johann pulled out a chair and sat down next to him. Their heads bent together as they read through the text. At the end, Johann sat back, dissatisfied. "I was told he wrote great organ music. This man says nothing of that."

"It is the nature of encyclopedias," Brother Johann replied, "that they are summaries. There will be more detail available elsewhere in the library."

"And I am not mentioned in this *Encyclopedia Britannica*?"

The monk shrugged. "There are five articles about

Bach musicians in the encyclopedia: this one, and articles about four of his sons. Nothing about those who came before."

Johann drummed his fingers on the table. He looked up at his namesake. "There are those who know the library, who do research?"

"Aye."

"I want to know everything there is to know about this man and his ancestors and his music. How long to produce it?"

The monk thought for a moment. "Perhaps a week to do the initial search and indexing. Perhaps two, maybe three weeks after that to gather all the material. Another week or two to put it in final form."

Johann frowned. "I will be back in Magdeburg before then."

"No problem," Brother Johann smiled as he used the up-timer phrase. "The bank offers a service. You deposit the fee into an escrow account. When we are done preparing the research, we take it to the bank, the escrow officer reviews it, and if it looks good, she releases the money to us and sends the results to you."

"Hmm. That might work." Johann fingered his beard.

"Oh, we do this kind of thing all the time."

"Indeed." Johann thought about a world where knowledge was a commodity to be bought and sold. He wasn't sure he liked the idea.

The more he stared at the picture, the more disquieted Johann became. It didn't matter if he looked from left to right or top to bottom, every time his eyes got near the center of the picture everything twisted and suddenly his perspective would change. He tried again, and it resulted in a frown. He turned to his host. "Master Wendell, please, what is the purpose for this picture?"

"Call me Marcus. It's called *Convex and Concave*, and it's by a Dutch artist named M. C. Escher who died in the 1970s."

"An up-timer, then." Just as he finished his response, Johann realized that it was a silly observation. Of course the artist was an up-timer. No down-timer would think of drawing such a mind-twisting picture.

"Oh, yes," Marcus continued. "He was well known for making drawings like this, representations of things that would be impossible in real life. Sort of like jokes on those who look at them. I keep that there to remind me that things are not always as they seem."

"Indeed." Johann looked at it one more time, then turned away. "I think it is a good thing the Inquisition holds no sway here. That picture might bring them visiting." Marcus laughed, but Johann wasn't sure he was joking.

"So, Herr Bach," Marcus said as he led his guest to the chairs, "you are interested in old Johann Sebastian Bach."

"Please, call me Johann." Johann took a seat. "Of course I am. As soon as Frau Marla and Herr Franz and their friends told me of him, I knew I had to come to Grantville and learn as much as I could about him."

"So, what do you know so far?"

"Only what the encyclopedia could tell me. He was apparently fairly well known in his later career, fell out of public favor for about a hundred years or so, then was restored to prominence."

"Are you related to him?"

"Probably, but the encyclopedia did not have that knowledge. I have asked Brother Johann at the library to find everything they can about him and his family."

"That's good," Marcus nodded. "Either he or Father Nick will dig out everything there is to be found."

"But that is still only words. Still only dry and dusty knowledge. I need to hear the man, feel him, feel his art and his passion. From the article I know that he wrote much music of different kinds, and I want to hear it all. But most of all I want to hear what he wrote for the King of Instruments."

"The organ." A slow smile crossed Marcus' face. "Oh, Johann. I envy you hearing him for the first time."

"That is what Marla said." Johann sat forward. "Is there someone who can play for me?"

"I don't think so," Marcus replied, "not as the music deserves. However," he held up a finger as disappointment crossed Johann's face, "I do have some recordings."

Johann's breath came a little quicker. "Ah, yes. Frau Linder and the others mentioned these 'recordings.' I look forward to seeing and hearing them."

Marcus levered himself to his feet. "Then come with me. No time like the present." He pulled a few flat parcels off of a shelf, then led Johann out of the office and into the band room. "Take a seat over there while I get ready." Johann walked to the area of chairs that Marcus' hand had generally waved at and sat down.

"Are you ready?" Marcus looked to him from beside a cabinet loaded with up-time devices. Johann nodded, although he wasn't sure what to expect. So far he hadn't heard a single note. Marcus pushed on something, then lifted a thin arm and carefully positioned it over the edge of a black disk. A faint hissing sound came from a couple of large wooden boxes that flanked the cabinet. *Ah ... this is something like the Trommler player, then. But where is the horn?* He was proud for a moment that he had made that deduction based on seeing a Trommler player once at a burgher's home in Erfurt.

Music came out of the air. Marcus grinned at him, so he relaxed and listened.

The opening motif was a simple tremolo, followed by a downward run of notes. It was repeated twice, an octave lower each time.

*Hmm. The registration is different each time—so the figure was played on three different manuals. Probably a three-manual organ, then: Schwellwerke, Hauptwerke, Brustwerke.*

Johann's eyes widened as a pedal tone was played to lay the foundation for a chord that was rapidly built. It was a large chord, very full of resonant timbre, very loud. That the instrument in the "recording" didn't lose wind in playing that chord meant it was a good organ, well designed and well built.

The chord moved and changed and resolved into a D minor tonic chord. Johann wasn't sure yet if this piece would be a Dorian mode work in the D tonality, or if it would actually be in D minor. Either way, he expected to be pleased with it.

The chord ended. The recording reproduced echoes and reverberations, as if the work was being played in a great cathedral. *How odd to hear that in this square room.*

The organist in the recording was a man of great skill. The next passage was a bravura passage of fingers moving in patterns up the keys, followed by several chords. This figure was repeated on a different manual. But to break pattern, the figure went down the keyboard next, played in octaves on two manuals, then melded into another of the thunderous loud chords, followed by a ripple of single notes and ended in yet another massive chord.

A new motif began, rapid runs of notes on the *Brustwerke*, leading into chords first on the *Brustwerke*, then on the *Hauptwerke*, finally leading into a slow run on the *Pedal* which culminated in a slow series of heavy resonant chords on the *Hauptwerke* and *Pedal*. The toccata had come to its conclusion.

Johan took a slow breath in the moment of silence. Master Marcus said nothing, waiting.

The fugue began. It was a light rapid figure begun on the *Schwellwerke*. It began passing back and forth between the manuals, still at that rapid tempo. Johann abandoned trying to analyze the music as it was played. He sat back, closed his eyes, and let it pour into him.

It was like listening to the springtime flood of a river—ironic, since Bach meant brook. Figure followed figure, seemingly tumbling along. The voicing jumped from manual to manual to manual. The music flowed, almost bubbling. The pedals came in, like large rocks the music had to flow around.

Still it poured along, rapid, even joyous in nature. The sound invaded Johann's mind, his heart, his soul. His fingers and feet began to twitch involuntarily, reaching for keys as he listened to this...this masterpiece. He had no other word for it.

The pedals came back in, rumbling along below the work of the manuals. Soon enough—or an eternity later, Johann wasn't sure—the flow poured into a series of heavy chords. The pedals sounded again, with the *Hauptwerke* coming in on top of them. One more rapid figure, then chords, many chords with little ripples between them. It was as if the river had reached the sea.

A final series of massive chords sounded. Johann felt the gravitas of them as they slowly moved from one to another. The player in the recording let up on the keys, and once again Johann heard the reverberation of a great space.

Marcus had arisen toward the end and stepped to the cabinet. Now he lifted the thin arm from the disk. The hissing sound disappeared from the cabinets. He turned to Johann.

"Before the Ring of Fire, this was the single most widely known piece of organ music; not in America, not in Germany, but in the entire world. Six billion people in our world, and if they knew any organ work at all, this was it."

Johann struggled for words. "I . . . It . . ." He swallowed. "Magnificent. It is truly a masterwork. A bravura piece that tests the organist as much as the organ."

Marcus chuckled. "Yeah, it does. I play at the piano, but I've never had the finger control to attempt this one, never mind the feet. There is some question as to whether Bach actually wrote that, but most people believe—believed—that he did. Oddly enough, there are—were—some music historians who think that old Johann wrote that specifically to test organs, to test their registrations and in particular their wind-delivery capabilities."

"Indeed." Johann nodded thoughtfully. "It definitely has me thinking about the design for the new opera house organ."

"That's right, you're doing that, aren't you? How's it going?"

"Ideas only at this point. A few doodles on paper. I will not begin the serious work until I get back to Magdeburg."

"Cool. Keep me posted on how it goes. I'd really like to hear it when you're done.

"Now, what do you want to hear next by old Johann: instrumental music, choral music or more organ work?"

"Oh, organ, by all means."

As Marcus turned back to the cabinet, Johann had a thought occur to him. "Master Marcus?"

"Yes?"

"You keep referring to 'old' Johann? How old was he when he wrote what we just heard?"

Marcus looked over his shoulder with a grin. "Music historians think he was twenty-two, maybe a little older, when he wrote that."

It was night out. Johann wandered down the streets of Grantville with his hands in his pockets. He had been hit in the head once, hard. He remembered how he felt then: woozy, disoriented, not certain what was real and concrete.

He felt that same way now. That a Bach, a member of his family, possibly a descendant of his own loins, could write that music... He shook his head, trying to clear his thinking.

Marcus had explained the Butterfly Effect to him. This Bach—this Johann Sebastian—would never exist in his future. He had been stolen from them by the Ring of Fire. Marcus had explained how little of his music had come back with Grantville. Johann could weep at the knowledge of what had been lost.

But what had come back—ah, what greatness. The world of music would be changed by this.

Johann stopped at the edge of town in a place where there were no nearby houses and no bright lights. He looked up at the sky. The moon hadn't risen yet, and the stars were shining brightly in the velvet black of the night.

"God," he said. "All the great men say that Grantville is your doing. That the Ring of Fire is a divine work, a miracle either of blessing or of judgment. But what if it is a test?"

He lowered his head and brooded on that. After a while, he looked back up at the sky. "Are you an Escher, God? Is Grantville like that picture in Marcus' office? We cannot see it straight on, we cannot look at it from the side, everything is different and twisted and not what we expect?"

Johann took his hands out of his pocket and pounded a fist into the opposite palm, then looked up once more.

"Escher or not, God, the music is real. You cannot play with our ears like Escher does with our eyes. I have heard the music. I have heard the work of Johann Sebastian Bach. I claim him as ours. He will not languish in our time. His renown will be as great now as it was in Grantville's world before the fall of the Ring."

He gave a definite nod. "He is ours." He turned and began striding back toward Grantville, toward his room. He had work to do. And a picture to buy.

# Adagio

*Magdeburg*
*August 1634*

Johann Bach left his rooming house in the sprawling exurb to the west of the Magdeburg city walls. He nodded to old Pieter the porter as he hurried down the wooden steps and stepped onto the graveled road that ran through the built-up area that by now was several times larger than the city proper. Magdeburg itself, the area within the walls, covered only about a square mile. The arc of land around the walls, beginning with the Navy Yard to the north of the city and ending with the refinery and chemical complex to the south, was full of new construction, much of it in raw lumber.

The rebuilding of Magdeburg after the almost total destruction of the city by Tilly's troops and the subsequent withdrawal of Pappenheim's occupation forces had drawn workers and their families from all over the Protestant territories. The eruption of manufacturing concerns that sprouted from the intersection of up-time knowledge, down-time skills and interests, and the support of Emperor Gustavus Adolphus turned a stream of workers into a flood, and much of their initial labor went into raising the buildings they now lived in outside the city.

He stopped at a bakery on the corner and purchased a roll for breakfast. Fresh and crusty it was, and he devoured it with gusto as he walked toward the city walls in the early morning light.

The bridge over the moat was busy with traffic today, as it was most days. Johann joined the stream of men heading into the city. He looked down from the peak of the bridge and watched the water boil around the columns that supported the span. The gates into the city were open, as they were most of the time these days. Magdeburg was a city that was beginning to never sleep.

Johann stepped through the gates, and immediately felt closed in by the walls. It was funny; he never would have felt that way even six months ago. Walled cities and towns was the way things were everywhere; it was the way things were done. But having lived in the "Boomtown," as the up-timers called the exurb outside the walls, now for several weeks, and mixing with the up-timers on a frequent basis and hearing them complain about how crowded and cramped the old city was, he had started to absorb some of their attitudes. He shrugged his shoulders, and hurried on down the street. He had finally found a whitesmith who was rumored to have the knowledge he needed, and he wanted to speak with the man soon.

"Johann!"

He stopped and looked around. He was one of several men doing so, and he wasn't surprised at that. His name was one of the more common men's names among Germans. Sometimes he wished his parents had used a little more originality in selecting his name. They did so with his brothers, Christoph and Heinrich, after all.

"Johann!" the voice called again, and he saw Marla Linder waving at him, two other women at her side. He waved back and walked to meet them.

"When did you get back from Grantville?" Marla asked.

"Wednesday."

"And today's Friday, so you've been back for two days and you didn't let us know." Marla shook her head. "What are we going to do with you?"

Johann grinned and shrugged.

"So, what did you find out?" Marla lifted an eyebrow.

Johann sobered. "I heard many of the recordings, and you are right. Johann Sebastian Bach is truly a great composer and musician, whatever his relationship to my family might be."

"And?" Marla looked at him expectantly. "Did you listen to the one I told you to?"

A slow smile crossed Johann's face. "The Toccata and Fugue in D Minor? Oh, yes," he said with reverence. "Many times. One of the reasons I was so long in returning was I was copying it out from the printed copy in the library of your Methodist church."

"Hah. I forgot they had one," Marla replied. "Gonna learn to play it, are you?"

"A silly question, Frau Marla. It may take a while, of course. I share a name with the man, but I am not at all sure I share his talent." Johann grimaced a bit.

"So what's next for you?"

"Organ design and building. In fact, I am on my way

to meet with a whitesmith. There is one in Grantville, but I would rather work with one here in Magdeburg. It will make testing and tuning easier. We have a lot of pipes to build."

"How many pipes in a pipe organ?" one of the other women asked.

"I'm sorry," Marla interjected, "I haven't introduced you. Anastasia Matowski," she pointed to the woman who had spoken. She was very short, petite, slender, with a long neck that lifted her head above her collar. "And this is Casey Stevenson," Marla pointed to the other woman. "Meet Johann Bach."

"Really?" Casey looked to Marla.

"No, he's not that Bach," Marla said.

Johann gave a slight bow. He knew his smile was a bit twisted, but he was getting so tired of that reaction from the up-timers. The two women nodded back. "So how many pipes in a pipe organ?" the question was repeated by Fräulein Matowski.

"That depends on the organ," Johann smiled. "I do not yet know how many will be in my organ, but . . ." He thought for a moment about the space he had to work in. "If I realize my dreams it would not surprise me to see three thousand pipes, perhaps as much as two hundred more."

"Wow." Fräulein Matowski blinked. Johann noticed that her eyes were large, golden hazel, and gleaming in a heart-shaped face framed by shoulder-length walnut-hued hair stirred by a breeze. "Sounds like a good job for a Bach."

"Thank you, Fräulein Matowski." Johann bowed to her. With what he knew now, she had delivered him quite a compliment whether she meant to or not.

"Call me Staci."

"Thank you, Fräulein Staci." He bowed again.

"But enough of me," he continued. "What is happening with you? What is new in the musical life of Magdeburg since I left?"

"We're going to perform Händel's oratorio *Messiah* either in late December or early January." Marla pointed at him. "You should either be in the choir or in the orchestra. I know you said you play."

"Orchestra," Johann said. "Viola."

"Good. Come by the house tonight and talk to Franz. Meanwhile, we've got to get back to school and you've got a whitesmith to talk to. We'll see you later."

"'Bye, Herr Bach," Staci said as they walked away. "It was nice to meet you."

Johann watched them move off, Marla setting the pace. Just before they turned the corner, Staci looked back over her shoulder and smiled.

Johann stood for a moment, thinking of a pair of dancing hazel eyes. Then he shook his head and took off down the street. Once he got to the Gustavstrasse, the wide boulevard that bisected the Altstadt, the old part of the actual city of Magdeburg, he turned north.

In a few minutes he was crossing the moat again, this time into the Neustadt. He smiled at the thought of calling that part of the city "new." It was also surrounded by the city walls, and was older than his grandfather.

He hadn't learned every street in Magdeburg yet, but he knew enough to find the building he was looking for. He knocked on the door.

"Yes?" A young man answered the door.

"Herr Johann Bach, to see Master Phillip Luder."

"Come in, Herr Bach." The youth gave a slight bow as he opened the door wide. Johann stepped through into a wave of heat. "The master is at the forge at the moment, but will be with you very quickly."

He conducted Johann to a chair set to one side, then stepped over to the forge set against the back wall of the building and spoke to a man of middle years who was stirring something in a crucible set above the coals. The man looked over his shoulder, handed the ladle to the younger man, and bustled toward Johann.

"Herr Bach! I am Phillip Luder." The master wiped his hands on his leather apron and extended one to Johann. Johann stood to clasp hands with the man. Master Phillip had a strong grasp, but didn't attempt to crush Johann's fingers. As a musician, he appreciated that.

"And what can I do for you, Herr Bach?" The whitesmith's eyebrows climbed his forehead for all the world like two bushy caterpillars. Johann had to bite his tongue for a moment to keep from grinning at him.

"Pipes, Master Luder. I need pipes—many pipes."

The master's eyebrows contracted downward. "Pipes." A vertical line appeared between the brows. "For water? For oil? For..." He looked expectantly at Johann.

"For music, Master Luder. I need pipes for a pipe organ."

"Ah!" A concerned expression appeared on the whitesmith's face. "Are you the one who will build the new pipe organ in that fancy new building that is beginning, or are you the one who will be rebuilding the organ in the Dom?"

Johann was taken back. "Rebuilding?"

"Oh, yes." The whitesmith nodded. "You are not from here, so you may not know that that black-souled Pappenheim, may he rot in Satan's hands, favorite tool that he is..." Luder spat into the forge. "Where was I?"

"The organ in the Dom?"

"Right. Pappenheim stripped all the metal work from the organ and sold it off to a jobber before he fled like a jackal with his tail between his legs."

Johann was horrified. "I hadn't heard. Was not that a Compenius instrument?"

Luder nodded again. "Aye, built by old Heinrich himself—the son, not the father—thirty years ago, they tell me. And a sweet instrument it was, although I'm no musician to say so. But no more, no more, thanks to Pappenheim eviscerating it..." The master's voice trailed off into muttered curses.

"I have met Master Heinrich the younger," Johann said. "He came to visit his son Ludwig, who lives in Erfurt. I learned much from the two of them."

"Ach, well, according to the word in the halls of the Dom, Herr Christoff Schultze, him who used to be *Möllnvoigt* for the archbishopric and is now the hand of Ludwig Fürst von Anhalt-Cöthen, Gustav Adolf's administrator, has been in contact with the Compenius family, trying to get either Ludwig or his older brother Johann Heinrich to come and lead the repairs."

"If all the pipes were stolen, it will be more like building a new organ."

"You would know better than I would," Master Luder smiled. "But your name is Bach, not Compenius, so now that I think about it, you must have something to do with the new organ rather than the old."

"Indeed." Johann smiled back.

"Should I congratulate you or commiserate with you?"

"I will let you know in a few months, but probably the latter." The two men laughed together. Johann decided he liked Master Luder.

"So you come to me to talk about pipes."

"To talk about making the pipes, yes."

"Hmm. And how many pipes are we talking about?" One of those expressive eyebrows climbed a level, but the grin was still in place.

"Three thousand, maybe a bit more."

The eyebrow dropped and the grin faded. "Three..."

"Thousand. Maybe a bit more."

Master Luder stripped off his apron and threw it on a peg on the wall. He rolled down his shirtsleeves, took down a jacket from another peg, and crammed a hat on top of his bristling hair. "Come. This needs ale."

Johann followed the craftsman out of his shop and down the street. Luder said nothing until after they entered a tavern—it was the Green Horse, Johann noted—and ordered their ale.

"Three thousand pipes." Master Luder began as they sat down at a table.

"More or less," Johann replied.

"All different sizes, I suppose."

"Many sizes, yes, but not individually unique, no. Many pipes can be made and tuned from one size."

"Good. That will speed the work. Do you know yet how many sizes you will have?"

"Not yet. I may use wooden pipes for the largest ones, and I won't know how many metal sizes there will be until I make that decision."

"Pipe metal? Tin and lead alloy?"

"No. No lead in it. It dulls the sound. I want a

bright sound to the pipes, so I want only tin, the purest tin you can get. English tin if you can get it."

"I can get it." Master Luder pursed his lips as his eyebrows crouched close together. "But enough for three thousand pipes will cost you. And I can't get it all at once."

Johann shrugged. "It costs what it costs. And as long as the pipes are done when I need them, it doesn't matter when the tin is available. But do you know how to make pipes?"

The craftsman took a healthy swallow of ale, then wiped his mustache and beard. "I do. I was a journeyman in Leipzig when my old master provided repairs to the university church organ. We had to replace a number of the pipes. I still remember what we did."

"Good. Then how much to put to use what you remember?"

Johann took a swig of his own ale as the bargaining began.


Marla looked up from the piano keyboard at a noise in the door. School was done for the day and she was relaxing a bit by playing.

"Hi, Staci. What's up?"

"Nothing. I just stopped by to see what you were up to."

Marla smiled as she always did when she heard Staci's voice. The powerful contralto was so surprising coming from her tiny frame. She waved her friend into the room. "Come on in."

Staci Matowski hesitated. "I don't want to interrupt anything."

"You're not interrupting. I was just improvising a little."

"Improvising?" Staci stepped over to the piano.

"Yeah. You take a musical theme, then try to make music out of it with variations and stuff."

"Sounds hard."

"It can be. Hey, what was your phone number?"

"Huh?"

"What was your phone number in Grantville?"

"534-3468. Why?"

Marla picked notes out on the piano keyboard. "G-E-F-E-F-A-C. There. That's the notes for your phone number." She set both hands on the keys and played with the resulting melody, adding chords and rhythms to it. After a minute or so, she brought it to a close.

"That was cool," Staci smiled.

"I'm not very good at it, so I work on it as often as I can."

Staci stepped back from the piano. "I didn't mean to interrupt you," she repeated.

"No problem. What do you want?"

Staci turned away and walked over to the window. She stared out for a moment, then she turned to face Marla. "This Johann Bach...what do you know about him?"

Marla leaned over and rested her arms on the music rack of the piano. "Not a lot. A good musician by anyone's standards. Seems to be a nice guy. Probably related to *the* Bach, but he hasn't heard from the researchers in Grantville to prove it yet."

Staci turned back to the window. After a moment, she asked, "Is he married?"

Marla's eyebrows rose in surprise. "No, not that I know of. Not all down-time men wear wedding rings, though, so it's hard to tell for sure."

"Franz does... wear a ring, I mean."

Marla blushed a little. "Yeah, well, Franz isn't your typical down-timer, either."

"Yeah." There was a long silence. Marla wasn't sure what Staci was getting at, but she was willing to wait for her to get to it in her own time.

"Marla..."

"Yeah?"

"Do you believe in love at first sight?"

*Oh, my.* "Um, maybe," she responded with caution. She didn't want to sound too out-in-left-field, here.

"I mean, when did you first know you loved Franz?"

Marla wasn't able to suppress the smile she always got when she thought of their first meeting. "Okay, you got me. He had me the night we met and he showed me how his hand had been crippled."

Staci turned with surprise on her face. "Pity? That's how it started for you?"

"No," Marla said with heat that surprised her. She calmed down. "No, it wasn't pity or sympathy. Empathy, now, that was probably a large part of it."

Staci tilted her head to one side. "What do you mean?"

"Understand that Franz lives for music. He *is* music, you might say. And that had been ripped away from him. You could see it in his face, in his eyes. There was a raw hole in his soul that he was bleeding from. I could see the pain in him, could *feel* it. And I knew that pain, because I thought I had lost the music when the Ring fell." She swallowed, reliving that moment. "It wasn't a moment of decision, of thought. I just..."

"You just stayed with him."

"Yeah." Marla nodded. "I stayed with him after

that. Mind you, I don't think he was that fast to recognize it."

"But he did, eventually."

"Oh, yeah." Marla smiled a bit at the thought of that night as well.

There was another long moment of silence. Marla broke it with, "So, are you feeling...something... for Johann?"

Staci looked back out the window. "Something, I guess."

"So the wind trunks come up from the wind-chest," Alfonso Parigi mused, tracing his finger over the rough drawing Johann had just done, "and feed into the small wind-chests under the manuals."

"Right," Johann nodded.

"Where does the wind go from there?"

"The player has to open one or more stops to open up passages from the small wind-chest to the pipes. Pulling the knob pulls the slider out and aligns holes in the slider with holes in the top of the chest and the bottom of the wind trunks to the pipes."

"Hmm." The architect pulled on his little spike of a beard. "So the routing of the wind in an organ is not unlike an exercise in fluidics."

"So I've been told." Johann smiled. "At least if this system springs a leak, nothing floods."

Parigi chuckled. "True." He tapped a finger on the papers. "So how have you progressed in moving from the concept to the reality?"

"The carpenters are ready to begin the main wind-chest, but that will have to wait until we are closer to the completion of the chamber that will hold it. I still have not found a reliable man to make bellows." Johann frowned at the thought. This was on the verge of becoming a problem, which he did not need this early in the life of the organ design and build.

"They mentioned using an electric fan," Parigi reminded him.

Johann sighed. "I know. But I do not know anything about that. I am not certain how to incorporate that into what I do know."

"A not uncommon problem for those of us born in this time," Parigi chuckled. "The building project has an electrician assigned to it. Talk to her."

"Her?"

"Her."

Johann grimaced and shook his head.

"Excuse me, please? Are you the electrician?" Johann had been pointed toward a table where coils of wire and odd metal fixtures were piled in haphazard towers that leaned in various directions.

"You're talkin' to her." The head that was bowed over a contraption on the table didn't move.

"I am Johann Bach."

The head rose, and eyes blinked at him from behind small rectangular glasses. "Oh. You're the organ guy, right?"

"Yes."

"Just a sec." The head bowed back down for a moment; a screwdriver was twisted. "Ah, that's got it." The contraption was pushed aside as she looked up at Johann. "What can I do for you?"

The woman looked familiar to Johann, but he knew

he'd never seen her before. He pushed that thought aside. "I need to move air to fill the wind-chest for the organ. In other times I would use bellows, several of them. But now they tell me I should use an electric fan. And..."

"And you need to know what one is, right?"

"Yes." Johann suppressed the irritation that flared from being interrupted.

She picked up a flat piece of metal and waved it at Johann. He felt air stirring against his face. "That's a fan, right? It moves air?"

Johann's irritation flared again, and he had to step on it harder. "I understand that, yes."

"Sorry, didn't mean to be patronizing." The electrician set the metal piece back on the table. "Okay, now an electric motor can turn very fast." She picked up a tool from the table and squeezed a trigger, which produced a whining sound as the pointed end began to spin rapidly. "Like so."

"And if one can figure out a way to attach a fan to that motor," Johann pointed to her now quiet tool, "one can move a lot of air rapidly."

He was rewarded with a bright smile. "Right."

"So what would it take to build one, and how much air would it move?"

"How much air gets moved would depend on the size and speed of the fan. We'd need to talk to an engineer about that. But I can't see that building one would be all that difficult. A medium-sized electric motor with a fan-blade assembly on it wouldn't be hard."

"An engineer. You mean like Herr Otto Gericke, the mayor of Magdeburg?"

"No, I was thinking more along the line of Herr Haygood."

"Ah, Frau Haygood's husband?" Johann was aware of the oddness of the up-timers, where the wife would take the husband's surname when they married.

"Right."

"But who would build this for me?"

The electrician steepled her fingers. "I can get the motor, once we know what we need to build. Who builds it depends on what you make the fan part out of—wood, sheet metal, even tin."

Johann nodded. That made sense. And wood would probably be the cheapest material and the quickest to work. He nodded again.

"So, I need to consult with Herr Haygood."

"Yep. I can't help you with the calculations for designing it."

"Good. I will seek him out." Johann gave a short bow. "Thank you very much for your assistance, Fräulein..." He realized he didn't know her name.

"Matowski. Melanie Matowski." She stood and offered her hand.

Johann grasped it, to have his own firmly shaken. "Are you related to Fräulein Anastasia Matowski?"

Another bright grin. "My sister Staci. She's the teacher, I'm the hands-on person."

Fräulein Melanie was perhaps an inch or two taller than her sister, and her face was somewhat rounder than Fräulein Anastasia's heart-shaped visage, but now that his attention had been drawn to it, he could see the resemblance.

"My thanks again."

"No problem."

Johann glanced back for a moment, to see that Fräulein Matowski had resumed her seat at the table and
was again head-down over her work. An ... interesting
young woman, he mused to himself as he walked out
of the workspace.

"Hey, Bach!"

Johann looked up from where he had stooped to
enter the Green Horse. He saw a hand being waved
and waved back. After collecting a mug of ale, he
made his way toward the table.

"Hey, Johann," Marla said. "Pull up a chair and
sit on the floor."

Johann stopped halfway down to the bench, frozen
as he untangled that thought in his mind. He decided
after a moment that it was more of the ubiquitous
but slightly off-pitch up-time humor, and continued
his descent to his seat. The others nodded or waved
a hand at him, and he nodded back.

It was Marla's usual crew, the musicians who accompanied her in her singing, plus a couple of extras.
Johann's eyes lit upon two familiar faces. At the
other end of the table sat the two young women who
had accompanied Frau Marla several days ago. He
considered them over the rim of his mug. Fräulein
Stevenson was laughing, leaning across Franz Sylwester
to say something to Frau Marla. Fräulein Matowski—
Anastasia Matowski, he reminded himself—sat across
the table from them with a slight smile on her face,
fingers laced around a coffee cup.

Something was different. It took Johann a few
moments to realize that Fräulein Anastasia's hair
was short. Very short. Extremely short. It looked as

if someone had cut all her hair to less than finger length.

Now it was understood that up-time women, among their many freedoms and licenses, were much more casual about the treatment of their hair than the women Johann had known all his life. And outside of Frau Marla, he hadn't seen many of them who wore their hair long. But shorter than Marla's hair left plenty of room for length—which Fräulein Anastasia's hair no longer possessed.

Johann considered the young woman. Perhaps she had been ill, and they had cut off her hair for some reason to help her heal. Doctors had been known to do stranger things, he knew.

The other thought that attempted to cross his mind he pushed away. Surely if she had committed some sin that a pastor or congregation had levied this as a punishment she would not be here surrounded by her friends. Perish the thought.

He let the conversations flow around him, content to sip his ale and look from under lowered lids at the young woman. Whatever the reason for the cutting of her hair, Johann had to admit it gave a certain charm to her.

Marla raised her head and looked toward the bar. "Woops! Okay, folks, time to do our thing. Let's go." Instruments were pulled from cases and bags, and Marla and Friends trooped to the open spot at the end of the tavern.

Johann found the evening enjoyable. He still wasn't very familiar with the songs that Marla and the men that clustered around her liked to perform. They were for the most part bright and bouncy songs, many of

which would have had people dancing to them had
they been done at a town fair or village market. He
remembered being told they were mostly from up-time
Ireland, which he had some trouble crediting. Irish-
men in the here and now weren't exactly common
in Wechmar and Erfurt where he grew up, but the
few that he'd met here in Magdeburg did not seem
to fit with bright and bouncy. A more moody, surly,
snarling group of men he'd never met before, and
never wished to again.

Regardless of their origin, by now the songs were
familiar to the crowd in the Green Horse, enough
so that they were singing along with some of the
choruses. Johann hummed instead, foot tapping and
fingers wagging in the air.

The music reached a resting place after the musician's finished "Nell Flaherty's Drake" with a flourish.
Marla was panting from the rapid pace of the song
with its intricate lyrics. "Staci!" she called out.

Johann watched as Fräulein Matowski looked around.
Marla beckoned her. She shook her head, and Marla
beckoned more energetically. Fräulein Stevenson reached
across the table and nudged her. "Go on. You know she
won't take no for an answer."

Fräulein Matowski shrugged, drained her coffee
cup and stood. As she walked toward the musicians,
Johann picked up his mug and slid down the bench
to sit closer to Fräulein Stevenson. She looked over at
him and smiled, then returned her gaze to her friends.

Marla waved for quiet. "We're going to do an old
song from up-time America," she said. "Leastways,
it was old for us, before the Ring fell—close to two
hundred years, anyway. Listen to 'Oh Shenandoah.'"

The musicians rearranged themselves, with Franz and Marla stepping forward and placing Fräulein Matowski in the middle. Franz lifted his bow and began playing a haunting melody. It soared and fell, flowed and ebbed, and at length paused for a moment of silence, delicately balanced, as if it stood on the head of a pin.

> *Oh Shenandoah,*
> *I long to hear you,*
> *Away you rolling river,*

A woman's voice began, and Franz played a descant. Johann was caught by surprise nonetheless, for it was not the voice he expected. It was Fräulein Matowski that he heard, singing in a strong alto.

> *Oh Shenandoah,*
> *I long to hear you,*
> *Away, I'm bound away*
> *'Cross the wide Missouri*

Marla's friend was not a vocalist to be a peer with Marla; Johann pursed his lips. Still, he nodded. Very few singers would equal Marla, and one could be less than Marla and still be very good. Fräulein Matowski was good—maybe even very good. He relaxed and listened to the song.

> *Oh Shenandoah,*
> *I love your daughter,*
> *Away you rolling river,*

When the second verse began, the other instruments joined Franz in providing a musical platform to lift Fräulein Matowski's voice to a new level. Marla came in as well, singing now the descant that Franz had played in the first verse.

> *I'll take her 'cross*
> *Your rolling water,*
> *Away, I'm bound away*
> *'Cross the wide Missouri.*

Johann closed his eyes to avert distractions and listened with concentration. This was not a bravura performance; this was not something that he would take to the courts of the emperor or the *Hochadel*. Still and all, it was beautiful, presented with no affectation by the musicians, and he drank it in.

The remaining verses followed the pattern of the second.

> *'Tis seven years,*
> *I've been a rover,*
> *Away you rolling river,*
> *When I return,*
> *I'll be your lover,*
> *Away, I'm bound away*
> *'Cross the wide Missouri.*

> *Oh Shenandoah,*
> *I'm bound to leave you.*
> *Away you rolling river,*
> *Oh Shenandoah,*
> *I'll not deceive you.*

*Away, I'm bound away*
*'Cross the wide Missouri.*
*Away, I'm bound away*
*'Cross the wide Missouri.*

After the last verse, Rudolf Tuchman's flute carried the melody again as a solo line, rising and falling, falling and rising, to fade away on the final note. Johann—indeed, the whole audience—sat in silence for a long moment, until applause broke out from the back of the room.

Johann leaned toward Fräulein Stevenson under the cover of the applause. "That was well done."

She nodded vigorously. "Marla and Staci did that as a duet for choir contest their senior year in high school." She counted her fingers. "That was three years ago, I think. Hard to tell exactly with the Ring of Fire in the middle of it." She flipped her hand in the air. "Anyway, they got the highest rank possible from the judges." Her shoulders heaved in a sigh. "I wish I could sing half that good."

"Are you not a musician, then, Fräulein Stevenson?"

"Call me Casey. Fräulein makes me feel like an old maid aunt. And no, I'm not a musician. I mean, my mother taught me some piano, but the real talent skipped me and went to my brother, I think. I'm just a school teacher." She paused for a moment. "Although I think I'm pretty good at that."

"And is Fräulein Matowski a musician or a school teacher?" Johann was intrigued.

"Neither one." Casey gave a wicked grin. "She's a dancer, she is, and everything else is just what she has to do to be able to dance."

"Dancer?" Johann wasn't sure what to make of that.

"Sure. Didn't you see the performance of *A Falcon Falls* back in July? I think you were in town then, maybe."

Johann thought back, then shook his head. "No, just some glimpses of it. Some kind of big staged thing with many set dances, is what I gathered. Was it an opera?"

"No, it was a ballet of sorts, a production consisting solely of dances. Staci danced one of the lead roles in it. Staci's mother Bitty produced it. She's taught dance in Grantville since forever. Everybody who's studied dance started with her, including me."

Johann's eyes drifted back to Fräulein Matowski—Staci. She was smiling and singing along, clapping her hands as the musicians played another fast song. "She looks so young."

Casey followed his glance. "Yeah, I know what you mean. She looks like she's a pixie, about twelve or thirteen years old, especially since she got her hair cut. She's younger than I am, but she's actually older than Marla, by at least a couple of months." She counted her fingers again. "Yep. She's twenty-three now."

Johann watched as the song dissolved into laughter. His gaze narrowed until his vision was filled only with the shining face of the smallest performer. His mouth curved in a small smile.

The evening came to a close, and Marla's friends packed up their instruments, laughing and talking loudly to each other. Johann watched with a smile. They reminded him so much of his younger brothers: full of enthusiasm and energy, one moment boasting of how well they performed, and in the next pointing to a friend and claiming that he was the root of all musical evil because he bobbled a note. Of course, the friend responded in like kind, and laughter arose from around them.

Johann's eyes never strayed far from Fräulein Staci. She pulled on a faded blue jacket while she chattered to Marla and Casey, then picked up a cap of the style the up-timers called baseball and placed it on her head. It was black, with a large orange P symbol on the front of it. It occurred to him that she looked even more like a boy than before. She caught him looking at her, and grinned at him.

He pointed to the cap. She looked puzzled and pulled it off.

"What does the letter stand for?" he asked, stepping closer.

"Pittsburgh." Staci put the cap back on and tugged it into place.

"Pittsburgh." He rolled the word around in his mind, and made the obvious translation. "Fort Pitt?"

"Yep. That's what the first structure was for a city in the up-time state of Pennsylvania. Became a very large city, about a hundred miles north of where Grantville was before the Ring fell. This," Staci touched a finger to the bill of the cap, "is from the city's baseball team, called the Pirates." She started closing snaps on the front of the jacket. Casey stepped up beside her and they started toward the door.

Johann fell in on the other side of her. "Did someone in your family play for this baseball team?" He'd been to Grantville. He congratulated himself on knowing what baseball was.

Both the young women broke out in laughter. "No, no," Staci gasped after a few moments. Johann held the door open and followed them out into the night air. "Not that my dad didn't try to get my brothers interested in the idea. No, Dad is a big fan of the Pirates." She tilted her head and looked over at Johann. "Actually, I guess *was* a big fan is the way to say it. About the biggest in Grantville, and that's saying something. And he and all his baseball buddies went into mourning when the shock of the Ring of Fire wore off and they realized they'd never see another Pirates game. No more games on TV, no more weekend trips up to Pittsburgh to see them play. It was downright gloomy around the house for a long time. They picked up on the local games when those started, but it wasn't the same. That was one of the reasons why I took the teacher's job here in Magdeburg."

"One of them," Casey snickered.

Staci shoved her friend's shoulder, causing her to stagger a step or two. "You should talk. You were the one egging me on. You just wanted a roommate so you could be closer to Carl Schockley."

"So you teach?" Johann prompted.

"Yeah, that's my day job."

"Day job?"

"It's what I do to feed myself and pay my expenses. It's not who I am, though. I don't want to be known at the end of my life as a teacher. Not that there's anything wrong with that," she hurried to say. "It's just that I'd rather have something on my tombstone besides 'She taught grammar to five thousand four hundred and ninety-seven snot-nosed little girls.'"

Casey laughed again.

"I'm serious," Staci maintained. She looked around as they wandered down the street. Johann knew more or less where they were, but wasn't sure where they were going. He was content to let them guide his steps.

Staci shivered. "I still have trouble getting used to how crowded the houses are here in Magdeburg."

Crowded? Johann looked around. Everything looked normal to him.

"I mean," she continued, "they're all built right next to each other, walls touching. There's no yards, there's no space. You've been to Grantville," Staci appealed to Johann, "you know what I mean. Even in the downtown district there's room. Here, except for the new boulevards, most of the streets are so narrow I can stand in the middle and almost touch the buildings on both sides."

Johann tried to see through the eyes of an up-timer, and began to understand what she was talking about. He remembered all the open spaces in the town, all the wide avenues and large lawns and gardens. He also remembered thinking that the up-time must have been very rich for everyone to live on private estates. Now he looked around with that vision, and understood why Staci shivered. The only wide-open spaces in Magdeburg were the space around the Dom, and Hans Richter Square and the Gustavstrasse that led into it. Well, and the places where buildings that had burned in Tilly's sack of the city had not been rebuilt yet, but he supposed those didn't count.

"It is the way it is done here and now," he said with a shrug. "Perhaps in time it will change, but not soon."

Staci shoved her hands in her jacket pockets and kicked a stone down the street. "Oh, I can deal with it. It just makes me feel claustrophobic sometimes, is all." She raised her head up and the moonlight lit her smile. "Of course, having everything built close together like this does mean that no place in town is very far away from anyplace else. It's easy to walk."

And so the three of them continued walking. "Where are we going?" Johann finally asked.

"Home," the young women both said at the same time, which occasioned another spurt of laughter. "Not too far," Casey added.

Staci nodded. She looked up at Johann again. "So, Johann, have you figured out yet how you're related to Johann Sebastian?"

He shook his head. "No, the report from Grantville hasn't arrived yet. But soon, soon I will know."

"What's so important about him, anyway?"

Johann stopped still, astounded. The two young women went a step or two further, then turned and faced him.

Casey laughed, he presumed at the expression on his face. "You'll have to forgive her, Johann. She's a dancer. To her, real music begins with the Romantic-era composers, a hundred years after Master Bach."

Staci slugged her friend in the shoulder again. "I'm not that bad! And you're a dancer, too."

"Are too!" Casey slugged her back. She looked over at Johann. "I already told you I'm not much of a musician, but I know this much. Do you want to tell her, or do you want me to?"

Johann shook his head. "How can I say this to make you see?" It amazed him that someone with Staci's talent for music didn't immediately grasp this understanding. A thought occurred to him. "Let me state it like thus: if music were a religion, Johann Sebastian Bach would be its Moses—no, Saints Peter and Paul combined."

In an age where what religion a man professed might determine whether he was breathing by the end of the day, that was a strong statement. He could see that Staci was impressed.

"Okay," she said. "I'll have to take your word for it. Casey's right. If I can't dance to it or sing it, I don't pay much attention to music. But that...if that's how important that old man is to you, then go for it. Build your organ and play his music."

"I intend to," Johann said, pleased at her encouragement. "It may well become my life's work."

They wandered on in silence for a space, until the ladies stopped in front of an ornate door. Johann looked at the imposing building, then back at them. He tilted his head to one side, and they laughed.

"I'd call it our rooming house," Staci offered, "but it's actually the school, and we have an apartment in it. Thanks for seeing us home."

Johann gave a slight bow. "It was my pleasure, Fräuleins. Good night to you, and until another time." He dipped his head again, then watched as they stepped up to the doorway and entered the house.


Casey closed the door to their room and whirled on Staci. "You, girlfriend, have got an admirer."

"Do I?" Staci took her cap off and tossed it on the wash stand. She started unsnapping her denim jacket.

Casey threw her hands in the air. "Staci, the man spent the entire evening watching you. Almost everything he said while you were performing were questions about you. I could barely get him to look at me."

"What of it?"

"What of it?" Casey snapped. "What of it? He's

literate, he's educated, he knows the arts well enough that he has a chance of understanding you, and he doesn't come across as a down-time Lothario looking to conquer an up-time maiden. You might consider giving him a bit of encouragement."

"Mmm." Staci hung her jacket on a peg in the wall, then turned back to her roommate. "First of all, you're not supposed to be flirting with other men. You're pretty locked in to Carl, as I recall. And second of all...look, I admit the man is presentable, if not exactly handsome, and I'm flattered that he's asking about me. But he's years older than I am, and he's a down-timer."

"So?"

"So, I'm not sure he's flexible enough to accept me for what I am. I'm a dancer, I'm always going to be a dancer, and any man who comes into my life has to accept that. No, he has to do more than accept that—he has to support that."

Staci crossed her arms and looked at her roommate. "I'll give Bach points for not being a down-time version of a jock. He's polite and well-mannered. And he appears to be everything you say he is. I'll even give him points for being passionate about his art. If anyone can understand that, I can. The question is, will he allow me to be equally passionate about my art?"

Casey saw the expression on Staci's face shift through fleeting impressions of loneliness and fear before settling into one of resolution.

"Can *he* understand *me*?" Staci asked.

Although it was not a rhetorical question, Casey had no answer.

❖    ❖    ❖

For a long moment Johann observed the closed door, then gave a sharp nod and turned away.

Staci, he mused to himself. She was a woman of passion, he decided. A woman who knew what she wanted and was not afraid to say so and to work to that end. He liked that she understood his passion in turn.

Thoughts crossed Johann's mind of Barbara Hoffmann, daughter of Johann Hoffmann, *Stadtpfeifer* in Erfurt, his former employer. He knew there was an assumption on the part of the father and daughter that he would marry Barbara. It was such a common thing, that an ambitious musician would find an assistant's place with such a man as the *Stadtpfeifer*, marry one of his daughters, and eventually assume the place of the father when he died or retired.

Johann tried to bring Barbara's visage to mind: round face, almost doughy in complexion, framed by limp brown hair, with weak short-sighted eyes peering out at the world in constant confusion and startlement. Another's face kept forming in his mind: heart-shaped, with golden hazel eyes shining dancing gleaming above smiling lips.

His steps slowed, then stopped. Could he even think of returning to Erfurt now? Could he even think of returning to Barbara—poor, placid, insipid Barbara?

He became aware of someone standing nearby, and looked over to see a city watchman scrutinizing him. "Are you drunk, fellow?"

"No, merely reaching a decision."

The watchman looked at him some more, then nodded. "Be on your way, then. Night streets are not for good citizens."

Johann took his advice and headed for his lodgings.

Grantville, Johann mused as he wandered, such changes you have wrought. You have rocked the crucible of Europe, winnowed the ranks of the mighty, disconcerted the minds of the philosophers and scholars and pastors. Yet even in the midst of that you have deigned to reach down and touch the life of one poor musician.

His steps slowed, then stopped again. "God," Johann whispered. "You are indeed an Escher. What would have been my life is now revealed to be merely a figment, a parody, of what will now come to pass. I do not know your will for me for the future, but I pray that it includes both the music of Sebastian and the presence of Anastasia Matowski."

# Interlude

*Magdeburg*
*Early December 1634*

Johann Bach stepped into the room. He saw Lady Beth Haygood glance toward the door, notice him, and immediately begin moving in his direction even as she continued her conversation with a woman Johann did not know.

"Master Bach, so good of you to come." Frau Haygood held out her hand.

Johann knew enough not to bow over her hand; up-timers by and large were rather egalitarian, he had found. Instead, he simply gave her the warm handshake he would have given another master musician. "Thank you for inviting me," he replied. He looked around, then looked down at his plain coat. "I fear that I may be out of place."

"Nonsense." Lady Beth gave a ladylike snort, if there was such a thing. "You were invited, you came, therefore you are exactly in your place. Everyone knows the rules by now, but if anyone sneers at you, feel free to sneer right back at him—or her, as the case may be."

The expression on her face could only be described as a grin, and a large one at that. Johann returned a smile to her grin, and nodded. "Now, find yourself a glass and join the throng. There must be someone here you know." She turned away with another grin.

The invitation to attend one of Frau Haygood's *salons* had been unexpected. Twice a month or so she would gather an eclectic mix of people from Magdeburg and its growing exurb for an evening of conversation, sometime collaboration, and occasional confrontation. The practice had actually been started by Mary Simpson early in 1634 in order to bring together people that she felt should know each other, and had been continued by Lady Beth after Mary had begun her travels. The attendees included some of the most influential, important, prominent, and accomplished people in the land, drawn from all manner of disciplines and offices.

Johann was aware that his being issued an invitation marked his arrival in the highest levels of Magdeburg society, and his approval by its guardians. It was flattering, and for all that he had dealt with influential patrons several times in his past, a bit daunting as well. He squared his shoulders and straightened his spine, looked around once more, and stepped into the current.

"Would you care for wine, sir?"

Johann looked toward the voice and saw a youth dressed in a short white jacket and up-timer-style long pants balancing a tray. He nodded. "What do you have?"

The youth pointed to various glasses as he spoke. "Black Muscat, Riesling, and Elbling."

Johann fingered his chin, read the name on the young man's pewter badge, and said, "What do you suggest, Barnabas?"

The young man looked around, turned slightly and leaned his head close to Johann's. "The Muscat is barely drinkable," he murmured, "and the Riesling and Elbling are not much better than okay." There was that American slang again, Johann thought. "The war, you know. But my friend Jacob is at the bar in the corner, and he has a couple of bottles of a good Hungarian *Aszú* under the bar. Tell him I sent you and he'll fix you up."

Barnabas straightened, and continued in a normal voice. "The bar also has coffee and purified water, sir." He pointed in the direction of the bar.

Johann nodded his thanks and made his way to the bar, which looked like nothing so much as a wide board laid over two barrels and draped with a table cloth. He knocked once on the bar. At the sound, the young man behind the bar straightened. In dress he was the twin of Barnabas, except that his badge read "Jacob." Physically, however, he was shorter and stockier, but looked to be about the same age as his friend.

"May I help you, Master Bach?"

Johann was taken a bit aback. "How do you know me?"

Jacob grinned. "Frau Haygood always makes sure we know who was invited, and usually sees to it that we have a description. Besides, I heard her greet you when you entered." He pointed to a couple of small kegs on stands. "I do have some schnapps and *Weinbrand*, as well as some fresh coffee if you desire it."

Johann nodded, impressed by the organization and

attention to detail this implied. "Barnabas said you had some *Aszú*." He kept his voice low.

"Yes, Master Bach." Jacob busied himself, selecting a yellow wineglass, holding it below the level of the counter as he pulled a decanter from under the counter to fill it. He placed it in front of Johann. "Here you are, sir." He glanced at a clear glass jar at the end of the counter which contained several coins and a few of the Grantville bills. Johann took his meaning and felt in his pocket. He pulled a single one-dollar bill from the money clip he was now carrying and placed it in the jar. Jacob smiled at him in return. "Thank you, sir."

The *Aszú* was good, Johann decided after taking a sample of the wine. In fact, from his limited experience, it was better than good; well worth his contribution to the "tip" jar—another innovation from the up-timers. It was not the kind of wine that an assistant small-town music master was offered very often, and he decided that he would savor every drop.

With another nod to Jacob, Johann turned away from the bar and began a slow stroll around the perimeter of the *salon*. Frau Haygood, as had Frau Simpson before her, varied the *locales* of her gatherings. One night might be at the house of a prosperous burgher; another in the town home of one of the Adel. He had heard that an early *salon* had even been held at the newly rebuilt Rathaus. The *salon* before this one had been held at the Duchess Elisabeth Sofie Secondary School for Girls, where Frau Haygood was headmistress.

Tonight—Johann grinned for a moment—tonight was held at the guild house of the Brewer's Guild. He knew that the up-timers had a pronounced taste for beer over wine, so it didn't surprise him that Frau

Haygood had chosen to favor this particular guild. Too, from what he could tell, the way the guild would license anyone to brew beer, from the largest brewery to the youngest house frau who wanted to brew for her husband and his brothers, would appeal to the open-mindedness of the up-timers.

But the reality of it, he decided, was that the weightiest factor of the choice of the guild house as tonight's venue was the simple fact that it was one of the few spaces in Magdeburg, outside of the churches, that was with purpose designed for gatherings of people. There were rooms of various sizes in the building, and he knew from experience that the guild made more than a bit of coin from renting those rooms to families and groups for celebrations and meetings. He'd made a bit of coin himself playing with other members of the Magdeburg Symphony Orchestra at wedding celebrations and other parties.

Johann looked into the various side rooms as he strolled past them. Here and there through his promenade he noticed people that he knew, most of whom were engaged in conversation with others. One or two who caught his eye nodded to him, but none offered to bring him into their immediate circles. But before long he heard the sound of a piano cutting through the hum of voices.

His attention firmly attracted, Johann followed the sound to a corner of the room. Where before he had drifted on the currents of conversation, now he was as a vessel driven by the wind to his destination where he found Marla Linder seated at the keyboard of a piano. It was not a grand piano; not of a length that would compare to the Zenti piano that had been gifted to the emperor by that famed Italian craftsman. Rather, it was of the type called a baby grand by the up-timers. For all that it was smaller, he decided, it had a nice tone.

Frau Marla was playing something very slow, not quite a *largo* tempo, but not far from it either, with a slow arpeggio in the right and plain chords in the bass, over all of which was a melody that almost sang. It was a simple piece, really; a child's piece, almost. Yet in her charge it was an offering of lyrical beauty; not exactly understated but a work so bare of disguising adornment that Johann knew that the composer had to have been an up-timer of superlative skill, for no down-timer could have written the harmonies in the piece—not yet, anyway.

Johann's steps had carried him to stand behind the young woman as she drew the piece to a close with a series of quiet chords in the bass. She finished the last one, and let the resonances of the strings ring out and gradually fade away. At length she lifted her hands from the keyboard and let the strings damp.

"*Brava*, Marla." Someone spoke before Johann was able to open his mouth. He focused on the area just to the right of the piano, and saw what looked for all the world to him to be a musical tribunal: Maestro Giacomo Carissimi, master of the Royal and Imperial Academy of Music, was seated in the center, flanked on the right by Master Heinrich Schütz, *Kapellmeister* to the Vasa court in Magdeburg and on the left by Master Andrea Abati, the noted *gentiluomo* from Rome, now a teacher and producer here in Magdeburg.

"*Brava*," Maestro Carissimi repeated. His fellow "judges" nodded in agreement.

*"Bellissima,"* Abati added. His soprano voice never failed to take Johann by surprise. Abati was his first contact with a *castrato*, and whenever he thought of what had been done to the young boy who grew into Andrea Abati, Johann wanted to fold his hands over his groin in protection. But he had to admit the man had a superlative voice of a most beautiful, almost haunting timbre.

Master Schütz looked beyond Marla. "Ah, there you are, Master Bach. Come, pull up a chair and join us. Frau Marla has been arguing for some little time now that all arts, but most particularly music, need no reason for their existence but their existence. It seems to become a topic of discussion every time we are at one of these little gatherings. And she has just played this . . . what was the name again, my dear?"

"*'Sonata Quasi una fantasia,'* otherwise known as the *'Mondschein'* or 'Moonlight' Sonata, by Ludwig van Beethoven."

"And when was it written?"

"I believe it was in 1801," Marla replied with a bit of a grin on her face. Johann had learned that Marla loved to tweak down-time musicians with the thought that so much of this new music that so many of them were having to adjust to came from times that were well beyond their life spans. In truth, his own mind still spun from time to time with the thought.

"So, Master Bach," Schütz continued, "let us hear your thoughts on the idea."

Johann started to beg off, but the others encouraged him to join them. At length he settled himself into the chair brought forward from the wall by Franz Sylwester, Frau Marla's husband.

"Since I have come in *in medias res,* so to speak,"

Johann began, "I think it only fair to ask Frau Marla to restate her case." He gestured with his wineglass—carefully, so as not to spill a drop of what he was coming to think was really an excellent vintage of *Aszú*. He watched as the young woman straightened on the piano bench and squared her shoulders. She took an obvious deep breath, and began.

"You all know how much I love the music brought back in the Ring of Fire. And you know that I've made it my life's work to spread that music throughout Europe. So I obviously feel some passion about music. I believe that music is its own reward. This idea used to be called 'art for art's sake' in the up-time. There should be no constraints on what can be written or performed, that whatever the mind of a composer can conceive of should be expressed."

Marla paused for a moment. Johann heard the sound of murmurs, and looked around to see several other guests gathering behind the others. His attention returned to the young woman as she continued. "Music should be performed just because it's music. It has no function other than to be music, to provide that avenue of enjoyment, to be a balm for the soul. And all things musical should be free, unhampered by requirements to justify their existence. Composers should be able to write what is in their minds and hearts without restrictions from a patron. All people—men, women, boys, girls—should be allowed to perform—to sing or play or dance to the best of their abilities. Music requires no justification. It simply is."

The murmuring was a little louder now. Johann did not turn his head, but he could see more people gathering behind the Schütz-Carissimi-Abati line.

"So, Master Johann," Schütz gathered the thread of conversation to himself, and the surrounding eyes as well. He gestured to Bach, and said, "So. How would you respond to that?"

Johann postponed his response, sipping at his wine almost in panic. How to address this question—ah, it must be done with care.

He lowered his glass from his mouth and held it with both hands. "Masters," he nodded to Carissimi, Schütz and Abati. "Frau Linder," he nodded to Marla with equal gravity. "It is not a new proposition, I believe. I know my own grandfather said words somewhat like those at least once, and I daresay that if one could call King David, the greatest singer of old, to the witness bar, he would say something alike that. Especially after King Saul threw the spear at him." A chuckle sounded round the group that was observing. "All those who create beauty feel that beauty is all that is needed. But '*Quodcumque potest manus tua facere instanter operare*,' as the great preacher said—'Whatsoever thy hand findeth to do, do it with all thy might.'"

Johann raised his glass again and moistened his lips. "I submit to you that music is a created thing, as indeed are all things called art. And as such, we as musicians are addressed by that scriptural ordinance. It is not enough that we make music, for in truth we can be lazy and careless and slothful and reckless and devil-may-care about how we do it, just as a farmer or a joiner or a seamstress may be. But when we are, we are guilty of disregarding this stricture: that whatever we do, we should do to the best of our ability."

Heads nodded around the circle that had gathered

as Johann took a slow breath, which he then released just as slowly.

"But, Johann," Marla turned on the piano bench to face him, "you didn't talk about why the music should be made. You only talked about how we should make it. That's not the same thing." She faced back to the other men. "I still stand by what I said."

Carissimi looked to Abati, who smiled and shrugged before nodding back toward Carissimi's right hand. The Italian master then looked to Schütz and made a gesture with a smile of his own. The German sat up straight and harrumphed. Amber Higham came up behind him and placed a hand on his shoulder. Schütz almost absently lifted his empty hand and laid it atop the hand that rested on his shoulder while he directed his gaze toward the up-timer woman.

"Let me attempt to build upon the foundation laid by our young Master Bach, then. It is indeed true that we who make music should take most seriously that instruction from Ecclesiastes which he mentioned. But you rightly point out that your issue is not about the crafting of music, but more about why music is made. And to discuss that, we must step even farther back; to first principles, as it were.

"Tell me, Frau Marla, who created music?" At her puzzled glance, Schütz smiled. "'Tis obvious, child. Think back to your lessons: Who created all things?"

"God." Johann watched as Marla's eyebrows drew down, as if she were suspicious about something.

"Indeed, yes," Schütz replied as he raised a finger. "First point: The Holy Word says 'And God said, Let us make man in our image, after our likeness: and let them have dominion over the fish of the sea, and over the fowl of the air, and over the cattle, and over all the earth, and over every creeping thing that creepeth upon the earth. So God created man in his own image, in the image of God created he him; male and female created he them. And God blessed them, and God said unto them, Be fruitful, and multiply, and replenish the earth, and subdue it ... '"

Johann nodded, and heard murmurs of agreement from around him.

"So, God created us as we are. Therefore there is nothing that we can do that is outside the boundary of God's intent. We must assume this includes the ability to make music." Schütz smiled as another finger was raised. "Second point: Why would God do so?" He looked around the people grouped around the discussion. "No one has an answer?" A longer pause. "Oh, come now; one cannot read God's Word without seeing the commands to praise God, to sing unto the Lord, to play instruments in His praise. So one is therefore forced to the conclusion that at least part of why God created man was for the creation to praise the Creator."

Johann nodded in acknowledgment of the point, visually echoed by others in the crowd.

The *Kapellmeister* lifted another finger. "To the third point: Is the making of music unique to man?"

Johann raised his eyebrows. He could think of birds making musical songs, but he was not going to interrupt the older master.

"Birds ... whales ... maybe wolves ..." Marla said thoughtfully.

"Angels," Franz Sylwester spoke from behind his wife.

Schütz smiled again. "The natural and the supernatural together, eh? But let us first consider the natural."

He pointed a finger at Marla. "We have all of us heard birds making sounds that we call singing, particularly in the spring. But is that singing truly music, or only musical sounds? Is 'birdsong' truly music as you think of it, or is it just pleasantly tonal noise?"

Johann watched Marla's eyebrows draw down again as she spent moments in obvious thought. At length her chin lifted and her brow smoothed. "I guess I have to say that when you look at it like that, it's not music."

"And can you say differently about your whales and wolves?"

"Err...no," Marla admitted with obvious reluctance.

"I would agree with that statement," the *Kapellmeister* nodded. "I have heard the CD of the 'whale songs' in Grantville, and I found it interesting but unmusical."

"He should listen to John Cage," someone muttered behind Johann. He turned his head to see a bland smile on the face of Isaac Fremdling.

"I heard that, young Isaac," Schütz intoned. Johann looked back to see what could only be called a wicked grin on the master's face, mirrored by the expressions on the faces of Maestros Carissimi and Abati. "And I have heard some of what that man created. I found him both uninteresting and unmusical; *außer*, to say the least."

The *Kapellmeister* returned to his original subject. "Still on the third point, having disposed of the natural, let us turn to the supernatural. We are all of us, up-timers and down-timers alike, conditioned to think of choirs of angels in heaven. But have any of you ever looked at the original languages behind either our good Luther's translation of the Holy Writ or the more recent translation authorized by King James of England?"

Johann saw heads shake all around him.

"I am neither a Hebrew scholar nor one of Greek, but I know men who are. And when one fine day I asked them to help me scratch a curious itch about this matter, imagine my astonishment when I discovered that there are passages in scripture that speak of angels praising God, but none that unequivocally speak of angels singing."

An astonished murmur ran through the crowd, and Schütz's wicked grin reappeared. "Doubt me? Then find your own scholars and prove me wrong."

"I believe there is a verse in Job that might gainsay you, Master Schütz." The speaker was a portly man dressed in sober clothing.

"Ah, good evening to you, Pastor Cuno. Master Bach, have you met the pastor of St. Peter's Church? Pastor Tobias Cuno, this is Master Johann Bach, a musician with much promise. Master Bach, Pastor Tobias Cuno." Johann stood to give a slight bow and shake the hand that was offered him. They exchanged murmured pleasantries. He resumed his seat as the pastor turned back to Schütz.

"Well, Master Schütz? What have you to say about my thesis?"

The older man sobered. "Is that the one that says something like, 'When the morning stars sang together, and all the sons of God shouted for joy'?"

"Indeed." There was a note of surprise in the pastor's voice, and Johann could see his eyebrows had raised.

"I did say that I had consulted scholars," Schütz said with a smile. "As to the verse, I would say that although 'the morning stars' might be interpreted as meaning angels, it also very well may not. After all, the very God that could raise stones to be sons of Abraham and to praise Our Lord would doubtless have no trouble in arranging for stars and planets to sing." The smile disappeared again, and then he was serious. "But if not outright undeniable truth, it is at least a matter of interpretation, and one can make a case that music is unique to mankind, something given to the descendants of Adam that not even Lucifer or Michael or Gabriel can possess."

Franz stirred. "The last trump—"

"Is a battle call," Schütz interjected, "not a fanfare. Read the context."

Amber Higham stirred from behind her husband-to-be, lifting a glass of wine from the tray of one of the attendants and handing it to Heinrich. He cradled it in his hands and took a sip. "Ah, thank you, my dear." He reached up and patted her hand where it rested on his shoulder, and the glance he gave her left no one in doubt as to the affection of their relationship. "Now then, where were we?"

"You had just finished point the third," Johann said, leaning forward in the chair.

"Ah, yes. Thank you, Master Johann. Point the fourth," and another finger was lifted in the air. "This one circles back to the words of Master Johann. Music is a creation, the product of craft and, sometimes, art. Young Isaac," Schütz said as he directed his gaze past Johann. "Let us bring you into the discussion, since you have found your voice. Is the natural world the creation of God?"

"I believe it to be so," Isaac returned in a strong voice.

"Is the natural world itself God?"

Johann shook his head as Isaac responded, "No. Although there are pagans who might say so, it strains the bounds of credulity to think so."

Marla half-lifted a hand. "There were these ecology extremists in the up-time..."

Schütz shrugged. "There will be apostates in the future, why not pagans as well?" He looked back to Isaac. "May we then abstract a principle from this that the Creator is not the creation?"

"Aye," Isaac voiced as murmurs of assent were heard around them.

Schütz sat back in his chair. "Let us pause there for a moment. Frau Marla, have you anything else for us tonight? Something else for piano, or perhaps a song?"

Marla said nothing, but looked down at where her hands rested on the keys of the piano. After a moment, they began to move as if by their own volition. Again, quiet chords, nothing the up-timers would have called flashy. Just as Johann began to wonder what Marla was doing, she smiled and said, "In honor of both the season and the discussion," then opened her mouth and sang.

> The angel Gabriel from Heaven came,
> His wings as drifted snow,
>    his eyes as flame;
> "All hail," said he, "thou lowly
>    maiden Mary,"
> Most highly favored lady,
> Gloria.

Johann was struck by the simple beauty of the melody. Anyone with a voice could have sung it. Any child, any mother, any deacon of the church.

> *"For known a blessed Mother*
> *thou shalt be,*
> *All generations laud and honor thee,*
> *Thy son shall be Emmanuel,*
> *by seers foretold,"*
> *Most highly favored lady,*
> *Gloria.*

Listening, Johann began to truly understand why Marla's name was on the lips of everyone in Magdeburg who knew anything about music. Yes, anyone could sing the song; but how many could sing it with such purity? A tone that never wavered, every note absolutely on pitch, there were those who could do that—not least of whom was *Signor* Abati who was smiling and nodding his head. But the pure lack of ornamentation, the so simple rise and fall, ebb and flow, swell and fade of her voice, so simple and yet so hard. How many could make the song *sing* as she did?

> *Then gentle Mary meekly bowed*
> *her head,*
> *"To me be as it pleaseth God,"*
> *she said,*
> *"My soul shall laud and magnify*
> *His holy name,"*
> *Most highly favored lady,*
> *Gloria.*

Marla's voice and the piano faded away to an instant of pure stillness. Then the applause broke out from those standing in the circle. Johann gulped the last of his wine so he could set the glass down and join in.

The three older masters were smiling; Abati's face contained an expression that could only be called beatific.

"Oh, very nicely done, Frau Marla," Schütz said after the applause died down, "very nicely done, indeed." A brief smile crossed her face as she nodded in response. "Now, where were we?"

"The Creator is not the creation," Isaac responded.

"Yes. Thank you, Isaac." He shifted in his chair. "So, the Creator is not the creation. And inasmuch as man is created in the image of God, then the same principle must be held true for man and his works as well, must it not?"

Johann nodded with the others. Truly, the *Kapellmeister* was speaking well tonight. He hoped someone was making notes, as this discourse was enlightening and deserved to be made public in some manner.

Schütz took a sip of his own wine, then continued in a sober voice. "I have thought much on these things. My time in Grantville was ... difficult ... in some ways ..."

Johann had heard that the master had suffered some form of crisis, but from the expression that he saw on Schütz's face it must have been severe.

"... and it caused me to truly consider music," Schütz continued, "what it is, and what purpose it serves. And to confirm this thought: What was the purpose of man in God's creation?"

Johann looked around. No one was willing to answer. He mustered his courage, and said, "To have dominion."

Schütz flashed a smile toward him. "I perhaps misspoke, in that there are more purposes than one in God's design for man. Yet Master Bach has named the purpose I sought. Directly after God said 'Let us make man in our image . . .' He declared that man would be given dominion over all the earth. All the earth; others would say all of creation. Surely that includes music. And as proof, I offer this from the Holy Word: 'The Lord thy God in the midst of thee is mighty; He will save, He will rejoice over thee with joy; He will rest in his love, He will joy over thee with singing.'"

"Zephaniah, the third chapter," Pastor Cuno said thoughtfully. Schütz nodded. Johann pursed his lips and tugged on his beard. He would have to think about that one.

"So if the Lord sings, and we are created in his image, then one can infer that our music is an integral part of being made in the image of God. And here, Frau Marla, is where we perhaps begin to address your thesis—and the dangers contained therein." Schütz was now sitting up straight, staring at the young woman. "If the purpose of man is to have dominion, and the purpose of music is to praise God the Creator, then we must be very careful."

Marla was frowning now, Johann noted.

"In and of itself," Schütz continued, "music is morally neutral. An A-flat is an A-flat, regardless of what produces it or what the type of music in which it is used. It is the words we attach to the music, it is the staging we accompany with it, it is the behavior of those associated with it, that provide a moral valuation. But setting that aside, considering music simply as music as you wish to do in your ideas, we still must be very careful."

He paused for a moment, then lifted one hand palm

up. "Music is under dominion, under the control and shaping of man, of the musicians, yes?"

Marla slowly nodded, echoed by others in the group, including Johann.

"But music must never be allowed to *have* dominion."

The crowd became absolutely still. Marla, still frowning, at length said, "I don't understand, Master Heinrich."

Schütz sighed. "In this time, my dear, and perhaps in your up-time as well, music is all too often considered to be a tool. We who write for the church consider it an aid to worship, something to shape people, to mold them into the appropriate state of mind and emotion."

Johann nodded to himself. He had heard statements very like that from his old master Johann Hoffman, the *Stadtpfeifer* in Suhl.

"But there is a danger with that thinking, a danger most insidious. Music can progress from being under dominion to having dominion. When we credit to music capabilities that it, as a created thing, does not inherently possess, then we have crossed a line into idolatry."

Johann saw an expression of shock on Marla's face, and knew that its twin was on his own.

"I have spoken with Master Marcus Wendell and Master Atwood Cochran in Grantville at much length, and they have shared knowledge and wisdom with me, showing me how in their history-that-was musicians would turn their art and craft into idols." A wry grin appeared on the *Kapellmeister*'s face as he reached up again to touch his Amber's hands where they rested on his shoulders. "Of course, all the other arts and artists did as well: the painters, the actors..." Amber's low chuckle filled the space, "...those who made the movies and DVDs. But the fact is, Frau Marla; young Isaac; and you, Master Bach who so strongly pursues the music of a descendant who will never live, when you take a created thing and give it dominion over its creator, when you surrender causality to the music, you have created an idol. And if you do so with music, you have made an idol of the very thing that we are commanded to use to praise God. And that should never be permitted."

Schütz sat back, and tiredly waved a hand. "Or so this old man thinks."

Silence reigned in their group. All eyes turned toward Marla, whose face had returned to a frown. "So are you saying that we should do nothing but church music? That only religious music should be performed, that . . . that . . ." she stuttered, "that the only music acceptable is that which contains the name of God?"

Johann was wondering the same thing as he watched Master Schütz jerk up straight as if shocked by the up-timer's electricity.

"By no means, child, or I would not be sitting here listening to you play the piano and having this delightful conversation. By no means." He waved a hand. "Play your Beethoven and your Chopin on the piano. Play your flute. Sing your Irish folk songs with zest and vigor. Let your younger Grantvillers play trumpets and beat drums and march in the parades. Let some of your friends even learn *jazz*." The older musician shuddered a little. "Enjoy it all; have fun with it all; but when you make music, make the best music you can make; not for the glory of the music, but for the glory of God. Anything less cheats God and cheapens you. And neither of those things ought be."

Marla sat still, unmoving, for long moments. Johann watched as Franz at length reached out and touched a finger to her shoulder. She looked up, and Johann could see tears pooling in her eyes. "I have never considered that, Master Heinrich. I will think on what you have said."

"Indeed," Giacomo Carissimi said as he stood, followed by Andrea Abati. Johann almost lunged to his own feet, not to be caught sitting at this moment. "You are master of us all, Master Heinrich, and we will think on these things." He bowed with respect, followed a split second later by Andrea and Johann. Others in the group murmured support. Carissimi straightened with a wicked grin of his own. "But do not be surprised if the subject raises its head again, Master Heinrich. A good subject loves to be debated."

"*Ach*," Schütz said, waving his hand again. "Enough talk. Let tomorrow's talk take care of itself. Tonight, make music! Make joyful music! Who has more music for us? Frau Marla?" She shook her head with a laugh, and pointed at Isaac. "Young Isaac! How fitting! What do you bring to us tonight?"

Isaac lifted the violin he had been holding all along, plucked the strings to test their tuning, and said, "With all joy, Master Heinrich, I offer up to you and to God the chaconne from Partita No. 2 in D Minor, by Johann Sebastian Bach."

Without another word, Isaac launched into the great work. Johann sat back, bemused by the fact that Isaac had brought such a work as that. The music poured out, and he soaked it up. *Mein Gott*, he thought. *Such beauty, such power, as much with the violin as I had found in the organ works. This other Johann,*

*who will never be, was so good I cannot even be
jealous of him.*

As he rose and fell with Isaac's bow, Johann understood how close he had come to becoming idolatrous.
*But never again,* he decided. *I will celebrate the
greatness of the music, and the greatness of the man,
but most of all the greatness of God who by His grace
gave us both the music and the man, and gave us the
Ring of Fire by which both the music and the man
will be made known.*

A commitment formed in his mind, to be observed
for the rest of his days.

*Soli Deo Gloria.*

# Etude

Wechmar
December 1634

> To Christoph Bach
> In Wechmar
>
> Brother, word has come to me that Mama
> has died. Since Papa died of the plague
> eight years ago, that leaves me the head
> of the family. I have moved from Suhl to
> Magdeburg to pursue greater opportunities
> here. You must come to me immediately.
> Bring young Heinrich with you. I have a
> commission here to build an organ, and
> I need your help. With good fortune this
> will lead to other positions for all of us.

Christoph stopped reading and looked at his younger
brother Heinrich. "Johann is starting to sound pretty
high and mighty now that Mama is gone."

Heinrich sniffed. "Are you surprised? He is the
*eldest* brother. He's always been the *eldest* brother.

He has never let us forget it, and probably never will." The youngest of the three Bach children gave an evil grin. "Of course, Papa usually gave him the first lick whenever anything happened."

"Aye, and usually you had something to do with that 'anything' happening, didn't you?" Christoph grinned back. He agreed that their brother Johann, who was nine years older than Christoph, had a tendency to think that his chamber pot contents didn't stink, and he had more than once played second violin to his younger brother's lead when opportunities arose to puncture Johann's pomposity. Nonetheless, he had genuinely missed his big brother when he left for Suhl.

"Hmm," Christoph reread the first paragraph to himself. "Something big must have happened."

"What do you mean?"

"You know how Mama would go on and on about how Johann was so lucky to have his position in Suhl, how he would be able to become a Joshua to *Stadtpfeifer* Hoffmann's Moses, and how it was understood that he would marry the *Stadtpfeifer's* daughter."

Heinrich made as if to spit. "Ja, Mama was so looking forward to having that Barbara as her daughter-in-law. Nasty *Scheinheilige*, she is."

"Yes, well..." Christoph found himself in grudging agreement with his brother, although he might not have worded his opinion so strongly. "Hypocrite though she may be, it would appear from this..." he waved the letter, "...that our Johann has come to his senses."

"Ja." Heinrich's eyes grew dreamy, and he smiled the smile he wore when he watched girls walk down the street. "Magdeburg. The emperor's new capital... where fortunes and reputations can be made." His gaze sharpened and focused on Christoph's face. "When do we leave?"

Christoph scanned through the rest of the letter. "He says to give Papa's clavier to Uncle Andreas, store as much of the furniture as we can in his barn, and sell the rest. So, maybe a week, maybe two."

"Good! Let's get started."

"Not so fast," Christoph said. "Listen to the rest of what he has to say."

"He would," Heinrich muttered. "More eldest brother talk..." his voice trailed off.

"Shh. Listen."

> *When you come, wend your way through Grantville. You know by now the town really exists, and the location of it. You will be surprised at much of the town, and some of it will make you wonder why there has been such a clamor about the place. The people seem odd at first, but by their lights they are a decent folk.*

"Idiot," Heinrich said. "Of course we know about Grantville."

"Shh. You said it yourself; he's just being the *eldest* brother."

> *When you get there, have someone direct you to the High School. There seek out Masters Marcus Wendell and Atwood Cochran, lecturers and musicians. They will play for you music from the future such as you have never heard. And some of it is by a*

> *man named Bach. Go; hear it, then come*
> *to me in Magdeburg. The three of us will*
> *have much to talk about.*
>
> > *Johann Bach*
> > *Magdeburg*

Christoph lowered the paper. The two brothers Bach stared at each other, eyebrows raised and eyes wide, all complaints and gripes and slurs forgotten. Music from the future—by a Bach.

*Magdeburg*
*February 1635*

Franz entered the bedroom and closed the door to keep the warmth from the small stove in the room. He looked to where Marla sat on the stool before her dressing table, combing her long black hair in the candlelight. She looked up at him and smiled, which sent a flood of warmth through him. Even after almost a year of marriage, he still marveled that she, who doubtless could have had her pick of the available up-time men, had seen something inside a crippled and bitter down-timer; something that drew her to him. Or perhaps, something that drew him to her, as a moth circled a flame . . . the attraction to her was that strong, that natural, that intense. Almost it was enough to make him a Calvinist, for to his mind it would have required the sovereign hand of God to bring her to love him. Of a certainty, he found nothing in himself that deserved her.

"What are you thinking, love?"

Marla's voice drew him from his reverie. "How much I love you," he responded, then warmed again as her smile flashed wider. He walked over to her, bent to kiss her upraised lips, then reached to pick up the hairbrush from the dressing table. She sat up straight as he began to draw the brush through her thick mane with long slow strokes.

This had become one of their little rituals, something that they did for themselves. Marla's hair was long enough and thick enough that it was hard for her to tend to all of it, and Franz had early on taken over the brushing of it. He loved the silken feel of her hair, and from the expression on Marla's face in the mirror on the wall that she had brought from Grantville, she was undoubtedly enjoying it as well.

They didn't talk for some time, just enjoying the intimacy of the moment. Franz paused for a moment, lifting a tress of the liquid ebony before him. Half-crippled his left hand might be, but the nerves still worked, and the feeling of the hair sliding across his fingers and palm left them tingling. He bent to deeply inhale the fragrance of it.

When he straightened, Marla had opened her eyes and was watching him from the mirror with an expression that reminded him of the portrait the up-timers called the *Mona Lisa*. He smiled back and resumed brushing.

"So why were you late getting home tonight?" Marla asked.

Franz chuckled. "Johann Bach asked if he could talk to me after the orchestra rehearsal. We went to the Green Horse."

"I thought I smelled beer on you when you came in." Her smile turned impish.

Franz raised his right hand. "Oath to Heaven's throne, I only had one, and I did not finish it."

"So what did he want?"

"It took him forever to spit it out. He kept hemming and hawing and dancing a gavotte around the outside of it, but when he finally asked his question of me I nearly bit my cheeks bloody to keep from laughing."

"So what did he say? Out with it, and no dancing around from you!" In the mirror Franz could see Marla's eyes were dancing themselves.

"He wanted to know how to court an up-time woman." Franz kept his expression as straight as he could, and watched in the mirror as Marla's jaw dropped. The surprise lasted only a moment, then she began to laugh. Peal after peal of silvery laughter sounded in the room, and Franz felt his own face relax as he began to chuckle.

"Oh..." Marla finally said, gasping, "oh, that's too funny. After the way he's been circling around Staci for the last few months, it's about time, but still..." she started chuckling herself, "...wait 'til Staci hears about this."

Franz started the brush moving again. "Now, I would ask that you not tell her." Marla's eyebrows went up in the mirror, and he replied, "Let them find their own way, my dear. It would be best."

Marla's mouth quirked, then smoothed out. "Okay, I suppose you're right," she said. "But think of the fun I could have had with that." Franz grinned at her. "So what did you tell him?"

"Well, I thought of quoting that song from *Camelot* to him..."

"'How to Handle a Woman,'" Marla interjected.

"Yes, that one. And what it says about love is true enough; but I thought he probably needed a little more than that to serve as his ground for the music he would write with her. So, I told him that from my limited experience up-time women are less concerned about the property and the furnishings and the spices, and more concerned with equality and equitability and trust. I told him to treat her with the same respect and care that he would give Master Schütz, and to listen to her when she talked to him about the things that are important to her."

Marla sat for a while as Franz continued brushing. At length she said, "That's probably the best advice you could give him. I hope he listens to it. I'd be pretty unhappy if he or anyone else hurts Staci."

Franz shrugged. "We shall see. He's a fine musician, and appears to be a good man, but..."

"Yeah, but..."

Franz had been counting the brush strokes while they talked. "One hundred." He set the brush on the table and stepped back to admire his handiwork. Marla's hair gleamed like an ebon waterfall and it flowed to her waist. She stood and began to remove her robe. He moved the stool over and stood behind her, resting his chin on her nightgown-clad shoulder and crossing his arms beneath her breasts. She raised a hand to cup his cheek, and they stood thus for long moments, staring at each other in the mirror.

"I would wish them to love each other as much as I love you," he whispered after a time. "They cannot possibly love each other more."

Marla turned in his grasp and gave him a warm and lingering kiss. "Come to bed, love."

Franz watched her move to the bed, then bent and blew out the candle.

## March 1635

"Johann!"

"Brother!"

Johann Bach's head snapped up. There were only two men on the face of Earth who would call him that, and he knew those voices. "Christoph? Heinrich?"

"Here!"

And there they were, hurrying down the street toward him. In a moment they were exchanging hearty embraces and slapping shoulders. After the welcome, Johann stepped back, a hand on each brother's shoulder.

"Look at you. It has been what, over a year since I last saw you? Christoph, you are broader across the shoulders than I am now. And Heinrich, I am glad to see that you can finally muster a proper beard. My last glimpse of you, your face looked more like a moth-eaten scabrous fox pelt."

He dropped his hands and clapped them together. "So! What did you think of Grantville?"

"Amazing!" Christoph's voice was a light tenor, which climbed into his highest register whenever he was excited. It was as high now as Johann had ever heard it. "I mean, it was no eternal Jerusalem with golden streets, but it was so different from everything."

"The up-timers were . . . different." Heinrich's baritone had a diffident tone. He wasn't used to being part of adult discussions yet, Johann thought to himself. "They are different, and they are not different," he replied. "The things they know, their attitudes, those may be different. But their wants and desires and passions—those not so much. Their musicians love the music, for example."

Johann took his brothers by the arm, turned them, and headed down the street. "So, did you hear the music I told you to find?"

Both young men nodded vigorously. "Indeed," Christoph responded. "And it was as you said—music such as we have never heard. Instruments that do not exist, harmonies that are rare, tonalities that our masters say should not be used, and above all, the many new forms."

Johann looked at Heinrich. The youngest Bach brother shrugged and pointed at Christoph. "He said it all. Except that the music of this Johann Sebastian Bach was among the best."

Johann stopped for a moment. "Yes, I agree. Old Bach, as the up-timer musicians sometimes call him, was more than gifted, more than a genius. He was a phenomenon, and they owe more to him than they realize." He started walking again. "With that name, he had to have been some kind of relation to us, but I was not able to determine it while I was there. I commissioned a research to provide as much information about Johann Sebastian and his family as can be found in the great library there, but they were unable to complete the work before I had to leave. I really hoped to have the results by now, but it has not arrived yet. Soon, perhaps."

Christoph laughed, echoed by Heinrich. He pulled a packet of folded papers from inside his jacket and slapped it across Johann's chest. "Soon is today, brother. We were in the library ourselves, reading a book called

*Harvard Dictionary of Music,* learning more about the up-time music, when we met Brother Johann. When he understood who we were, he immediately took us to the bank because he had delivered the research results to them only the day before. The . . . what did they call her, Heinrich?"

"The escrow officer."

"Yes, the escrow officer accepted that we were your brothers after reading the letter you had sent to us. We told her we were coming to Magdeburg to join you, so she gave us the information."

Johann looked down at where his hands were holding the papers that Christoph had thrust on him. "You . . ." Words failed him at that moment. The realization that he might be holding the answers to his questions suddenly burst in his mind. He jerked upright. "Come!" He took off down the street at a pace not much below a run, with the sound of his brothers' steps behind him and people scattering to each side ahead of him.

"Well, that is clear enough." Johann took one more glance at the page he held angled to the light of the candle before he set it on top of the stack of other pages brought from Grantville. He took a pull at his mug, swallowing disappointment along with the beer.

The Green Horse was relatively quiet. It was full, but there was no music, so only the conversations were filling the air. Johann wished for a moment that Marla and Franz and the others were here. He could have listened to the music and put off the strange hurt he was feeling.

"What is clear enough?" Heinrich lowered his own mug.

"Well, according to what Brother Johann was able to determine, he," Johann leveled a finger at Christoph, "was the grandfather of Johann Sebastian Bach. You and I will have to make do with being known as the men who would have been the great-uncles of Old Bach."

Christoph looked very pleased with himself as Johann took another mouthful of beer.

"Do not get above yourself, brother," Heinrich murmured with a wicked grin. "The man will never exist. There is no fame from being the grandfather of one who is less than a ghost." Johann laughed outright at that as Christoph's brow wrinkled.

"It seems," Johann picked up the thread of his thought, "that in the up-time the Bach family was even more widespread in Old Bach's time than it is now. The three of us were the beginning of what was known as the Erfurt Bachs."

"Why?" Christoph questioned, looking down into an empty mug with a puzzled expression on his face.

"Well, in truth," Johann replied, "the Erfurt council has sent me a letter asking if I would be willing to be considered as director of music. If Grantville had not appeared, I probably would have left Schweinfurt and taken the Erfurt position."

"And married Barbara Hoffmann, no doubt."

Johann lowered his eyebrows in a glare at Heinrich, but did not respond to his dig directly. "I do not now intend to go to Erfurt, and I doubt that you will return to Wechmar. According to the up-timers, the river of time has been wrenched from its erstwhile banks by Grantville being sent back to us. It will not return to its previous bed, but instead is carving new channels.

The Erfurt Bachs will instead become the Magdeburg Bachs." He stared at the wall between his brothers, eyes unfocused, seeing with an inner vision. "And while we may not have genius equal to that of our now-never-to-be-realized grandson and great-nephew, we will collect all his work, we will preserve it, we will perform it, and it will become a cornerstone in the edifice of music from this time forward."

The younger Bach brothers were silent for a moment. "You have thought on this, obviously," Christoph at last ventured.

"Oh, aye," Johann's eyes focused back on his brothers' faces, "it has been near the forefront of my thoughts since I first learnt of Old Bach's music. God will not allow that brilliance to fade into obscurity. He preserved it in the up-time; He will preserve it in our time. We will be the tools by which He will accomplish it."

Johann knew his voice had become intense. From the expressions on his brothers' faces, he suspected that his own expression was in line with his voice. They had best get used to it, he thought, gazing again into the mists of the future. This was at one and the same time a legacy to be tended and a challenge to be faced.

God may be drawing an Escher work with Grantville at the center—He would not find the Bachs lacking. They were Bachs—that was enough.

"Well, what shall we do today?" Christoph asked as they left the rooming house the next morning. Johann stifled a yawn as old Pieter the porter shut the door behind Heinrich, who trooped down the steps to stand with his brothers.

"Bread first," Johann muttered. He led the way to *Das Haus Des Brotes*, cracking a huge yawn every few steps. When they arrived, Frau Kreszentia Traugottin verh. Ostermännin, the proprietress, was sweeping the steps with a broom. Her husband, Anselm, was the baker; she handled the sales of the bread.

"A good day to you, Frau Traugottin," Johann called out as they neared the bakery, which occupied a corner on one of the busiest intersections in the exurb of Greater Magdeburg.

Frau Kreszentia looked up and smiled. "Ah, Herr Bach. You are out and about early this morning."

Johann shrugged. "There is work to be done, and it won't get done if I'm sleeping while the sun is up."

"So true," she replied, "so true. And who might these young men be?"

"My brothers," Johann responded, "Christoph and Heinrich." The two bowed slightly as their names were given.

Frau Kreszentia looked at them for a moment. "A definite family resemblance. But with three of you, one must be a bit of a rascal, a trickster."

Johann and Christoph both pointed at Heinrich and said in unison, "Him." Heinrich didn't deny it, but did his best to appear innocent.

"Let me guess—the youngest?"

At that, Heinrich grinned and nodded.

"Aha," she said with a bit of a smile of her own. "I can see I need to be sending word to all the taverns to warn the girls who serve that there is a new rascal in town."

All of them got a good chuckle out of that.

Frau Kreszentia opened the door and led the way

into the shop, to step behind the counter. "Three of the regular?" she asked Johann.

He nodded, and she turned and pulled three of the small loaves and handed them out to the three brothers. "Thank you, Frau Traugottin," they chorused, as Johann pulled ten pfennigs from his pocket and offered them to the proprietress.

"Call me Zenzi," she said. "Everyone does. I'm the sister and cousin and friend to so many folk, I just let everyone use the name. So much so that when someone says Frau Kreszentia or Frau Traugottin, I look around to see who they're talking to."

Johann's brothers laughed as they followed him out of the bakery. The three of them walked down the street side by side, eating their bread, Johann in the middle.

"So," Christoph said after swallowing a lump of bread, "you said you're building an organ?"

Johann nodded, mouth full of bread.

"Isn't that a bit ambitious for you? I mean, you've not done that before, have you?"

Johann swallowed. "Not designed one, no, but when I left Suhl for Schweinfurt, I was involved in a repair and partial rebuild of the Schweinfurt church organ. And I did get to spend some time with two of the Compenius family and talk organs one night in Erfurt, and I made careful notes afterward. I think I can do this."

"You'd best do it," Christoph said around the bite he was chewing. "You will taint the name of Bach if you don't."

"*We* will do this," Johann said. "You have as much interest in seeing it happen as I do. As the up-timers say, a rising tide lifts all boats."

"I'm not a boat," Heinrich announced. "I'm a ship. See my sails?" He extended his arms to their full length to the side, and smacked Johann in the chest with one of them, which made Johann choke on the bite of bread he had just taken.

"Id . . . idiot," Johann gasped between coughs.

Both brothers pounded on Johann's back. When he finally got his breath back, he snapped, "Enough!" He caught a grin on Heinrich's face before the youngest brother could erase it. "Just wait until I find you coughing, Heinz. Two can play that game," he said with an evil grin of his own, lifting a hand.

Heinrich edged around to the other side of Christoph, who immediately stepped out from between them. "Don't try to hide behind me," was all he said with a smirk.

The youngest brother lifted both hands, palm out, shoulder high. "I'll be good," he said with a solemn face and a motion of the cross.

"Right," Johann snorted. "And if anyone believes that, I have a castle on the Rhine I'd like to sell them." Christoph laughed at that, and even Heinrich reluctantly cracked a smile. "Now come on," Johann continued. He turned, and headed down the graveled road that was Kristinstrasse, one of the major east/west avenues in Greater Magdeburg outside of the walls of the old city.

His brothers fell in beside him again. "So what are you doing today?" Christoph asked.

"Today we go check on the wind-chest for the organ."

"Ah, they've gotten that far with it, then?" Heinrich asked with interest.

"Yah," Johann answered. "The building of it is

basically complete, and they should be sealing the inside of it. That's what I want to check on. If they make a mistake, it will be much easier to correct if we address it before the glue sets and cures."

"Right," Christoph said with a nod, echoed by Heinrich. Although neither of them were instrument makers in their own right, they both had observed craftsmen at work on violins and claviers, so they had some idea of how that kind of work was done.

"So," Johann said, turning north on the ring road around the old city of Magdeburg, paralleling Der Grosse Graben, the moat around the Altstadt, the oldest part of the old city, and the walls around the Neustadt, the rest of the old city, "we shall see how well they are doing."

It wasn't long before Johann had led his brothers through the southwest gate of the Neustadt and into the west side of the construction site, where they found themselves watching the carpenters glue paper to the inside of the main wind-chest. The wind-chest had indeed been solidly built, but the cracks between the boards would allow for air to escape and weaken the pressure needed to make the pipes sound. So the carpenters had to seal the inside of the chest, and the manner in which they had chosen to do so was interesting to him. His brothers stood beside him, just as fascinated.

The little brazier under the carpenters' glue pot kept the chamber rather warm. Johann had taken his jacket off not long after they had arrived and laid it atop the carpenters' tool chest. His shirt-clad arms were crossed as he watched them.

It was a matter of some humor that both of the

carpenters working on the organ were named Georg. It wasn't the most common of names in Thuringia, after all. But Big Georg and Old Georg, as he thought of them, didn't seem to have any trouble keeping straight who was talking to each of them, and they were good at their craft, so Johann just smiled from time to time when the thought crossed his mind.

At the moment, Big Georg was brushing glue from the pot onto the back of a large thick piece of paper. His strokes were smooth and steady, almost like it was a task he'd done a myriad of times, yet Johann knew that this was the first organ the man had worked on.

Big Georg put the brush back in the gluepot and placed the pot back on the brazier, careful not to spill a drop. He then lifted the piece of paper with care by two corners and passed it to his partner.

Old Georg applied it to the inside of the wind-chest with equal care, overlapping with the piece he had just applied a few moments ago. He took up a brush and smoothed out the new application, then picked up a tool that was nothing more than a piece of thick leather folded over a brass blade and began smoothing the air bubbles out, pushing them toward the outside edge.

Johann's gaze was very intent, following every practiced move. It startled him when Big Georg chuckled.

"You know, Master Bach, you really do not have to stand around and watch us like my old schoolmaster. We will do the job right."

Johann looked over to see a wide grin on the big man's face.

"Nah, not like a schoolmaster," Old Georg's voice echoed from inside the wind-chest. "More like a first-time father when his wife is in labor." Johann could hear the humor in the older man's voice, and he did not doubt a smile was also present.

"How do you mean?" Big Georg asked.

"Well, he knows he's responsible for what is going on, and he wants to do something to make sure everything goes right, but he does not know what to do and is totally dependent on someone else who does not want or need his help to get it done."

The two Georgs broke out into raucous laughter, and Johann could feel his lips curling up, however reluctantly. "Not being married, I cannot say from my own experience if you have the right of it, Georg," he replied.

"Not married, are you?" Big Georg asked.

"Not yet. There was a girl in Erfurt, but..." Johann shrugged.

"You came to Magdeburg, and suddenly Erfurt does not look so grand, eh?"

Johann shrugged again, hearing muffled snorts from Christoph and Heinrich.

"Got your eye on a woman here?"

A vision of Staci's face crossed his mind. "Perhaps."

"I knew it." Old Georg crawled out of the wind-chest. "Side walls are done. Cap the brazier and set the pot to cool, Georg. We'll pick up from there in the morning." He straightened his slight frame and twisted his back, generating several loud pops. "Oog, I am getting too old to be crouched like that all day." The older man took his hands, grasped his head and jerked it to each side, generating more pops.

"You knew what?" his partner demanded.

"He is looking for a city girl, a *bürgemeister's* daughter, or maybe a younger daughter of one of the Niederadel. Or, even better," Old Georg leered at Johann, "he wants one of those uppity up-timer women. Am I right?"

Johann said nothing, just smiled.

"Hah! I thought so." Old Georg slapped his knee. "You just be careful, Master Bach. Them up-timers can be a tricksy lot at times. Everyone knows that. You think things through with care before you tie yourself down with one of them."

Johann picked his jacket up as the two Georgs lifted their tool chest to take it to the locked storage area. "I will take your advice to heart, Georg."

"You do that," the older man called over his shoulder as they maneuvered out the door.

Johann looked around. Solid progress being made at last. It had taken longer than he had hoped for the wind chamber to be built, but now that it was up and roofed the carpenters were making good speed. He bent over and peered into the wind-chest. Another day, maybe, to finish lining the chest with paper, unless they decided there needed to be two layers. Two or three days past that to make sure the glue was cured, then the varnish would be applied. Once that dried, he could rest assured that there would be no air leaks from the inside of the chest.

He slung his jacket over his shoulder and walked through the shell of the building, his brothers following, feet following the safe paths with unconscious thought as he mused. An uppity up-timer woman, huh? Is that what he wanted? Hazel eyes above an impish grin floated before him, sparking a smile of his own. Yes, if he was going to be honest, that was what he wanted.

"An up-time woman?" Heinrich asked. "When do we get to meet her?"

Johann heard the glee in his brother's voice, and groaned inside. He had really hoped to keep Staci a secret for a bit longer, but it looked like he'd let his own secret slip.

"Today is . . ." Johann began, then paused.

"Wednesday," Christoph said with a grin. "What of it?"

"I may be able to introduce you tonight, then," Johann said.

"What's her name?" Heinrich insisted.

"Later. Let's go see the whitesmith." And with that, Johann headed back out of the construction site and onto the Gustavstrasse.

Half an hour later, the three Bachs were standing against the back wall of Master Philip Luder's forge space, watching the master and his assistant work. The two men carried a crucible full of molten tin from the forge to the pouring table with great care. There was no doubt in his mind that the crucible and its carrying rods were weighty, and that the molten ore contained within the crucible added to the load. But there was also no doubt in his mind that the reason for their slow steps and gentle handling had nothing to do with the weight. No, he could see the heat waves above the mouth of the crucible, making wavy lines through which he could not see with clarity. The thought of what that molten metal could do if it spilled or splashed on a man's flesh caused his groin to shrivel and his stomach to attempt to climb up his throat. Despite the fact that he was well away from them, he still slid down the wall another step or two, pushing Christoph and Heinrich along as he did so.

The whitesmith and his journeyman came to the pouring table and positioned themselves with care at the head of it. They lifted the crucible so that the lip of it rested on the edge of the trough mounted on top of the table rim.

"Gently, gently," Master Luder breathed. "On the count of three . . . One, two, three, pour."

They tilted the crucible until the molten silvery-gray tin slowly poured out in a steady wave into the trough. Higher and higher the crucible tilted, until the pour slowed and the last few drops of it fell into the trough, making ripples in the molten metal.

"Quickly now," the master snapped. They set the crucible down on the stone floor with alacrity, then took positions on each side of the trough. "Ready?"

"Jah." The journeyman was focused on the trough, having grasped a handle on his side of it with both his gloved hands.

"Again on three. One, two, three, pull."

Johann saw Master Luder trip a latch as he said "pull," and the molten tin sluiced out the bottom of the trough as they pulled it on the raised rim down the length of the table. The last drops spilled out as they reached the end of the table.

The two smiths straightened and took off their heavy leather gloves. Master Luder walked the length of the table, peering at the shining sheet of tin. At the head of the table, he turned to Johann.

"It is a good pour," he declared, reaching up to take off his scarred leather apron. "That is the first of the English tin. I had to try it myself to see how it would melt and pour. Very few impurities in it, and I was able to skim most of them right off the top. So, somewhat cleaner than the locally produced tin, but also somewhat more expensive. I will do a pour of the local tin and compare them, then you and I will talk. The English tin is more costly, of course, and if there is little benefit to the cost increase, you may need to rethink your requirement. Either way, I will likely contract with other whitesmiths to make the sheet tin like this, and I will concentrate on making the pipes for you."

"Very good," Johann said. He stepped closer to the table and gazed at the shimmering metal through the heat waves. "I trust that we will start seeing pipes soon."

Master Luder shrugged. "As soon as this cools and I can start working it. First pipes in a week, first tunable pipes the week after that."

Johann calculated in his mind. "That will do for a start. But you may have to work with other smiths to make the pipes as well. Three thousand pipes is a lot for you and your workers to make by yourselves."

Master Luder shrugged again. "We will cross that ford when we come to it."

Johann said nothing, but observed to himself that the crossing of that ford would not be far off—not if he had anything to say about it—and he did. Still, this was a good beginning. "My thanks, Master Philip. Shall we go to the Green Horse and celebrate this auspicious beginning?"

"Nah," the whitesmith replied with a smile. "I have much to do yet before this day's light is done." He held up a hand with a raised index finger. "However, the day that you pass the first completed pipe, then we will all go to the Green Horse!" He waved his hand broadly to include both his journeyman and the two younger Bach brothers. The journeyman nodded his head with a vigor that matched Heinrich's echoing nod.

"As you will," Johann replied with an answering smile. "Until then."

Johann was still smiling when he stepped out into the evening light. He had carried his jacket from the construction site, and had left it off in the warmth of the forge. For all that it had been a sunny spring day earlier, clouds were covering the sun now and the air outside was cool, so he shook the jacket out to put it on, shrugging his shoulders to get it to settle.

"Herr Bach!" someone called out. "Johann!"

Johann looked around to see Marla Linder waving at him from where she stood with her husband, Franz Sylwester. He started to cross the street to where she was, only to have Christoph grab his collar and yank him back just as a large pair of horses moved into the space he'd been about to step into, pulling a rather large and laden wagon behind them.

The wagon driver looked down at him. "You..." The rest of the driver's monologue established a masterful command of profanity, scatology, and blasphemy as he assessed Johann's intelligence, likelihood of siring children, legitimacy, general maleness, and prospects of making any significant contributions to the German people or to the human race in general, all in a few short pithy sentences that trailed away as the wagon trundled on.

"You might want to watch where you're about to step," Christoph said, voice slightly strained. Johann wasn't sure if that was from concern at almost seeing his elder brother stepped on or run over, or from suppressed laughter at the same cause.

Johann looked to his younger brother, where he observed widened eyes and lips moving soundlessly as he stared after the wagon. He was undoubtedly trying to memorize parts of what he'd heard. Johann shook his head.

"Come on." After a moment, Johann started forward again, this time carefully looking both ways. He suspected he would hear about this again.

Marla grinned at Johann as he and his brothers joined her and Franz on their side of the street. "Got to watch where you're going, man."

"Indeed," Johann admitted with a bit of a sour grin of his own. Christoph nudged him. "Ah, these are my brothers, Christoph and Heinrich." They each nodded as their names were called. "These are Franz Sylwester, *dirigent* of the Magdeburg Symphony Orchestra, and Marla Linder, leading treble singer of Magdeburg, superb musician and master of the piano, and one of the leading lights of Magdeburg's music establishment."

The two young men bowed, receiving nods in reply from Marla and Franz.

"Nice to meet you, boys," Marla said. She looked at Johann with another grin. "You going to put them to work?"

"They're going to help with the organ project, yes."

"Good. I suspect you're going to need the help."

Johann shrugged.

"We're going to be at the Green Horse tonight," Marla continued. "You planning on being there? Staci said she was going to come." Marla's grin reappeared, this time with an edge of humor to it.

"Ah, yes," Johann said, not missing the glances his brothers gave each other.

"Good. We'll see you then." Marla slipped her hand around Franz's arm. "Meanwhile, we've got to run to Zapff and Sons printers and get some more staff paper. See you tonight. And nice to meet you, Christoph, Heinrich."

And with that, the two of them turned and moved off.

"Is she the one?" Heinrich asked.

"No," Johann said in a quelling tone.

"She is that good a musician?" Christoph asked, watching them leave.

"Frau Marla, as she insists everyone call her, may be the best musician in the city," Johann responded. "And Herr Franz is not far behind her."

"Up-timer, I assume from her accent," Heinrich said. Johann just nodded in response. "He said nothing. Is he an up-timer as well? Does he hide behind her?"

That jarred a laugh out of Johann. "By no means. Franz is one of us. He is no weakling. He is as strong-willed as she—he had to be, to win her—but he is somewhat quieter, so that he sometimes seems to be the shadow to her sunshine. Let him stand at the head of the orchestra, though, and you will see him in all his strength."

"*Dirigent*," Christoph mused.

"We will talk about that later," Johann said.

"Staci," Heinrich murmured with an evil grin.

Johann sighed. "Fräulein Anastasia Matowski," he said reluctantly.

"I thought you said she was an up-timer. Is she Polish?" Christoph wrinkled his forehead. "Russian?"

"Up-timer," Johann said, gritting his teeth. "And the up-timers use Fräulein as a common form of address for any unmarried woman, so do not be thinking she's a child of rank or anything."

"So is she a musician, too?" Heinrich asked, his grin broadening.

"No, not like Frau Marla. She's a teacher. And that's all I'm going to say for now. Now come on, we need to go talk to Herr Jere Haygood."

It was evening, and Johann and his brothers had just stepped into the Green Horse. He was chewing the last of a piece of sausage he had bought from a street vendor who had been about to close for the evening. His hand was greasy, so he wiped it on the seat of his trousers.

"Johann! Over here!"

He could see Marla standing at the end of a table and waving at him. He waved back, but stopped first at the tavern keeper's bar to acquire mugs of beer for himself and Christoph and Heinrich. Once they were all suitably equipped, he led the way toward Marla's table.

In addition to the musicians of Marla's immediate circle, several other friends were there. Johann's heart seemed to skip a beat when he saw Staci Matowski and her friend Casey.

The two young women were wearing usual up-timer garb: trousers, rather snug-fitting sweaters, and caps that looked something like Staci's baseball team cap only covered with many rows of small reflecting things that bounced light from the lamps and candles into Johann's eyes. They had to be some form of sequin, he decided, albeit a bit smaller than he had ever seen before, and certainly more concentrated in quantity, since he could not see a bit of the bare fabric of the cap underneath them. Staci's hat was a dark blue, and Casey's was a brilliant red. Both were reflecting flashes of light around the interior of the tavern as they turned their heads in conversation and laughter. Staci's hair had grown out some since the short cut she had gotten several weeks ago, but it was still rather short, which left a fringe of the hair sticking out from the bottom edge of the hat.

Lights were also reflecting from the wire hoop earrings that Staci was wearing. They attracted Bach's attention, as he had never seen such before. Studs that nestled against the earlobes, yes. Dangling earrings, yes. But hoops, now...those were new to him. But then his attention was caught by something else.

Staci was sitting sideways on the end of a bench, left foot on the bench and arms wrapped around her left knee as she looked across the table at Casey and laughed at something her friend was saying. She was wearing a shoe much like a slipper which left the top of the foot mostly bare, since she wore no sock or hose on the foot. Johann's first thought was that the shoe was a bit impractical for the season. His second came as he stopped and tilted his head in the realization that there was a large mark on the top of her foot.

"Hi, Johann." Staci had looked around and seen him standing there. She caught the direction of his gaze. "Like my tat?"

"Your what?"

"My tattoo." She lifted her foot up and angled it so that the light shown across the top of her instep.

"See? It's a rose, and the stem runs up and circles above my ankle like a bracelet or anklet."

In the better light, Johann could see the artwork involved for what it was—a rather nice rendition of a scarlet rosebud, with a green stem complete with thorns that twined up the top of her foot until it reached her ankle and then circled her leg as she had described. The small shapely foot and slender ankle did stir him a bit.

"Interesting artwork," he said. "Do a lot of you up-timers have those?"

"Some," Staci said. "Don't people do tattoos in the here and now?"

"I think religious pilgrims may sometimes get some kind of symbol or icon when they do achieve a pilgrimage," he said. "And of course, sailors and soldiers seem to have a lot of them. But the regular folk, no, not that I've seen."

Staci shrugged. "Same with us. Lots of military folks, lots of biker types, and some other side groups of society, but not a lot of the regular folks. This was actually my eighteenth birthday present to myself, and I caught hell from Mom and my grandma about it." Johann raised his eyebrows at that, and Staci laughed. "Oh, for different reasons. Mom had a practical concern about it showing through any dance outfit I might wear. Dancers are in white and pastels so much that just wouldn't cover something so dark. I had to prove to her that there are stage makeups and creams that are opaque enough to cover it. Once she saw that, she was okay with it."

"And your grandmother?" Johann asked.

"I had to pull Reverend Jones in on that one," Staci

replied. "Like a lot of older church folks, she thought that the Bible teaches that tattoos are sinful because of one verse in the Bible somewhere in Leviticus. He was able to explain to her that the verse was specifically talking about the Jews not practicing pagan rituals about worshipping the dead, so that if the tattoo doesn't match up with pagan worship, it's okay from that standpoint. Then he told her that since we're not Jewish, we're not bound by that commandment anyway, especially since the Jerusalem council in Acts clarified that non-Jews are not bound by the Jewish law." She grinned again. "I'm not sure that she really believed him, but she quit muttering about it, anyway."

"It is a nice piece of artwork," Johann said, eyeing her foot again and admiring its smallness and slenderness.

"Yeah, I had to go all the way to Morgantown to find a guy who was good enough to do it." She shrugged as she dropped the foot back to the bench. "Cost me a pretty penny, too, but it was worth it."

"So does someone in Grantville not do tattoos? Is that why you traveled?"

"No one I trusted back then," Staci said. "I wanted to make sure that whoever did it was a good artist and kept his needles and equipment clean. I figured I was going to be living with whatever I did for a long time, so I wanted it to be good art, and I didn't want to pick up an infection from it."

"Needles?" Christoph asked, eyebrows raised.

"They use small-gauge needles to inject the color into your flesh," Staci said with a moue of distaste.

"That must have hurt." Christoph again.

"Not really."

Casey turned back toward the group. "It hurt like a big dog. Don't let her kid you."

"Did not."

"Did so," Casey retorted. "I was there, listening to every whimper you made, and holding hands with you until you about crushed mine. Watching you deal with it is one reason why I never got one."

Staci shrugged again. "Well, maybe it hurt a little. Tattooist said that it would probably hurt more there than if I'd done something on my arm because the tissue was so thin and there were so many nerves. But I wanted it on my foot."

Johann shook his head. "Does anyone in Grantville do it now?"

She shrugged again. "There are a few folks doing it. But I've got the one I wanted, so I haven't been thinking about it much." Staci pivoted and put her foot on the floor. "Have a seat...and who's that with you?"

Johann sat down and slid over. "My brothers, Christoph and Heinrich."

"Hi, guys," Staci said with a smile. "Sit down...I think there's room."

The two brothers nodded at Staci and returned her smile. Christoph took the end of the bench by Johann, and Heinrich sat on the other side of the table by Casey.

"Are you guys into music, too?" Casey asked.

All three of the brothers laughed. "We are Bachs," Christoph said. "Of course we are...how did you say it...'into music.'"

"There are Bachs scattered all through Thuringia," Johann continued. "And everywhere you find us, we are mostly involved with music. There may be one or two who aren't, but I do not know of them if there are."

"Wow," Staci said. "So you could make an all-Bach orchestra if you were all in one place."

"And a choir as well," Heinrich said with a grin.

"That's cool," Casey said. "My mom would have been thrilled at that kind of thing. So, Johann, did you ever figure out if you are related to Johann Sebastian Bach?"

At that moment, Marla stood and moved to the piano that stood against one wall of the tavern, followed by Franz and her friends. Johann quickly pointed to himself, "Great-uncle," to Heinrich, "Great-uncle," to Christoph, "Grandfather. Later."

Casey and Staci both nodded, and everyone turned their eyes to where the musicians were assembling.

"Good evening, everyone," Marla announced. The room was mostly full by now, and there was a rumbled response of various forms of greetings. "Glad you're here," she continued. "We're going to have some fun tonight, so hang on and let's get started." With that, she sat down on the piano bench and placed her hands on the keys.

"Play some soul music, sistuh," a voice drawled from the back of the room.

Marla spun on the bench with a surprised look, which was replaced by perhaps the biggest grin Johann had ever seen. "Nissa? Nissa Pritchard, is that you?"

"Ain't nobody else, child," came the response in a resonant voice that came from a Moorish woman who was dressed in up-timer clothing who made her way through the crowd.

Marla jumped to her feet and met the other woman at the edge of the front table line. They embraced in a strong hug, then stood back. The other woman's grin

was as large as Marla's, and her white teeth shone in
the midst of her dark face. Johann judged her to be
of rather mature years—there were wrinkles on her
face—but as with many of the up-timers, he hesitated
to judge her by down-timers' standards. Best he could
do was guess that she was over forty. Her face was
strong, and that combined with her short curly, kinky
hair gave her an exotic appearance for the middle
of Germany. Everyone knew of Dr. Nichols and his
daughter Sharon who had come back with Grantville
in the Ring of Fire, but this was the first that Johann
had heard that there had been anyone else of their
race among the up-timers.

"It's good to see you, Nissa," Marla said. "I've
missed seeing you."

"That goes both ways, you know," the older woman
said with a laugh.

"What are you doing here, anyway?"

"Oh, Mayor Gericke brought me and Claude and a
couple of the other power plant team guys up here to
talk about building a big power plant in Magdeburg."

"Cool." Marla's eyebrows popped up, and her eyes
gave an additional gleam. "Say, did you bring that
mouth harp with you?"

Nissa laughed and slipped a hand into an inside
jacket pocket to bring out something that shone in the
lamplight with a brassy golden gleam. "Now would I
be anywhere without this?"

"Great!" Marla enthused. She grabbed Nissa by
the arm and dragged her over by the piano, where
she looked around at Franz and the other musicians.
"Sorry, boys, there's been a change in plans." She
dropped onto the bench, and looked out at the room

with another big grin. "Okay, folks, hold onto your hats. This is going to be like nothing you've heard before. Tonight we're going to be doing some Southern music."

Johann was confused. Southern music? Swiss? Venetian? Roman? What did she mean?

Casey turned back to the brothers and murmured, "Southern up-timer music. It's good, but it's probably pretty different from what you're used to."

Marla played a few dissonant sounding chords, then looked up at Nissa. "What key are you doing 'Steamroller Blues' in this month?"

Those white teeth flashed again in Nissa's dark face. "Key of G sounds good to me."

What followed was an astonishing potpourri of some of the most unusual music Johann had ever heard. He was dumbfounded from beginning to end; when he looked at his brothers, they seemed to be even more astonished than he was.

It was one song after another, frequently with no breaks at all between them as Marla would play two or three transition chords to move from one to another. And they were all music that just gripped him, even as he struggled to assimilate what he was hearing. The rhythms were frequently so syncopated that he had trouble feeling the beat. The harmonies were frequently so dissonant that at times he almost lost the key feeling. Yet there was a power to the music, whether fast or slow, that just reached out and transfixed him.

Song followed song: "Steamroller Blues," "Crossroad Blues," "Swing Low Sweet Chariot," "Rockin' Chair Blues," "Down By the River," "Miss Brown to You," "Go Down Moses," "Preaching Blues," and on and on. Most of them were sung by Nissa with additional lines on what Marla called a harmonica, but Marla sang a few, and added descants to a couple of others.

Johann was almost exhausted by the time he felt they might be drawing toward a conclusion. They pulled into a slow-moving song where Marla took the lead. "Cry Me a River" was saddening in most ways, and the room grew quiet by the end. That was followed by Nissa doing one called "God Bless the Child" that the CoC members in the room seemed to appreciate, based on the thumps of fists on the table and boots on the floor when it concluded.

"Yeeoowww!" Marla almost screamed out as she stood up and knocked her bench over backwards, startling Johann and most of the room. She started hammering the piano keyboard in an almost berserk manner, a very heavy syncopation, with both hands moving almost independently, bringing them to a point where she was repeating the same chord rapidly. Then she opened her mouth and began singing a song about some boy who lived in the woods down by New Orleans, wherever that was. Nissa was playing the harmonica along with her, and the other musicians were falling into place as they began to pick up the harmonies.

They arrived at the chorus, which involved heavy chord repetition and syncopation again, and very simple words, repeating "Go!" and ending with "Johnny B. Goode."

Nissa took the second verse, they cycled through the chorus again, and Marla took the third and last verse. When they hit the chorus again, Nissa took the lead with Marla singing a descant over the top. The chorus was repeated a number of times, until they reached a place where Marla held the last word out for an extended time while she took the chords through another transition run into a final song. Nissa gave a short laugh when the chords resolved into the final pattern, but turned and faced toward the crowd to belt out the final song.

> *Oh, when the saints go marching in*
> *Oh, when the saints go marching in*
> *Oh, Lord I want to be in that number*
> *When the saints go marching in*

They cycled through a number of verses before returning to the original. By now everyone in the room understood the melody, and they started singing along with the words as that verse was repeated over and over again. Fists were beating on tables, boots were stomping on the floor. Even as he sang along with the others, Johann kind of wondered if the tavern building could withstand much of this. He found he didn't care. A glance out of the corner of his eye showed that Christoph and Heinrich were standing alongside him and singing at the top of their lungs as well.

> *Oh, when the saints go marching in*
> *Oh, when the saints go marching in*
> *Oh, Lord I want to be in that number*
> *When the saints go marching in*

Marla brought the song to a crashing conclusion with bravura keyboard work up and down the black and white keys. When she took her hands off the keys and straightened, the room burst into applause, and Nissa grabbed her in a big hug. The two of them embraced, then stood together side by side, arms over each other's shoulders, almost panting as they laughed together.

Johann found he envied them...at least a little. He greatly enjoyed making music, but he wasn't sure he'd ever had a time like this one, where he commanded such an outpouring of sound and energy and gathered the focused attention of so many people at once. That didn't reduce the pace or strength at which he beat his hands together, though.

The din finally dwindled as Marla and her friends, including Nissa and a large up-timer, settled at the other end of the table. As the rest of the room sat back and the bar servers began scurrying around picking up empty mugs and replacing them with full ones, Johann and those at his end of the table just looked at each other, almost worn out with what they had just witnessed and been a part of.

"Wow," Staci said. "I'd kind of forgotten just how much energy Marla can pack into a performance."

"You mean she does that a lot?" Johann asked.

"It doesn't come through quite as strongly in her classical performances," Staci said.

"Classical?" That from Christoph.

"Her serious stuff," Casey said. "What she does with and for Mary Simpson and the Royal Arts League. It's a different style of music, one more directly connected with the court music of this time."

"And the new stuff that Master Carissimi and Master Schütz write, too," Staci said. "I just wish they'd write a ballet or two."

"Your mom still wants to stage the old standards," Casey said.

"I know," Staci replied, "and I get that. I don't want to see them fade away, either. They're too important for dancers. But I think we need some new stuff, too."

"Ballet? Is that not something in France?" Heinrich asked.

"Sort of," Staci said, her mouth quirking for a moment. "But what we do is very different. It does involve a lot of dancing, a lot of very structured and choreographed movement by sometimes a lot of people."

"Dancing?"

Casey leaned forward. "Staci's mom was a professional dancer for a little while. Then she started teaching dancing to students. Since the Ring fell, she's been teaching a lot of people, including a few daughters of Adel families." She shrugged. "It's really good physical exercise and conditioning, and it requires some real discipline to practice and develop."

"So do you do this ballet?" Heinrich asked.

Casey smiled. "Yep. You see before you Mrs. Matowski's two most experienced female dancers."

"I thought you were teachers," Christoph said.

"We're teachers to support ourselves, to buy bread and the occasional mug of beer or glass of wine," Staci replied. "But speaking for myself, I live to dance. I want to keep up-time dance alive, and when I can't dance any longer, I want to teach it so it will live on."

There was a moment of silence after that, then Casey said, "Well, we need to call it a night. School starts pretty early in the morning."

"Right," Staci agreed.

The two young women stood up, stepping over the benches and putting on their jackets after they got untangled from the furniture. Johann stood as well.

"Good night, Johann," Staci said with a smile and a touch to his arm. "Nice to meet you, Christoph and Heinrich. I'm sure we'll see you again some time."

"G'night," Casey said.

"Good night," the Bach brothers chorused, and the two young women walked off together.

Johann sat back down. The three brothers looked at each other, and in unison picked up their mugs and drained the remaining contents. They stood, and Johann waved toward the other end of the table.

"You calling it a night, Johann?" Marla called out.

"Work to do tomorrow," he replied with a shrug.

Farewells were called back and forth, and Johann led his brothers out of the tavern. Once on the street, they flanked him as they moved down the street. It was late enough that there were no heavy wagons out, and only a periodic carriage or cab to contest them for the roadway. Hands in pockets, they walked along.

"How was your baptism in up-timer music?" Johann asked with a chuckle.

"That was an immersion, not a simple baptism," Christoph said. "Is it all like that? The up-timer music, I mean?"

"Surely not," Heinrich said from Johann's other side. "The Bach music we heard certainly wasn't."

"No, it's not all like that," Johann said. "But you have to remember that Old Bach lived and wrote seventy to one hundred and fifty years from now. But there was another two hundred plus years of musical development and changes after him. And a good many of the changes were apparently due to the influence of aboriginal and tribal music from all over the world, but especially southern Africa. Those influenced richer, darker harmonies and much more complex rhythms. But they take some getting used to." He chuckled again.

"Be honest, now," Heinrich protested. "You have not listened to that much of it, have you?"

"No," Johann admitted. "And I cannot say that I like a lot of what I have heard. But I have been told that familiarity will breed at least tolerance, if not a certain taste." He shrugged and held out his hands to each side, palms up. "The same miracle that brought us Old Bach also brought us the blues. We will have to learn from both, I believe. But our call is to preserve and spread abroad our Bach heritage."

"Agreed," Christoph said, and Heinrich threw in an affirmative grunt.

They were another half a block down the street toward the rooming house when Christoph said, "You are thirty years old, Johann."

"As of last November twenty-sixth, yes, I am. What of it?"

"She looks like a child. They both do. Is she really a teacher, or does she just tend children not much younger than herself?"

"Part of that is because Fräulein Staci is small—short, that is, and slender. The French word petite applies. And part of it is because she was raised in the up-time, with their abundance of good food and excellent medical care. Like most up-time women, she looks younger than she really is. No plague scars, either. But she's probably older than the two of you."

"What?" Heinrich exclaimed. "She cannot be that. Can she?" He sounded almost insulted from his august age of nineteen. Christoph was frowning a little, obviously thinking there was no way that Staci was older than he was.

Johann chuckled, taking a bit of pleasure from being able to puncture their pomposity. "I believe she is twenty-two. Frau Marla is a few months younger. I do not know about Fräulein Casey, but she is probably about the same age."

"I'm twenty-two," Christoph protested.

"Staci's birthday is in February," Johann said with a grin.

Christoph muttered as it was proven she was indeed older. The two younger brothers mulled that over as they walked.

"That is hard to believe," Christoph said at last, "but I must take your word for it. And it would explain their control and manners. But even so, even if we give her those years, that's a bit young to marry, is it not?"

"Not that much," Johann said. "Not by our standards, even, and definitely not by theirs. It was not uncommon in the up-time for up-timers to marry as young as eighteen, and sometimes even earlier. And it still is today."

"So at twenty-two Fräulein Staci is perhaps a bit ripe by their standards?"

Johann chuckled again. "Perhaps. But they tend to not think that way."

More steps in silence as his brothers mulled things over.

"She is pretty," Heinrich offered, "certainly much more so than Herr Hoffmann's daughter Barbara. But . . ."

"But what?"

"A dancer? One who performs in front of people? What would Mother have said?"

And that, Johann knew, was a question that he had to deal with.

The rest of the walk was made in silence.

Over the next several weeks, the two major concerns in Johann's life progressed in parallel. Christoph and Heinrich rapidly became as familiar with the building plans as he was, and before long were on a first name basis with the construction crew, especially the carpenters and electrical workers, and most especially the cabinetmakers who were doing the fine and detail work for the organ works. Christoph had begun to take over the monitoring of that work, which freed up some of Johann's time to begin working with the carpenters on the exact placement of the pipe ranks and the routing of the air pipes from the primary wind-chest to the smaller reservoirs behind the keyboard console and from the keyboard console to the ranks of pipes.

Heinrich, meanwhile, had become an unofficial almost-apprentice to Master Luder. He was spending much of his time at the whitesmith's operation, watching the preparing and pouring of the sheet tin and the work to shape the sheets into the pipes. After a few false starts, the whitesmith had recalled the knack of shaping the voicing openings of the pipes, and true to their agreement, the night of the day that Johann had passed the first pipe had been a night of celebration at the Green Horse. Johann still remembered the head he had had the next morning.

So the organ was progressing well. His courting

of Staci Matowski was progressing...or at least, he thought it was. Staci would meet with him once or twice a week, always in the company of others. She appeared to be enjoying his company...at least, she laughed a lot when they were together. But there were no signs that she was encouraging his courtship.

Of course, she was an up-timer. Her understanding of courtship was probably different than his. He wasn't sure he knew what signs she would give.

The conversation he'd had with Franz Sylwester floated through Johann's mind for perhaps the umpteenth time, to use one of Staci's phrases. Give her equality, equitability, and trust. Listen to her. Well, perhaps he needed to give her that opportunity.

And so it was, in the third week of April, that Johann delivered himself to the front steps of the Duchess Elisabeth Sofie Secondary School for Girls late in the Wednesday afternoon. He looked up at the front of the elaborate townhouse that currently housed the school, plus provided rooms for some of the teachers, and shook his head. Such grandeur, compared to the rooming house he was living in; for that matter, compared to the house in Wechmar he had spent most of his childhood in.

He shrugged, opened the door, and entered. As it happened, Lady Beth Haygood was moving down the hallway toward him, papers in hand.

"Herr Bach," she said in surprise. "Are you here to see me?"

"No, Frau Haygood," he said. "At least, not this time." They met fairly frequently to review the progress of the organ construction, so it was an easy assumption to make. "Actually, I would like to have a few words with Fräulein Matowski. Is...does...would she have time to see me now?"

Lady Beth looked at the up-time watch on her arm and smiled. "The teaching day is about over. She should be free in a few minutes. I'll send a note up to her room to tell her you're waiting on her. Why don't you have a seat in the parlor?" She gestured to a wide doorway behind Johann.

He took her advice and entered the parlor room. Looking around, it was very rich, in a restrained sort of way. The walls were paneled in rich wood—he looked closer, even going so far as to touch one of the walls, and verified that it was a very nice walnut. Caryatid figures stood around the room against the walls, with paintings on the walls between them and smaller statues on rich stands scattered among some very elaborate furniture.

Johann didn't dare sit down in the room, for fear that some dirt on his clothing would besmirch the fine fabrics on the furniture. He simply stood in the center of the room in the only clear spot, and turned slowly, taking in everything, and wondering how even up-timers could take this for granted. Then his gaze was drawn to the ceiling, where an incredible plaster expanse was painted with a bucolic scene of a group of women and children in a garden. The skill of the painter took his breath.

He didn't know how long he stood gazing up, enraptured, before, "Johann?"

Johann turned back toward the fancy archway through which he had entered. Staci stood there, so slight, so small in a skirt and a tailored shirt, hands clasped in front of her, with a slight smile on her face. Her head was slightly tilted as she gazed at him. And for that moment, just that one timeless moment, Johann wanted to do nothing more than enfold her and take her into himself forever. The intensity of the feeling almost frightened him.

"Johann?" she said again.

"Umm," he began, then had to stop and clear his throat. He looked around. "How can you live and work with this?" he said.

"Easy," Staci said. "My room isn't nearly this fancy, and my classroom just has plain tables and chairs in it. This is the fancy room for the important people to sit in." She grinned, and it transformed her face from heart-shaped beauty to gamine in that instant. "Lady Beth must like you. She usually uses this room to receive people that she wants to impress."

"Oh, I am impressed," Johann muttered. "So impressed I am afraid to touch anything."

"You've never been in a patron's home before?"

"I have never had a patron like this." He shook himself. "And that has nothing to do with why I'm here."

Staci's grin flashed again. "So why are you here?"

"Umm," Johann took a deep breath, "to ask you to join me at Walcha's Coffee House tomorrow evening for an evening of conversation, and . . ." he reached into an inner pocket of his jacket, "to bring you this." He handed her a book.

"What's this?" Staci took it, but didn't open it like he had expected her to.

"A book," he said with a bit of a grin of his own.

"I can see that." She lightly slapped his arm with the book. "What kind of book?"

"Poetry, actually."

With that, she folded it within her arms against her breast. She looked at him for a moment, head tilted again, hazel eyes gleaming above her solemn mouth.

"Yes."

Johann looked at her, startled for a moment. "Yes?"

"Yes, I'd like to spend tomorrow evening with you at Walcha's Coffee House." Her smile this time was somehow soft, with a sweet light that almost seemed to enfold her like a halo.

"Umm..." Johann was beginning to hate that sound, and it had come out of his mouth a lot tonight. For someone with his self-confidence, that was more than a bit unsettling. "Thank you."

He felt a smile grow on his face to match hers, and they stood there for a moment sharing the moment.

"Staci?" Casey appeared in the doorway. "Oh...I'm sorry, I didn't know you were here, Johann."

The moment was broken, and Johann gathered himself. "It is of no moment, Fräulein Casey. I must leave now anyway." He turned to Staci. "Tomorrow evening, then? About this time?"

Staci looked at her watch. "A bit later, perhaps. How about six o'clock?"

Johann bowed his head slightly in acknowledgment. "I will arrive then."

Staci held a hand out, and Johann took it in his not to shake, but simply to hold and press for a moment. Then he nodded to Casey and took his leave.

"What was that all about?" Casey asked.

Staci continued to gaze at where Johann had left her field of view. "I have a date tomorrow night."

"A date? What do you mean, a date?"

"I have been invited to an evening of conversation with Johann Bach at Walcha's Coffee House tomorrow evening at six o'clock."

"Pfffpt!" Casey uttered, followed immediately by, "Ow!" as Staci slapped her arm much harder with her new book than she had slapped Johann.

"Seriously?" Casey said, rubbing her arm.

"Seriously."

"I dunno about that guy," Casey muttered. "Conversation. Geez."

"Actually, I think I'm going to like it," Staci said.

Casey had the wisdom to not say anything more as she was still rubbing her arm.

Staci folded her book back to her breast and left the room, the small soft smile returning to her lips as she trod the stairs toward their room.


The next morning, after their usual stop at Frau Zenzi's, the three Bach brothers were walking down the Kristinstrasse chewing on their morning bread.

"Oh," Heinrich said suddenly. "I forgot to tell you last night. Master Luder wants to see you today."

"What about?" Johann said after he swallowed the bite he'd been chewing.

"Don't know. He didn't say."

"Well, did he look mad, or sad, or serious, or happy?"

Heinrich had a mouthful of bread at that point, and it took a bit for him to get it chewed up. "More serious than anything," he finally said. "Not mad, anyway."

"Something about the pipes?"

Heinrich shook his head. "No, when he was working on the pipes was the only time that he didn't look serious."

"Hmm," Johann muttered. "Wonder what he has on his mind. Tell him I will come by before noon."

Heinrich nodded.

And it was a moment before noon when Johann stepped through the doorway into Master Luder's forge. The master was bent over something with his journeyman. The young man looked up, saw Johann standing by the doorway, and murmured something to his master. Master Luder looked up in turn, saw Johann and held up a finger. Johann nodded that he would wait a moment, and the master returned to his conversation with the journeyman. Before long, they both straightened; the master clapped his journeyman on the shoulder, then turned and stepped toward Johann.

"Master Bach."

"Master Luder."

The whitesmith was not smiling. Johann grew concerned at the seriousness of his expression. Master Luder slapped his heavy gloves on a shelf, took his jacket from the nearby peg, and said, "Come. We need to talk, and it needs beer."

Johann smiled to himself as he followed the whitesmith out of the forge. For Master Luder, most conversations seemed to need beer.

It wasn't long before they were seated at a table in a corner of the Green Horse and Master Luder was taking a long pull at his large flagon of beer.

"Working in the heat of the forge gives you a thirst," Luder said.

"I can see that," Johann replied after taking a smaller sip of his own flagon. "Heinrich said you wanted to see me? I hope he hasn't been any trouble."

"No," Luder said, waving a hand in the air. "He is actually proving to be of at least a little bit of help, which is useful, since my apprentice broke his leg a few weeks ago and isn't up to doing the work yet." The whitesmith looked down to where his large blunt-fingered hands were wrapped around his flagon on the table, then looked back up again to face Johann squarely. "We have a problem . . . or rather, you have a problem that will affect the work I am doing for you."

Johann leaned back on his stool. "And that is?"

"You remember how I told you that it looked like they were going to bring in Ludwig Compenius to rebuild the organ in the Dom, the one that Pappenheim gutted?"

Johann nodded.

"Well, they struck a deal, and it will happen. Compenius is in Magdeburg this week, examining the Dom and assessing the damage. He will probably go back to Erfurt while he thinks things over and determines what his plans will be, but it will not be long before he returns to begin the work." Luder picked his flagon up and took another pull of its contents.

Johann considered that. "So we are going to be competing for the same resources, most likely?"

Luder gave a firm nod. "I expect the prices for the partially refined tin ore from the Ore Mountains to rise. We have not been buying enough yet to cause the demand to rise greatly and prices to jump. But if he starts buying as well, especially in large quantities, that could change. But it is not just the tin ore. He is also trying to line up the local smiths to work on his project."

"He approached you already?"

"He did indeed, yesterday afternoon. I told him I

had already given my word to work for you. I don't think he was happy about it, but he was polite in his leave-taking."

"But the other smiths that you were going to use to make the sheets—they are not bound to us, are they?"

Luder shook his head. "I had talked to them, but without binding them with money or a project, they can accept his work. And if he demands they work for him exclusively, as long as he pays for that, they will do so."

Johann frowned and crossed his arms, considering what he had been told. This could be a real complication to his plans. After a moment, he unfolded his arms and leaned forward. "First, buy up as much ore as you can get—if that nudges the prices up a little, we will just have to live with that. I would rather make sure we have the ore than worry about paying a bit more for it. If you do not have room to store it all, I think we can find a place in the opera house grounds to store it. We may have to throw up a shed or get some barrels or something, but we will find a way.

"Second, try to get one of the others to commit to my project. If it takes money, as long as what they want is not totally outside of reason, pay it or promise it, and I will have it covered by the opera house project."

"You can do that?" Luder's eyebrows rose.

"I think I can," Johann said. "I need to talk to Frau Haygood soon, though."

Luder shrugged. "I will do my best. How well I succeed will depend a lot on how quickly Master Compenius is moving, and how much silver he is willing to lay out right now."

"Understood," Johann said. "Do your best, though. And let me know immediately if anything else changes."

"That I can do." Luder picked up his flagon and finished off his beer, setting the empty flagon down with a definite thump. "And now, I must get back to the forge. Regardless of what else happens, I still have a lot of work to do."

The whitesmith strode off, whistling tunelessly enough that Johann was wincing until he was out of earshot. Johann remained at the table staring at a half-full flagon of beer, thoughts awhirl. He really didn't need this complication right now. He had hoped that the rebuilding of the Dom organ would be delayed by some kind of bureaucratic issue or some kind of disagreement among the pastors. After all, that kind of thing happened with fairly great regularity. But of course, something like that would never happen when he would derive some benefit from it.

"God," Johann muttered with a quick upward look, "it would be nice if You would at least slow them down a little bit."

There was no answer—not that Johann was expecting one.

He finished off his flagon of beer and headed out the door himself.

Driven by a sudden urge, Johann walked to the cathedral, which lay in the very southern end of Old Magdeburg facing Hans Richter Plaza and just inside the southern walls of the Altstadt, the old city. He could have hired a cab to take him, but the early afternoon was nice with a cloudless sky and a very light breeze, and there was enough traffic that a cab wouldn't have saved him a lot of time. Besides, it gave him some time to think.

One of the western doors into the nave of the cathedral was open when he approached, so he walked on in. It was his first time in the cathedral, the Dom as everyone referred to it, although the formal name was *Dom zu Magdeburg St. Mauritius und Katharina*. Once inside, he had to stop and gaze around.

The Dom was the largest cathedral in the eastern Germanies. From where Johann stood, he could see down the length of the building over three hundred fifty feet to the presbytery at the eastern end of the building. Looking up, he could see the vaulted ceilings which rose over one hundred feet above the floor. He drank in the sight. It was an impressive building, despite the damage that he could see in various locations where some of Tilly's soldiers had made off with some type of valuable.

As Johann stood and absorbed the experience of the cathedral, he gradually became aware of others talking.

"... Gustav appointed *Fürst* Ludwig von Anhalt-Cöthen to be the administrator of the archbishopric's properties. The Swede now claims to own the *Erzstift* of Magdeburg, and of course we are in no position to gainsay him." The speaker's voice was nasal and penetrating, even at low volume.

"Does the *Fürst* not provide for Magdeburg's needs, then?" The second speaker's voice was a bit rough.

"He does," the first speaker replied, "but he keeps the purse strings tight and only allows one project at a time. The churches of St. Nikolai and St. Katherina were destroyed totally, and the church of St. Sebastian was badly damaged in the fire set by Tilly's vandals. The *Fürst* has placed a higher priority on getting at least the major repairs done to St. Sebastian before it collapses."

"One perhaps cannot blame him for that."

"In other circumstances, I would agree," the first speaker said stiffly. "But to put that ahead of restoring the cathedral was a mistake, I believe."

"Regardless, those repairs must be mostly done if he is advancing the funds for the organ restoration."

At that, Johann turned and faced toward where two men were standing together staring up at where the organ had previously stood in the western end of the cathedral. It was obvious where it had been, as there was this hideous gap in the wall where the pipe ranks should have stood. There was no screen, no grill, no facade of false pipes, only a huge opening in the plasterwork that had been laid over the stone. Johann could dimly see what appeared to be some wooden pipes back in the darkness of the recess of the pipe chamber, but he couldn't see clearly. It did look like many of those were leaning or had even been knocked off their fittings.

A sudden flare of rage shot through Johann. Now he understood the Magdeburgers' hatred for Tilly, and even more for Pappenheim, who had been left to command the garrison of the city after Tilly's troops had sacked it. It was Pappenheim who had ordered the sale of the metal from the cathedral, which had resulted in the gutting of the organ. Johann now understood that hatred at a very visceral level.

One of the men was dressed in rather fine black clothing and was holding a large Bible in one hand. Obviously that was the minister.

The other was a stocky man dressed in sober clothing. He was facing slightly toward Johann, which allowed Johann to view his profile and recognize him as Ludwig

Compenius, the youngest of the current generation of the organ-building Compenius family. He was also the only one of the family that Johann had met; having had the opportunity to speak with Ludwig when he had left his position in Naumburg and relocated to Erfurt, at least temporarily.

Compenius must have caught sight of Johann out of the corner of his eye, for he turned his head to face him, which in turn caused the pastor to turn and see who the organ builder was looking at.

"Herr . . . Bach, is it not?" Compenius' brow wrinkled a bit as he strove for recall.

"Yes, Master Compenius. Johann Bach."

"We had a pleasant conversation over a bottle of wine a couple of years ago, I believe."

"I am flattered that you remember me," Johann said. And that was the truth. Master Compenius, for all that he was only a bit older than Johann himself, had an enviable reputation and was renowned throughout Germany as being "one of *those* Compeniuses." The fact that he recalled a conversation from almost two years ago provided a bit of encouragement and ego lift to Johann.

The organ builder chuckled. "Of course, if Heinz and I had realized that you were going to become a competitor, we might not have been so freely spoken in our conversation."

"Competitor?" the pastor interjected, looking confused.

"Ah, Herr Bach, have you met Magister Matthias Decennius, the *Caplan im Dom*?" Compenius said.

The pastor was the head pastor for the cathedral, then, which in essence made him the head pastor in

Magdeburg. This was not an unimportant man in the city, Johann thought. Even Mayor Gericke walked with some care around Decennius, word of whose uncertain temper had reached even Johann.

"I am honored to meet you, Magister Decennius," Johann said with a slight bow.

"And this is Herr Johann Bach," Compenius concluded, "a member of the widespread clan of Bach musicians, a performer of some skill, I believe, and now a designer and builder of organs."

Decennius said nothing, simply nodded. Johann decided that was acceptable to him. He had no desire to get crosswise with the pastor.

"At that time I had no idea myself that I would," Johann confessed. "Become a competitor, I mean. But after I came to Magdeburg, and the Arts League sent out the proposal for the new organ, I thought there was nothing to be lost by making an offer. I was very surprised to find out that I had been awarded the contract."

Compenius chuckled again. "Herr Bach, you should never be *surprised* to find you've won a contract. You should be *gratified*."

"I shall endeavor to do so, Master Compenius."

The two men shared a grin before Compenius looked back up at the ravaged pipe loft. "The vandals were thorough, I will give them that," the master builder said.

"Unfortunately," Johann agreed.

"Well, the scale of the theft actually does help in one respect," Compenius said. "Since they took everything down to bare wood, it will actually make it easier to design and build new ranks." He shrugged.

"It will still be an awful lot of work, and rerunning the air feed pipes will be almost as large a challenge."

"They took those as well?" Johann said, astounded.

Compenius nodded. "At least part of them, the parts that were easiest to reach."

"I begin to understand why Pappenheim's name drives people in Magdeburg to blasphemy."

"Indeed."

Decennius had frowned at the mention of blasphemy, but forbore speaking at the moment.

Compenius continued to stare up at the organ loft, fingering the beard on his chin as he did so. "Herr Bach," he said as he moved his head slowly from side to side, obviously scanning the entire structure, "I have heard tell that there is music from the future in Grantville by a Bach."

"Correct," Johann said. "Actually, there is music by three or four Bachs, but most of it is by one Bach, the greatest of them, one Johann Sebastian Bach."

"The greatest of Bachs?" Compenius said.

Johann shrugged. "He would have been born fifty years from now, in 1685, and would have lived a very full life, dying in 1750. And he wrote...would have written...some of the greatest music ever composed."

"Greater than our best?" Decennius said. "Greater than Praetorius or Schütz? I doubt that."

"Magister, a few weeks ago I told someone that if music was a religion, Johann Sebastian Bach would have been its chief apostle, Peter and Paul together." The *caplan* seemed to swell up. "I have reconsidered the notion. I now think the man would be the chief saint...or better yet, the archangel."

"He was that good?" Compenius said.

"Master Compenius, he was so good I weep at the beauty of his music, and I despair of ever approaching his skill and craft and art."

"You hear that, Magister Decennius?" Compenius said. "That is the judgment of a Bach, and one who is not the least among them."

"His judgment verges on blasphemy," the *caplan* muttered, turning his head away.

"Of course it does," Compenius said after a snort. "He is a musician. That goes without saying."

There was a moment of silence, then Compenius looked up at the pipe loft again and heaved his shoulders in a big sigh. "Well, there is no help for it but that I must climb up there and examine what little remains. I cannot assess the damage from down here. Good day to you, Herr Bach. We will meet again, I am certain." The organ builder nodded at Johann, then looked to the pastor. "Magister Decennius, the door to the loft, if you would."

Johann watched as the two men crossed to a door barely visible in the side wall of the end of the nave and disappeared through it. He shook his head, looked around the nave once more and up toward the vaulted ceiling, then made his way out the doors he had entered through.

Well, he thought, that hadn't gone as poorly as it could have. But it was clear that while Master Compenius respected the Bach family as a whole, he had no reason to be accommodating to them or to Johann in particular. And Johann doubted that he would be. So his instructions to Master Luder would stand. But he needed to have a conversation with Lady Beth Haygood now. And at this hour of the day—he glanced at the position of the sun—she was probably at the school, so that was where he headed.

It was nearing six o'clock when Johann made his way to the Duchess Elisabeth Sofie Secondary School for Girls for the second time that day. He felt his neck and face where the barber had trimmed his beard and shaved his neck and cheeks to give a somewhat cleaner appearance. It all felt good. He checked his fingers. No traces of blood, so he hadn't been cut or scraped by the razor, which was a good thing.

Johann's earlier conversation with Frau Lady Beth had gone well. She understood the implications of having yet another project in town competing for scarce resources, especially one that competed for the same things needed for the organ. At the end of their conversation, Johann had the approval for what he had already told Master Luder to do.

That conversation had been relatively short, and he had left the school without seeing anyone else. The remainder of the afternoon had been divided between checking on the carpentry work at the construction site and working on learning the pieces he would need for the inaugural performance on the organ. He hadn't determined the final selection of works yet, much less the sequence in which they would be performed, but he already knew the piece that would open the concert, and the piece that would conclude it: the Toccata and Fugue in D Minor to open, and the Passacaglia and Fugue in C Minor to close. Those would not be quick pieces to learn, so he had begun the process already, working with the small clavier in his room. That would at least let him get the manual parts ingrained in his hands and arms.

Learning the pedal parts would require having access to an organ. Obviously the Dom was out of the question, but maybe one of the daughter churches still standing had a small organ that he could at least begin the learning on.

In any event, other than the pedals, Johann about had the Prelude portion of the D minor ready, and the Fugue was beginning to take shape. The Passacaglia, on the other hand, was still very rough. Johann chuckled. It could be worse. He could have decided on doing the entire *Art of Fugue*—all eighteen fugues and canons of it.

Even though he had thoroughly brushed off his jacket and pants before he left the rooming house, Johann still brushed off the front of his jacket with his hands, and took his hat off to make sure that it was clean before he opened the door and stepped into the school.

A young girl stuck her head out of the door of Lady Beth's office for a moment, only to retract it immediately. This was followed by both Lady Beth and Staci stepping out of the office a moment later, both pulling on coats. For a moment, Johann was afraid that Lady Beth planned to come along, but then his common sense asserted itself when he remembered that she did not live in the school building as Staci and some of the other teachers did. She and her husband had a small town home of their own in the northern quarters of the Neustadt in the Old City not far from the school.

"Good night, Herr Bach," Lady Beth said as she brushed by him. "Y'all have fun."

Johann looked at Staci, who gave him her gamine grin. "No, she wasn't being a chaperone," she said. "We were just talking about an idea I had for teaching a unit on economics. I think we're going to bring the Monopoly game into the class."

"Shall we leave, then?" Johann said, gesturing toward the door.

Staci walked by him, and he followed her out the door and closed it behind them. "Is there someone still in the office?" he inquired as he moved up alongside her.

"Oh, yes," Staci replied. "Whenever anyone is out, there will be one of the staff or the night porter waiting to let them back in and make sure they get home."

"You do not let the girls out at night, do you?"

"Only for a reason approved by Frau Haygood, and only when accompanied by an adult member of the immediate family or by one of the teachers." She sidestepped something in the roadway. "We do take the safety of the students pretty seriously."

"That is good," Johann said. "So, Monopoly?"

They made the turn onto the Gustavstrasse, which ran along the inside of the city wall in the Neustadt, and progressed south.

"It's an up-timer board game," Staci said. "There were several sets in Grantville when the Ring of Fire happened. It used to be very popular. I played it a lot with the family when I was a kid. Anyway, it can be used to teach some basic principles about owning property and handling money."

"In school?" Johann hoped he didn't sound too incredulous.

"Yes, even in a girls' school," Staci replied. "These girls are mostly from well-off families—major merchants, guildsmen, patricians, even some of the Niederadel. They will need to be grounded in the practical aspects of their families' businesses or properties, if for no other reason than to keep someone from taking advantage of them."

Johann nodded. He could see that. He remembered some of the things his mother had had to take control of after his father had died.

"So how is the organ building going?"

"Progressing well," Johann said. He gave her the high points of where they were; the cabinetry progressing, the main wind-chest completed. The air pipes between the main wind-chest and the main console completed, and some of the pipes actually being produced.

By the time he completed that recital, they were stepping through the southwest gate of the Neustadt onto the ring road that circled the outside of Old Magdeburg. The road angled to the southwest for several yards, then intersected a major east/west street in front of Magdeburg Memorial Hospital, the up-time designed hospital that was being expanded. The two of them turned onto that street and headed west.

"And how is Frau Marla?" Johann asked. "I mean, as far as being..."

"Pregnant?" Staci responded. "She says she feels as big as a house, but that's ridiculous, because she's not that far along, and she hasn't gained that much weight yet. Plus she's been lucky enough that she hasn't had much trouble with morning sickness. So all things considered, she's a typical first-time mom, somewhat nervous, but seems to be doing okay. She's still putting in her regular schedule as a teacher, anyway."

"That's good," Johann said.

Walcha's Coffee House was two blocks west of the hospital, he remembered. Johann had never been there before, though, so he was a bit relieved when he saw the shop's sign, and he sped up his walking a bit. He held the door open for Staci and followed her inside.

The shop was larger on the inside than he'd expected; larger than the Green Horse tavern, even, which made it very sizable for a public space in Magdeburg. Standing inside the door, he saw several people whom he knew. He'd heard that the coffee house had become a favorite place for musicians and artists and people of letters, as well as those who liked to be seen with such. That did indeed seem to be the case, as he could see a fairly well-known writer and his friends at one table, and two or three of Frau Marla's musician friends at another with some more players.

There was a small table with a couple of chairs to one side, against the wall. Staci looked up at him and pointed to it. "There?"

"Why not?"

They made their way there, beating out another couple. Staci was able to slip through the crowd and the other seated patrons and plop down into one of the chairs just moments before the others could, which collected her a couple of serious frowns. Johann noted that that didn't seem to bother her, as her gamine's grin was back in place on her face when he took the other seat.

"You enjoyed that, I think," Johann remarked with a bit of a smile of his own.

"Too right, I did," Staci said.

At that moment one of the servers arrived at their table. "First time here?" the young woman asked.

"Yes," Johann said.

"Well, then, tonight we have coffee, Dutch chocolate, and American chocolate. The American chocolate is a dollar more, because of the extra sugar in it. If you want something to nibble on as well, we have a few of the oatmeal cookies left, and I could probably find some bread and butter. We normally have more, but a bunch of the army officers came in earlier, and ate most everything we had prepared for the evening."

"Coffee for me," Johann said, "and two of the cookies." He looked to Staci.

"The Dutch chocolate," she ordered, "and I was hoping for a piece of the chocolate candy I've heard so much about."

"Up-timer, are you?" the server asked. That should have been a rhetorical question, Johann thought with a suppressed snort. Staci's unmistakably accented Ami-deutsch should have left no doubt in the server's mind. At Staci's nod, she smiled and said, "I'll see what I can do."

As the server bustled off, Johann looked at Staci. Just by chance, she was wearing the same hoop earrings she had worn to Marla's performance at the Green Horse Tavern, and his attention was caught by how they swung in the light, and how the little bauble on the loop slid freely forward and back as she tilted her head.

He caught her looking at him with a quizzical expression. "Sorry," he said, "it's just . . . your earrings are so different."

"Are they?" Staci looked around for a moment, then returned to gaze at him. "I guess maybe they are. Now that I think about it, I've never seen anyone else wearing hoops of any kind, much less these big two-inch jobbies."

"Pendants, yes, but not these . . . hoops. And especially with the little . . . whatever it is hanging from them."

Staci grinned, reached up with both hands and a moment later had one of the earrings removed and was holding it before him so he could see it closer.

Johann for a moment wished it was still in her ear but that he was that close to it.

"See?" she said. "It's a little teddy bear charm. I've had these for years. I wear them for luck."

Johann looked at the charm. He knew what up-timer teddy bears were. He had seen originals of them in Grantville, and had seen inspired imitations of them in various places in Magdeburg. The charm did resemble them, in a unique fashion. "Very interesting," he said. "Very...cute?" He wasn't sure that was the right word, but he tried it anyway.

From the look of pleasure on her face, he gathered that he had gotten that much right, anyway. Staci busied herself in restoring the earring to its proper location. After that, she looked to Johann, and said, "So, I've met your brothers. You look to be older than they are."

Johann nodded. "Eight years and some months older than Christoph, a couple of years more than that to Heinrich."

"Eight years is a big gap."

Johann shrugged. "One stillborn child, one winter birth that caught the croup and did not survive until spring."

"I'm sorry."

Johann could see the sadness on Staci's face. Another mark of the up-timers, he thought, to be so affected by what was a part of life. He shrugged again. "It happens. It is a part of life for so many."

"And your parents?"

"Papa died of the plague in 1626, and Mama died last year. She had pneumonia two winters ago, and never really was the same after that."

Staci shook her head. "So you and your brothers are all that are left of your family?"

"Of the immediate family, yes."

They both paused as the server appeared with a tray. Johann sat back a bit to allow the server to slide a cup of steaming coffee in front of him, and a saucer with two cookies. A moment later saw a cup with dark chocolate sitting in front of Staci, and another saucer with a slab of very dark something sitting on it beside her cup. Johann took up his cup and blew on the steaming liquid before taking a cautious sip of the hot liquid, watching as Staci took up her candy and nibbled on the corner, then closed her eyes as a most blissful expression crossed her face.

Staci opened her eyes. "Oh, that is heavenly. I have really missed chocolate."

"You must have," Johann said with a chuckle, "to order both the liquid and the solid form of it."

Staci laughed. "No, I didn't order the coffee because this late in the day if I drink coffee I'll be up all night."

"Coffee does that?"

"Oh, yeah." Staci took a sip of her chocolate, and laughed again. "Actually, this might as well. Pretty strong chocolate . . . a lot of difference between this and what we knew up-time."

She took another nibble of the candy. "So you said you and your brothers are all that is left of your immediate family. Some extended family, then?"

Johann swallowed the bite of cookie he had been chewing. "Oh, yes. We have cousins all over Thuringia."

"That's good. It's nice to know you're not alone."

Johann nodded. He'd never thought of it like that.

He'd always taken it for granted. "And what of you? What is your family like?"

"Mother and Father still living, and they moved to Magdeburg not too long ago. Older brother Joel serving with a State of Thuringia-Franconia National Guard force in Fulda. Younger sister Melanie works for Kelly Construction as an electrician on the opera house project, and youngest brother Josef works as an apprentice for Kelly on the same project."

"A family affair, then? I have met Fräulein Melanie, as it chances."

"Well, almost," Staci said with a smile. "And my roommate Casey Stevenson is getting ready to marry Carl Schockley, who's the project manager for the opera house project for Kelly."

"I have met Herr Schockley," Johann said with a bit of a grimace. "I think he does not like me very much."

"Oh, I think he likes you fine," Staci replied. She took a sip of her chocolate, then continued, "He's just afraid that you're going to do something that will mess up the construction schedule."

"And Fräulein Casey is a dancer?"

"Yep. One of Mom's senior dancers, along with yours truly."

It took Johann a moment to realize Staci meant herself.

"So, we don't have anything quite like the dancing you do. What does it involve? Why do you like it?"

Johann picked up his coffee cup and settled back.

"Did you see the dance program in the July fourth program last year?" Staci asked. At Johann's nod, she continued with, "Well . . ."

And from there the conversation wandered as conversations often do. Staci spent time telling Johann about dance. Her eyes sparkled, and her voice was very animated. From the gestures of her hands, Johann could see her passion about it, and from her descriptions he began to see that there was art to it—it wasn't just bodies moving, it wasn't just like people dancing at fairs and parties—there was a skill and a craft to the dance as Staci described it that was above and beyond what his people thought of as dance.

Johann didn't know how much time passed as he watched Staci. His cookies were long gone when he checked on them, and he was working on his second cup of coffee. He didn't care if he was awake all night. Any excuse to sit and watch the young woman across the table from him was fine with him. Cheeks flushed, broad smile, leaning forward to emphasize something she was saying—it was like he was falling into her eyes, drowning in her joy and zeal and passion.

Staci finally paused long enough to finish her cup of chocolate. She looked around as she did so, and her eyes opened wide. Johann glanced over his shoulder, only to discover that they were the only ones left in the coffee shop.

Staci put her cup back on the table with a *thump*, and pulled back her shirt cuff to reveal a watch. "Oh, no," she said. "It's after nine o'clock. I need to get back to the school...I have an early day tomorrow."

The server appeared at their table as Staci pushed her chair back. She had a small piece of paper which she used to wrap up the piece of candy which Staci had barely nibbled on, which she then presented to Staci with a flourish.

"Thank you," Staci said with a smile. "It is really very good, and I would have eaten more of it, if someone," she lowered her eyebrows at Johann, "hadn't got me started talking."

"Think nothing of it, ma'am," the server replied, with the up-time courtesy. "We are used to that happening."

"And I'm sorry we kept you so late," Staci said with an apologetic expression on her face and a touch of her hand to the server's arm.

"We stay open until the last customers leave," the server said. "Georg says he wants people to feel comfortable here." She gave a wicked grin. "Of course, there's been a time or two where he was out sweeping the floor with a broom, too."

"I bet!" Staci said with a laugh. "Anyway, thank you, and I'll tell everyone that your chocolate to drink is wonderful and your chocolate candy is to die for!"

"That's all we can ask," the server responded with another smile. Johann had seen the price board when they entered the room, so when the server looked his way with one eyebrow raised, he passed her twenty dollars, folded so the bill numbers were visible. That was enough to cover their drinks and food and provide a gratuity in the up-time style. The server's smile broadened just a bit, the bills disappeared with a deft move of her hand, and she gave a small bow to Johann.

"And you are?" Johann asked.

"Anna," the server replied. "Georg is my husband."

"We will be back," Johann said.

"Thank you, and good evening to you," Anna said as they turned to go.

"Good evening," Staci said over her shoulder.

Johann preceded Staci out the door to make sure the way was clear, then held the door for her to step out of the coffee house. They started walking down the street together. The evening was quiet. There were a few other pedestrians in view on the street, but none were close by. The sky was clear; no clouds hid the stars, and the golden light of the crescent moon shone down on them from low in the eastern sky.

After a few steps, Johann was almost startled when he felt Staci's hand slip onto his arm. He instinctively crooked his elbow, and felt her grasp settle and rest in that crook. They walked that way for a couple of minutes or so. He felt his chest tighten a bit.

"You shouldn't have let me ramble on and on like that," Staci said. "I did all the talking."

Johann chuckled. "Fräulein Casey warned me some time back that you were all dancer."

"She's a fine one to talk," Staci said with a snort. "She's just as fixated on it as I am. But you still shouldn't have let me monopolize the evening."

"I enjoyed it," Johann said.

After a moment, "So did I," softly. A few more steps. "But next time, I get to ask the questions and you have to talk."

"That is fair," Johann conceded.

The rest of the walk to the townhouse the school was in passed by in silence. Johann could feel a grin on his face. He kept trying to suppress it, trying to be serious, but the happy feeling in his chest kept rising and making the corners of his mouth curl up. He kept his arm tight, feeling the presence of Staci's hand pressed between his arm and his side.

All too soon they had arrived in front of the building. Johann walked Staci up the steps to the portico, where she removed her hand from his arm. It was a slow withdrawal, and Johann was certain that was an expression of a certain reluctance. That resonated with him, for he was certainly reluctant to have it release its contact with him.

They turned to face each other.

"I had a very good time tonight, Johann." Staci had a smile on her face, and her eyes were bright in the lamplight. "Thank you for inviting me."

"Thank you for accepting my invitation," he replied. He started to raise a hand, but stopped with the movement barely begun.

Staci's mouth quirked. "It does feel a bit odd, doesn't it? You and me, I mean?" She held her hands out, and after a moment, Johann took them in his.

Her hands were of a scale to match the rest of her; slender, slight, and very fine-boned. He felt as if he were holding the wings of a dove in his hard long-fingered hands, and he forced himself to hold them gently, for all that he wanted to grasp them firmly.

"I . . ." Johann couldn't settle on the right words. Strange, that, given how self-assured he usually was.

Staci freed one hand and lifted it to place the tip of her index finger against his lips. "Shh. We don't need to say anything tonight. No great protestations or promises. Whatever we might have between us, let's let it grow on its own, without forcing it."

Johann reached up and recaptured the hand in his own. He looked at her for a long moment, head tilted slightly. "All right. We have some time, I think."

"All the time we need," Staci said with a warm smile, the moonlight glinting from her eyes. She squeezed his hands, then dropped them. "Thank you for tonight." Johann opened the door for Staci; she laid a hand atop his for a moment, then slipped inside.

The door closed. Johann stared at it for a moment, then turned and moved down the steps to the street, where he turned and looked back up at the town-house, where lights glimmered in a few of the upper windows. He was sure that one of them was Staci's, and he felt nearer to her for a moment.

Sticking his hands in his jacket pockets, Johann turned and started back toward his rooming house. "God," he muttered, "what kind of Escher are You making out of my life? When I am with her, I feel suspended between Heaven and Earth; yet when she is not near, I feel as if life is upside down. What are You doing to me?"

The door clicked shut behind her. Staci sighed, and leaned back against it, arms wrapped around herself.

Wow. What an evening. It had been so mundane, on one level; just the two of them—well, mostly her—talking. Yet she had never talked like that before to anyone—not her mother, not Casey, not any of the male dancers she had known in the up-time. Certainly not any of the typical high school jocks who'd thought she was cute or that they'd make a good couple.

Johann didn't know dancing, not like she did. She could tell that he hadn't really grasped a lot of what she had talked about. But everything had registered with him. She could almost see things sink in with him, or into him. Nothing had bounced. No one had ever listened to her like that. No one. Not even her mother. And because of that, she had opened her heart, and poured out all her dreams and fantasies, and even her fears. And he had taken them in. All of them.

Wow.

Staci didn't know how long she stood there, but she became aware of a face staring at her from the door to the office. It was Casey, of course, waiting on her. When she saw that Staci had finally noticed her, she stepped out into the hallway.

"You okay?"

Staci nodded. "Yeah. I think I am."

"So how did it go? Give." When Staci didn't reply right away, Casey frowned and walked toward her. "Did he try something? Was he rude? Was he a jerk?"

"No, no," Staci said after a hiccough of a laugh. "He was fine all night long. He was better than fine."

There was a moment of long silence after that, before Casey said, "So what's up, then? Is this it? Are you done with him? Are you going to see him again? Come on, tell me what's going on in that pointed little head of yours."

"I . . ." Staci took a deep breath. "I think . . ."

Another gap of silence. Casey advanced and placed her hands on her friend's shoulders to give her a little shake. "Earth to Staci. Tune back in, girl."

"I think he's the one." And with that a big smile broke out on Staci's face. "I think he's the one."

Casey grinned at her, and shook her head. "You've got it bad, don't you, girlfriend?"

*June 2, 1635*

"Johann!"

Johann jerked back to awareness and looked to Christoph and Heinrich seated across the table from him. It had been a long day, and he had a lot on his mind. "What?"

Christoph snorted. "I have asked you three times now what the holdup is in testing the wind connections through the console cabinet. I know we do not have the pipe ranks ready to go, but we could at least test it as far as the console, make sure that the keys and pedals will release air."

"Compenius has hired away the whitesmith who did the first pipes for the run from the main wind-chest to the smaller reservoirs behind the console," Johann replied. "They do not connect correctly and need to be modified, but he now says he cannot promise he can work on them any time soon because of his commitment to Compenius."

"In other words, he did shoddy work and now he is hiding behind Compenius to keep from having to fix it for nothing."

"That is Master Luder's guess," Heinrich contributed. "And he is not half happy about it, either."

"The good news, such as it is, is that we at least should not have to buy any more material for them," Johann said. "The lead alloy in the pipes should be sufficient—they just need to be reformed."

"Why do all the up-timers flinch whenever we talk about using lead pipes?" Christoph asked.

"That stupid game...Claw, or Flue, or something like that," Johann said with a frown.

"Clue. And one of the murder weapons in the game is a lead pipe," Heinrich said with a grin. "I like it."

"You would," Johann muttered. "But it is also because the up-time medical knowledge has proven that using lead to store water or food will taint the water and food and make people very ill, if not kill them. But we will just be pushing air through them, so there is no risk there. I already checked."

Heinrich snapped his fingers, and Johann and Christoph both looked at him. "That is why the tavern keeper at the Chain was arrested the other day. He had been adding sugar of lead to his rotgut wine, saying that it helped the flavor of the wine. From what I heard, it couldn't have hurt it. Anyway, apparently some people died, and somebody got the new *Polizei* department involved. Word is that the up-timers are involved with that, and one of them figured out what happened pretty quick."

Johann's eyes narrowed. "You stay away from that place. People who spend much time there usually get found floating facedown in The Big Ditch. I do not want to have to explain to Mama's ghost how you came to die such a stupid death."

Christoph choked from where he was taking a pull at his mug and sprayed beer across the table, fortunately missing Johann. They all laughed a bit, then flagged the server down to bring a bit of rag or towel to wipe the table down.

"You were saying?" Johann said with a look to Heinrich. "About the pipe fixes?"

"Master Luder says he thinks one of them can be bent slightly to bring it into alignment." Heinrich shook his head. "I'm not sure, myself, but he says it can be done. The other long pipe needs to be shorter, so he thinks that will be a cut and solder job."

Johann frowned. "As long as the pipes let the air pass, don't leak, don't burst, and fit the design, I don't really care what he does to fix them. When does he think he can have them done?"

"That will depend on when he can come take the measurements. For the bending, a day or so after that. For the cut and solder, a day or so longer. It's not just the work, you understand. It's also the testing for leaks. He said he'll use water for that, so that will be an additional preparation he'll have to make. If the worst happens and he has to start over, he can just melt them down and recreate them, but that would take a lot longer."

Johann shrugged. "As long as he gets it done. Tell him we really need them done and installed by..." he thought for a moment, then looked to Christoph, "...next Wednesday?"

Christoph's mouth quirked. He obviously wanted it sooner than that, but he acceded to Johann's directive with a nod.

"You are spending more time with us and not with Staci," Christoph commented. "Are you not progressing in your courting?"

Johann sighed. "Yes and no. I think we are continuing to draw closer together, but her dance company will be putting on a show next month as part of the July the Fourth Arts Festival, and she has been very busy with rehearsals. She does some of the dancing and much of the teaching and...what was the word... coaching, that was it. And the rehearsals mostly happen after school." He shrugged. "So I only get to see her during those moments when she is not involved either with the school or the dancing...which are not very many, at the moment."

Christoph shook his head. "Sounds like Mama muttering about when Papa had to go off to do some special music."

"This dancing, it is that special?" Heinrich asked.

Johann thought back to the show that was done in the previous year's arts festival. "I guess it is. Certainly Frau Simpson and her backers in the Magdeburg Arts League think it is. They put up some pretty serious money last year to produce a show, and it was not one of the big shows that Staci talks about, but a number of smaller scenes that they strung together."

"So you saw that?" Heinrich again.

Johann nodded. "I got to Magdeburg right before the festival, and just wandered around seeing things. The dance was done on an outdoor stage, so when I chanced upon it, I watched bits of it. It was . . . interesting."

"You say that like Mama said Frau Schmidt's bread was 'interesting,'" Heinrich said with a grin.

"I did not know what I was watching," Johann said, "and that was not why I had come to Magdeburg. I kept hearing that there was going to be some kind of big concert, so I kept looking for that."

"And you found it?" Christoph asked.

"Indeed," Johann responded. "I was able to act like I was a member of someone else's party and slip into the palace. I stood in the back of the room and listened. It was . . . powerful."

"I bet," Heinrich said, with a bit of longing. "I want to hear the orchestra perform."

"In a few weeks," Johann said. "Patience."

"So when will you see Staci again?" Christoph said.

"Her friend Casey is getting married in a few days, and she asked me to attend, partly so we could spend some time together. If nothing else, then."

Johann drained his mug and stood. "I am going

back to the room and getting some sleep. I have a long day scheduled tomorrow."


*June 7, 1635*


Johann stood with a glass of wine in his hand. He should have taken the beer instead, but Staci had wanted wine so he had done the same. He looked down at her where she stood beside him. Her wineglass wasn't any emptier than his was.

"The wine..." Johann muttered out of the side of his mouth.

"Just drink it," Staci responded. "It was the best Carl and Casey could get."

That, Johann could understand. Good wine was rare in the Germanies right now, although some of the winemaking areas were starting to produce again. That was hope for a few years from now, but at the moment good wines had to come from outside the region.

"So are Casey and Carl going on the...honey... month?"

"Honeymoon," Staci said with a smile. "Honeymoon. And yes, they're going to take a few days off and take the train back to Grantville and stay at the Higgins Hotel. They'll catch up with family and friends, have some time by themselves, and then come back to Magdeburg."

"Can you afford for them to be gone from the dance rehearsals that long?"

Staci quirked her mouth. "If you ask Mom, the answer is no, but she's the biggest worrier on the planet. They both know their parts cold. What we're mostly doing now is drilling the corps, the dancers that are the equivalent of a chorus. Those are younger girls, many of whom have not danced a big dance before, and most of the rest have only done the summer show last year or the Christmas show, so they don't have a lot of experience."

"So this year, it is this . . . Schwein Lake?"

Staci's eyes got really big for a moment, then she busted out laughing. "Swine Lake! No, no, no . . ." and she laughed some more. "It's *Swan* Lake! Tell me that you didn't just make that up."

Johann shrugged. "Okay, I did not just make that up. Really, I did not. But I could not remember exactly the name, so I guessed."

"Oh, but that's so funny. And that is something that cropped up as a joke before. P.D.Q. Bach may have done something with that . . . or was it the Muppets . . ."

"P.D.Q. Bach?" That caught Johann's attention. "Who is that? Or was that? Or whatever?"

Now Staci's eye widened again, and this time her jaw dropped.

"You haven't heard about P.D.Q. Bach yet? Oh, oh, oh . . . come on, we have to find Marla."

With that, she grabbed Johann by the arm and dragged him around the room until they finally ran down Marla and Franz, who were standing talking to Lady Beth and Jere Haygood. Johann noted with some small jealousy that Franz had taken a stein of beer. He thought about setting the wineglass down somewhere to lose it and going after his own beer, but wasn't sure he could manage that discreetly.

He did eye Marla, and noted that she did seem to have put on some weight, so the pregnancy was showing a bit. He hoped things were going well for her and Franz.

"Hi, Lady Beth, Mr. Haygood," Staci said. "Marla! Johann hasn't heard about P.D.Q. Bach! How could you not have told him about him?"

Wide grins appeared on everyone's faces. Johann was now rather confused.

"Oh, you poor deprived soul!" Lady Beth exclaimed. She turned toward Marla. "Marla, how could you?"

Marla stood there, hand pressed to her mouth as if in horror, but Johann could see the corners of her lips curling up and the crinkles in the corners of her eyes as she struggled to suppress a laugh. A struggle that she lost after a couple of moments when Johann looked at her and raised his eyebrows. That in turn triggered laughter in the others, especially Franz Sylwester, so it was several more moments before the conversation could continue.

"You mean Marcus never told you about him?" Marla finally responded.

"No," Johann said. "I think I would have remembered if he had."

"Oh, you'd have remembered it," Marla said after another chuckle. "Trust me on this, you would have remembered."

There were firm head nods and sounds of agreement from the others in the group.

"I'm sorry," Marla said. "I should have done this a long time ago, but the thought never occurred to me for some reason. I guess you were never around when he came up before. Tell you what . . . you come over to the house tomorrow night, and I'll introduce you to the man properly. Staci, you come, too."

Johann looked at Staci, and seeing her grin of anticipation, all he could do was nod in agreement.

"Wait . . . wait . . ." Johann gasped from where he was sitting on the floor in front of the sofa in Franz and Marla's parlor. "Please . . . no more. I am in pain."

He had been laughing for most of the last couple of hours as Marla had played selection after selection from the P.D.Q. Bach albums. Toward the end, he had slid off the front of the couch as *The Art of the Ground Round, S. 1.19/lb.* had played, wrapping his arms around his ribs and howling. "My Bonnie Lass She Smelleth" from *The Triumph of Thusnelda* was the pièce de résistance that did him in, forcing him to stuff the corner of a pillow in his mouth to muffle his laughter.

"Oh . . . oh . . ." Johann said as his breathing began to slow down. "That man is a genius."

"Most up-time musicians thought so as well," Marla said with a big grin on her face. "I only have a few of his albums, but Marcus has them all back in Grantville—or everything that had been done before the Ring of Fire, anyway—and he promised me he was going to leave them to me in his will. One of the things I really regret about the Ring falling is we have missed any new albums that might have been produced." She took the CD out of her boom box and put it back in its case. "I haven't been able to get Marcus to put any of this stuff on the priority publication list for the Grantville Music Trust yet."

"Oh, that must happen," Johann said. "I can tell I did not understand a lot of the humor because I do not understand enough about specific up-time music pieces or up-time English idiom yet, but still, from what I did understand, it was so funny. This has got to be published. And that supposed biography of P.D.Q. Bach has got to be published again. Musicians all over Europe will take this up. Patrons will never understand this, but musicians will petition to have Herr Peter Schickele in his persona of P.D.Q. Bach made a saint, even if he never lived or never lives in our time.

"Perhaps we can work together," Johann ended.

"That might work," Marla exclaimed. "You take one arm and I'll take the other, and we'll both twist."

Johann held his hands up together and twisted them in opposite directions, exchanging a grin with Marla.

Staci slid off the front of the sofa where she'd been sitting to settle alongside Johann. Before he really realized what he was doing, he'd placed his arm around her shoulders. She nestled in beside him. That caused his eyes to widen a bit and his breath to quicken for a moment.

Johann didn't move for the rest of the evening until it was time to leave.

## July 1, 1635

"The wind-chest tests are complete," Christoph said. "The new fan works fine after Fräulein Matowski had the fan blades reworked and the seals around the fan channel reinforced."

*Fräulein Matowski? Staci?* Johann thought. Then a light dawned. "Oh, you mean Fräulein Melanie."

"Uh-huh. It is a bit confusing, having two of them around."

"Right," Johann said. "I assume the carpenters have

resumed work on the cabinet case for the keyboards and for the pipe chambers."

"Yes," Christoph said. "But Old Georg says they are going to need to know the measurements for the keyboard and pedal assemblies soon."

Johann made a note. "Right. That friend of Franz Sylwester's, Friederich Braun, has come up from Grantville to work those for us. He had roughed them in in the Bledsoe and Riebeck workshops, and then accompanied them to Magdeburg. He got here a couple of days ago, and has been waiting for the opportunity to start putting them in the case. I will have him come in tomorrow so he can get with you and Georg and Georg."

He turned to Heinrich. "Pipe production?"

"As of today," the youngest Bach said, "one hundred and forty-seven pipes completed, thirty-six more ready for tuning, and nineteen roughed in."

"And Master Luder is still working the lowest-register pipes?"

Heinrich nodded. "He understands that getting them done first will speed things up later as he moves to the midrange and treble pipes. He will be able to get more pipes out of a single sheet of tin, and he's gotten very good at bending the tin and sealing the edges. To the point where he is about to let the other whitesmith, Müller, out of their agreement. He says that he spends so much time going over Müller's work and either fixing it or arguing with him about it that he can pretty much do the work himself as fast or faster. He also muttered something about it was obvious why Compenius hadn't hired Müller for his work."

"Any word on how the Compenius project is going?" Johann asked.

"I have not heard anything," Christoph replied.

"Someone told Master Luder that they have finished clearing out and rebuilding the pipe loft, and the whitesmiths have started making pipes, but nothing more than that."

"We still have not had that much conflict with him," Johann mused. "I am glad about that, but also nervous." He thought about it for a few moments longer, then shrugged. "Nothing says we have to get in each other's way. We will see."

He placed his pencil in its loop in his notebook and closed it. "You two are on your own tonight. There will be a small performance at the Duchess Elisabeth Sofie Secondary School for Girls tonight, involving Frau Marla and a few of her friends in something for the Arts League and the school. I suspect they are trying to raise money and using Frau Marla's cachet to do it."

"And we poor humble Bachs are not on the invitation list," Christoph said with a mock frown. "Imagine that."

"So how are you getting in?" Heinrich asked his oldest brother.

"Staci is part of the performance group and asked me to come along."

"It is always who you know," Christoph said with a smirk.

Johann looked at the two of them. "So stay out of trouble, all right?"

His brothers looked at each other, grinned, and looked back at him. He shook his head.

There was light applause as Marla led her group of performers into the great room of the townhouse. Of course, as great rooms go, it wasn't huge, but there were easily twenty Adel and patricians seated in a crescent around a piano, leaving some space.

There were more people than that in the room, of course. There was one steward at a table with several bottles of wine and other comestibles, and there was a table laden with food in what the up-timers called "buffet style," with servants to serve the food and even deliver full plates as needed.

Marla and her friends were obviously experienced at this kind of affair, Johann noted. They gathered around the piano, Marla standing at the fore. She had her hands clasped before her.

"Good evening," Marla began. "Thank you for coming tonight. We will be presenting a short program of up-timer music of the sorts that were called 'popular' prior to the Ring of Fire. We hope that you will find it enjoyable. For some of these songs, this will be the first time we have done them in Magdeburg."

And with that, she settled on the seat at the piano, placed her hands on the keys, and the music began.

Johann didn't recall a lot about the evening after it was done, other than the sheer mastery of the music as the musicians moved from song to song. A few of them stuck with him: Staci singing "Norwegian Wood," Marla singing "Big Yellow Taxi," Isaac and Rudolf doing a duet on "Mommas Don't Let Your Babies Grow Up to Be Cowboys," and others.

In the middle of the evening, Marla stood up and moved around before the piano, where she was joined by Staci, Isaac, and Rudolf.

"And as a real change of pace, just so you'll know that there were some really weird guys out there, here's a bit of musical humor." She looked directly at Johann where he stood in the back of the room and gave a quick grin. For a moment he was apprehensive, uncertain as to what was going to happen. Marla hummed a pitch, gathered the eyes of the other three, and gave a nod.

They broke into a rendition of "My Bonnie Lass She Smelleth." Johann had to bite the knuckle of his forefinger to keep from bursting out in wild laughter as they progressed through the verses detailing both the beauties and the shortcomings of the lass. When they hit the line about her sounding like a crow, he nearly drew blood trying to suppress his guffaws. As it was, at least one or two moans escaped him, which drew some sidelong looks from some of the servants.

The song was finished in a few minutes, and he sagged in relief. Marla returned to the piano keyboard, and the next couple of songs passed in a blur while he regained his composure. He straightened up and paid attention, though, when Marla said, "This is the next to the last song of the evening. It's a superb song, with a rich reputation in the up-time. 'Hotel California,' two three four."

What followed was a tour de force of syncopated rhythmic piano work, impassioned violin playing, especially in the long extended coda, and Marla's surgically tuned voice bending tones and placing lyrics as if they were gemstones in a matrix. Despite himself, Johann was caught up in it, hunching forward and rocking back and forth as the currents of the song ebbed and flowed. When the coda died away, he was almost limp.

Marla stood again. "For the final piece, we are going to do something a bit different, perhaps more than you expected. Since one of the program events coming up in the next few days will be the ballet *Swan Lake*, we thought we would present one of the dancers doing something for you tonight. It won't be ballet, and it will be rather different. Please give us a moment to prepare." She looked toward the side door and nodded. A veritable procession responded to her nod.

First came a couple of male servants carrying a rolled-up carpet, which they took to the far side of the piano, set it down, and unrolled it. It extended far enough that Johann gained an insight as to why there weren't more chairs in the room.

Those two men were followed by four very brawny men who were lugging in what appeared to be . . . a slab of metal? It was perhaps four feet wide by six or eight feet long, and from the way they were straining with it had to be very heavy, which meant it was thicker than he had at first assumed it would be. They carried it very carefully over to the carpet, lowered one edge down with great care to rest on the carpet just inside the front edge of the carpet itself, then lowered the back edge of the metal plate to rest on the carpet. There was a final soft *thump* as it settled into place.

The men exited, and Staci reentered the room. Johann hadn't even noticed she'd left. Her steps were very loud—much louder than normal—and she was followed by a musician Johann hadn't seen before, carrying a viola da gamba. Two of the others stepped forward, holding flutes, to cluster behind Marla while Staci moved to stand behind the metal plate.

"This is a style of dancing you've not seen before," Marla said. "It's called tap dancing, for reasons that will be very evident in just a few moments. The song is 'Take Five,' and I give you premier dancer Anastasia Matowski."

Marla sat down and without further ado began playing a very unsettling rhythm, very syncopated; a pattern that repeated over and over. As she did so, Johann's attention was drawn to Staci reaching to the left side of her waist, unfastening something, and swirling her skirt off to reveal her legs clothed in black hose that progressed to where they disappeared under an extremely brief garment which clad the bottom of her torso. It was as if her legs were nude, but painted black. He could hardly grasp what he was seeing.

By now the viola da gamba player had joined in, and was providing a ground of plucked notes over which Marla was now elaborating a bit. Johann finally pinned down what was unsettling him about the music: the meter was not two, or three, or four—it was five! No one wrote in five, but this song had been.

That conundrum solved, his mind immediately fixated on the other thing that was unsettling him—Staci—just as the flutes joined the performance, which was apparently Staci's cue to move.

Her petite figure erupted into an outpouring of rhythmic clicking from the shoes she was wearing on the metal plate. The sound was almost overpowering. In the back of his mind, Johann was astonished to hear that she was tapping her feet in very complex patterns that still fit into and flowed with the five meter, adding to the complexity of the music and making a true multisensory experience, one that he had never even considered was possible.

That astonishment lasted but a moment, though, for in the next moment Johann saw every man in his field of view tense up. The seated guests all twitched, heads turned toward Staci, and to a man they leaned forward at least a little bit. He glanced quickly at the servants who stood to one side of him by the tables, and saw the same tension in them, the same slight shift in posture. And there was no evading what they were all focused on, to a man.

Fräulein Staci Matowski dancing—but such dance—legs flashing, moving, kicking, swinging out from side to side, from front to back—legs so nearly nude that one could see the cords of muscle in them as she moved. There was no question what the others were fixated on.

For all that the back of Johann's mind was growing increasingly uncomfortable with what he saw, the front of it was so wrapped up in visual presentation of the dance, in the movement of Staci's body—in the sensuality of it—that his mind was overloaded. He felt as if his skull should be bulging, like a wineskin that had been overfilled.

The song finally came to an end. Johann knew that it couldn't have lasted more than a few minutes, but it had felt to him as if it had lasted forever, with Staci up before the audience capering around and displaying herself. When Marla stood, the audience applauded, some louder than others. Johann, head spinning, slipped out the door of the great room.

Johann didn't know what to think. He didn't know how to feel. He wasn't numb, but he felt as if he couldn't move, respond, act. After a long moment, he wandered down the hall toward the front door to the school, wavering as he did so, bumping into first one wall and then the other until he finally walked through the doorway and down the steps to the street.

Outside, in the night air, the coolness seemed to help slow down the currents of his mind, reduce the churning of his thought. Johann stared straight up to see the spangling of stars on the black velvet of the sky. No moon was visible yet. But as his thoughts slowed down and returned to some sort of order under the starlight, something darker began to form, to grow in him.

"Johann! There you are!"

Staci's voice sounded behind him as the door to the school opened, and the musicians all exited in a throng. Staci skipped down the steps ahead of them and almost bounced over to Johann and placed a hand on his arm. "Did you see me dance? What did you think?"

Johann shook her hand off and took a step back. Her smile disappeared into shock as her mouth dropped open. Before she could say anything, the darkness found its outlet.

"How could you?" Johann demanded in a hard tone that nonetheless shook. "How could you put yourself on display like that? You were practically naked, dancing like Salome in front of all those people, those men." He heard his voice become vicious, and at just that moment he didn't really care. "I thought you were an artist. I thought you danced for joy, for beauty, not for tawdry lascivious lust. You . . . you little hypocrite."

Johann was surprised to find that his hands were fisted, clenched at his sides, as his breath poured in and out of him in torrents. At least the pressure inside was gone. But then he saw Staci's face. Tears flowed in slow procession down her cheeks, her eyes looked bruised in the lamplight from the lamps by the door, and her cheeks looked sunken. She looked like a starveling, someone famine-struck, and it dawned on him that he had just taken from her the nourishment of her soul.

The tableau was still. Johann, Staci, and the musicians behind her all stood motionless for a long moment. Then Staci sighed.

"I'm . . . sorry you feel that way," she said in a very quiet, almost dead tone. "You need to find your girlfriend somewhere else, I guess. Don't bother calling." She turned, took two steps, then turned back. "Oh, and I wouldn't shave my legs for you if you were the last man on Earth."

She turned again, head high, and walked down the street. The musicians all flowed around Johann, avoiding contact with him, although Marla's fulminating glance should have left him as a pile of charred bones in the street.

Johann stood in the dark, alone, empty.

# Toccata

"Pipe production?"

Johann Bach was having another meeting at the Green Horse tavern, this time with his brothers. He looked at his younger brother Heinrich, who was still his connection to the whitesmith Luder who was producing the pipes for their organ project.

"Four hundred ninety-seven produced, voiced, tuned, and passed," Heinrich said with a certain note of pride. "That is over three hundred more than we had a month ago. Plus there are another twenty-nine ready for tuning, and at least a dozen in various stages of production."

Johann stared at his brother. "How did Master Luder manage that?"

Heinrich grinned. "The owner of the rolling mill contacted him and offered him a really good rate for them to roll out the sheet tin. Even after paying for that it saved him so much time that he and his journeymen and the one associated smith who has remained committed to him have been able to focus

329

on cutting and forming the pipes. They've caught up with the schedule, and expect to be ahead of it by the end of the month."

"Excellent." Johann turned to his other brother, Christoph. "And how is the construction going?"

"The wind-chests are done, and all the pipes between them have been fitted and tested. The console appears to be ready," was the reply. "The cabinet part has been ready for weeks, and Herr Braun from Bledsoe and Riebeck says that the keyboards and the sliders and trackers are as ready as they will be until there are some pipes installed and he can do the final testing."

Johann turned back to Heinrich. "How many ranks of pipes has Master Luder completed?"

"At least four of the deeper-register ranks," was the reply. "The treble and mid-voice ranks, it may take a couple of weeks for the first of them to be ready. I'll tell him he needs to shift to producing full ranks rather than all pipes of a size. That may slow things down a bit."

"If it does," Johann responded, "it does. We have to be able to start testing the complete ranks and making any final tuning adjustments."

"Right," Heinrich said. He made a note on his clipboard. "He did thank me yet again for the steel rules and precision-measuring calipers."

Johann shrugged. "He needed them to do his best work; we could get them from Grantville wholesale. Helps him, helps us."

He closed his folder. "Stay on top of things," Johann said as he pushed back from the table. "I am going to go practice. You know where to find me if you need me."

With that, he left them without a backwards glance.

His brothers watched him leave, then turned to face each other. They shook their heads in unison.

"I do not know what is going on in his head," Christoph said as he took a drink out of his mug. "I mean, I thought he was all ready to wed Fräulein Staci. I thought they were about ready to sign the nuptial agreement."

"Ja," Heinrich said. "Me, too. I expected to be told to get my best suit cleaned and be ready to stand with him in church just any day now, and then..."

"Then all of a sudden it is all off," Christoph said. "And he turns into a golem."

"Ja," Heinrich said. "I mean, I have never seen him like this before. I have never seen him react to a disappointment like this. It is like his heart has been ripped out of him, or something."

Christoph shook his head. "The bad thing is, I was starting to get to know Fräulein Staci's sister Melanie, from working around her and working with her on getting the blower going for the main windchest. Then whatever happened, happened, and now she will barely even talk to me."

"He will not tell us what occurred between them," Heinrich said. "It must have been pretty bad, though. He was never like this before, even when that strumpet Madeline Hoffmeier rejected his suit and married the butcher's son instead."

"Well, as to that one, I think even Johann realized pretty soon thereafter that he had actually escaped hell on Earth by the skin on the back of his neck," Christoph replied. "Even Mama did not like her, and you know how she was about getting him married soon."

"True." Heinrich took a pull at the beer in his own

mug. "Have you been able to find out exactly what happened yet?"

"No." Christoph drained his mug and thumped it back on the table. "Fräulein Melanie will not talk to me, and I do not know anyone else to ask. Well, Frau Marla, maybe, but since she is one of Fräulein Staci's closest friends, that might not be a good idea."

Heinrich followed suit by finishing off the beer in his own mug. "Utter truth there, brother. From what I have seen, if there is one person in Magdeburg I do not want angry at me, that would be Marla Linder."

"From your mouth to God's ear, Heinz," Christoph laughed.

The two of them stood and left the tavern together, headed back to their respective work.

Marla Linder beckoned to Casey Stevenson in the hallway of the townhouse which currently housed the Duchess Elisabeth Sofie Secondary School for Girls. A flood of students had just washed by them as the classes completed for the day and the girls whose families lived in Magdeburg headed for home. The girls who were boarding at the school were now moving past them in the opposite direction, headed for the stairs to the upper levels.

"How's Staci doing?" Marla asked quietly.

Casey shook her head. "She won't talk about it, but I don't think she's doing so hot. It's kind of bad that this happened right after I got married and moved out. I think she does okay during the day, because the girls and the teaching keeps her busy and she doesn't think about it much. But at night, she's alone. I'd bet she spends a lot of nights crying."

Marla shook her head. "Not good."

"Yeah." Casey nodded in response. "She was so skeptical of Bach at first . . . she really tried hard to not fall for him."

"I remember," Marla said. "We talked about it when she felt like she was heading that direction."

"He was so serious, so constant, so attentive to her." Casey shook her head again. "She really thought Bach was going to be the man for her. After all the years of jocks and nerds hitting on her, she thought he was the one who could understand her."

Marla's expression turned to one that qualified as grim and bordered on sinister. "He's lucky I haven't turned Gunther Achterhof loose on him to massage his kneecaps with a six-pound hammer. Or even better, arrange for a double orchiectomy." A hint of an evil grin touched her face for a moment.

"Staci wouldn't like that," Casey said with a reluctant smile. "And although I certainly sympathize with your feelings, it wouldn't be quite fair."

"Fair?" Marla snorted. "What's fair got to do with it? The man basically abused Staci in front of all of us."

"Not abused," Casey said. "Not intentionally, anyway. Bach's from small towns, his background is in the church, and whatever dancing he'd seen in the past, it certainly wasn't anything like what Staci was doing that night. And you have to admit that her outfit didn't leave much to the imagination, at least from the waist on down. So it had to have been somewhat of a shock to him."

"Are you taking Bach's side?" Marla demanded.

"No!" Casey said. "But I can kind of see why it happened."

"Well . . ." Marla drawled reluctantly. "Okay." She reached out and slapped Casey on the upper arm.

"Hey! What was that for?"

"For making me see the other side. I hate it when people do that to me." She gave an exaggerated sigh. "Okay, so Bach may not be the most evil villain in the history of mankind...although as far as I'm concerned, the jury is still out on that...but he's not the issue. What are we going to do for Staci?"

"I think we need to schedule a girls' night out."

Marla smiled. "Right. Can you make it tomorrow night?"

Casey's brow furrowed as she thought. "I think so. Carl's really tied up with a major project developing, so he probably won't even notice I'm gone. Why?"

"It just so happens that Brendan Murphy is trying out his new stand-up comedy routine at the Green Horse tomorrow. You and I and Staci and Melanie can go sit in on that. That work?"

Casey was grinning. "Yeah, that works. We'll take her out, keep her talking and laughing, and maybe when she gets back to her room she'll have enough of a buzz from beer and wine or brandy that she'll just collapse and get a solid night's sleep. I think that would help her as much as anything."

"Okay," Marla said. "You get word to Melanie and see if she can come. After classes are over tomorrow."

"Yes," Casey agreed. "I'll double-check with Lady Beth to make sure none of us are on evening desk duty tomorrow as well."

"Good thought," Marla said. "We don't want to get tripped up by that, either."

"Tomorrow evening, then," Casey said.

"Yep."

❖     ❖     ❖

Johann opened the music and set it on the stand of the clavier, then sat before it and placed his hands on the keys. After a moment he began, fingers moving through the opening phrases of the "Little" Fugue in G minor by the never-to-be-seen-in-this-universe Johann Sebastian Bach, purported and now theoretical grandson of his younger brother Christoph, who at this point in history was unmarried and had no descendants of his body at all.

It was an occasional source of amusement to Johann that his namesake's music had survived and come back through the Ring of Fire. It was more often a source of awe, and of wondering at just what God had wrought. This piece, the so-called "Little" Fugue in G Minor, was one of his favorites of all the Bach works that had come back; not because it was grand and glorious, but because it almost felt like laughter to him. He could see in his mind's eye the young man, no older than Christoph was now, smiling and chuckling and chortling as he wrote the notes, as he tried the phrases, as he developed the motif, and that humor came through to him. He'd never understood why so many up-timer musicians thought that minor keys were "sad." Nothing could be further from the truth, he thought.

The opening phrases passed under Johann's fingers on the clavier keys, with his feet moving on the floor when the pedal line came in, which he hummed to give himself the sense of tone, since of course the clavier could not.

He'd wanted to practice at St. Ulrich's Church. The church and its small organ had managed to survive the 1631 Sack partially intact, which was more than could be said for much of the town.

The cathedral had taken some damage and much

vandalism. St. Katherine's, St. Nikolai's, and St. Johann's churches had all been so severely damaged in the great fire that they were basically destroyed. The efforts of the occupying troops to find anything of value had completed that destruction. St. Sebastian's Church was severely damaged, but repairs were progressing on it. St. Ulrich's, Heilig-Geist, and St. Peter's churches were damaged to some extent, but were usable and had received early repairs. Only little St. Jacob's Church, in the poorest district of the Altstadt, had escaped damage from the Sack, the resulting fire, and the subsequent vandalism, primarily because it was upwind from the source of the fire and was the poorest church and had little the occupying troops wanted.

St. Ulrich's, being located in one of the richest quarters of the city, had taken damage, but had also been supported by the wealthy families who had returned to the city after Gustavus Adolphus had liberated it from Tilly and Pappenheim's occupation troops. Consequently, it had been one of the earliest to be repaired, since its congregation, led by its returning pastor, Gilbert de Spaignart, was willing to put up the funds to have the repairs done.

But as with everywhere Johann had served, the needs of the church or of the congregation took precedence over his need to practice on the organ, and today it chanced that there was a wedding occurring. The wedding was occupying the nave during most of the block of time he had to practice, which meant that the organ, even though it wasn't in use for the wedding, was not available to him. So he was back at the Royal Academy of Music in one of the side rooms, practicing on a small clavier.

Johann could have found a piano, possibly. The academy now had at least four of them—maybe five, if he remembered rumor correctly, with some coming from Bledsoe and Riebeck but the latest from the studio of Girolamo Zenti—but for what he was doing, a piano didn't have the right touch. A clavier gave more like the effect of an organ, at least for the purpose of practicing. So he settled for the first clavier he could find.

He finished his first run-through. It wasn't as smooth as it should have been, so he went back to several places in the music and played those sections again, usually where there were transitions or where there was a new entry of the theme. After several repeats, the passages felt smoother, and his hands seemed to have the patterns down.

Again, from the beginning this time. The lilt and the bounce of the fugue just lifted his spirits, almost as if dancing.

And at that point Johann's fingers stumbled and he totally lost the flow and feel of the fugue. His hands froze. He hunched forward, almost as if he had been struck. And his mind flashed back to the events that had occurred over a month ago.

Johann saw again Staci strip away her long skirt and stand revealed in the close-fitting hose that had left her looking as if her legs were painted black, with no skirt covering her lower torso, simply more form-fitting clothing that would have been indecent as underthings to most of the women Johann had known in his life.

She stood there like that, before a room half-filled with men, and then proceeded to dance, energetically, feet flashing, tap sounds happening as her shoes contacted the metal plate she was standing on, kicking her legs up at moments.

It had shocked Johann. Shocked him deeply, truth to tell, and he hadn't responded well. He had heard that the up-timer women were more liberal in their dress than most down-timers, but he thought he had seen the limits of that with the short skirts that were sometimes worn in Magdeburg. The occasional tight-fitting top had its down-time equivalents, certainly enough. No, it was the short skirts and tight-fitting trousers that Johann had mostly found somewhat inappropriate. But even that he had accepted as somewhat in the norm of things.

But what Staci had worn that night...it had shocked him. There was no other word for it. And for someone like Johann, someone who was a thinker and a planner and who liked to have everything in life fitting into its proper place in the harmony of life, that shock had stripped away all his control, all his knowledge, all his assurance, and left his bare emotions exposed so raw—so almost-bleeding—that for the first time in a long time he had simply reacted without thought. He had spoken from his shock, his hurt, his confusion, his bewilderment; and because he did so, he struck out to cause hurt to match his own.

For perhaps the first time since that night, Johann admitted that to himself. That he had struck to hurt as a way to assuage the hurt he was feeling.

He remembered the expression on Staci's face when he savaged her—the stark desolation, the slow tears, the dark pain he saw in her eyes in the combined lamplight and moonlight. And today...today for the first time Johann admitted to himself that he had been wrong to do so...that he had, in fact, done evil.

Johann leaned forward, placing his elbows carelessly on the clavier keyboard and creating a jangle of sound. He ground the heels of his hands into his eyes. The pain that he felt as he did so was welcome, because for that bare moment it gave him something else to feel, something else to focus on, something that wasn't the result of a really bad choice on his part.

Johann ground his teeth so hard that he was surprised that some of them didn't just shatter or crack. That produced another ache, another physical feeling that he embraced. Yet as with the first pains, nothing could blot out the deeper ache, the deeper shame.

The need was there to make amends, if for no other reason than what Scripture required of him. Matthew chapter seven verses 2, 3 and 12 alone put him on notice of what God expected of him. But how? That was the operative question now. And that needed some thought. Much thought. Because the last thing in the world Johann wanted to do now was compound the evil he had already created. So he would move slowly, he thought. But he would move. He took his hands from his eyes and gave a definite nod.

To mark that decision, he set aside the music for the "Little" Fugue in G Minor, and set his mind on the first piece of Johann Sebastian's music that he had learned—the first piece he had heard—the Toccata and Fugue in D Minor. He placed his fingers on the keys, and after a moment, began.

And as always, once he was into it, he became swept up in the riverlike flood of the music, feet tromping on the floor as he hummed the pedal lines. It flowed, it danced—and this time the thought didn't break his performance, but buoyed it up, instead—it rushed in a spate, and for not the first time in playing the music of his almost-descendant, Johann experienced a moment of time out of time where he wondered at the Escherness of God at allowing Johann to know and play the music of a descendant who would never be, the Escherness of God at allowing that music to be available to Johann, the Escherness of God at allowing that beauty to not be lost with the Ring of Fire, but to be brought back.

"*Soli Deo Gloria*," Johann whispered as he played the final chords.

"All right, y'all," Brendan Murphy said as the laughs started to die down. "Here's one you haven't heard yet. You all know that the army uses a whole bunch of mules, right? In moving all that army stuff from one place to another, I mean, right?"

Nods from all around the Green Horse common room, and grins all over the place in anticipation of what his joke would be.

"So, there was this one army mule named Hermann, right? Well, Hermann died..."

Brendan waited, and sure enough he got an "Awww," from the table where his wife Catrina was sitting with Marla and Staci and Melanie and Casey. It was almost like homecoming week. He loved it when there were up-timers in the audience, because they always knew when to laugh.

"Yeah, Hermann died, and he'd been such a great mule for the army that they actually put up a memorial for him." That got snorts from some of the men around the room who obviously had experience with the down-time armies. "No, seriously, it was engraved and everything. Here's how it read:

"In memory of Hermann, who in his lifetime kicked..." Brendan started ticking the list off on his fingers, "one general, four colonels, two majors, ten captains, twelve lieutenants, forty-four sergeants, five hundred thirty-nine privates and corporals, and one bomb."

Brendan ended the joke with a straight face, and it took a moment for the punch line to sink in. When it did, there was a groan from the girls' table and a shout of laughter from almost everyone else in the room.

Almost everyone else in the room wasn't everyone, though, and Brendan took a swig of ale while the audience laughed at the joke, glowering over the rim of his mug at the old farmer sitting at the table right before him. The man had obviously brought a cart or wagon full of something to Magdeburg for the local markets, and had stopped in at the Green Horse for something to eat, or, more likely, something to drink. And he'd sat there like a frog on a log all through Brendan's new routine. Everyone else was laughing, but this guy could be a statue, for all Brendan could tell.

*All right then, time to pull out all the stops.*

"So," Brendan began again as the laughter started to die down, "General Mike Stearns was riding along at the front of the Third Division one day. He looks over to his left, and he sees a herd of pigs, with an old swineherd leaning on a staff watching them. Then he sees something remarkable; something so unusual he can't believe his eyes. He throws up his hand and brings the whole column to a halt. 'Colonel Higgins, do you see what I see?' he says to Jeff Higgins.

"'Well, General, if you see a pig with a wooden leg, then yes, I do.'

"'I thought so,' the general said. 'Come on, I've got to see what this is all about.'

"So the general and the colonel rode over to the swineherd. 'Good afternoon, old-timer,' General Stearns said. 'What's the story with the pig with the wooden leg?'

"'Oh, Herr General, sir, that's the finest pig in the world, the greatest, smartest, bravest pig that ever was or ever will be,' the swineherd replied.

"'Friend, I don't want to buy the pig,' General Stearns said back to him, 'I just want to know about the wooden leg.'

"'Well, Herr General,' the old man said, leaning on his staff, 'you see, that there pig really is special. One day some bandits came upon me and the herd out in the trees somewhere over there, and started to steal the pigs. They drew their knives, and came after me, too, and I was really afeared for my life. But that pig, that one there with the wooden leg, why he started to snorting and bellowing and pawing the ground and roaring and gnashing his teeth, and after he did all that, he rose up on his hind legs, and then he leapt forward and started biting and slashing at the bandits, until they all ran away bleeding and crying for their mothers. Then he trotted back and helped me up, and picked up my staff and handed it to me with his mouth.

"'Yep,' the old swineherd said, nodding at the pig with the wooden leg, 'he saved me and the rest of the herd from murder and slaughter.'

"'Old-timer,' General Stearns said, 'he sounds like a very fine pig indeed, a veritable Hercules among pigs. But why does he have a wooden leg?' The general was getting a little put out with the old man by this point.

"'Well, Herr General, sir,' the old swineherd said..."

Brendan paused for effect, watching the farmer, timing his punch line. *Now*, he thought.

"'...you don't eat a pig like that all at once.'"

*Gotcha*, Brendan thought with a grin as the farmer spewed ale from his nose and mouth and the room erupted in laughter as much because of the farmer's spew as for the joke itself.

"That's it for tonight," Brendan said, waving a hand over his head. "I'll be back next week. Tell your friends."

And with that he stepped down off of the little platform that was at one end of the Green Horse's common room. The tavern keeper had put that in about the third week after Marla and her friends had started performing there back in late 1633, and it had seen a lot of use since then.

Brendan walked over to where his wife was sitting with the other up-timers, pulled up a free chair and turned it around, then straddled it and sat down—carefully, because he was a large guy—and laid his arms across the top of the chair back. "Hi, y'all," he said. "Did you come down to see me shine, or was this just a serious drinking night?"

That got chuckles all around, because none of the women at that table did much drinking other than a mug of beer or a glass of wine at meals, and he knew it.

"Good job tonight, Brendan," Marla said. "You're getting pretty good at the stand-up stuff. I really liked those last two jokes."

"I'll take praise from you, Marla," Brendan said with a grin. "And yeah, it's kind of funny doing stand-up, and kind of odd as well. The down-timers have stuff kind of like stand-up, but it's usually combined with other stuff at the same time, like jugglers or tumblers or in between songs from a minstrel or singer. Just having someone standing up and telling jokes for an hour or so is unusual to them, and it's taken a while to get people used to it. But Ernst," he nodded at the owner of the Green Horse who was doing duty behind the bar tonight, "was good about giving me time to build a following. And now it's starting to take off."

"You still working for the transportation department?" Casey asked.

"Yeah, for a little while longer at least," Brendan said, "at least as long as the Army will keep me there. We're expecting," he nodded to where Catrina sat with a hand on a very pregnant belly, "so we need a little more reliable income than I'm likely to make just doing the stand-up."

"Must be something in the water," Marla said putting a hand on her abdomen where her own pregnancy bump was beginning to show.

"Or the wine," Brendan said with a grin.

Johann watched from where he had been leaning against the wall beside the door of the Green Horse. He'd been there for close to half an hour, watching Brendan's routine...and watching Staci as well. He hadn't planned on seeing Staci tonight. It's just that the tavern had become a common stop for him on the way home on those nights when he knew that Frau Marla and her friends were not performing there. He didn't have the courage to face her any more than he did Staci, so he had been avoiding the tavern on those nights. Just his luck they'd both be here tonight.

His first impulse when he saw them there, all of the up-timer women in a group, had been to leave. Almost Johann did, but he was drawn into the room despite himself. He stood there in the back, looking at the back of Staci's head, occasionally getting a glimpse of her full or partial profile when she turned to speak to someone else. A couple of times Johann saw the corner of Staci's lip curled up a bit, but even from the side her face appeared a bit drawn, and he could tell from the set of her shoulders that she was tired ... perhaps weary, even.

When Brendan brought his act to a close and stepped down off the stage, Johann took one last look at Staci, just as she started to look behind her. He sharply turned away and pushed his way out the door.

Outside, night was well fallen, and even for August the air was a bit cool. That fit Johann's frame of mind just fine, for in his heart he felt it was winter.

Staci turned back around with a quizzical expression on her face.

"What?" her sister Melanie asked.

"I thought I saw Johann in the back of the room," she replied.

Marla stiffened and jerked around to check. "I don't see him now," she said after a moment. "And he'd better not be anywhere I can lay eyes on him."

"You mean that Bach fellow?" Brendan asked. At the volley of nods from the women, he said, "Yeah, he was in the back. He stepped in the door, maybe a half hour or so ago, almost left, but hung around until just a few seconds ago." He caught a frown from all of them, and held up his hands. "He didn't act like a stalker, okay? He just stood back there listening to the jokes for a while, then left without talking to anyone or doing anything."

Staci drew her feet up on the front of her chair seat, wrapped her arms around her knees, and leaned her forehead against them. Marla and Casey looked at each other over her, and Casey shook her head.

## September 1635

Christoph pulled Heinrich to one side in the echoing space that would be the main performance auditorium of the opera house. Johann was down by the organ performance console talking to the two Georgs and to Friederich Braun. They looked to be set for a long discussion, but Christoph kept an eye on them anyway, not wanting Johann to get in the middle of what he was about to say.

"I got a little more out of Fräulein Melanie about what happened between Johann and Fräulein Staci."

Heinrich's eyes cut toward Johann as he leaned closer. "And?"

"Apparently our esteemed eldest brother was somewhat offended by both a dance costume Fräulein Staci wore and the manner in which she performed the dance. And when she asked him for his opinion, he pushed all his ire off on her and then had the rank foolishness to call her a hypocrite."

Heinrich's eyes pulled back to Christoph and grew larger. "He what?"

"You heard me."

"*Scheisse*," Heinrich muttered.

"Indeed," Christoph said.

"What was he thinking?"

"I am not at all certain that he was," Christoph replied. "He always was one who would...what is that up-timer phrase...go off the deep end if something really caught him unawares or off-guard."

"Hoo, yes," Heinrich said with a grin. "Remember that time when—"

"Shush," Christoph murmured. "He is coming this way." And so he was, but then one of the Georgs called him back. "So, what do we do about this?"

"What can we do?" Heinrich asked. "It is a problem of his own making, is it not? And even if it were not, I somehow doubt that our esteemed *eldest* brother would appreciate either of us intervening in the matter."

"I fear you are right, Heinz," Christoph said quietly. "He would view it as interference, and probably rightly so. And," he turned away from the view of the four men at the console, "I do not particularly want to be the person he gets angry with right now. He is bad enough to deal with as it is; let us not make the situation worse."

"Agreed," Heinrich said feverishly. "My lips are sealed, my teeth are locked, my voice still...about this, at any rate."

"I was about to declare a miracle," Christoph said with a sardonic grin, "until you qualified that last statement."

"Do not ask for too much, brother mine," Heinrich said with a matching expression. "Leopards and spots, you know."

"Indeed."

❖　　❖　　❖

"What did you say?" Johann looked up with a frown. His brother Heinrich was standing next to the spinet clavier with the soberest expression on his face.

"I said," Heinrich repeated with no trace of his usual sardonic attitude, by which Johann knew that the matter was serious indeed, "that they need you at the opera house construction site right now."

"What about?"

Heinrich took a deep breath. "Someone stole some of the organ pipes."

"*What?*" Johann spun around on the bench and sprang to his feet. Heinrich took a step back. "Are you sure about that?"

"I did not see it with my own eyes. That's just what Herr Carl and Christoph said."

"Come on."

Johann grabbed all his music and notes and stuffed them into his portfolio every which way, then stuffed that all under his arm, grabbed his hat, and headed out the door, almost running over two students in the hallway.

"Sorry, sorry," Heinrich said as he eased by the angry students. "He just got some bad news. Sorry." He looked back over his shoulder as he turned the corner in the hallway. The two girls were kind of cute, in a partly down-time partly up-time way that a lot of the younger women in Magdeburg were starting to develop. He certainly would not have minded getting to know them, but approaching them right after Johann had almost left boot marks on their backs was probably not a good idea. Heinrich shook his head. He hoped that Johann's bad luck and current bad behavior did not poison the well for him and Christoph. He really didn't want to have to move back to Erfurt or Wechmar to find a bride.

By the time that Heinrich got outside the music academy, Johann was already across the plaza and going up the steps to the opera house. Heinrich broke into a trot and went up the steps two at a time, catching up with his older brother just as he burst through the main doors into the auditorium.

"Christoph!" Johann bellowed, which caused Heinrich to wince. "Christoph!"

The middle Bach brother appeared from the side of the stage, waving his hands in a downward motion. Johann ceased yelling, but headed toward the stage. "What is this about some of the pipes being stolen?" he demanded as soon as he got within normal conversational range of the leading edge. He continued moving to the side where there were some temporary steps in place, and a moment later was on the stage facing Christoph. Heinrich joined them.

By now Carl Schockley had come out to stand by Christoph, and he responded. "Your pipes aren't the only things that were taken last night. Whoever it was managed to make off with some tools and some other supplies, as well, so there were probably several of them in on it. They didn't get into the ranks installed in the pipe lofts," the project manager said. "But they did manage to find the storage space where we were staging the next round of pipes to be installed, and they took several of them."

"*Scheisse*!" Johann cursed. "That bastard Compenius has to be behind this." He started to turn away, but Christoph grabbed him by the arm. "Let go of me!" Johann said, trying to pull his arm free.

"No, Johann," Christoph said. "Herr Schockley has already sent for the *Polizei*. They will handle this matter."

"And here they are now," Carl said, looking toward the back of the auditorium.

Johann and Heinrich turned to see a stocky man in close-fitting clothes coming down the aisle they had entered through. Carl pointed to where the temporary steps were fitted, and in a moment they were joined on stage.

The newcomer reached inside his jacket and pulled a small leather wallet out of an interior pocket. He flipped it open to show a bronze badge with a snarling lion's face. "Kaspar Peltzer, detective sergeant, Magdeburg *Polizei*," he announced in German pronounced with a strong Polish accent. "I understand there has been a theft." He folded the wallet closed and placed it back inside his jacket, then pulled a small notebook and pencil out. He pointed the pencil at Carl. "You are?"

"Carl Schockley, project manager for Kelly Construction. We're building this opera house."

The pencil made notes, then pointed at Christoph. "You are?"

"Christoph Bach. I am assisting my brother," he pointed at Johann, "in building the organ for the opera house."

More notes, then the pencil pointed at Johann. No words this time, just lifted eyebrows.

"Johann Bach, musician, contracted to build the organ for the opera house, and apparently part of what was stolen were pipes for the organ. Compenius had to have something to do with that!"

Peltzer didn't look up from the notes he was making.

"We will talk about that in a moment, Herr Bach. In the meantime, please be patient." This time he didn't point with the pencil, but he turned his head to look at Heinrich.

"Heinrich Bach, also his brother," he nodded at Johann, "also assisting in building the organ."

The pencil jotted a few more notes, then Peltzer looked up. "So, what has occurred?"

Carl Schockley began. "There are a number of items missing that we believe have probably been stolen."

"Items..." Peltzer said. "Such as?"

"Several hand tools, a keg of nails, and apparently some tin pipes that had been fabricated for the organ that is being built."

Peltzer made notes. "Show me the scene of the crime, please."

"This way," Carl said. He went toward the back corner of the stage area, where he opened a door and led the way down some stairs. Heinrich followed at the tail end of the procession. He could tell from the set of Johann's shoulders that he was probably angry. Which was not a surprise.

There were several lanterns lit in the lower level, so they could see where they were going pretty well. Heinrich continued to follow the group until they arrived at a couple of storage rooms near where the main wind-chest for the organ was located.

"Here," Carl said, pointing at two doors sagging in splintered door frames. "We discovered this this morning. This one," he pulled open one of the doors, "was a tool closet. As best we can tell we are missing a couple of hammers, a couple of heavy pry bars, and at least one shovel."

"Any identifying marks on the tools?" the investigator said.

Carl nodded, and picked up another shovel to display a mark on the handle. "These were all owned by Kelly Construction, and they were all marked like this."

Peltzer quickly drew that mark in his notebook. Carl returned the shovel to the tool closet, and turned to the other door. "This one," he said as he opened it, "we have been using to stage the organ pipes as they get completed, because the builders," he nodded to the Bach collective, "build and set and connect a rank of pipes at once, so they wait until all the pipes are available. According to Christoph, it appears that perhaps as many as a half dozen of the pipes that were here yesterday are now gone."

"Herr Schockley insisted that I wait to examine the remainder until after you arrived," Christoph said to the detective.

Heinrich craned over Johann's shoulder to take a look at the closet. It was certainly disarrayed and not in the neat order he had seen it in yesterday. He backed away from Johann after his brother growled something that wasn't intelligible.

Peltzer made a quick sketch of the appearance of the pipe closet in his book, then looked up. "How quickly can you determine what is missing?"

"Less than a quarter of an hour, I think," Christoph said, "especially if Heinrich helps."

The look that Heinrich caught from Johann over the older brother's shoulder made it very clear that he would be helping. He started forward, only to stop when Carl said, "Aren't you going to check for fingerprints, or run any kind of tests?"

The sergeant sighed. "Herr Schockley, we do not yet have any trained fingerprint *technicians*," he was careful in pronouncing the American word, "and it will be some time before we get some trained. Plus we do not have any of the supplies. So, no, I will not be checking for fingerprints. Besides, how many men do you have on your work crews? And how often do they come by these closets? How many men could have touched these doors since they were hung?"

Carl's mouth twisted, but he nodded. "Gotcha," he said. "Trying to figure out who all the prints belonged to would take forever."

"Exactly," Peltzer said. "So let us focus on what we can do and on the practical. Now, a pipe count, please?"

With that, Heinrich slipped by Johann and joined Christoph in the closet.

"We had the pipes for two ranks in here," Christoph said, pulling a notebook of his own out of his jacket. "And since Master Luder started stamping numbers into the pipes, I think we can identify what is missing pretty quickly. You start on the back side and read the numbers and arrange them as you go. I will verify against my list, and whatever you do not read will be the missing pipes."

"Right." Heinrich made his way to the back of the stacks with some care. "Ready?"

"Ready."

"Number six forty-nine."

"Yes."

"Number six fifty..."

✦      ✦      ✦

Sergeant Peltzer stood and watched the count occurring. Johann stood and fumed, waiting for the detective to talk to him.

"Bach . . ."

Johann looked around to see Carl beckoning to him from several feet away. Johann moved over to face the up-timer.

"Look, it's really none of my business," Carl began, "but I'm not too sure you realize just how badly you've stepped in it."

"Stepped in what?" Johann asked with a bit of confusion.

"How badly you've screwed up with this thing with Staci."

"Oh." Johann looked down for a moment, then back up to meet Carl's eyes. "Tell me, then."

"First of all, Staci is a dancer. That's her passion in life, just as much as music appears to be the passion in your life. She takes it very seriously, and she works at it very hard. And right now, she's the best we've got. Casey's close, and maybe I shouldn't say it because Casey is my wife, but Staci is just a bit better."

"Was she one of the best in the up-time?"

"Honestly, no. But then, I wasn't exactly a primo dancer myself. We were both very good for where we were at the time, but the people who had been dancing for twice our lifetimes were just better. But she could have made the prima ballerina ranks in time. She has the size and the build and the carriage and, perhaps most importantly, the passion. She was starting to attract attention in the state, and we were close enough to the capital, Washington, D.C., that it wasn't out of the realm of possibility that she could have joined one of the big dance companies there. But the Ring of Fire took that away."

That thought took Johann back a bit. He had always considered the Ring of Fire from the standpoint of what it had brought to his time. It had never really occurred to him to think about what the up-timers had lost in the event.

"Think about it," Carl continued. "If you had been chosen to be the *Kapellmeister* for Gustav Adolf, and then suddenly something happened, and not only were you not going to become that, you were now in a place where no one recognized your music as good or your art as worthy... how would you feel?"

That punched Johann in the gut. That got through to him in a way that none of his previous considerations had ever reached him.

"That," Johann said slowly, "that would be hard."

"Too right it would," Carl said. "And it was hard for all of us, but for a very few of us it was killer hard."

"Staci..." Johann said.

"Was devastated," Carl said. "About the only person out of our group that took it harder was Marla. Oh, some of the older folks in town had some real mental problems adjusting. In fact, there are a handful that can't be left alone even now, five years later. But the younger folks, those just out of high school or younger, for the most part adjusted... not well, but okay. Except that Staci and Marla both had futures planned out that would have taken them to the heights, and then they didn't. Staci had a really hard time dealing with that."

"And Frau Marla?"

"She had an even harder time, and some of us were afraid that she was going to become one of the mental cases, until she met Franz Sylwester. He drew her out, and she finally found her balance again. Staci never had a Franz, but even though it took her a while, she did come out of her funk."

Carl gave Johann a hard look.

"Staci had started thinking about how to bring dance about again. She was trying to work up ideas with her mom for staging some of the great dances. She is the prima ballerina, now—the best in the world—and if she wants a dancing career, she's going to have to create it from scratch, much like Marla is doing with music. And frankly, we were all a little surprised when she took up with you—not because you're a down-timer, but because you have no connection with the dance. But she saw something in you that caused her to connect with you, to open up with you, in a way that she never had with anyone before, either up-timer or down-timer. She was as happy as I have seen her in a long time. And you destroyed that."

Carl's voice had turned very cold, and Johann flinched. Carl closed in to loom over the shorter Johann, and he jabbed a very hard finger into Johann's breastbone. "Understand me, Bach," he said in a low tone that the others wouldn't overhear, "I'm working with you because I have to as the project manager. But it wouldn't bother me at all if you disappeared. It wouldn't bother me at all if you died. You really hurt Staci, and she's very important to me and my wife, and if I were a different kind of man I'd have already hauled you off and left you bleeding and broken somewhere, or maybe left you floating facedown in The Big Ditch." Jab. "I am actually somewhat surprised that someone else hasn't done that, like Brendan Murphy.

He was sweet on Staci at one time." Johann winced, not at the following jab, but at the thought of the oversized Murphy putting his outsized hands on him with mayhem in mind. "Yeah, you get it. And there are still people around who might do that. But that's really the least of your problems. That's just your body. Where you really stepped in it is professionally."

Johann looked up sharply.

"Ah, that got your attention, did it? Then wrap your head around this. Mary Simpson is a huge supporter of the arts in Magdeburg, right?"

Johann nodded at that.

"But do you know what her favorite art form is?"

That Johann had to shake his head at. "I assume music, but I do not know for certain."

"Her favorite art form is ballet," Carl said with an evil grin. "Dance. She's a ballet aficionado to the ultimate degree. She's been trying to get Bitty to stage major ballet productions for the last three years, and she finally got *Swan Lake* done this year. She's also responsible for the fundraising for this building and for the construction of it. She signs your checks. Now, you have made her prima ballerina very unhappy. This is going to make her unhappy. And let me tell you from painful personal experience, when Mary gets unhappy, she tends to share that unhappiness...in a very polite, polished, and oh-so-refined way, of course. You could lose the contract for the organ. You could also find yourself blackballed."

"Blackballed?" Johann asked. Carl spent a minute or so explaining the term. As it turned out, Johann was familiar with the concept. "Blackballed," he said at the end.

"Yep. If Mary really gets a mad on, you may have to move to France, Spain, or Russia to find work, and maybe not even then."

Johann sighed. "I confess that I do not handle surprise well. My brothers will delight in telling you that I do not, and will happily recount times when I have reacted badly. But even for me, this time I acted very badly. I was very surprised, and jumped to a conclusion without thinking everything through. I was surprised, then I was angry, and before I could wrestle the anger into submission, Staci approached me, and I . . . said some very bad things."

"Yeah, you did, from what I've heard." There was no give in Carl's voice, no sympathy. That was okay with Johann. He didn't deserve any.

"I want to apologize. I need to apologize. Even if Fräulein Staci will never accept me again, I need to do that, because I treated her very badly. But she told me, ah, 'not to call.' I've sent letters, they were sent back to me unopened with the word 'Rejected' written boldly across the address. I've tried to go to the school and meet her, and Frau Haygood herself met me at the door, told me I was unwelcome, and that if I did not leave immediately she would call for the police and have me arrested."

Carl whistled. "Wow. If Lady Beth is acting like that, she's seriously pissed. That's not good, man. She's Mary Simpson's right-hand woman, and has a lot of influence with Mary."

"I understand," Johann said, "but how can I apologize if I cannot make contact with Staci?" He spread his hands in helpless hopeless frustration.

Carl snorted. "Dunno, man. You put yourself in

this mess, you're going to have to get yourself out."
He started to turn toward the pipe closet, where it
looked like the count was about done, then froze.
After a moment, he looked back at Johann. "Actually,
there may be one thing you can do."

"Name it. Anything." Johann stared the up-timer
in the eyes.

"Talk to Mary Simpson. If you can convince her of
your sincerity, she can probably bring about a meeting."
Carl's mouth quirked, and he held both hands before
him and did a balance-weighing motion. "Of course,
if you can't convince her, having attracted her specific
attention may be the end of your career."

"I understand," Johann murmured as they turned
together to face the closet. "But do I have any choice?"

He closed up with the rest of them in time to hear
Christoph announce, "The good news is we appear to
only be missing four pipes: numbers six fifty-seven,
six fifty-nine, six sixty, and six sixty-two. A few of the
others have been dented from being knocked around,
but I am not certain that will affect the tuning. Even
if it does, Master Luder should be able to restore
them fairly easily.

"The bad news is . . ." Christoph turned to Johann,
". . . the missing pipes were some of the larger pipes.
If the thieves were looking for material to resell, that
was the most metal available."

"Probably," Johann said. He found that his temper
had cooled some as a result of his conversation with
the up-timer. This meant he could more easily see the
reality of the situation. "And unless the *Polizei* could
catch them quickly, they've probably been fed into cru-
cibles already and we won't be able to prove anything."

"You made reference to someone," Sergeant Peltzer said, looking up from his notebook, "someone you thought might be involved?"

And so Johann found himself explaining how there were two different organ projects in progress in Magdeburg, and how he had found himself competing with the Compenius family for both resources and workers. "So you think this Compenius, or someone who works for him, might have directed or instigated this robbery?" Peltzer observed.

Johann sighed. "Honestly? Despite what I said earlier, I do not really think that Herr Compenius would have ordered it or participated in it. That does not mean that someone else in the community or in his associates does not see a way to profit from something like this. Can I accuse anyone now? Not really. And as I said, unless you can catch someone with the pipes, it is all supposition. But I will say that if something like this happens again, either here or in connection with Master Luder and the work he does for us, then there will be reason to ask some very pointed questions of Herr Compenius."

Peltzer nodded. "I have the Kelly Construction mark that is on the tools; I have the numbers that were on the pipes. Is there a maker's mark on the pipes?"

"Yes," Heinrich said. He picked up one of the smaller pipes and showed the mark to the sergeant, who pretty carefully sketched that into his notebook as well. Johann looked at the sketches over the sergeant's shoulder—the man was decent at it. Much better than he himself was, Johann admitted.

Peltzer closed the notebook and put it back in his jacket packet. "We may be able to find the tools," he said. "The pipes..." he shrugged, "...that is more iffy. If they were stolen as a matter of opportunity, perhaps. But if they were stolen for the value of the metal, then most likely, as you said," he nodded toward Johann, "they have already been cut up and fed into a crucible to be turned into some other item or into anonymous ingots. We will look, but I cannot promise anything."

"Understood," Carl said. "Let me know if anything comes up or if you find anything."

The detective nodded and touched a finger to the band of his hat. "This way out?" he said nodding back down the hallway.

"Yes," Carl said. "Let me show you."

"No need," Peltzer said. "I can find my way. Good day to you, *meine Herren.*"

As the detective walked away, Carl looked at the Bachs. "Well, I suppose it could be worse," he said.

"Indeed," Johann said. His brothers nodded in support. "But it is bad enough. Replacing the stolen pipes is going to eat into both our schedule and our finances, as Master Luder will probably have to buy more ore."

"He told me recently that he has quite a few of the tin cakes that the local miners produce when they partially smelt the ore." Heinrich sounded confident about that, Johann noted. "So he can probably get the pipes replaced fairly quickly. What that does to the long-term schedule, though, he will have to address."

"Right." Johann nodded, then looked at Carl. "Meanwhile, can we find another storage location for these pipes that is perhaps a bit more secure just in case our visitors come back?"

"I was about to suggest the same thing," Carl said. "Leave me your brothers, and we'll get that taken care of. I've already sent a preliminary report to Lady Beth about the theft, but I suggest you go turn in a personal report on it. She'll appreciate it, and right now you need all the brownie points you can get in that court."

An idea that had slowly been growing in the back of Johann's mind for some little while that morning finally arrived. He paused with his mouth open just before his response to Carl came out for an awkward moment, then turned to his brothers. "How soon can we have enough ranks of pipes set up in the pipe lofts that we could give a...what do they call it...a demo of the organ?"

Both of his brothers stared at him in confusion. "We do not have anywhere near enough installed to provide the full voicing," Christoph said. "You know that."

"We barely have a thousand pipes yet," Heinrich said. "You know that. We are a long way from being done with this build."

"Yes, yes," Johann said with a wave of his hand and an unfamiliar smile on his face. "But do we have enough that we can have most of the tonal ranges covered, even though we do not have all the voices or stops or registers covered yet?"

The two younger Bachs looked at each other. Christoph shrugged. "You are the pipe man," he said as he pointed an index finger at Heinrich. "You get to answer that."

Heinrich's brow furrowed in thought, and he turned to stare at the pipes in the closet for a long moment, then his head swiveled and tilted up, brow still furrowed.

He was obviously considering the installations that had already occurred. Johann and Christoph waited. Surprisingly, so did Carl.

Heinrich finally brought his eyes back down to their level and his brow smoothed. "With what is here," he gestured toward the closet, "and what is already in place, I think we might."

"Will Master Luder need to replace the stolen pipes for that?" Johann asked.

"Probably," Heinrich said.

Johann nodded. "Well enough, then. Get these pipes to a more secure location, then you get to Master Luder's shop," he pointed to Heinrich. "Tell him what has happened, and warn him he might ought to take some precautions around both the pipes in progress and around the stock of his ore. Thieves might not take the cakes, but if he has refined ingots or bars, those could be targets for anyone looking to seize an opportunity."

"And you?" Christoph said.

"I," Johann said with a deep breath, "am going to go face Frau Lady Beth Haygood."

"Good luck with that," Carl muttered.

"Indeed."

"Herr Bach," Lady Beth Haygood said in a decidedly frosty tone of voice. That, combined with the fact that she was using his surname when she had previously called him "Herr Johann" or just "Johann" in conversation, was an indication of just how—one hesitated to use words like "upset" or "irritated" with Lady Beth—angry she still was with him.

"Frau Haygood," Johann replied formally, following

Lady Beth's lead. He gave a slight bow, and remained standing before her desk. She pointedly did not invite or direct him to sit in the visitor's chair.

"You said this was official business," Lady Beth said, voice still cold. "Get on with it."

"You had word from Herr Schockley earlier today I believe, about a theft at the opera house construction site." Johann paused long enough to allow Lady Beth to nod, then continued with, "After some investigation of our own and by Sergeant Peltzer of the Magdeburg *Polizei*, it was determined that the crime appears to be limited to breaking into two storage closets on the lower level of the building."

"Lower level?" Lady Beth said. "That almost makes it sound like someone knew what they were looking for."

Johann gave a small shrug. "Quite possibly, but there is no way to prove it at this point."

"What did they take?"

"From one of the closets they took several hand tools belonging to Kelly Construction."

"I can imagine how happy Carl was with that." A very small smile flitted across Lady Beth's face.

"Indeed."

"Since you are here, am I to assume that this has affected your project?"

Johann nodded. "From the other storage closet they took four of the larger pipes that had been formed and were waiting to be installed in ranks up in the pipe lofts."

"Four pipes?" Lady Beth was surprised by that.

Johann nodded again.

"Why on Earth would they do that? What good can they get out of four big pieces of tin pipe?" Now she sounded irritated. Her voice had warmed to reach that level, at least.

"Our guess, which Sergeant Peltzer agrees with, is that they stole the pipes to either melt down themselves and sell the resulting ingots or to sell to someone who will melt them down and either reuse or sell them."

"Ah." Lady Beth reached up and tapped her right index finger against her lips a few times. After that moment, she focused on Johann. "Is there a connection with the Dom organ project here?"

Johann nodded in respect of her quick perception. "It is possible, but unless the *Polizei* actually locate the pipes, it is impossible to prove. Once it is melted down, how can anyone tell where an ingot of metal came from?"

"Yeah," Lady Beth said. "We had some troubles like that in the up-time, where folks were stealing copper wiring and stuff from construction sites. Once they got off the sites, one piece of wire looks like another, and it was very hard to prove anything."

She sat up straight. "But only four pipes. That's not too bad, I guess. It could definitely have been worse. But what does that do to your project and your schedule?"

"Nothing good, obviously," Johann said. "They took four of the larger pipes in the closet. It will take some time and a noticeable amount of the ore stock to replace them. The time may not be too bad, as Master Luder is actually a bit ahead of schedule." Lady Beth looked surprised and pleased at the same time at that news. "But the impact on the ore stock cannot be worked around, I am afraid."

Lady Beth's mouth quirked. "I have a certain amount of cushion built into the project plan, so this won't kill it. And it doesn't sound like it would take a lot of money to buy the material to replace whatever gets used. But I really don't want to hear about any more of a delay than absolutely has to happen. We're already three weeks behind schedule. I don't want any more."

Johann nodded at that.

After a moment, Lady Beth said, "And tell Carl this is why he has insurance."

"I will do that," Johann said.

Johann started to turn, when Lady Beth said, "Hang on a moment."

He turned back and faced her. She leaned back in her chair and steepled her hands in front of her, the tips of both forefingers resting on her lips and touching her nose. After a moment, she lowered her hands. "I'm pretty pissed off at you, and you know why."

Johann took a deep breath. "Yes, I do. And you should be."

Lady Beth's eyebrows rose. She obviously hadn't been expecting that response. "Then why?"

"Rigidity. Pride. Lack of understanding. Stupidity. A down-timer caught in an up-timer world for a moment. And probably not least, disregard for the worth of another person when her passions conflicted with mine."

Johann clenched his hands tightly behind his back, strong organist fingers clamping and compressing flesh and bones almost to the breaking point. Lady Beth folded her hand across her stomach, and stared at him for a long moment. Johann bore that stare as best he could, even though he most wanted to evade her gaze and look anywhere but in the eyes of this powerful and influential woman.

"What are you going to do about it?" Lady Beth at length asked. "Staci won't see you."

Johann sighed. "If I were her, I would not see me, either. I suspect her conversations about me are rather unflattering."

"Oh, she says nothing about you," Lady Beth said, the corner of her mouth quirking up after she spoke. "Her friends, on the other hand . . . the mildest word I've heard is 'jerk,' and they go downhill rapidly after that. Some of them are using German words that I don't know . . . yet."

Johann winced. "Not undeserved, I am certain." He brought his hands before him and held them out. "I have an idea that I am going to pursue. To that end, would you please tell Frau Simpson that I will be doing a 'demo' of the organ in the near future, to which I would like to invite both her and yourself?"

Lady Beth considered that, then nodded. "I will pass the word. I assume you'll let us know a specific date and time before long?"

"Yes," Johann said.

"Very good," Lady Beth replied, sitting up again. "Thank you for bringing me the news yourself, Herr Bach."

Her voice still wasn't very warm, but it was much more so than it had been at the beginning of the conversation. Johann counted that as a gain.

"You are very welcome, Frau Haygood. Good day."

"Good day, Herr Bach."

Christoph watched Johann stride away confidently the next morning after they left Frau Zenzi's bakery. "He seems to be in a better mood," he remarked to Heinrich.

"Umm-hmm," Heinrich mumbled around the mouthful of bread he had just taken out of his roll. He chewed manfully, and swallowed the lump before it was half ready to be swallowed.

"Do not do that," Christoph said, looking at the lump moving down his brother's throat. "That hurts to watch."

"He does seem a bit happier," Heinrich responded, ignoring Christoph's interlude. "Or at least is less desperately unhappy. If I did not know better, I would say he has thought of a way to address his problem."

Christoph shrugged. "Possibly. But what?"

"You know Johann," Heinrich said. "He will have a plan. He has a plan for everything, even using the chamber pot."

Christoph snorted, and took a bite out of his own roll.

### October 5th, 1635

As it turned out, it was a bit over two weeks before Johann could issue his invitation to the Fraus Simpson and Haygood. It had taken Master Luder a bit longer than expected to replace the missing pipes, and it turned out that the missing pipes were definitely required to finish the ranks that Heinrich had determined were necessary for the "demo." Then, once they had the pipes, it had taken a bit longer to install the ranks in the pipe lofts than Heinrich had anticipated. One of the fittings on the air flow pipe from the second wind-chest didn't seal correctly, and it took another day or so to come up with a solution to that, by which point Johann was rather grateful for the presence of Melanie Matowski, as she was the person who made the suggestion that provided the fix.

Johann sent his invitation to Frau Lady Beth's office, and the next day received a reply that the two women would be available in two days after the noon hour. So he made his plans.

When the appointed day arrived, Johann was almost shocked to discover how nervous he was. He hadn't had fluttering stomach as a performer for years, so it was definitely different to feel it on this day. Maybe because this would be judgment on his craft as an organ builder rather than as a performer. Or maybe because more than just his reputation rested on how he would be received today.

Johann had wrestled with where to be to welcome the ladies upon their arrival. His first inclination had been to allow Christoph or Heinrich to greet them at the doors and escort them to the auditorium, where he would meet them before he took his seat at the console. But after consideration, he decided he should meet them when they arrived, and personally escort them. Given that he was in serious need of support from both of them, both personally and professionally speaking, he didn't want to risk alienating them by appearing to be standoffish or reserved or, God forbid, proud or arrogant. It was a time to treat them less as garrulous and gregarious up-timers and more as the patrons that they truly were.

And so, he found himself standing on the front portico of the opera hall between Christoph and Heinrich. They were all dressed in their best clothing, which had been recently cleaned. He'd even made his brothers get their beards trimmed, while he had opted for the clean-shaven look that was becoming more of a thing as the up-timer influence continued to spread in little ways.

"Where are they?" Heinrich muttered. "When are they going to get here?"

Johann gave a strained chuckle. "Lesson number one in dealing with patrons: Their time is more important than your time. They will usually be late. Assuming they show up at all, that is."

"But are the up-timers really patrons?" Christoph asked. "And do they act the same way?"

Johann shrugged. "These two women are decidedly patrons by anyone's standards or measurements, and we should not lose sight of that fact. And whether or not they act out of patron-like behavior or custom, or whether they are truly delayed by other issues, either way we must simply make allowances for that. And," he concluded as a cab entered into the curved driveway before the opera house, "it appears they have arrived."

This was one of the fancier cabs on the streets, several cuts above the usual wagon or cart with a couple of bench seats on the back. This looked like someone had thought out what a people-moving conveyance should be like if it were to be good but not opulent like some nobleman's carriage. There was an actual seating compartment, with sides to provide some stability for the passengers and assurance that they wouldn't just go sliding off the seat. And the seats, although wooden, looked more like formed chairs than flat benches. The driver sat in front of that compartment on a short bench, guiding his pair of horses with ease. The horses were well tended and healthy. The driver was neat and well presented, for all that his clothing had some mending marks on them. Everything about the rig said there was care and forethought in it, which made it obvious why someone like Frau Simpson would use it.

The driver pulled the team to a halt, set the brake, and jumped down with a small stool that he set below the door, which he opened to the passenger compartment. The cab was relatively low slung, but it was still a bit of a step up or down for someone as short as Frau Simpson. The driver offered a hand, and both Frau Simpson and Frau Haygood took advantage of it as they dismounted from the cab.

Frau Simpson passed a bill to the driver, who grinned and bobbed his head in thanks. "Can you be here in about an hour, Horst?" she asked.

"Yes, Frau Simpson. I will do that."

"Good. We'll be waiting."

Frau Simpson turned toward the steps as the driver hopped back up onto the driver's seat. By now Johann was standing at the bottom of the steps, Christoph and Heinrich to either side and slightly behind him. "Herr Bach," she said in a cool voice.

"Frau Simpson," Johann said with a more than perfunctory bow. "Frau Haygood," he repeated the bow to the other woman. "Thank you for making the time to hear our little presentation."

"Given the time that has passed since you began, this is a timely progress report," Frau Simpson replied. She looked to his brothers. "And these are?"

"My brothers, Christoph," who nodded from where he stood at Johann's right hand, "and Heinrich," who echoed the nod from the other side. "They have been of great help in preparing the organ and getting it ready so quickly."

"Bach brothers," Frau Simpson said with a bit of a smile. "So, the men who would have begun the Erfurt Bachs are now in Magdeburg, are they?" The smile broadened a bit. "Do you intend to become the Magdeburg Bachs, then?"

Johann wasn't surprised by Frau Simpson's knowledge. He had already decided the woman was scary smart and probably knew more about music and the arts than any one person he knew, not even excepting Marla Linder or Heinrich Schütz.

He gave a slight bow again. "We do indeed have some aspirations in that direction," he said. "But that lies in the future."

"Maybe," Frau Simpson replied.

That caused a bit of an awkward moment, and Johann was afraid he knew exactly what she meant. He took a slow breath, but didn't respond directly. "Shall we go inside, then?" he said instead.

Mary inclined her head a bit and headed up the steps. Johann fell in beside her, with the others following behind. When they reached the top he stepped ahead to open the door and usher the two patrons through into the foyer. He repeated the action at the door into the auditorium, then led the way down the aisle. The main seating had not been installed yet, so there was a small grouping of chairs set most of the way down in the middle section of the seating areas.

Frau Simpson and Frau Haygood took their place in the middle of the first row of four chairs and seated themselves. Christoph stood beside the second row. Johann descended to the organ console, which was now in its permanent place in the orchestra pit. Heinrich followed, carrying the folder of sheet music. They both stopped and faced their very small audience to take a bow, then Johann seated himself and Heinrich set the sheet music for the first piece on the music rack.

Johann flipped the switch to turn on the blower that put pressure in the wind-chest system, adjusted the necessary stops, placed his hand on the keys, and took a deep breath. Releasing it, he began.

The first piece he had chosen was the chorale prelude "Wachet auf, ruft uns die Stimme." Johann had chosen this one because it was light and had good movement, yet moved over the tonal range well. It wasn't an extremely lengthy piece, either, usually running between four and five minutes when timed with a good watch.

Heinrich turned the pages at the right moments, so there were no interruptions or stutters there.

It almost felt like a dance, with its pulsing beat. And he forced down the thoughts that brought into his mind. It wasn't time to deal with those.

That piece wound to its conclusion. Heinrich removed the pages and set the next piece in place. The pages were darker with notes than the first piece had been.

Johann adjusted the stops, bared his teeth at the piece, again set his hands on the keys, and launched into "Wir glauben all an einen Gott," another chorale prelude, but with a very different feel to it. It had a faster pace, was louder, and was martial in tone, sounding almost like triumphant fanfares. It was also shorter, taking between three and four minutes using the good watch again to time it.

That ended with a flourish. Johann adjusted the stops again while Heinrich again replaced the sheet music. And this time the piece was the very favorite "Little" Fugue in G Minor. Of all the pieces he was learning and practicing, this had perhaps become the one that gave comfort to him. Even the dancing nature of the themes no longer disturbed him. It was such a joy to play that he didn't even nod at Heinrich to turn the pages. He was playing with his eyes closed most of the piece, just reveling in it.

The fugue came to its inevitable rousing conclusion. Johann held the final chord for a long moment, then released it, opening his eyes as he did so.

"If you are not going to look at the music," Heinrich whispered, "why do you have it up there?"

"Just in case." Johann reached over and turned off the fan switch.

"Ah. So I'm a just-in-case page turner," Heinrich murmured as Johann turned on the bench and stood up.

Johann didn't respond to that last comment. He stepped down from the console and mounted the steps at the end of the orchestra pit to return to the seating level.

"Very nice, Herr Bach," Frau Simpson offered. "Very nice, indeed. Ignoring the missing registrations and tonal stops, that was as good a performance as I've ever heard. And a very nice selection of pieces from the work of your namesake, Johann Sebastian."

"Thank you, Frau Simpson," Johann said, adding a short bow to it. "As you realize, this is not the full capability of the designed instrument, but it is enough to establish that the work we have done so far is sound, and all that needs to be done is to finish the instrumentation."

Frau Mary nodded. "I'd say that has been reasonably demonstrated. Congratulations, by the way. Everything had a very nice sound. So how long before you can have enough of it done to perform a full concert of Sebastian's music?"

"Heinrich?" Johann looked to his brother.

Heinrich stepped up beside Johann. "To finish

fleshing out the primary registries will require perhaps another five to six hundred pipes. Fortunately our whitesmith, Master Luder, has gotten very good at producing the pipes, so unless there is some kind of problem..."

"Like someone stealing pipes or ore," Johann commented.

Heinrich shot Johann a hard glance, and continued, "...we could have enough pipes on hand in the first week of December."

Christoph picked up the discussion. "It would take another week or so to install the ranks in the pipe lofts, and perhaps a few days to test and possibly adjust tuning."

"Tuning," Frau Mary said. "What temperament are you using?"

"That," Johann said, "was undoubtedly the hardest issue of the design. I...we..." he waved his hands to include his brothers, "have broken with the tradition of Johann Sebastian Bach, and decided to strive for equal temperament rather than well temperament."

Frau Mary's eyebrows rose. "Have you, now? How remarkable. But who established the tuning base for you?"

"Frau Linder tuned the initial set of pipes," Christoph offered from behind the women. "We have simply matched tones with those as best we could."

"Ha," Frau Mary said with a bit of a smile. "I see you have anticipated me. I was going to offer Marla as a source. She really does have perfect pitch, and she really does understand temperaments, so she can absolutely tell when something is as right as it's going to get. Of course," Mary's smile grew wider at this point, "she is also seriously pregnant at the moment, so it's probably best that you not be bothering her with tuning questions right now."

"Organs by their very nature tend to be approximations of tuning, anyway," Johann said. "So many separate voices, so many separate throats, that unless Frau Linder goes through and tunes each one individually, there will be differences even between the octaves. And we cannot ask for that commitment of time from her, and even more importantly, we cannot afford to pay her for that service."

"Agreed," Frau Haygood contributed. "I've negotiated with her before. The project can't afford her prices."

Frau Mary gave a refined ladylike chuckle. "Oh, I can see that. I know the girl well enough to know that she is just a bit on the strong-willed side."

"Yeah," Frau Haygood said. "That should be carved on a mountain somewhere."

That got a surprised laugh out of Frau Mary. She then looked back at Johann. "So when could you do a full concert?"

He looked at his brothers—first Heinrich, then Christoph. "If we can get the pipes done as Heinrich says, and get the installation done as Christoph says, allowing me a few days to practice with the full voicing and stops, then by perhaps mid-month."

"Hmm." Frau Mary looked to Frau Haygood. "Schedule?"

Out came an up-time style loose-leaf notebook from Frau Haygood's portfolio. She rested it on her lap, flipped it to one particular section and turned several pages. "Nothing scheduled yet. And good news, no apparent major church saint days around that date."

"What day would the fifteenth be?"

Frau Haygood's finger traced across the page.

"Saturday."

"Good." Frau Mary looked back to Johann. "Put December fifteenth on your calendar, Herr Bach. Do you have a program list firmed up yet?"

Johann grinned, forgetting for a moment how serious this conversation was and what his additional goals were.

"In addition to what I just played, I plan to open with the Toccata and Fugue in D Minor..."

Frau Mary clapped her hands. "Of course," she said. "What else could you open with but the most bravura of the fugues." She laughed. "But what would you close with?"

"The Passacaglia and Fugue in C Minor."

Now her face got sober. "Oh, my. That...would be stupendous, I believe. So three fugues and two organ chorales. What else would you consider?"

"I would like two more works like the chorales," Johann said.

"One of my favorites is 'Schmücke dich, o liebe Seele,'" Frau Mary said. Johann pointed to Christoph, who pulled out his notebook and jotted that title down. "But for the other, rather than another chorale, you might consider one of his works entitled 'Komm, süsser Tod.'"

"Come, Sweet Death"? Johann wasn't sure that was a title he was interested in putting in his performance list. Some of his reservation must have shown in his face, as Frau Mary tilted her head in regarding him.

"I don't think you'll find it in the organ literature," she said. "There might be some arrangements of it for organ, but I doubt if any of them made it to

Grantville. It was a vocal work originally, but one of the most well-known instrumental arrangements was made by Leopold Stokowski for orchestra, and that album was pretty popular, so someone like Marcus Wendell might actually have it. If they do, I'm sure the Grantville Music Trust people could notate it for you. It might take you a little work to adapt it for organ, but it's not complex, and it is a striking piece of music. Shall I send a telegram to inquire about it?"

"Please," Johann said. What could he say? The leading patron, the woman who was paying for his project, wanted a particular piece of music. He was going to say no? No. He just prayed he could learn it quickly.

"I've got it," Frau Haygood said as she pulled a pencil out of her portfolio and made notes in her journal.

"Good." Frau Mary stood. "I understand you might have a need for a private conversation, Herr Bach." He said nothing; simply gave a nod. She returned a small smile. "Shall we draw aside, then?"

He nodded again, then gestured for her to lead. Frau Mary chose to move to the right rear corner of the main seating floor, so Johann followed behind her.

"So, you asked for this meeting," she said as she turned to face him and crossed her arms.

For just a short moment Johann considered who he was facing. As a music and arts patron, she was without peer in Magdeburg, which meant probably the entire USE, which meant she was in the top five of all of Europe, including the Russias. Her whims, her choices, her decisions could make or break careers and leave men—and now women, Johann reminded himself—either exulting or broken and despondent.

For all that, she wasn't particularly beautiful, by

either up-time or down-time standards. She was petite, albeit not so much as Staci—short and slender, despite having enough years to be Johann's mother. Her face was regular, perhaps even handsome, but it was a bit long and her nose was more aquiline than even classic beauty would accept. And he could see the traces of her age in the wrinkles around her eyes, the skin of her neck, the silver filaments in the dark hair that curled under her jawline, the prominence of bones and veins in her hands. But her carriage was strong enough that none doubted that she was what she was called by allies and opponents alike: the Dame of Magdeburg.

Johann saw her fingertips tap where they were folded along one arm, and he hastened to get to his point.

"I would not ordinarily ask you to intervene in a personal matter," he said in a halting tone, "especially one where I dug my own pit, but I need to set something right and I am unable to get the person I wronged to—"

"You're talking about the Matowski girl, aren't you?" Frau Mary interjected. Johann, train of thought derailed, just stared at her mutely for a moment. "No, she didn't talk to me," the up-timer continued. "She didn't need to. Lady Beth is my assistant and right hand, and Marla Linder is my protégée and confidant. How quickly do you think I heard about what happened?"

Johann shook his head. "I was . . . harsh."

"You were brutal, from what I heard." Mary's arms were still crossed, and her face was now cold. "Inexcusably so, I would say."

"I cannot argue with that," Johann managed in a low tone.

"Indeed." There was a moment of silence, then she

sighed. "Nevertheless, I can't say that I'm surprised. Oh, not that you specifically were involved, Herr Bach," she said as Johann stiffened. "It's just that the collision of Grantville with the Germanies is going to be fraught with these kinds of conflicts of standards, understandings, and cultural assumptions. And it is our women who seem to be on the receiving end of most of it, because for all their complaints about it, their lives were so much freer in the up-time, and there are so few of them now in proportion to the vastness of down-timers they have been dropped among. The great surprise is that there has been less of it than there could have been."

She leaned back against the wall and clasped her hands before her. "It's one of the reasons I have pushed myself into this position." She grinned for a moment. "Not that I wouldn't have done it anyway, just for the fun of it." The grin dropped. "But because of who and where I am I can offer some protection—a shield or aegis, if you will—for people like Marla and Staci, until they reach their full bloom and maturity and can stand on their own two feet in the midst of the storms of the world."

"Except it failed Staci," Johann said with some bitterness.

"Because you had connected with her and she had let her shields down." She directed a strong glance at him. "Make no mistake about it, Herr Bach. You betrayed her."

That got through. Johann felt as if he had been kicked in the gut. He hadn't thought of it that way before, even in his darkest of recriminations. He was robbed of voice, was shaken, and simply stared at Frau Mary.

"You see it now," she said. "Good." There was no

note of satisfaction in her voice, though. "At least you're honest with yourself. We might be able to work with that." She tilted her head and gazed at Johann for a long moment. He clung to her gaze. "What do you want, Herr Bach? Just to apologize?"

"That much, at the very least. I would hope for more, but that much I must do, even if she does not accept it. I cannot leave things as they are." Johann stopped talking.

Frau Mary continued to look at him, reading him like a book, Johann suspected. "Do you love her, Herr Bach? Do you love Anastasia Matowski, the dancer, the singer, the pixie who enlivens everywhere she goes... or did, before you quenched her light?"

"What is love?" Johann wasn't trying to be difficult or sardonic. It was just that his understanding of love wasn't as secure as it had been.

Frau Mary pursed her lips for a moment. "Fair enough. So we're back to what do you want, Herr Bach? What do you want for Staci?"

"I..." Johann paused. How could he say what he felt? "I want her to be whole. I want her to be well...no, beyond well. I want her to be radiant, to be brilliant, to shine above the firmament. I want her life to be a fountain of joy, where she blesses all those around her. I want her to live a life that marks a boundary point in history, so that in the future people divide time into Before Anastasia and After Anastasia. I want her to dance before the very throne of God, to hear 'Well done, thou good and faithful servant.' I want..." His voice tapered off, but the yearning ache remained. He wondered where the words had come from, how they had poured through his lips.

But having said them, he couldn't take them back; nor would he, if he could, for they were indeed the desire of his heart.

After a moment, Frau Mary stirred. "Well, if that's not love, I think it will do until the real thing comes along. But you didn't say anything about your place in all that."

"I have forfeited the place that might have been mine," Johann murmured. "Any place I receive will be due to grace and mercy on her part. But whether I have a place or not, that is what I desire."

"Well enough," Frau Mary said as she straightened up from the wall. "Let me think about this, Johann." He noted the change of address with an internal surge of happiness. It meant her perception of him had changed. "It may take me a while to think of a way to bring it about without it being a forced meeting, but I believe I can manage that. In the meantime, you focus on your organ and your playing, all right?"

"As you say, Frau Simpson."

"Call me Mary, Johann."

"Frau Mary."

She shook her head with a bit of a smile. "Germans. Always so formal."

Johann shrugged. What could he say? And even among Germans, he was always one for the formality.

Frau Mary passed by Johann. "Notes done, Lady Beth?" she said as she approached her companion.

Lady Beth patted her portfolio. "Done and tucked away."

Frau Mary looked at her watch. "Hmm. Looks like we may have kept Horst waiting for a few minutes." She looked around. "Good day to you, *meine Herren*."

"Good day, Frau Simpson," the three Bachs chorused back. They followed her back into the foyer and out through the main doors onto the portico. Horst was indeed waiting for his passengers, and as soon as they walked through the doors he hopped down from the driver's seat with his little stool. Placing the stool and opening the door to the seating compartment, he beamed a large smile toward them.

A moment later, the ladies were seated and Horst was shaking the reins and clucking at his team to get them moving. As the cab moved off, Frau Mary looked their direction and waved a hand. All three of them raised a hand in response, and then the cab was out on the street and out of sight.

"Well, that seemed to go well," Christoph said with a sidelong look at Johann.

"Yes, it did, did it not?" Johann knew he was smiling. He couldn't help himself. And truthfully, he didn't care. For the first time in weeks, he felt a cautious optimism. Whistling the theme to Old Bach's Contrapunctus No. 1, he turned and headed back into the opera hall. As long as he was here, he might as well get some more practice in.

Christoph and Heinrich looked at each other behind him. Neither said a word, but after a moment they shared a shrug.


*October 8, 1635*


Late in the afternoon three days later, Johann was again seated at the opera house organ console when Heinrich hustled in. "Johann! Have you heard?"

"Heard what?" Johann said, not looking up from the Passacaglia sheet music.

"Frau Marla lost her baby! She went into labor last night after the concert, and the babe was stillborn this morning."

Johann froze for a moment, then laid down his pencil and dismounted from the organ bench. "*Mein Gott.* That poor woman," he murmured.

Should he go to the house, offer his condolences? The mental answer was swift: No. His presence would undoubtedly not be welcome.

"We must add them to our prayers, Heinrich," Johann said. He looked at his brother. "Which, of course, means that you should make some."

"For this, I will pray," Heinrich said. "No one deserves this."

"Indeed."

*October 9, 1635*

Johann turned over the envelope that was addressed to "Johann Bach, Christoph Bach, and Heinrich Bach." He opened it and drew forth a card.

"What is it?" Christoph asked from the other side of the table.

"An invitation to a funeral."

"Funeral? Oh . . ." Heinrich realized what it had to be.

"For the funeral of Frau Marla's child. A daughter: Alison Wilhelmina Sylwester."

"When?" Christoph again.

"Tomorrow; midmorning."

"And?"

Johann knew the question that was being asked. "I will not intrude, but I will be there."

"And I." Christoph nodded.

Heinrich said nothing, just added a nod.

"That poor woman," Johann murmured.

*October 10, 1635*

The brothers Bach were standing on the outskirts of the gathering across the open grave from the family. Johann could see the family group clearly. Franz Sylwester looked haggard; hair and beard somewhat rumpled, red-rimmed eyes over a drawn face. Marla Linder, if possible, looked even worse, with her hair hanging limp around a lifeless expression centered on dead eyes. Her lips were drawn tight, looking as if they were as hard as forged metal.

There was an up-timer standing beside Franz whom Johann assumed was Marla's brother-in-law Byron Chieske, the one who had been so instrumental in getting the Magdeburg *Polizei* in operation so quickly, and more importantly, had helped lead them into becoming a surprisingly effective organization. The man looked like a warrior, Johann decided: lean hard body, large strong square hands, and a face that for all it was now cast in lines of sorrow also showed ingrained lines of strength and authority. All in all, a man Johann would not want to cross. And now he understood Sergeant Peltzer a bit better, for this was the man he reported to.

Staci Matowski stood beside Marla. Dressed in black trousers and jacket over a simple white blouse, she was a sober figure. For all that her eyes were red-rimmed as well, even at the distance Johann was standing she radiated strength.

Behind them stood Mary Simpson and Lady Beth Haygood at the head of a phalanx of up-timers. Every up-timer in Magdeburg appeared to have come to the funeral.

Johann was somewhat surprised at first that the funeral was not being conducted in a church; but then he realized that the Lutheran church did not consider a stillborn child as being a soul bound for heaven, so they would not allow burial in one of the church cemeteries, and most likely would even refuse to allow a requiem mass to be performed. So they were standing at a graveside in a public cemetery, and the man standing at the head of the small grave was an up-timer. He had been speaking for several minutes, words of comfort, readings from scripture, a prayer. Now he was coming to an end.

Closing his Bible and holding it in both arms against his chest, the speaker said, "In the end, we all return to whence we came, and we all come into God's hands. Alison simply made that journey rather sooner than we will. We must trust that the God who said 'Suffer the little children to come unto me' will know His own and receive Alison as such. Let that be our prayer. In the name of the Father, the Son, and the Spirit, amen."

"Amen," Johann chorused with everyone else. He heard his brothers' voices in echo around him.

He stared once more at Marla and Franz, and he saw Franz tending to his stricken wife, gently guiding her steps away from the end of a dream, all the while his own loss and his own pain shrieked from his eyes. *I want that,* Johann thought. *Not the pain, but to be that kind of man. I want to be that.* And almost his own heart broke at the thought of how close he had come to that possibility, and how it had come to slip through his fingers.

As the crowd around them began to disperse and the figures before him began to thin out, Johann became aware that Staci was looking at him.

Staci was about to turn and follow her bereaved friends, when a bit of motion caught her eye, and she looked over to see Johann Bach across the way, staring not at her, but at Marla and Franz. His face had an expression that was...not grieved...not sober...in some weird way almost seemed to be yearning. She tilted her head as she considered him. He looked a bit thinner; not gaunt, but perhaps a bit wan. Her mouth quirked. It was appropriate, since much the same could probably be said of her.

His head turned and suddenly he was looking at her. After a moment, he reached a hand up to settle his hat, then he brought the hand down to rest on his breast as he gave a slow nod that she was certain was for her and no other. In the next moment, he had turned and was leaving, followed by his brothers.

The rest of the month of October passed very quickly, between the work to get as much of the organ assembled as possible and trying to get the music ready to perform.

It was a week or so after the funeral that Johann had to ask for more of Frau Lady Beth's time.

"What's up, Johann?" She had followed Frau Mary's lead in relenting a bit in how she related to Bach.

Johann took a chair, following the wave of her hand. "I may need to correct an unfortunate impression."

"How so?"

"The organ will not be completed by the December fifteenth concert. Oh, we will have much of it done," he hastened to add as a large frown crossed her face. "Much more than I was able to play in the 'demo' earlier. But it will not be the full complement of pipes."

"Why not?" The frown had eased, but Lady Beth could not be said to be looking happy or joyful.

"Because the original plan was to have it completed in the spring of next year at the earliest," Johann replied.

"Oh," Lady Beth said as she sat back in her chair. After a moment's thought, she said, "You're right. That's what the schedule said. Well, that's a bust. How'd we lose track of that?"

Johann shrugged. "I have spoken with Master Luder, and even with replacing the stolen pipes he will still be a bit ahead of the original schedule."

"But not enough to make up that kind of time," Lady Beth predicted.

"Alas, no. It will be some time well after the first of the new year before he has all of the remaining pipes manufactured."

"And then you and your brothers have to install them."

"And then we have to install them, and do a final tuning, and make all the final little adjustments—what Herr Carl calls 'the tweaks.'"

"Got it." Lady Beth sat forward again. "Mary will be very disappointed that the concert's not going to happen."

"Oh, we can do the concert," Johann said. Lady Beth shot him a suspicious glance. "We will not have the full range of tonalities and voices, but we can do the concert. What we have done and what we will add in the next few weeks is more than many church organs have today. It is just not everything it will have when it is completed."

"But it's enough to perform everything?"

Johann nodded.

"Then why are you here trying to scare me to death?" Lady Beth semi-growled, but Johann was not affected by that at all, because the smile on her face belied her words.

"So that if you heard one of us talking like we would still be working on the organ in March you would not panic." Johann grinned.

"Smart aleck." Lady Beth pointed a finger at him. "You are beginning to think too much like an up-timer."

"God forbid!" Johann said with just a frisson of real horror. She laughed.

Johann set his hands on his knees, ready to get to his feet, but paused when Lady Beth motioned him down. "Hang on a moment," she said. "I have something here for you. Came in today's mail."

She reached behind her and picked up a large brown envelope from the table there, then pushed it across her desk to Johann. He picked it up and looked at her. "Go ahead," she said. "Open it up. I don't have a clue what's in it—just that it came from Grantville."

Johann examined the front of it. The initials GMT were written in the upper right corner with a Grantville address below that. That didn't mean anything to him, so he lifted a letter opener off of Lady Beth's desk and opened the envelope up across one of the short ends. The opener went back on the desk, and Johann reached into the envelope and pulled out a sheaf of white paper.

"Music!" he exclaimed. He pulled a hand-scrawled note page out from under the paper clip holding everything together, and made his way through the American English. "Ah, I see. The Grantville Music Trust," he picked up the envelope and waved it, "before they got the recording notated they found a copy of an organ arrangement of 'Komm, süsser Tod' in the music library at the Methodist church, so they copied that and here it is." He held it up.

"Great," Lady Beth said. "Guess I know what you'll be doing now."

Johann looked at the pages in anticipation.

"Indeed."

*November 1635*

Johann's work intensified after that. Having an additional piece of music to learn and take to the level of performance he wanted it all to be at took more time out of an already fragmented schedule than he had anticipated it would. For all that the new song was not a bravura technical show piece, it was longer than the three organ chorales he already had in his program list, and one of them was still pretty new to him as well.

With the performance less than two months away, Johann had no choice but to reduce his supervision of Christoph and Heinrich's work to not much more than a periodic review. Short periods, of course—he wouldn't leave them unsupervised for extended periods—but instead of daily meetings he only followed up with them twice a week, and the discussions were very short.

The rest of the time, if it was light outside, Johann was at a keyboard practicing. Most of the time he could work at the organ console in the opera hall, but that was still an active construction site, so there were times he just couldn't use it: If the power was off, the wind-chest fan wouldn't blow; if the carpenters were applying varnish to any woodwork the fumes would seep everywhere; or occasionally there would just be so much noise that he couldn't concentrate. So on those occasions he might be at a church, or sometimes back at the Royal Academy of Music.

And so it was on an early November day he was approaching the academy's door when it opened and Franz Sylwester exited the building, followed by most of his and Marla's immediate circle of performer friends. Johann stopped, and said, "Herr Sylwester."

Franz stopped and looked at him. The young *dirigent* still looked very worn, despite the passage of almost a month since the event of the miscarriage. His face was drawn, his eyes were sunken, and there was no spark in his gaze. From what little Johann had heard of how Marla was doing, that was not surprising.

"Herr Bach," Franz responded.

"I realize that I am not exactly persona grata to your family, but I just want to extend my deepest condolences over what has happened and to tell you that you and your wife and your daughter are in my prayers."

With that, Johann gave a short bow, then stepped to one side to allow the others to pass.

Franz took a deep breath, then said, "Thank you,

Herr Bach. I appreciate your consideration and compassion. I could only wish..." With that, he quit talking, waved a hand to one side, and moved on.

Johann turned to watch him go. "That poor man," he murmured.

"Indeed," Johann heard from beside him. He turned and saw that one of Franz's companions stood there, a short stocky man with a bushy beard.

He racked his brain. "Hermann...forgive me..."

"Katzberg. No reason to apologize for not remembering a name that was shouted at you once in a crowded noisy tavern. And that was well said. On their behalf, thank you."

Johann shrugged. "Words. All I can offer, especially since I am not acceptable company otherwise."

Hermann looked up at Johann with a tilted head. "Maybe so, but a kind and gracious word can be balm for a man's wounded soul, especially from an unexpected direction. If that is what is in your heart, Herr Bach, be patient. Things will resolve."

"As you say, maybe so," Johann said with a sigh. "Maybe so. But the waiting is hard."

Hermann clapped a hand on Johann's upper arm. "You are a good man, Bach. It will happen."

And with that, he nodded and broke into a trot to catch up with his friends.

"Johann!" Heinrich burst into the main seating floor of the opera hall from the doors at the back. "Johann!" he called out as he ran down the stepped floor toward the orchestra pit.

"What?" Johann took his hands off the manuals and looked over his shoulder.

"Someone broke into Master Luder's forge last night and stole some pipes."

By the time Heinrich finished the sentence, Johann had turned off the wind-chest fan switch and was on his feet headed for the steps out of the pit. "Come," he said as he brushed by Heinrich.

Once they were outside, Johann said, "What do you know?"

"He said he had eight smaller pipes completed and four roughed in when he locked the forge up last night, but when he opened up this morning the four smallest finished pipes were gone."

"Only four? And the smallest?"

"Ja," Heinrich replied breathlessly, trying to keep pace with his older brother.

"That makes no sense," Johann muttered.

"That's what Master Luder said, only louder and with more blasphemy."

"Someone who steals pipes usually does so for the metal to melt down to either sell or reuse. So the larger pipes are what would be taken, like last time."

"You think so," Heinrich said, "I think so, Master Luder thinks so, but apparently whoever broke in to the forge does not."

They were getting close to the forge, and Johann could see a familiar figure dismounting from a cab. "Sergeant Peltzer," he called out. The sergeant paused at the door to the building. "Any news yet?" Johann asked.

The sergeant's mouth quirked at one corner. "I just arrived, Herr Bach. It has been a busy morning for the *Polizei* investigation department, I am afraid, and I was just now able to break free and come over. Shall we enter together?"

Johann followed the sergeant through the door into the forge area of the building, with Heinrich treading on his heels. A thought crossed his mind, and he turned toward his brother. "Where's Christoph?"

Heinrich shrugged and held out his hands. "I thought he was at the opera house with you."

Johann resisted the urge to slap his forehead. Of course he was at the opera house! But the news had flustered Johann just enough that he hadn't thought of calling Christoph out to come with them.

Peltzer led the way through the door, and Johann was on his heels.

Master Luder was waiting. The sergeant introduced himself and began his questions. Having been through a similar routine with the earlier theft, Johann's attention wandered. A low cabinet set to one side attracted his attention, and he sidled that direction until he could see what lay atop it, which were some of his organ pipes—four of them, to be exact. They must have been the four that were not taken. And they were small, flue pipes that were somewhat larger than his thumb, and perhaps as long as his forearm. The larger ranks were mostly completed at this point, and now they were filling in the smaller pipes, focusing mostly on flue pipes without the reeds at this point, creating the variety of different length and width pipes which produced the different timbres of the organ sound. These looked like the pipes for the string ranks, open-ended rather than closed so they would produce higher-pitched notes.

"Johann," Heinrich said from beside him. Johann looked up, startled. "Sergeant Peltzer has a question for you."

"Master Bach, do you still think there may be

some connection between these thefts and Master Compenius?" Peltzer's pencil was poised to make notes.

"No more than I did before," Johann said. "But two thefts now involving this project is perhaps pushing the limits of coincidence."

The pencil made some marks, then was caught up in the notebook as the sergeant put it away. "We shall make some inquiries," Peltzer said. "Good day to you, Master Luder, Master Bach."

Johann looked at Luder after the detective left. "Well?"

"Numbers thirteen seventy-one, thirteen seventy-three, thirteen seventy-four, and thirteen seventy-six," the whitesmith counted them off on his fingers. "I have the milled sheet tin in hand to do the work; I can rebuild them in a day." He turned and spat into the forge. "At least this time they took little ones—not much metal and flue pipes at that, so easy to replace."

"That makes me wonder if it was the same people," Johann mused. "Not much gain, really, in lifting the small pipes. You might give the *Polizei* a little time... they might actually find these."

Luder shook his head and spat again. "Stupid either way, but very stupid this, ja."

"If they are stupid, maybe the *Polizei* will catch them this time," Heinrich said with an evil grin.

"I'd like that," Luder said with an answering smile. "I would pay money to see them standing before Gericke in his magistrate role."

And with laughing agreement on that, Johann and Heinrich took their leave and headed back to the opera house.

❖   ❖   ❖

"So, Herr Bach."

It was two days after the most recent theft. Johann was having one of his brief reviews with his brothers at the Green Horse. He looked up to see Ludwig Compenius looming over their table.

Compenius continued without interruption. "Is it you I have to thank for the visit from the *Polizei* yesterday? Something about stolen organ pipes?"

"I was asked if I suspected anyone. I said I did not suspect you, but that when two projects are in competition for the same resources, which you must admit we have been to some extent, then it is possible that someone in a low rank or peripheral position might perform or instigate something that he thought was to his advantage."

Compenius' frown deepened. "So you said that I could not manage my workers? Is that it?"

Johann stood and faced the other. "No, Master Compenius. I did not say that. But you must admit that someone who knows about your project but is not part of it might see a way to gather some coins by taking pipes from us and melting them down to sell the new ingots to one of your smiths with no one being the wiser."

A grudging look of acknowledgment crossed the master's face. "Perhaps, Bach. Perhaps." His eyebrows lifted, as if a thought occurred to him. "What is this I hear about your organ having no bellows?"

"An up-time device called a fan fills the wind-chest and maintains the pressure," Johann said.

"A...fan..."

"Ja. A fan."

"And how does this work?"

"Talk to one of the up-timer engineers or mechanics," Johann said with a grin. "They will be happy to work with you."

"For a price, I am sure," Compenius grumbled half-heartedly.

"The way of the world, Master Compenius."

A few nights later Johann was sitting in the Green Horse again, this time poring over some of his music by the light of a lantern, when he felt someone move up beside him. He looked up to see Marla Linder staring down at him, but it was a revivified Marla, one who looked much more like the Marla of old than the Marla he had seen at the funeral—the Marla he had heard report of. He sprang to his feet, almost knocking his bench over backward as he did so.

"Careful," Johann heard her say.

"Frau Linder!" he replied. "It is good to see you out and about again. But how..." He bit off the beginning of the question two words too late.

"You can blame or give thanks to Maestros Abati and Carissimi," she said with a bit of a smile. "Andrea would not allow me to 'wallow in my grief,' as he put it, any longer, and so he and Giacomo intervened. Good friends..." Her voice died away and her gaze grew distant.

Johann didn't know quite what to say, and there was a bit of an awkward silence between them before Marla's eyes refocused and she cleared her throat. "I, ah," she paused, then started again. "You're not one of my favorite people, you know, after what you did to Staci."

Johann said nothing. He wasn't going to defend himself, and anything else he said would seem fatuous.

"But..." Marla continued, "...Franz told me what you said to him. That was kind of you. It showed a level of compassion I didn't know was in you... that I was sure wasn't in you after what you said to Staci that night. So now I'm torn. I'm still very angry with you, but I'm also grateful for what you said and prayed for me... which almost makes me angry all over again, because I'm not used to having to change my feelings about folks."

She gave another small smile at that point. It was quiet, it was sad, but there was some warmth to it as well, and it stirred Johann's heart to see it on her face. It was a mark on how far she had come.

"Thank you," Marla said at the last. "It was kind of you, and I do appreciate it. I just wish you..." She broke it off there.

"Thank you in turn," Johann finally said. "And your wishes are no stronger than my own."

Marla looked at him for a long moment. "I think," she finally said, "that I shall pray for you as you prayed for me."

"Thank you," Johann said in as sincere a manner as he knew how to express.

## December 1635

On December 1st, Johann's meeting with his brothers was short.

"As of this moment, we are not making any more changes to the organ until after the concert," he said. "I need it to be stable now, so that I can finish preparing and know exactly how everything is going to sound."

Christoph nodded. "We have caps on the end of the wind pipes that do not have ranks installed yet, so that should not be a problem. The ranks are reasonably balanced between the two pipe lofts. I can have the two Georgs finish building the final rank frameworks, but we will simply store them until after the concert."

"Ja," Heinrich said. "I am surprised that you had not shut it down before now." He shrugged. "No problem with Master Luder. He will simply continue making the pipes needed to finish it. Since these are mostly the small pipes, he has little problem in storing them for a short time until we need them."

Johann looked at his brothers, and saw only commitment and encouragement, even from Heinrich the japester. He held his fist out and they placed their hands atop it.

"Do this thing, brother," Christoph said. "We will be—we are—the Magdeburg Bachs, and it begins now, with you, with this music."

"What he said," Heinrich concluded.

Every day now consisted of practice time. Johann had for the most part learned the notes. Now he was exploring the best ways to translate the written notes into music, for he had determined that while the notes might be what the future Bach had written, they were only an approximation of how the music was to be played, to be realized. It was up to him to find the spirit of how Old Bach would have wanted the music to sound. He had a total of ten works: three organ chorales, three preludes, three fugues, and "Komm, süsser Tod."

It was a grueling challenge, but it was exhilarating

as well. Piece by piece, Johann would take them apart, line by line—sometimes measure by measure—and try different emphases, different volume gradations, different phrasings, different stop settings, even different fingerings. More than once, something that he determined worked best for one of the pieces made him go back and revisit one of the earlier pieces to try another approach in something he had previously settled.

Day after day Johann did this as long as there was light enough to see the keys, light enough to read the sheet music if he needed to refer to it. He began drinking coffee, large cups of it, one after another, throughout the day. His stomach most evenings was a roiling mass of acid, so his evening meals were seldom more than a portion of bread, more often than not the remainder of his morning roll which he hadn't finished because he was so intent on getting to the music.

Bit by bit, line by line, page by page, Johann began to arrive at his performance interpretations. To some extent they were shaped by some of the up-time recorded music he had heard in Grantville, especially those performances by Helmut Walcha and E. Power Biggs, two musicians whose hands he greatly wished he could have shaken. They were very different in their approaches to performing the music of Old Bach, but they both played with élan and with authority, and the impressions left in his memory both inspired and challenged him.

From time to time Johann was aware of his brothers standing behind him or to one side just watching him; sometimes together, sometimes singly, and never speaking, just watching. Finally, one day he looked up at a time when they were both there. "What?"

Christoph looked at Heinrich, who shrugged, then back at his older brother. "Just trying to understand you," he said. "You have never been like this before. Proud, yes. Pushy sometimes, yes. Arrogant know-it-all big brother at times, oh, yes. And other things like organized as a Jesuit and focused on your goals like a terrier on a rat as well."

"Thank you, I think," Johann responded drily.

"But you have never been this focused. You are losing weight, you look gaunt . . . feverish, even. It concerns us—both of us," he waved a hand to include Heinrich in the conversation.

"It is almost enough to make you think of the old legends of soul-stealers or Loreleis or lamias," Heinrich added. "You were focused on that Matowski woman before . . ." he stumbled at the frown on Johann's face, then continued with, ". . . but that was nothing compared to now."

Johann crossed his arms. "Is it not enough that I am striving to build our future, that I am reaching for something that would not otherwise exist for our family for two more generations?"

Christoph shook his head. "No. Not for what we see. Not for driving yourself to the precipice of exhaustion day after day after day. I would blame it on a woman, but there is no woman."

"There you are wrong," Johann said in a low voice. "There is a woman . . . the same woman who has been part of my thoughts for over a year: Fräulein Anastasia Matowski. And yes, she is my Lorelei, my lamia. She haunts my dreams at night. She stole my soul long ago. And I foolishly...oh so foolishly...drove her away. That, my dear brothers, is proof that I can be as folly-ridden as anyone. And my one desire now is to convince her to accept me again, to forgive me, to allow me to make the great amends to which she is oh so entitled."

His brothers looked at him. Heinrich finally said, "You have a plan, then?"

"Call it an idea," Johann responded, hands clamped tight to his elbows, "a plea, an outreach. Not a plan, not a ploy, but a desperate forlorn hope."

"And it involves the concert?"

"It rests totally upon the concert," Johann said. "And so I bend all thought, all energy, every waking moment to make the concert as extraordinary as I can."

"Ah," Christoph said, eyebrows lifted. "That is the way of it?"

"That is the way of it."

"She was better than you deserved before, you know," Heinrich said, "not to mention now."

"I know."

"We will wish you well, brother," Christoph said after a moment as Heinrich nodded. They stepped forward and clapped their hands on his shoulders in affirmation. For a moment, Johann's throat was thick, and all he could do was nod himself.

The younger Bachs slipped away, leaving Johann to understand that perhaps he had more in his brothers than had been apparent to him before. After that quiet moment of appreciation, he slipped back onto the organ bench, took a deep breath, and set his fingers on the keys. There was much yet to do before dusk.

❖   ❖   ❖

Staci followed Casey into Lady Beth's office at the school. She stutter-stepped to a stop when she saw Mary Simpson sitting in a chair beside Lady Beth's desk. Lady Beth herself, of course, sat in the chair she'd had custom made for herself behind the desk. It wasn't padded, but the wood of it had been shaped to perfectly conform to her body and her build when she sat in it, and she swore that it was more comfortable than any padded desk chair she had ever had in Grantville.

"Sit, ladies," Lady Beth said, pointing at the two armless chairs that sat across from the desk. Wondering what was going on, Staci moved across and sat in the furthest chair. She heard Casey close the door behind them, and a moment later settle into the other chair.

"What's up, Lady Beth?" Casey asked with a grin. Staci was content to let her friend do most of the talking. She'd gotten somewhat out of the habit herself in the last few months.

"I actually asked for you," Mary said.

That got both their attentions, and Staci stiffened a bit. After seeing Mary work with, through, and around her mother in previous years, she knew that there was more to Mary than the smiling, friendly, gracious, glad-handing "hostess with the mostest" that was Magdeburg's usual perception of the admiral's wife. If she was here, there was a reason, and if she asked for them, she wanted something. The question was what?

"We will be having a concert on December fifteenth, Saturday, at the Opera House. The Royal Arts League is very involved in all of that, as you know, so we would like representation for all of the league's activities there."

*Aha. Translation: Mary and her arts cronies want*

*some dancers at the concert to dress things up a bit and put a smiling pretty face on it for the money people*. That made sense to Staci, and she relaxed a bit. It wasn't as if she hadn't been paraded out on display before. It was a pretty common part of being a dancer, doing things to keep the art in the public eye. Even in the down-time it seemed fundraising was a perennial activity.

Lady Beth cleared her throat. "The school calendar is clear that evening. The Christmas concert will be on the thirteenth this year."

"And boy am I glad that Marla's back," Casey said. "I wasn't looking forward to having to lead that. I mean, I could have gotten it done—I helped enough with church children's choirs to be able to fake it as a director—but the girls just do better when Marla's standing in front of them."

Mary smiled. "They undoubtedly respond to her authority."

"Who wouldn't?" Staci said, finally contributing to the conversation. "Authority ought to be Marla's middle name: Kristen Marlena Authority Linder. Has a nice ring to it, actually."

That got laughs started from everyone in the room, and it was a few moments before things settled enough that the conversation resumed.

"Actually," Mary said as she wiped at one eye, "I could have seen something like that if she'd been around in the Puritan colonies in about a hundred years. 'Goodwife Authority Linder, of Salem, Massachusetts.'" A couple of chuckles surfaced after that one, but Mary had everyone's attention again, which was undoubtedly why she had made the remark.

"So who's doing the concert?" Casey asked. "Franz and the orchestra?"

Out of the corner of her eye, Staci saw Lady Beth freeze for just a moment, and her heart sank. She didn't know why or what yet, but this was undoubtedly going to be something they didn't want to hear.

"No," Mary said without a pause. Staci noted just how smooth she was about it. "This will be a solo performance." She paused for a beat, then concluded with, "An organ recital."

It took a moment for that to register, but when it did Staci flinched and leaned forward a bit as if she had been hit in the stomach.

"What?" Casey sounded incredulous. "Who's going to play it? That bastard Bach?"

Mary lifted her hands. "He's the designer of the organ, and he's probably the best organist in the city... probably even the province."

"Oh, hell no!" Casey said. Staci turned her head enough to see that her friend was red-faced. "No way are we..."

"Case..."

Staci's voice cut her friend short. Casey turned toward her. "Stase, you can't do this. After what he did to you, you can't put yourself there."

"Case, it's not like we live in New York City. Magdeburg's not that big. I've already seen him more than once. And with both of us being in the arts, that makes the circles even smaller." Staci took a deep breath, then looked from Mary to Lady Beth and back again. "If I go, I will not approach him, I will not talk to him, I will not make polite conversation with him. And you *will* owe me for this."

Mary nodded once. "Believe it or not, I do have some idea of how you feel. Remind me to tell you someday about the first society fling I ever staged. I snubbed a former friend for years after that one." She tapped the tip of her nose a couple of times with an index finger. "Your stipulations are accepted. And you are right, I will owe you for this. You'll find I always pay my debts." Staci wasn't sure how to take that, but Mary's smile seemed genuine, not her hard-polished professional smile, so the knot in Staci's gut eased a bit.

"Unless you have other questions, that's all for now," Lady Beth said. "You can go find dinner or a glass of wine."

"Wine," Casey said as she stood with alacrity. "Definitely wine."

Staci shared a smile with Lady Beth as she followed her friend out the door. She missed the nods that the two older women exchanged, though.

"That went well," Mary said after the door closed.

"About as well as could be expected," Lady Beth replied, leaning back in her chair. "I wasn't sure how Staci would take it. I mean, she's never been a drama queen, and even now that she is center stage in the spotlight has never had the prima donna attitude. But after what Bach did, I wouldn't have blamed her if she'd had a hissy fit."

Mary shook her head. "Not her temperament. She's the consummate professional, or at least on her way to being that. The worst she would have done is said no."

"And I don't doubt she would have done exactly that if she'd chosen to," Lady Beth said with a ladylike snort. "Marla might be the queen-empress of hard-nosed artistes at the moment, but Staci would most likely be crown princess. Between growing up under her mother's hand and then hanging with Marla the last few years, she has a spine and she's not afraid to use it."

"One of Marla's pack of performers has said that Marla has sword steel for a backbone."

Lady Beth snorted again. "I hadn't heard that before, but boy, does it fit. And Staci's not far off that mark, I'd say. But what would you have done if she said no?"

"If I'd thought there was a real possibility of that," Mary said, "I would have used a different approach."

"Hope Bach turns out to be worth this," Lady Beth said.

Mary stood and brushed her hands down the front of her dress. "Oh, I think he will. You said yourself that he seems to be really messed up by what he did. If that's really the case, then the situation can be salvaged. And if it's not, then we deep-six him, to use one of John's naval sayings. Either way, it's resolved. Binary solution set."

"Heh," Lady Beth responded as she stood herself and moved out from behind the desk. "So, you going to tell him about this?"

"No," Mary replied with a grin. "He can wait on tenterhooks until the concert. He may have come to his senses, but that doesn't mean he still shouldn't pay a bit of a price for being such a cast-iron bastard."

"You're a hard woman, Mary Simpson."

Mary shrugged. "I was the Lady of Pittsburg. I'm now the Dame of Magdeburg. Comes with the job description."

Lady Beth laughed.

*December 15th*

Johann stood in the wings of the opera house stage. There was nothing on the stage, of course, other than the plain curtain backdrop. That was okay, since other than prefatory remarks, he wouldn't be on the stage anyway. Once he moved to the organ console in the orchestra pit, every focus would move to that location, especially since the spotlight operator would set a light on him there.

He spared a moment to look upward and think, "God, You who created both Escher and Johann Sebastian, if ever You have looked after me, let it be tonight."

Johann raised his arms in front of him, checking one more time that his new coat didn't bind his arms. And as it had done in all the previous checks, his arms moved freely through the needed range of motions.

He had thought about his dress for the concert with some care and consideration. He had worked with a tailor who was used to the mélange of clothing styles that were present and prevalent in Magdeburg. The decision to go with up-time-style long trousers had not been difficult to make. He'd even had the tailor put stirrup straps under the instep of his boots to help them stay in place when his feet were dancing on the pedals.

For a coat, though, he had stayed somewhat more traditional, eschewing the shorter coats and short-waisted jackets of the up-timers in favor of something more like the longer frock coats of the down-time. He shrugged. He just liked the way the coat hung and looked on him. It was a more substantial look. A simple linen shirt with a simple pleated neck cloth completed the ensemble.

Johann ran his fingers through his hair and over his smoothly shaven face, then adjusted his cuffs.

"Nervous?" Heinrich asked from where he stood beside him.

"About the music? No. Never." He held his right hand out before him; it was rock solid steady.

"But about Fräulein Staci . . ."

"Not nervous, but . . . uncertain." No bravura gestures this time. He had no word from anyone as to who would be here tonight. He simply had to trust that Frau Mary would deliver on her promise.

Heinrich's mouth opened, but closed again a moment later after no words were said. Apparently he was uncertain as to what he could say in the face of that. Johann certainly understood that feeling, for his own lack of certainty as to what he could or should say was rather strong.

They stood together, then, waiting for the moment. And that moment arrived before long. People had been filtering into some of the box seats on the second level for some little time, and now Frau Mary Simpson and Frau Lady Beth Haygood, accompanied by several others, including their brother Christoph, moved down the stepped floor from the main doors and took seats in the central section toward the front.

Johann could see Fräulein Casey and Fräulein Staci standing behind Frau Mary, and his heart soared. His heartbeat surged so strongly that for a bare moment it felt as if it was going to shatter his chest.

Everyone took their seats as the older woman took hers. The two younger women settled directly behind Frau Mary. Frau Mary looked toward the stage, and gave a firm nod.

"Go." Johann gave Heinrich a nudge, then stepped forward toward the front of the stage while Heinrich carried the music portfolio toward the steps down to the orchestra pit and the organ console. He came to a stop near the front edge of the stage where the spotlight flared on and focused on him, and essayed a formal bow—a bit more florid than his usual, but not wildly so.

"Good evening," Johann said. He pitched his voice a bit deeper than his normal speaking voice. He heard just a bit of echo from the back wall, which indicated his tone was strong and was carrying well. "Thank you for coming to this small affair. Our purpose tonight is twofold: first, to inaugurate the organ here within the opera hall, providing the first of what we believe will be many such performances over the years to come; and second, to celebrate the music of an up-timer composer, one Johann Sebastian Bach, one of the greatest geniuses in the history of music as brought back and told by the musicians of Grantville. And I must immediately clarify that no, despite our great similarity of names, this Bach is not me, and I am not him, much as I wish I could lay claim to both his talent and his genius."

Johann had a self-deprecating grin on his face at that point, and there were several chuckles heard from those in the seats.

"Nor is, or was, the man descended from me. That honor actually belongs to my brother Christoph Bach." Johann gestured to where Christoph was seated. Christoph stood and took a bow, to the sound of a light spattering of applause and more chuckles.

"Lectures concerning the man and his music will occur at later times," Johann continued. "Tonight is for the music, not for talking. But I must first of all thank the Royal Arts League as led by Frau Mary Simpson for supporting the building of first the Royal Opera House and the organ itself." There was another round of applause at that.

"And second, I must dedicate this concert to another performer: Fräulein Anastasia Matowski, the prima ballerina of the Magdeburg Ballet Company. Her skill and art are of a consummate level, and if you have not seen her dance, you are an impoverished soul. She is worthy of the music you will hear tonight."

Johann could see that Staci had stiffened at that final announcement. He hoped that it hadn't distressed her. He gave another formal bow which he subtly directed toward Staci, then turned for the steps.

"Well!" Casey huffed. "The gall of the man."

"Shh," Staci whispered.

She leaned back in her seat, and considered what she had just seen and heard.

Johann didn't look well. His face was very hollow-cheeked, bordering on gaunt. His eyes looked a bit sunken, but for all that, there had been a feverish gleam to them. What he'd said . . . that touched her, strongly, despite her intention to avoid the man.

At that moment, the music began.

Johann settled onto the bench and looked down to place his feet. He looked up to where Heinrich had placed the sheet music on the music rack, and took a deep breath.

"Courage," Heinrich whispered from where he stood to turn pages.

Johann released the breath, gave a firm nod, and placed his hands on the manuals. He paused for just a moment, waiting for . . . now.

He played the opening for the Toccata and Fugue in D Minor, the simple trill followed by the downward run. And from there, the music just flowed from him. Statement followed statement, chords built, resolved, and poured into cadences. New statements followed, new chords, new resolutions. Complexity increased, lines crossing, pedal tones entering to buttress harmonic structures, then leaving to allow the higher voices more room to work their magic.

Pages turned. Johann heard it, and realized that he had his eyes closed again. He smiled at that, but didn't open his eyes. He felt closer to the music this way, as if what was pouring out was really part of his own soul rather than that of a man who had not yet lived, and never would now.

The prelude whirled its way through to its conclusion. Johann waited a bare moment, giving the audience the space to react, then began the fugue. In moments Johann was caught up again in the feeling that the music was like bobbing along on a stream or a river. He remembered feeling that the very first time he'd heard the work in Marcus Wendell's band room. He still felt it now, even after practicing it for months. And it was, after all, appropriate, since Bach meant brook.

Staci had never been a particular fan of classical music in the up-time before the Ring of Fire. Oh, she danced to it, but it hadn't been something that she would listen to for fun, like Marla did. And especially anything pre-Mozart just wasn't on her list of things to spend time on. But she had heard this piece. The Toccata and Fugue in D Minor was perhaps the mostly widely known piece of classical music in the up-time world. Staci, like a lot of her generation, had first heard it in the soundtrack to the movie *Fantasia*. Ironically, seeing that movie as a young child was one of the influences that had awakened in her the desire to dance, as one of its episodes involved animals doing ballet.

Tonight, for the first time, Staci really listened to the piece, listened to the bravura of the toccata, then followed through to listen to the currents of the fugue. And for the first time, she began to see what Marla had always loved about the great organ works of Bach, that there was at the same time a majesty and a light-heartedness.

Being a dancer, she was very aware of kinesthetics, and she found herself watching Bach's movements as he performed, the rises and dips of his shoulders, the shifting of his head positions, the leaning to one direction or another to balance the movement of his feet. It occurred to her toward the end of the fugue that Bach was, in a way, dancing on the organ, especially in the pedal passages. That caused her mouth to quirk, since she had seen a demo once of a mat that laid on the floor but was marked as if it were a musical keyboard and people could dance from key to key and make sounds. It would take a team of dancers—a team of very good dancers, she decided—to match what Bach was doing before her. Just for a moment, that thought amused her.

Johann brought the fugue to its resounding conclusion. After holding the final chord for a moment, he lifted his hands and feet at the same moment and sat back on the bench. The final vestige of the chord echoed in the auditorium, then faded away to inaudibility, and at that exact moment the applause began.

He opened his eyes and grinned up at Heinrich, who returned a quick lopsided grimace of his own, then spun on the bench and shot to his feet to acknowledge the applause.

Frau Mary and Frau Lady Beth seemed to be leading the response, but most others seemed to be clapping with a will. And Johann's heart lifted when he saw that Fräulein Staci was clapping—not as energetically as Frau Mary, to be sure, but more than a desultorily polite recognition as well. His vision blurred for just a moment, and he folded into one of his formal bows to hide it, and take his eyes off the cause while he rapidly blinked his eyes to clear them.

Each of the people attending had been handed a program of the pieces to be played, including brief notes about each of them. True to his promise at the beginning of the event, Johann spent no time discussing them but returned to the bench at the console, where Heinrich had already arranged the music for the next piece.

No deep breath this time; simply position the feet and the hands and launch into it.

Staci looked at her program. The next piece was something entitled "Wir glauben all an einen Gott," which translated to "We All Believe in One God," a reminder of the pervasive nature of religion—particularly Lutheranism in its various flavors—in the USE, and in Magdeburg in particular. It was apparently something called a chorale prelude, whatever that was.

At that moment, Bach began the performance.

It proved to be quite a contrast from the opening piece. It felt like it was in four-four time, and almost felt like a march—very definite, very strong character, very much an "in your face" kind of piece. Assertive, aggressive, even, she thought. Inevitably, stray thoughts of trying to choreograph something to it crossed her mind, and she toyed with the idea. It could be done, she decided, but it would take a corps of really strong male dancers to do it. Too bad they didn't have one of those at the moment.

She shelved that thought and followed the progression of the music to its conclusion, watching Bach all the while.

Johann brought the chorale prelude to its rousing conclusion. The applause started this time as soon his hands left the keys. He grinned at Heinrich, who grinned back. Johann came to his feet to acknowledge the applause. Again it was led by the older up-timers, but again Staci was also clapping, this time a little harder than before.

Another formal bow was in order, so Johann made it, this time with a very evident smile. His eyes still remained fixed on one particular part of the audience, though.

The applause lasted a bit longer this time, so he gave another bow, then returned to the organ and once again almost immediately launched into the third work, another chorale prelude, "Wachet auf, ruft uns die Stimme."

Hmm, "Awake, the Voice Is Calling Us" . . . as a religious song title, it wasn't any worse than some of the hymn and praise song titles Staci had heard in the Grantville churches.

For all that this chorale prelude was also in four-four time, it had a lilt and a bounce to it. Staci began to think that Johann *Sebastian* Bach must have had a sense of humor, because this one made her smile.

She could dance to this one, she decided. And so she did, head moving in time to the music, feet flexing and shifting a bit on the floor, shoulders shifting a bit, in time with the movements of Bach's body where he sat on the bench.

The congruity of that did not escape her when the piece came to its joyous conclusion.

Johann bounced to his feet immediately upon finishing the chorale prelude. The applause increased more, and he heard a "Bravo!" or two as he took his bow. Again he was smiling. It was hard not to with that piece. It absolutely danced, and for the first time it occurred to him that what Staci felt in dancing had to be much like what he experienced when he played that work. It was a startling moment of insight to him, and his eyes whipped to where she sat. There was a bit of a smile on her face . . . the first he had seen since the evening of the disaster.

That he took in, that he placed in the core of his heart, and the hope that it fueled increased, twofold, threefold, maybe more.

Staci examined her program as the applause died down and Bach returned to the organ bench. Next up was something called "Little" Fugue in G Minor. She had always thought of fugue as being some kind of old-fashioned antique of music. But listening to what Bach presented tonight was beginning to show her that maybe she was being just as judgmental about that as her grandparents had been about the music she listened to.

*Again with the four-four,* she thought as Bach launched this work. There was no toccata or prelude or other work paired with the fugue. It stood alone.

The opening theme was strong, and while it was almost martial in its feel, it also had somewhat of a bounce to it, so she could see why it was positioned in the program to follow the previous chorale. It was also a very busy work, with the rapid themes and statements being passed from hand to hand to the pedals and back again.

She found herself beginning to weave a bit again, shoulders moving, hands twitching in her lap, feet wanting to kick out. It wasn't until she focused on Bach, watching his head jerk back and forth as he performed this one, that she began to pull herself out of it.

Johann loved this fugue. It was so strong, so passionate, that he was caught up in it as soon as he began it. The stops he had set gave it a very strong voice, and he found himself bouncing on the bench as he pounced on the keys and trod the pedals with enough force that he was almost surprised he didn't break one.

But he had designed the organ too well. It held up to the pounding of his feet and the pounding of his hands, and the gorgeous music poured out of the pipes above him.

It crossed Staci's mind in one of the pedal passages that she wished she could see Bach's feet. The notes of the line were so rapid they had to be absolutely dancing. That thought gave her pause for a moment—could he really have come to see just from what he was doing?

A bubble of ... something ... floated free, and a feeling of joy followed it.

Johann charged to the finish, head shaking as he hammered the last few notes and brought everything to its rousing conclusion.

The applause that broke out when he lifted his hands was very strong; more so than anything he had yet heard that night. And the smile on his face approached the status of a grin as he took several bows. This time he heard more than one or two "Bravos" as he took those bows.

Frau Mary was applauding with great vigor, and judging from the smile on her face was both enthused about the performance and about the success of the organ. Frau Lady Beth was not far behind her, either. But Johann lifted his eyes to the figures behind them. Fräulein Casey was giving a little more than the polite applause that had been her standard for the evening, but Fräulein Staci was applauding with more energy.

Johann's heart almost stopped when he realized that Staci was looking directly at him with a small smile on her face. She did nothing else—no other acknowledgment—but for the first time that night she connected with him. And that took him to another plane altogether.

It took a longer period of time for the applause to die down before Johann could return to the organ console. It was a heady feeling, having that much acclaim thrown at him. But at length the noise died down, and he gave a final bow.

He took his place on the bench, looking up to verify that Heinrich had the correct sheet music in place. He did, of course: another chorale prelude, this one entitled "Schmücke dich, o liebe Seele."

Johann took a deep breath and released it. Heinrich flashed him a thumbs-up that they had learned from the up-timers. Johann nodded with a brief grin, adjusted the stops, placed his hands on the keys, and began.

"Adorn Yourself, O Dear Soul" Staci read the translation in the program. This one was slow, and quiet, in four, but with a triplet lilt to the slow beat. The organ almost sounded like a woodwind choir to her, low, mellow, and smooth.

Staci leaned back in her seat and relaxed. This one didn't call her to dance. This one called her to float and enjoy the music.

She closed her eyes, and just let the music flow through her, giving her a feeling of tranquility.

It may have been her imagination, but it seemed like the piece went on for a very long time...almost as long as the first fugue. But it did finally come to its quiet ending. She sat up and began to applaud.

"Boring," Casey muttered out of the side of her mouth.

"Shh," Staci replied.

The level of applause was less, which didn't surprise Johann at all, although Frau Mary was very pleased with it, he could tell. And since it was one of the two pieces she had recommended, it was good that she liked it.

From his own viewpoint, the contrast between the styles of the piece compared to the previous fugue was interesting, but also gave him a chance to settle a bit, which he was going to need before long.

Johann returned to the organ after just a couple of bows, this time to address the other piece that Frau Mary had requested.

"Komm, süsser Tod." Staci read it twice to make sure that she was reading it correctly. "Come, Sweet Death." Wow, not exactly an uplifting title, she thought.

But then the music began. And this one, this one reached out and grabbed her. Slow though it was, it had more movement than the previous one, and Bach had set the organ stops to give more of a feel of strings.

The music ebbed and flowed, and it had a very definite feeling of elegy to it. It almost reminded her of some of the Adagio for Strings piece that the orchestra had done in the 1634 summer concert, the one that had left her in tears. But strangely, she could sense a choreography for this one, a slow mass movement of dark dancers, almost like a funeral scene from an opera or something, yet with a single dancer in white moving against the flow of the mass, giving movements that contrasted, and ended with the dancer lifted on the hands of the mass, lifted high above them.

That vision gripped Staci, and when the music came to an end and the vision faded, she almost cried out.

When the applause began, hers was the strongest, the fastest, the loudest, and she was on her feet.

❖      ❖      ❖

When he came to the end, Johann lifted his fingers from the keys, but just let them rest lightly there for a moment. For all that it was an easy piece to play, "Komm, süsser Tod" demanded an intensity from him. Not the subject matter, as such. Death was; death is. But the calling for death, the yearning for the peace of the end, the yearning for the union with God—to pour that out through his hands, to make that sing out through the wordless notes of the organ, that called upon his very soul, and for that moment after the end he was empty.

But then feeling rushed back in, buoyed on the wings of the applause, which was as great as any that had been given so far that evening. Smoothly he turned and rose to his feet, stepped away from the organ and took his bow.

Staci wasn't the only person on her feet. Someone else in the row behind her was standing, she noticed out of the corner of her eye. She didn't care. For just that moment, it didn't matter that Bach had been so cruel to her. For just that moment, his betrayal didn't matter. For just that one moment, the music carried all before it, and she gave it its due.

The first thing Johann saw after he gained his feet was Staci standing and clapping. His gaze remained fixed on her even as he took his bows. She wasn't smiling, and she quit clapping after a long moment, but she looked directly at him the whole time.

Staci at length returned to her seat. Johann finally looked around the room as the applause faded, then returned to the organ console.

❖     ❖     ❖

Casey leaned over. "What are you doing?" she muttered. "The man is scum, girl."

"Shhh," Staci replied, not wanting to get into a discussion. She picked up her program. Last piece: Passacaglia and Fugue in C Minor. She wasn't sure what the first word meant—probably something like toccata or prelude. But fugue she knew. This was the third fugue of the evening, and given that it had been saved for last, she had a feeling it was going to be a big piece. She found herself looking forward to seeing what Bach considered to be a climactic work.

Johann took his deliberate time in setting the stops for the Passacaglia. It was the pièce de résistance for the evening, and its arrival meant the night was drawing to a conclusion, as was his plan. He would soon see if his goal was attained, or rejected. All he could do was his best, and now it was time to do so.

He looked up at the sheet music and caught a wink from Heinrich. "Do it," his brother whispered.

Johann quirked a smile back at his brother, leaned back to position his feet on the pedals, and began.

The opening to the Passacaglia was slow, and totally played on the pedals. That was different, Staci decided, compared to everything else that had come before. But for a change, the time was in three-four, as opposed to the four-four that almost everything else had been in. Too slow to be a waltz, though, she thought with a small grin.

It was a long theme—eight measures, it seemed like. Very low, very rumbly. She liked that, Staci decided. When it reached the end, it started over again, and now Johann leaned forward to play notes on the manuals with his hands. It grew more complex, with the additional moving lines.

She watched as Johann progressed the piece. It was almost like watching a weaver, she decided, as Johann folded in line after line of music, body moving on the bench as he continued to play the repeating motif on the pedals, seeming to almost reach out in midair to each side to pull in threads as he started new treatments of the melodic material with every iteration of the motif.

Staci couldn't feel a dance to this one, though. A procession, yes, but not a dance. It almost felt like some kind of huge wedding processional, or something.

She sat back, and watched Johann's body move, jerk, and sway as he continued to weave the tapestry of the music.

Johann's eyes were closed again, but he knew the moment was approaching. The motif completed in the pedals as the phrase came to an end, and, "Now," he said quietly.

Heinrich moved around him, pushing and pulling stops to change the tonal settings per the performance plan that Johann had mapped out. The sound of the organ changed within a couple of beats as it entered the section where the motif moved from the pedals to the lowest manual. Now that he didn't have to constantly shift to address the pedals, he remained stationary, eyes still closed, almost crouched as the music poured from his soul through his hands and fingers into the organ— this organ—his organ—his king of instruments—and resounded in the space of the room.

✧　　✧　　✧

Staci watched Bach's body as things changed. He wasn't dancing, no . . . but the shifting of his hands from manual to manual, the changes in the tilt of his head as musical phrases rolled out, the tensing and relaxing of his shoulders and neck, all gave a sense of . . . something.

The pedals started again, and Bach's physical movements got larger as he had to constantly shift to play up and down the range of pedals. The stop settings now were stronger and almost harsh, but the force they added to the music was undeniable.

The tension continued to build, the intensity continued to grow, until there came a series of final sounding chords. For a moment, Bach seemed to clench into a single lump on the organ bench, then his hands lifted and the chord ceased. An instant later, a new theme began, one lighter than the original but obviously related to it. And after just a few beats the theme was heard again, and Staci knew the fugue had begun.

Johann was . . . not lost in the music . . . perhaps abandoned to the music was a better phrase. There were no thoughts now, no words, no perceptions of what was outside him or around him. There was only the fugue. There was only the flow of the lines, the climbing ascending phrases that were constantly moving the mass of the music forward, upward, onward. There was only the fugue.

The only reason Johann knew that Heinrich was still with him was the changes in tone and voice that occurred when stops were moved according to his plan. He saw nothing but the lights behind his closed eyelids; he heard nothing but the music; he felt nothing but the movement of air in and out of his lungs, the beat of his heart, and the rush of the fugue.

The music drove him, or he drove it, or they drove together until they reached the penultimate chord, which was held for a long moment, before being released to create a very short pause. Heinrich feverishly changed stops before Johann leapt into the ending, driving it through to the final slow adagio arpeggio that led into the concluding thunderous chord.

The chord was held for what seemed like a moment out of time, until Johann knew the moment was over, and released it. Reverberations rang and slowly died away.

Staci sat frozen, stunned. The conclusion of the work had broken a gestalt. Her own eyes had been closed as she floated with the fugue. She gave a quick shake of her head as she opened her eyes, to discover that everyone around her was on their feet applauding—applauding loudly and longly. Even Casey was standing and clapping.

She rose and joined the applause, but then her hands faltered as she saw that Bach was still sitting on the organ bench, motionless. Was there something wrong? Her heart skipped a beat, until she saw his brother reach over and lay a hand on his shoulder.

It was almost like watching an ice cube melt at high speed. The tension seemed to drain out of Bach; he slumped for a moment before straightening and turning on the bench to stand and step forward.

Staci eyed Bach carefully even as she clapped. His hair was slightly disarrayed, and even in the December chill he was sweating. His eyes were wide, and his head almost jerked as he looked around. After a moment, he took a deep breath, smoothed his hair back, smiled and took a bow.

The applause intensified, and shouts of "Bravo!" were heard from several directions, including from Mary Simpson right in front of Staci. Her own hands were starting to sting a little, she was clapping them so hard.

Johann took yet another bow—it was at least the fourth, maybe the fifth. He was breathing hard still, which was making him a bit dizzy, which in turn meant he had to be careful bending into the bows. He really didn't want to fall over.

Finally the applause started to die down. Johann darted a glance over at Heinrich, to discover that he was standing beside the console, hands clasped behind his back and grinning like an idiot. A check of the audience revealed Christoph standing and clapping like the others, likewise with a broad grin on his face.

As the noise tailed away, Frau Lady Beth stepped out and around the rest of the seats to move to the edge of the orchestra pit. She raised a hand.

"Quiet! Quiet, everyone!" Silence fell pretty swiftly. "Thank you for being here today. There is a reception set up in the foyer area. Feel free to join us there to talk to Herr Bach, or his assistants, or anyone else associated with the Arts League." She made shooing motions with her hands.

This was news to Johann, but he was game for it, especially since it would hopefully provide him with an opportunity to approach Fräulein Staci.

By the time he had climbed out of the orchestra pit

and made his way to the doors to the foyer, there was a throng of people there before him. A small throng, granted, but rather more than he had expected. There must have been more people in the box seats than he had realized.

"Herr Bach! Johann!" Frau Lady Beth called out with a wave. He made his way to where she stood beside a table. She took a glass of wine from a servant behind the table and handed it to him. "Here. You look like you could use this."

Johann was indeed thirsty, and took a big gulp of the wine. It was better than he expected. After a moment's thought, he realized that shouldn't have surprised him, given who was sponsoring this affair. If anyone in Magdeburg could get good wine, it would have to be the people associated in the Arts League.

Frau Lady Beth hooked her arm through Johann's, and guided him around the foyer slowly, introducing him to many obviously well-to-do individuals—men, women, couples, both patrician and Adel. He received many compliments and comments, various proposals concerning music and organs, and by the time they were halfway around the room he'd agreed to take three students for organ lessons and another for composition.

Christoph and Heinrich were standing together near one of the wine tables, eating some small food items and chatting with a couple of young women—probably more dancers, from the look of them. They had the build, anyway, and were dressed similarly to Fräuleins Casey and Staci.

Johann caught glimpses of Fräulein Staci from time to time. She seemed to be circulating with Frau Mary, and always seemed to be on the opposite side of the foyer space from where he was. Every time he tried to go to her, Frau Lady Beth would tighten her hold on his arm and pull him in a different direction. He was growing increasingly distracted and almost frantic, trying to get free.

Staci walked with Mary, stopping and talking to whoever Mary brought her to. She understood the fundraising gig very well; that she was expected to make pleasant and smile at the patrons, and answer their silly redundant repetitive inane questions over and over again.

Time passed; they made several circles around the space. She did get to talk to Johann's brothers for a few moments when Mary paused to refresh their wineglasses. They were still just as funny as she remembered.

Johann she spotted from time to time. Lady Beth was apparently doing the drill with him. Her mouth quirked at the harried look on his face. She'd have thought that he'd be used to this by now, given how much patronage was a part of the life of down-time musicians.

There came a point where Mary just drew her out into the center of the foyer space. "What did you think?" Mary asked.

"Of the performance?"

"Umm-hmm." Mary took a sip of her wine, looking away from Staci.

"I'm not a good judge of organ music or organists," Staci said slowly, "but I was . . . impressed. Reluctantly . . ." she added. "What did you think?"

"Mmm," Mary said. After a moment, she continued with, "It was good. Bach made some voicings that departed from the usual up-time performances. He does seem to grasp the feel, the core, the ... essence, I suppose, of the work. And the organ is good, as well."

Staci looked away. She still wasn't sure how she wanted to feel about Bach, after having been treated so badly but having seen a side of him in the evening's performance that hadn't touched her before.

Mary took her arm, and Staci looked around sharply to see Lady Beth and Bach approaching, arm in arm. She started to withdraw, but Mary's grip held her fast. She couldn't pull away without causing a scene, which she didn't dare to do in front of the patrons. So she froze.

Lady Beth and Bach—Johann—came to a stop in front of them. His eyes clung to her gaze, his face was solemn, his free hand seemed to be shaking just a bit, judging by the dregs of wine in the bottom of his glass.

"Fräulein Anastasia Matowski," Mary said, "allow me to introduce you to Herr Johann Bach." Mary's glance turned to him. "Herr Bach, Fräulein Matowski."

Johann bowed, deeply. "Fräulein Matowski, I am very honored to make your acquaintance," he said, his voice husky and with the faintest of tremors in it. "I understand you are a dancer. I think that is wonderful. I am certain that you are superb at your art, and I wish you the best of fortune as you pursue your art and your dreams."

He transferred his glass to his left hand, and held his right hand out. His hand trembled a little; he could see it, but try as he might, he couldn't hold it still. The smile he tried to make also felt a bit shaky.

Johann, at the end of his hope, at the end of his

plan, at the end of his strength, looked at his dream, and waited.

Mary and Lady Beth had released them and stepped back.

Staci looked at Johann. His hand was shaking; his wobbly smile slipped away.

She had never seen yearning so rawly expressed before. She had never seen naked pleading in a pair of eyes before. It hurt to look at him, he was so exposed before her.

"Are you sure you want to do this?" she asked in a quiet tone.

Johann gave a sharp convulsive nod. His hand remained outstretched.

Staci looked at Johann. Her heart resisted for a long moment, then the walls around it melted. She smiled, reached out and took his hand.

His smile was like the dawning of the sun. It almost blinded her.

# Coda

## From "The Fall of Fire: The Coming of Grantville and the Music of Europe"

Charles William Battenberg, B.A., M.A.,
Fellow of the Royal Academy of Music,
Schwarzberg Chair of Musicology, Oxford University,
1979, Oxford University Press

### CHAPTER 9
### THE GENERATIONS THAT CAME AFTER

...of the clans and families that arose in the aftermath of the Ring of Fire that were prominent in music and the arts, second only to the Linder-Sylwester clan were the Magdeburg Bachs, descended from three brothers: Johann, Christoph, and Heinrich. They took up the challenge of the heritage and legacy of Johann Sebastian Bach from the future. They founded the Bach Gesellschaft, which vied with the Grantville Music Trust for over two hundred years in providing guidance and leadership to the music scenes of Europe. They were also prominent in ballet and the dance, especially the percussive tap dancing.

...for one hundred fifty years after the Ring of Fire, every male child of the Magdeburg Bach clan was named either Johann or Sebastian—but never both at once.

# Cast of Characters

**Abati, Andrea**

Noted *castrato* from Rome, known to Francesca.

**Bach, Christoph**

Second-oldest of the three Bach brothers who will be known as the Magdeburg Bachs, purported grandfather of Grantville's Johann Sebastian Bach, who will never be born.

**Bach, Heinrich**

Youngest of the three Bach brothers who will be known as the Magdeburg Bachs.

**Bach, Johann**

Oldest of the three Bach brothers who will be known as the Magdeburg Bachs.

**Bandini, Carlo**

Friend of Davit's in Brescia.

**ben Israel, Jachobe**

Jewish merchant and moneylender in Bologna who assists Francesca.

**ben Jachobe, Davit**  Son of Jachobe.

**Bocchardi,**  Rider and guard for
  **Benvenuto**  Jachobe.

**Bonaro, Marcello**  Captain of the USE airship.

**Brenzona, Ercole**  Palace guard at the Grand
  Duke's court, duped by
  Francesca.

**Brother Johann**  Benedictine monk who
  specializes in researching
  the Grantville libraries.

**Caccini, Francesca**  Leading musician at the
  court of the Grand Duke
  of Tuscany in Firenze
  (Florence), known as La
  Cecchina, and sometimes
  called the Nightingale of
  Firenze.

**Callas, Barbara**  Actress at the Teatro
  Mediceo who performed
  under the stage name of
  Isabella.

**Carissimi, Giacomo**  Noted composer from
  Rome, known to Francesca.

**Charducci, Antonio**  Driver for Jachobe.

**Chastelina,**  Christine's attendant and
  **Maria da la**  seneschal.

**Cintoia, Sansone**  Employee of Jachobe.

**Comagni, Guillermo**     Medic on the airship.

**Compenius, Ludwig**     Member of the organ-building Compenius family.

**Corsinis, Giulio**     A driver who helps Francesca begin her journey.

**Cuno, Tobias**     Pastor of St. Peter's Church.

**Dauth, Georg**     Big Georg, carpenter on the Royal Opera House project.

**de Joseph, Bigliamino**     Another man who helps Francesca, part of a network of associates.

**Decennius, Matthias**     Caplan Im Dom, senior pastor in Magdeburg.

**Tazzera, Piero del**     Ferdinando's page and attendant.

**Falconieri, Cesare**     Captain of the palace guard in Firenze.

**Fremdling, Isaac**     Musician friend of Marla and Franz.

**Furttenbach, Josef**     Architect, senior partner of Furttenbach and Parigi.

**Gagliardi, Paolo**     Roberto's sergeant from his condottiere days, now his companion.

**Haygood, Jere**     Up-timer, engineer, and Lady Beth's husband.

| | |
|---|---|
| **Haygood, Lady Beth** | Up-timer, assistant and right-hand woman to Mary Simpson, headmistress at the Duchess Elisabeth Sofie Secondary School for Girls. |
| **Higham, Amber** | Up-timer, wife of Heinrich Schütz. |
| **Iacho, Clara** | Jachobe's cook. |
| **Jordan, Elizabeth** | Up-timer musician, married to Carissimi. |
| **Katzberg, Hermann** | Musician friend of Marla and Franz. |
| **Köppe, Georg** | Old Georg, carpenter on the Royal Opera House Project. |
| **Landa, Giuseppe** | Palace guard at the Grand Duke's court, duped by Francesca. |
| **Langfeldt, Jacob** | Bartender at Lady Beth Haygood's *salon*. |
| **Lenzi, Bartolomeo** | Employee of Jachobe. |
| **Linder, Marla** | Up-timer musician, superb vocalist, married to Franz Sylwester. |
| **Lorraine, Christine de** | Dowager Grand Duchess of Tuscany, Ferdinando's grandmother, and Francesca's real employer. |

**Luder, Phillip** — Whitesmith who will help build Johann's organ.

**Matowski, Anastasia (Staci)** — Up-timer, dancer, teacher at the Duchess Elisabeth Sofie Secondary School for Girls.

**Matowski, Melanie** — Up-timer, Staci's sister, electrician on the Royal Opera Hall project.

**Medici, Ferdinando II de** — Grand Duke of Tuscany, and Francesca's official employer.

**Del Migliore, Roberto** — Minor noble, former condottiere, now palace major for Ferdinando.

**Mozo, Guido** — A bakery boy Marco meets in the streets of Firenze.

**Murphy, Brendan** — Up-timer, comedian.

**Murphy, Catrina** — Up-timer, Brendan's wife.

**Nerinni, Alessandro** — Roberto's assistant.

**Nofri, Bastiano** — Palace guard from the Grand Duke's court.

**Odermann, Barnabas** — Bartender at Lady Beth Haygood's *salon*.

**Parigi, Antonio** — Architect, junior partner of Furttenbach and Parigi.

**Peltzer, Kaspar** — Detective Sergeant, Magdeburg Polizei.

**Pritchard, Nissa** — Up-timer, employee at the Grantville Power Plant.

**Rusche, Anna** — Server at Walcha's Coffee House.

**Sabatini, Marco** — Young attendant and traveling companion of Francesca Caccini.

**Salvi, Ricardo** — Driver/smuggler who helped Francesca travel to Bologna.

**Schockley, Carl** — Up-timer, project manager for the Royal Opera House project for Kelly Construction.

**Schütz, Heinrich** — Down-timer German composer, Father of German Music.

**Simpson, Mary** — Lady of Magdeburg, wife of USE Admiral John Simpson, head of the Magdeburg Arts League.

**Stevenson, Casey** — Up-timer, dancer, teacher at the Duchess Elisabeth Sofie Secondary School for Girls, fiancée to Carl Shockley.

**Sylwester, Franz** — Down-timer musician from Mainz, husband of Marla Linder, *dirigent*/conductor of the Magdeburg Symphony Orchestra.

**Terci, Renata** — Another actress at the Teatro Mediceo.

**Toro, Ernani** — Palace servant in Firenze.

**Traugottin, Kreszentia** — Baker the Bachs patronize.

**Wendell, Marcus** — Up-timer, Grantville high school band director.

# ERIC FLINT

## ONE OF THE BEST ALTERNATE HISTORY AUTHORS TODAY!

---

### *THE RING OF FIRE SERIES*

## THE RING OF FIRE ANTHOLOGIES
### Edited by Eric Flint

## THE WARRIOR'S APPRENTICE
TPB: 978-1-4767-8130-3 • $16.00

## CETAGANDA
PB: 978-0-6718-7744-6 • $7.99

## ETHAN OF ATHOS
PB: 978-0-6716-5604-1 • $7.99

## BROTHERS IN ARMS
TPB: 978-1-4814-8331-5 • $16.00
PB: 978-1-4165-5544-5 • $7.99

## MIRROR DANCE
PB: 978-0-6718-7646-3 • $7.99

## MEMORY
TPB: 978-1-4767-3673-0 • $16.00
PB: 978-0-6718-7845-0 • $7.99

## KOMARR
HC: 978-0-6718-7877-1 • $22.00
PB: 978-0-6715-7808-4 • $7.99

## A CIVIL CAMPAIGN
HC: 978-0-6715-7827-5 • $24.00
PB: 978-0-6715-7885-5 • $7.99

## DIPLOMATIC IMMUNITY
PB: 978-0-7434-3612-1 • $7.99

## CRYOBURN
HC: 978-1-4391-3394-1 • $25.00
PB: 978-1-4516-3750-2 • $7.99

## CAPTAIN VORPATRIL'S ALLIANCE
TPB: 978-1-4516-3915-5 • $15.00

PB: 978-1-4767-3698-3 • $7.99

## GENTLEMAN JOLE AND
## THE RED QUEEN
HC: 978-1-4767-8122-8 • $27.00

PB: 78-1-4814-8289-9 • $8.99

". . . filled with a satisfying blend of strong
characters and wry humor."
—*Publishers Weekly*

# Robert A. Heinlein

"Robert A. Heinlein wears imagination as though it were his private suit of clothes. What makes his work so rich is that he combines his lively, creative sense with an approach that is at once literate, informed, and exciting."
—*New York Times*

| | |
|---|---|
| **ASIGNMENT IN ETERNITY** | 978-1-4516-3785-4 TPB $13.00 |
| **BETWEEN PLANETS** | 978-1-4391-3321-7 $7.99 |
| **BEYOND THIS HORIZON** | 978-0-7434-3561-1 $6.99 |
| **EXPANDED UNIVERSE** | 978-0-7434-9915-6 $7.99 |
| **FARNHAM'S FREEHOLD** | 978-1-4391-3443-6 TPB $13.00 |

**THE GREEN HILLS OF EARTH & THE MENACE FROM EARTH**
978-1-4391-3436-8 $7.99

**THE MAN WHO SOLD THE MOON & ORPHANS OF THE SKY**
978-1-4516-3922-3 TPB $13.00

| | |
|---|---|
| **THE ROLLING STONES** | 978-1-4391-3356-9 $7.99 |
| **SIXTH COLUMN** | 978-1-4516-3872-1 $7.99 |
| **THE STAR BEAST** | 978-1-4516-3891-2 $7.99 |
| **STARMAN JONES** | 978-1-4516-3844-8 $7.99 |
| **WALDO & MAGIC, INC.** | 978-1-4767-3635-8 TPB $14.00 |

# Master of Dark Fantasy

*Queen of Wands*                    (pb) 978-1-4516-3917-9 • $7.99

# Master of Bolos

*The Road to Damascus* with Linda Evans
                    (pb) 978-0-7434-9916-3 • $7.99

■ ■ ■

# And don't miss Ringo's NY Times best-selling epic adventures written with David Weber:

*March Upcountry*           (hc) 978-0-6713-1985-4 • $24.00
                    (pb) 978-0-7434-3538-3 • $7.99

*March to the Sea*          (hc) 978-0-6713-1826-0 • $24.00
                    (pb) 978-0-7434-3580-2 • $7.99

*March to the Stars*        (pb) 978-0-7434-8818-1 • $7.99

*Throne of Stars*     (omni tpb) 978-1-4767-3666-2 • $14.00
*March to the Stars* and *We Few* in one massive volume.

# RING OF FIRE SERIES
### (with Eric Flint)

**1635: The Papal Stakes**        978-1-4516-3920-9 • $7.99
Up to their necks in papal assassins, power politics, murder, and mayhem, the uptimers need help and they need it quickly.

**1636: Commander Cantrell in the West Indies**
                                  978-1-4767-8060-3 • $8.99
Oil. The Americas have it. The United States of Europe needs it. Enter Lieutenant-Commander Eddie Cantrell.

**1636: The Vatican Sanction**    978-1-4814-8386-5 • $7.99
Pope Urban has fled the Vatican and the traitor Borja. But assassins have followed him to France—and not only assassins! The Pope and his allies have fled right into the clutches of the vile Pedro Dolor.

# STARFIRE SERIES
### (with Steve White)

**Extremis**                      978-1-4516-3814-1 • $7.99
They have traveled for centuries, slower than light, and now they have arrived at the planet they intend to make their new home: Earth. The fact that humanity is already living there is only a minor inconvenience.

**Imperative**                    978-1-4814-8243-1 • $7.99
A resurrected star navy hero attempts to keep a fragile interstellar alliance together while battling and implacable alien adversary.

**Oblivion**                      978-1-4814-8325-4 • $16.00
It's time to take a stand! For Earth! For Humanity! For the Pan-Sentient Union!

---

# TIM POWERS